Made In Myrtle Street

B A Lightfoot

Published by

Ranelagh Books

Made in Myrtle Street

First published in 2009 by Ranelagh Books Ltd

Cover design by Phill Watson

Photograph on the Front Cover courtesy of the Imperial War Museum,
London. (negative number Q5242)
Photograph of Myrtle Street on the back cover adapted from one
supplied by Salford Archives.

ISBN 978-0-9561468-0-9

Printed and bound by RPM Printing, Chichester, UK

www.ranelaghbooks.co.uk

Ranelagh Books Ltd
PO Box 163
Poulton le Fylde FY6 6DF

To Pippin – thanks for your lovely family.

With special thanks to Liz Noble for so patiently reading and proof checking the manuscript, to Eileen and her Pendlebury readers group for their encouragement in reviewing the first version, to Phill for his technical help and advice and to my family and friends for reading and commenting on the various offerings.

Chapter 1

Autumn 1914

Edward looked on uneasily as his wife Laura carefully washed the bacon rashers under the cold water tap, dabbed them with the pot towel, and then placed them, spitting and raging, into the hot fat of the cast iron frying pan. She turned the bacon over with a fork and the fat sprayed with a renewed vigour over the cooker and down the pinafore that protected her long black dress. She stared implacably at the spluttering frying pan, barely seeing its contents; locked into her unshared thoughts.

He was crouched in the small square space between the living room and the scullery that he used as a temporary workplace; just for small to medium jobs like fixing mops and brushes, cleaning shoes, varnishing chairs and repairing drawers. When it came to actually making things such as rocking horses, breadboards, toy prams and tea caddies he worked down in the cellar. Occupying this area in the winter he would get the smoky warmth from the living room with its rich smells of baking bread and burning coal. In the summer he could open the cellar door and benefit from the cooling air that came from its whitewashed depths. From this space a step led down into the scullery and he would often sit here, leaning his back against the wall where the lead gas and water pipes ran along the skirting boards, to read the newspaper or to talk to Laura. If the weather was hot he might choose instead to sit on the step that led into the paved back yard.

Now, with jobs to complete before he left, he had positioned himself in this space at the top of the cellar steps to repair the clogs for his younger son, Ben. He rubbed his thumb nail vigorously on his dark head and cursed quietly so that the children wouldn't hear. Distracted by his wife's alien silence, he had just inadvertently hammered his thumb. His eldest brother, Jim, had told him years ago to rub a hammered finger on his hair to prevent bruising. It always seemed to work although he didn't know why.

Positioning the clog on the cast iron last, Edward extracted another tack from between his teeth and hammered it into the clegg that he was fixing on the heel. He felt helpless in the face of her silence; her normally warm and communicative lips seemed set in a grim, cold line.

The bright sun outside was throwing shadows onto the slightly uneven, white distempered walls of the scullery. The speckles of fat from the bacon gleamed like raindrops on the wall around the gas stove and over the grey stone flags of the floor. Laura turned the rashers once more before finally lifting them onto a plate. She replaced them in the pan with two rounds of bread. Fried bread as well. This was a special treat for a special day. Like the condemned man's breakfast, he thought grimly.

He heard his seven year old daughter shouting angrily from the back yard where she had gone to clean the rabbit hutch. She was also Laura but nicknamed Pippin by her Dad to avoid confusion. His eldest son was named Edward, like him, but his wife's tone of voice seemed, somehow, to make it clear who she was addressing. He was also out there, polishing the greengrocer's bike that was the prized acquisition of his new job. He could just about handle it. 'You leave my Floppy alone our Edward, or I will let the tyres down on your horrible bike.'

The nine year old lad was mocking and unrepentant. 'Don't be such a big soft girl. This is how you're supposed to hold them. That's why they have these big ears like handles. Look, it smiles when you jiggle it up and down.'

The shriek from his daughter drew no response from her mother who continued ladling fat over the yolks of two eggs. 'Stop pulling my hair you stupid girl. Pack it in or I'll belt you.'

The moistness that appeared on his wife's eyes and ran down her still immobile face forced Edward into a relieving response. Normally, Laura would have rebuked the children to stop them arguing but the tenseness in her face and the occasional gulping movement in her throat showed her struggling with some deeper turmoil. He didn't want the memories that they would hold after he had gone to be of an angry, bullying father but he would have to intervene. 'Look, you two. Stop arguing or you will be frightening the coalman's horse in the yard at the end.'

'Our Edward is frightening my Floppy,' his daughter protested.

'Edward, just give the rabbit back to Pippin and you get on with doing your bike. You'll be needing it later.'

He listened to his son's mumbled provocations as he handed the rabbit to his sister and felt a deepening guilt over the decision that he had made to sign on as a regular. When the declaration of war against Germany and her allies had been announced the choice had seemed clear and straightforward. He had been at the annual camp with the Territorials in Prestatyn at the beginning of August when the call had arrived to become full time soldiers. They were needed to give support to the regular army in dealing with the worsening situation in Europe. It had posed a serious dilemma for most of them when they were approached as there were many who, like himself, had got wives and young families to support but the supplications that had followed, urging them to fight for King and Country, had resulted in almost all of them signing on immediately. It had seemed so much the right thing to do at the time. The assassination of the Austrian Archduke Franz Ferdinand in Sarajevo by a group of oddball fanatics, a place and person that none of them had even heard of before, had seemed to have little relevance to their lives in the rapidly growing Lancashire town of Salford but the German invasion of Belgium and then of

France changed things. Almost overnight it had become a sudden and alarming threat to their own homes, families and freedoms,

They had willingly agreed to take up the cudgels, to go 'over there' and give the Hun a bloody nose and to be back in time for Christmas but they had had no real appreciation of the possible scale of the war, little understanding of its causes and no concept of its potential cost in human lives.

Since they had been brought back from camp, the newspapers had been carrying stories daily about the unbelievable brutality of the Germans, the bayoneting of babies and the raping of women. They also read the reports on the efforts that were being mounted by the British Government for the biggest mobilisation of armed forces that the country ever had seen. Transport, food, medical supplies, weapons, tents and blankets had all to be put into place to support an army of hundreds of thousands of men.

In the hectic days since, though, doubts had started to build in Edward's mind. Times were already tough and they now had five children to support, including a young baby. His departure would impose a heavy burden on his wife and on the shoulders of his nine year old son. He worried over whether Laura would be able to get enough coal for the fire when the weather started to get colder. It was a good job that during the previous winter he had shown young Edward whereabouts to go at the gas works to get a pram of coke. Now, so quickly, it was the 2 September and almost time for him to leave. New doubts crowded into his mind as he struggled to put a shape to the silence that gripped his wife.

Laura took a loaf out of the white enamelled breadbin and placed it in the centre of the sycamore cutting board. Holding her hand across the top of the bread in a way that always caused him alarm, she cut a thin slice, buttered it carefully, halved it and placed it on the small plate that she had taken out of the cupboard. He preferred it plain as he liked to dip it into the fat but he understood that the butter was to make it memorable.

Edward polished the clogs and lifted the shoe last back onto the shelf above the cellar door. He bent down to pick up the clogs and Laura's skirt brushed against his arm as she carried the breakfast plate through to the living room. She positioned it carefully on the green chenille table cloth, laid the knife and fork on either side and picked up his soft, khaki Lancashire Fusiliers cap from the centre of the table to replace it with the small bread plate. His army rucksack was also removed and placed on a chair, surmounted by the cap. His kitbag, containing all his army issue clothes and a selection of additional items that his wife had deemed to be essentials, stood on a second chair.

'Sit down, love, and enjoy that while it's hot,' Laura said gently but without meeting his eyes. 'You might not get another decent meal for a bit.'

He needed to tell her about the thirty pounds that he had brought home in his wage packet. She had been so thrilled to hold that much money that he had not had the heart to tell her that it was paying him off. He now had no job to come back to when the fighting finished.

A loud rapping on the front door thwarted his confession. Young Edward came charging through from the back yard, disturbing the sleeping cat into a spiky spitting bundle. He raced for the front door with Pippin hanging on to the back of his jumper. 'I want to get it,' she yelled. 'It'll be Amy calling for me to play out.'

'No it won't. It'll be Jimmy Horrocks coming to lend me his Dad's pump.'

Edward nudged his chair closer to the table as they battled past him to the front door. A gust of warm autumn wind swept over him and he waved a bacon sandwich to acknowledge Maggie Ellis from two doors down as she shouted from the street. Her mother had had a fall and could your Laura come and see what she could do for her. He relayed the message through to his wife then repeated her response to Maggie.

Edward looked around the small room that was the focus of their family life as he ate his sumptuous breakfast. The net curtains at the window created a heightening background to the rich green of the long, aspidistra leaves. The plant stood on a crocheted cover on the tall oak table with the barley twist legs. He enjoyed running his finger down the curving pattern that had been crafted by his father and thinking about the man that he had barely known, the Dad who had appeared so briefly in his life before he had died when Edward was only two.

The table where he now sat was pushed up against the wall between the front door and the door that led into the scullery. The flowers that he had bought for Laura two days before stood in a plain glass vase on the table in front of him. They were already beginning to fade. Laura swept past him wiping her hands on her pinafore. 'I'll be back in a minute, love. She must have had one of her turns again,' she said quietly, gazing resolutely ahead of her.

He had never been away for so long before. The two week annual camp was always a bit of a wrench but this would now be for much longer. He blotted up the remnants of the yoke with the last crust of the bread. Their living room was small but it was functional and cheerful. It was a room full of vigour and life, of argument and upset, of inquiry and discussion. Sometimes, with the noise of a young family, it felt oppressively small and he would escape into the backyard, the street or even the cellar. At others, it was filled with the glowing warmth and security of loving relationships.

Edward felt especially pleased with the decorating that he had only recently completed. His older sister, Sarah, was the cook for a family that owned a wholesale stationery business in Manchester. Their home, a large house in Seedley, had recently had the hall redecorated. When there had been some rolls of anaglypta left over, the owner, Mr Muir, had kindly agreed to Sarah taking them for her brother for 'just a small, nominal charge.' Edward had been thrilled and had covered the lower half of the walls with it. A rich brown paint bought from the Paint and Varnish Company on Cross Lane had given it a warm finish. The same source had supplied the cream gloss for the upper half and the distemper for the ceiling. He had toyed, for a while, with the idea of stippling the somewhat plain cream top section with the brown paint, but Laura had said that it would be far too flamboyant. He had settled, instead, for nailing up some pictures along with a framed sampler that her Grandma had made. It was getting a bit discoloured now but you could still clearly see the white rose stitched proudly over the title 'The Almonds of Morley.'

A big cupboard was built into one of the alcoves that flanked the cast iron fireplace with its heavy wooden mantle. Underneath the cupboard there were three large drawers with shell-patterned brass handles. The top drawer was crammed full of freshly ironed clothes – mostly children's – whilst the middle one was filled with towels, tablecloths, spare curtains, crocheted mats and tea towels. The bottom drawer had a varied collection of Edward's tools including his multi-sized shoe last, screwdrivers, hammers, an axe, various tins containing a range of tacks, nails and screws, a set of chisels, a rusting rip saw and a broken-toothed cross cut saw. A variety of part-used paint cans that he had meant to sort out filled the space in the left of the drawer.

In front of the fireplace the varnished wooden floor was covered by a colourful rag rug that Laura's mother had made. He took his plate into the scullery, came back into the living room and relaxed into the comfortable warmth of the rocking chair that had once been his Dad's. He closed his eyes, rested back onto the crocheted antimacassar and enjoyed the solace of the traces of ancient pipe smoke.

His eldest brother, James, had inherited most of their father's woodworking tools after he had followed him into his trade as a wood turner, but Edward was proud of the wooden mallet, pliers, awl, two old chisels, a spokeshave, two moulding planes and a sharpening stone that had been passed on to him. His Dad was thirty nine when he had died and it had left a void in his life that, despite their best efforts, his older brothers were unable to fill. He missed the guiding hand, the strong supportive presence, the special bond that counterpoints the mother's unquestioning love. On the other hand, when he saw some of his mates' fathers after they had had an excess of alcohol, he was grateful that he didn't have to contend with that darker side. Even now, as an adult, he felt a thrill when he used his Dad's tools and held the handles that his master craftsman father had held. He oiled and sharpened the blades with the same reverential care that he knew his Dad would have used. For a while he was the son of the father and the father was embodied in the son.

Pippin pushed the dummy back into the mouth of the protesting baby, Mary, who was demanding attention with reddening fury from a chair against the wall. The ungrateful baby, fists clenched and arms flailing, spat it out again. 'I haven't got all day to be standing here pushing this back in,' Pippin said, putting her hands on her hips and unconsciously mimicking the scolding tone of her mother. 'Mam has just gone an errand so you will have to wait for a minute.' She had wood shavings from the rabbit hutch still nestling in her red hair.

The baby, having woken to the stimulating smell of cooking bacon, was not to be appeased. Pippin picked up a wooden sheep from the pile of toys that was carefully stacked in front of the drawers. It had moving legs but the unfortunate, cross-eyed appearance of a bemused, white dog. 'Mary had a little lamb, its feet were white as snow,' she chanted, waving the tormented looking sheep in front of little

Mary. The baby continued crying but Edward declined his eldest daughter's invitation to nurse the unhappy infant, unwilling to risk the unblemished appearance of his new, khaki trousers.

He had made most of the toys that were in the stack though the dolls had been his wife's creations. The sheep had been one of his earlier efforts and was showing clear signs of abuse and neglect. He felt rather more proud of the fortress that he had created two years ago as a Christmas present for young Edward. The wood had been salvaged from the scrap bin at the sawmill where he worked and the lead soldiers had been made by his brother James using strips of lead flashing thrown away by roofers repairing a property near his home.

Jim had made the moulds from Plaster of Paris, building them up in two sections with grease proof paper in between. Edward remembered how even he had been excited when Jim had taken the molten lead out of the oven in his black-leaded range and poured it into the plaster cast moulds. Then he had been as thrilled as any schoolboy would have been when they were broken open to reveal the shiny lead soldiers.

'Dad. When you're away can I shift that wood out of the shed so that I can put my bike in there?' his son shouted, intruding into his reverie.

Edward had said his goodbyes to his widowed mother and his brothers the day before. She had told him to make sure that he got plenty of potatoes down him and not have too much of that foreign muck that they all eat over there. To send him on his way, his Mam had sat him down at the table and given him a large plate of hotpot, cooked with a thick, shortcrust pastry top, followed by his favourite custard tart.

As he had left, she had told him to watch his bowels and, in a rare show of emotion, had given him a big hug and a kiss on his cheek.

Edward now bent his head tentatively towards his wife's face but the hurt in her grey eyes made him hesitate and he turned, instead, and kissed the forehead of the sleeping baby that she was holding. Laura was embracing the child protectively against her breast but her gaze held Edward's steadily in wordless communion. They heard the clatter of a horse-drawn cart passing down the cobbled street outside. There was no thudding rumble in the note from the wheels. It would be the coalman returning empty to the yard at the top of the street.

'Laura. That money in my wage packet. I need to tell you. They paid us off. I have no job to come back to.'

She placed her hand on his shoulder and kissed him gently on the cheek. 'I know. We'll manage. Something will turn up.'

'I'm sorry love. You just seemed so pleased with the extra pay that I couldn't bring myself to tell you. How did you know, anyway?'

'Brig told me. You must have mentioned it to Liam.'

'It's not right really. The Corporation are keeping the jobs open for their lads but all the private firms round here seem to be laying their people off.'

'Maybe it is safer to have the money in your pocket now. A job to come back to won't help the families of those who don't come back.'

Edward suddenly sensed the deep dread that had gripped his wife. It had locked her into this silent world of fear where even the odd word spoken might betray thoughts that were too awful to air. She had seen more clearly than he had that this wasn't a rugby match with its bruising physical contact but limited dangers; it wasn't the pantomime heroics on the practise fields of the Prestatyn army camp. This was a real war, raw and brutalising. They would be facing an army of professional soldiers that had rampaged ruthlessly through Europe and men would be killed and maimed. The camaraderie and bravado of the pub, the rush of the preparations, had dominated the last few weeks and obscured the realities of the combat. He had dwelt on domestic arrangements – she had sensed sacrifice and feared for his life. He had dreamt of a heroic, vanquishing, Comic Cuts adventure whilst his wife was seeing his battered and lifeless body; unreachable and beyond her care.

The constricting tightness in his throat and chest crushed the words of his farewell. The kiss would be the final act of parting. Edward touched his lips into the fiery orb of her hair and deferred the moment.

He tousled the hair of young Edward who was gazing up at him, proud of the Dad who was going off to beat the Germans. He felt a twinge of guilt as he thought of the extra burden that was going to fall on the boy. 'Look after your Mam whilst I'm away, young fella' he said and smiled as he saw the shoulders bracing back in an odd contrast to the loud sniff and the quivering lip.

He bent down and kissed the upturned face of seven year old Laura who was getting to be more and more like the gentle but mischievous girl that her mother had been when he first knew her in Turner Street. 'Bye Pippin' he murmured. She reached up, touching his face for reassurance. Next to her was her younger brother Benjamin who, at only five years old, was finding it hard to be the brave soldier that his Dad was telling him to be. Finally, there was a hug and a squeeze for Sadie. She had been named Sarah after her Aunt but they had adapted it to Sadie because they liked it and it avoided any confusion. Sadie was crying because she didn't understand what was happening and anyway she was only three and her Dad was going off somewhere and her Mam was hanging on to him.

He pressed his face again into the soft, coppery red hair of his wife. After twenty years of sharing their lives as children and then adults, they were to be separated and it would probably be for some months. He was trying desperately to be calm and strong. It had been very difficult, telling her that he was going to fight in another country, even though she had been so supportive. Since then, the preparations for his departure had been hectic, almost exciting, but it was this inevitable final moment of farewells that he had been dreading.

A shaft of sunlight was coming through the freshly cleaned windows and it hung like a burnished frame around her head. He kissed her lips briefly as though extra seconds might expose more hurt. The thoughts that flooded around in his brain seemed to falter in his unresponsive throat and he clung to her in a silent intimacy of unspoken need. No words seemed adequate to express the tumult of emotions that flooded through his body. He told her not to worry and that he would be back soon. She whispered to him as she turned to kiss his cheek. Her tear stayed on his skin like a cold breath of air.

With a heavy heart he slung his kitbag on his back, went through the front door and down the cream-stoned steps into the bright sunlight. He barely heard his children's 'Bye Dad' because of his thudding heart and the echoing response from his studded boots on the stone paving flags. Numbed and confused, he walked the few yards down Myrtle Street and past the house of his in-laws. Laura's whispered 'Keep safe, Love' ran round his head like a mantra. She had spoken it so quietly. He felt as though he had heard her heart praying.

He kept telling himself that it would be just like going to summer camp but maybe for a bit longer.

On the corner he hesitated for a moment then turned. He needed the detail of the already familiar image fixed in his mind. The red brick walls, neat painted window sills and carefully stoned steps were strong and ordered. A warm, comfortable backcloth. Neighbours stood on their steps to see him off. The coalman, unhitching his horse at the top of the street, waved to him. Laura was at their front door. Her arms were locked around the baby. Long black dress with a white pinafore. A housemaid in a drama. Her glowing red hair framed her white face. The children were clustered round her legs. He waved briefly but they were frozen into this brief pastiche.

It was only a hundred yards walk to the left over the railway bridge and up Cross Lane to the Drill Hall but Edward opted instead to turn right, walk past the theatre and down to the crossroads. The concerns oppressed him – would Laura be able to manage on his 1/7d a day for the next few months; would she get a bit behind with the rent and be kicked out of the house? He would try to save something out of the one shilling that was paid directly to him so that he could sort things out when he got back and perhaps have a bit over for Christmas.

Each sector of the crossroads was fringed with tubular iron railings, thoughtfully built so that the top rail was a convenient height for the elbows of the out-of-work Salford men from the houses behind that corner. Like four tribes they gazed out with taut-faced resignation at the passing traffic. The groups were dotted with the khaki of enlisting soldiers.

Edward joined the cloth-capped men who stood around the Ship Hotel corner, their hands thrust deep into their pockets or cupped around sustaining cigarettes. They were mostly dockers who hadn't been chosen that morning in the inequitable daily lottery of gang selection. Every day they rose early and crowded hopefully around the Dock gates, shoulders shrugged against the chill mists that rolled across the canal, and prayed that today they might be lucky. Each morning, the dowdy gang stood in stark contrast to the showy opulence of the Dock offices and hoped that, if fortune had smiled on them, they could go home that night with their heads held high.

Now, the luckless rejects from that morning's selection had made their way up to the corner at the crossroads and were aimlessly discussing the weekend's sport, the runners in the dog racing and the injustices that burdened their lives. For the past two months, following the assassination on the 28 June of Archduke Franz Ferdinand and the subsequent outbreak of the rapidly escalating war, the conversation had increasingly centred on the fighting in Europe and the employment opportunities that this might offer. Some of the men had strong opinions about the political wisdom of Britain entering the battle but most of the talk was tinged with a sense of excitement at the prospect of a change in their personal circumstances and fortunes.

Muttered greetings were exchanged with Edward but the men respected the silence of his confused mood. To his left, Regent Road ran down into the bustling commercial centre of Manchester whilst to his right, the route ran past the huge, formidable Salford Workhouse and on through Eccles into Warrington. In front of him, Trafford Road was busy with the endless streams of carts ferrying products to and from the Docks; the horses leaving numerous, steaming markers to denote their passing. The rich warm vapour from the sweating horses hung like a thin cloud over the junction, contrasting sharply with the stale odours emanating from the open door of the Ship Hotel behind him. The cleaners had begun their daily struggle to free the pub of the evidence of the previous night's indulgencies. Woodbine smoke hung in the still September air, dulled by the smell of the grain flour that had lingered for the last two days in the dockers' jackets.

A motorised cart tumbled the clouds of damp haze and left behind the pungent traces of burnt fuel as it passed through. Edward was fascinated to see that these trucks were becoming more commonplace. His Dad would never have believed that, in his son's day, they would be seeing horseless carriages pushing the carters off the roads.

He watched the groups of coolies from the ships on their way up to the shops and pubs. They walked in single file like a line of sombre, grey geese. Their eyes were lowered submissively and they crossed the road maintaining the same order and distance between them. It was a deliberately non-confrontational and non-intrusive style, he reflected, as though it was a part of their shipboard training.

Edward stood with his arms resting on the rail, his hands clasped in front of him as if in supplication. His eyes were fixed on the church on the opposite corner where he had married his childhood sweetheart ten years before. He was not a regular churchgoer and Laura and the children now went to Salford Central Mission, the big new church that he could see just a bit further down Trafford Road. This imposing, three storey building with the domed roof above the central section, had been opened only six years before, yet already it was the hub of the community. Up to a thousand people attended the Sunday services and each day during the week there was a range of interesting activities for young and old alike. He had often joined the hundreds of men who enjoyed the thought provoking addresses given by the speakers at the secular Pleasant Sunday Afternoon Society meetings. The steaming jungles of South America, the exotic spices of India and the commercial brashness of New York had all been brought to their Salford doorstep.

When they were young lads, the racecourse had stood at the bottom of Broadway, the road that ran in front of the church. Since then, it had been relocated to Kersal and the land now housed the huge Number 9 Dock. The voracious growth was dizzying. His mother hated it and never came down further than the market.

The Mission did seem a friendlier place, and less formal in its purveying of the Christian message, but the statuesque, Victorian gothic pile of the building opposite elicited from Edward a special reverence.

This elegant edifice of Stowell's Church was imbued with the spirit of a thousand happy unions that had been blessed within its walls. There were fragments of both his and Laura's beings embedded in that majestic stone. He admired the skill of the masons that had gifted this building to the community as a repository for the golden threads of the mutual commitment that bound together their often drab lives. He wondered at the skills and learning of the artisans that had created this complete and unified whole out of the rough-hewn rocks that had been brought to them.

Occasionally, there would be a loud, metallic thudding as a monstrous steam traction engine rumbled by hauling a heavy trailer. They carried massive castings from Lancaster and Tonge's in Pendleton destined for one of the new factories in the rapidly developing Trafford Park industrial estate.

Many of the men shouted a greeting to Edward and wished him good luck. Some said that they would see him over in France sometime soon. Edward smiled bleakly and waved back at the many familiar faces.

He watched the horse drawn carts coming up Trafford Road with the loads that they had collected from the Docks. A lot of them were carrying large bales of cotton or crates of fruit, whilst others were weighted down with strangely shaped blocks of rubber. Some were loaded with timber and Edward mused as to whether any of these were on the way down to the Regent Road sawmill where he had worked.

Streams of carts were going back down towards the Docks with loads for the waiting ships. They were carrying the fruits of Lancashire's industries, the products of northern ingenuity, artistry and engineering skills. Edward was intrigued to see the number of gleaming gun carriages, the burnished steel coated with a thin, protective film of oil, being carted down to the Docks. They would be mated with the precision-milled barrels being brought in from the mighty engineering sheds of British Westinghouse in Trafford Park.

The carters sat hunched on the front of their vehicles, their elbows resting on knees covered by large leather aprons, reins resting loosely in their hands and the clogs on their feet hanging adjacent to their horses' plodding flanks. The men's faces almost invariably bore the baleful expressions of the disinterested, resigned to their tediously exploited existence. The older horses maintained the same stoic pace throughout the day, heads bowed like bored old men, but the younger animals occasionally raised a small objection with a skittish shake of the head. Their exuberance was quickly curtailed by a sharp rap on the rump from the carter's whip.

Along the side of the road there was a line of handcarts carrying the short distance loads. These were the entrepreneurs of the carting trade; men who had worked long hours and saved every penny to buy their own handcart and then grabbed every opportunity that was offered to move even the smallest load. They took unfettled forgings from the ironworks to the engineering shops where they picked up sacks of brass turnings that they then carted to the motor manufacturers. On the way back they collected window frames from the joinery company to take to the building site before returning again to the ironworks.

A sharp young voice penetrated his thoughts. 'Eh up, Mr Craigie. Yer must 'ave been up early to get that tidied up.' He looked down at the thin, but imperturbably cheerful face of his daughter's eight year old best friend. Her dad's worn and threadbare cap was perched coquettishly on her fair curls and her grey blouse, with cuffs that hid her small hands, was spread out over an ankle length skirt. The toes of her black leather clogs protruded from beneath the double frill around the bottom of her skirt and she beamed up at him with a mischievous smile as she banged her clog irons on the paving stone, trying to create a spark.

It was impossible not to be drawn in by her impish smile. 'Hello, Amy. Do I look smart enough then?'

'Aye. Yer look a real toff. But yer'll 'ave to do summat about t' socks. They're full of wrinkles,' she said, pointing at the puttees round his calves.

'Well, I think that they're supposed to be like that but I'll ask the Major when I get to the barracks. Where are you off to then?'

'I'm going to t' shop for a loaf for me Mam. Me Dad 'ad t' rest of it for 'is butties.'

'Here you are then,' Edward said, charmed by her irresistible good humour. He handed her a halfpenny piece. 'Buy yourself a liquorice stick.'

'Eh, ta Mr Craigie. I'll save 'alf of it for your Laura. Bye for now.' She waved cheerily and skipped off up the road.

Edward watched as she dashed past two women, shawls pulled round their shoulders, carrying a heavy cotton bag between them. She narrowly avoided two men in suits and straw boaters before colliding with the portly greengrocer in his brown overall. He heard her shout 'Oops, sorry Mr Artingstall' before she disappeared into the crowds on Eccles New Road. Mr Artingstall smiled and shook his head indulgently before returning to his task of artistically arranging the shiny red apples on the trestle in front of his shop.

Crossing the road, Edward hesitated for a moment. He had forgotten which foot he had started into the road with. It was usually his left. He adjusted his step and finished comfortably on his right. At the gateway to Stowell's Church he stood for a moment looking up at the commanding steeple and admiring its powerful, manmade presence. He was thrilled by the thought of the huge volume of free air that the masons had enclosed as they reached up to their God. Standing in the entrance he ran his hand over the joints of the heavily studded door and gazed at the precise carving of the lintel. His outstretched hand was resting palm downwards on the stone pillar at the side of the door when he heard Big Charlie.

'Hey, Eddie. Are you alright? Are you walking up to the barracks, then?' the big man boomed out. Big Charlie, like many men of his size, was formidable in appearance, clumsily rumbustious in approach, but gentle and caring in manner. He was going to war with enthusiastic gallantry because he had been told that it was the right thing to do and because he was convinced that it would all be over by Christmas.

Edward joined his pal and together they walked up Cross Lane towards the railway and the barracks of the Lancashire Fusiliers. 'How was your Dot, then?' he asked Big Charlie.

'Well, she wasn't right taken with my going. But she did do me a grand breakfast to see me on, like. And she'd got me a lovely bit of tongue for some butties for afterwards. Nice with some pickled onions. What about your Laura?'

'She was a bit quiet. Worried about things. She made me a nice breakfast though.'

'She'll happen be a bit mithered about how she'll manage if it goes on too long. You having the kids' like.'

'Aye. There's that. But I think that she's frightened that we might not come back at all.'

Big Charlie's face was suddenly sombre. 'We better had. Dot didn't say owt about that but I know she'll be scared. She gets frightened enough when I go to work and leave her in the house by herself.'

Passing Myrtle Street Edward saw his eldest son with some of his mates, kicking a ball against the coal yard doors at the bottom. His father-in-law, standing at the corner of the street, shouted across to him 'Take care of yourself, son. We'll see you soon.'

As they passed the Railway Hotel a soldier was being pushed gently through the door by the landlady. She put her arm around his neck and gave the younger man a quick kiss on his cheek. 'Come on, Liam. You can't accept a drink off all of them else they'll be carrying you up to Salford Royal and not the barracks.'

'Thanks, Edie. I'll have the rest for Christmas. And don't be changing your favours to anybody else while I'm away.'

'Go on, you daft sod,' she said giving him a quick cuff round the ear.

Liam shouted when he saw Edward and Big Charlie approaching. 'Well, blow me. Fancy seeing you two here. The Germans will be quaking in their boots when they know we're on the way.'

'Well, we've got the start of a good rugby team,' Edward admitted, 'But I don't think the Huns will be too worried about that.'

'We'll give 'em a good battering at whatever they want,' said the irrepressible Liam. 'And the sooner it's over and done with the sooner that I can collect some of those pints that I've just missed out on.'

Walking up Cross Lane towards the barracks and the area of all their childhood adventures, the three lifelong friends stopped on the railway bridge. The L&NWR Manchester to Liverpool rail link formed an important dividing line between the old and the new parts of this growing town. In the massive Salford goods yard near Manchester, the line met that of the L&NY which connected with Bolton and the north. Within the fork of the two lines stood huge, imposing edifices, symbols of northern industrial success and the economic might of Victorian England, including the Salford rolling mill and a large cotton mill.

Through the throbbing heart of this rail hub was pumped the fruits of the formidable British Empire and the products of northern industry. It reached out around the country and, through the increasingly important Manchester Ship Canal, it stretched out into the world.

'Have you thought,' Edward reflected, 'this might be the last time that we cross this bridge?'

'What?' Liam exclaimed, immobilised in the middle of the pavement by the thought. 'That's a right morbid idea. Where've you got that one from?'

'It was just something that Laura said. That it might be better to have been paid off rather than keep the jobs open like the Corporation lads have. In case some of us don't come back.'

Big Charlie rested his arms on the parapet of the steel bridge, his chin resting on his clenched fists. He gazed out at the smoky industry of the shunting yard. 'What do you mean… like… killed?'

'Either that or run off with some French Madam bloody Waselle,' Liam retorted tartly. 'There's probably about the same chance of either and that's no chance.'

'Well, maybe or maybe not,' Edward said thoughtfully. 'The papers have said that there's tens of thousands of French soldiers been killed. The German army has been mowing them down like skittles. Happen that Laura was right to be afraid.'

'A right game of soldiers this is turning out to be,' muttered Liam. 'There's none of us can afford to get killed.'

'Aye. It's a bit of a sod that is,' said Big Charlie ponderously.

The three soldiers walked on up Cross Lane accompanied by many greetings from friends and neighbours, some of whom applauded them as they passed. Salford was getting caught up in the fever of excitement as the country went to war. There was to be a big meeting that evening at which the citizens of the town were to be exhorted by grey flecked local dignitaries to register for the new Salford Battalions. The hate against the Germans was being stoked daily by the newspaper accounts of atrocities. The outrage grew as ever more lurid details were added when the stories were recounted in the Salford streets. The savagery of the Huns dominated the conversations in the pubs and factories, and on the corners of Trafford Road.

There was a consensus amongst both the men and the women that these brutes needed to be dealt a sharp lesson, that they must be stopped before they took it into their heads to invade Britain and to defile their wives and daughters. This was an honourable cause for any red-blooded male and the government's pleas for the security of freedoms and the defence of the realm and the British Empire added a noble and nationalistic veneer.

Nearing the castellated and imposing structure of the Victorian barracks their hearts started to pound. In a moment of passion, they had made a commitment that would change their lives. They would be introduced to experiences that they had only dreamt about as young boys when they had seen the soldiers marching down Cross Lane.

Heading towards the entrance, they joined other men from the Territorial Army that they had befriended over the last few years. Edward felt the pain and remorse of separation from his young family and yet the strange thrill of transferring into the secure and familiar, regimented life of the Army and the promise of adventure that it held. He stepped through the Drill Hall gates and he was a soldier – Private 2789 Edward Craigie of the Lancashire Fusiliers.

The transition as he walked through the majestic gates was almost brutally fast. It was only a short time before this that he had been a Terrier – a member of the Territorial Army – along with many of his friends, neighbours and workmates.

They were known locally as the 'Saturday Night Soldiers' because that was when they did their training.

Joining the Terriers and having the chance to go away to annual camp had been a bit of an adventure prompted, also, by an honourable determination to stand up for their families and for Salford if they were called upon to do so. When they had enlisted in the Territorial Army the concept of it was simply as a home defence force and with no obligation to serve overseas. The possibility of fighting for King and Country in a previously unheard of part of the World, or even of dying in some foreign field, had been merely the hyperbole of the bored upper classes.

Now the three friends were waiting to put their signatures to the documents that would bind them to become regulars in the 1/8 Battalion of the Lancashire Fusiliers, the '1' indicating the first line formations that had been created from the Territorial Forces. Soon they would be leaving for foreign fields with alien cultures and strange languages.

Long queues stretched out in front of the registration desks in the huge Training Hall. The hubbub of noisy chattering drifted off into the lofty, white-girdered roof space but to their right they could hear the strident, barking commands of the Sergeant Major as he ordered the new arrivals into their appropriate lines. They sheepishly joined the queue indicated and put their equipment on the floor; shuffling it along as they slowly progressed towards the form-filling officer.

They smiled uncomfortably as the officer in the adjacent desk yelled at an embarrassed youth who had replied 'my street' when questioned as to where he lived. The officer appeared to be the only person in the room who didn't know that My Street was just off Eccles New Road. The blushing youth, his clutching hands over his stomach belying the discomfort that he was now clearly suffering, was trying in vain to persuade the officer that it was a genuine address.

Progress in the queue seemed painfully slow and the over-vigorous nudge in his back almost sent the day-dreaming Edward stumbling over his rucksack. Big Charlie, chuckling loudly, was nodding towards Liam. 'See the little fella. Looks as though he's got labour pains and sucking a lemon at the same time.'

Liam's slightly crouching position, drawn in cheeks and puckered mouth did, indeed, suggest the misfortune that Big Charlie had described. 'Are you alright, mate?' Edward enquired with genuine concern.

'Not really. I'm seriously regretting those last two pints in The Railway,' Liam groaned.

'Why don't you nip off to the toilet then? It's going to be a while before we get to the desk.'

'I've just tried that but that big mouthed sod over there spotted me and gave me a right rollicking,' Liam answered, nodding towards the RSM. Gleaming beads of sweat were now standing out on their small friend's forehead. 'I can't hold out much longer.'

Big Charlie, more inclined to action than to words, picked up Liam's equipment and ushered his miserable friend to the front of the queue. There, his massive presence helped to persuade the man who was next in the line that allowing Liam to go in front of him was a suggestion that held great merit. The crisis was averted and within minutes Liam was rushing towards the exit door and heading for the toilet.

Once the registration was complete, however, they seemed to barely have time to think. Instructions and equipment came at them in an unabated rush. They were sent to the stables to clean and prepare the horses then, before that job was finished, they were despatched upstairs to the store rooms to carry down bales of blankets. Later, given a five minute break, they had hardly taken a couple of sips from their mugs of hot tea when they were sent off again; this time it was to clean and polish the big artillery guns in the yard at the back of the barracks.

'Bloody wars. This is worse than being at home with our Brig when her old granny is coming on one of her state visits,' Liam grumbled. 'At least, there, Brig is grateful to me afterwards and I can usually wangle a couple of pints in the Railway. These miserable sods won't even let you have a mouthful of your tea.'

'Stop complaining, Murphy, and get on with it.' Liam was galvanised into a renewed urgency as the RSM's rasping tones, now somewhat hoarser after his day of shouting at the unfortunate new recruits, emanated from a broken pane in the officer's toilet window. 'You have already put more liquid inside you today than your useless little bladder can hold,' bellowed the unseen but intimidating presence.

In the late afternoon, they were marched down to Cross Lane station where a crowd had gathered to wave them off. A lump came into Edward's throat when he saw his young daughter, Laura, and her friend sucking on their liquorice sticks amongst the enthusiastically waving throng.

'Ta ra Mr Craigie,' screamed Amy excitedly. 'Don't forget to pull tha socks up.'

The image of his daughter, her golden red hair framing her morose pale face, a tear gleaming in the corner of her eye, her hand waving uncertainly, haunted his mind throughout the journey to Bolton and on to the training camp in Turton.

29 Myrtle Street
Cross Lane
Salford 5
Lancs

5th September 1914

Dear Dad,
I hope that you like your new camp. Mam said that your beds are only bags full of straw so I hope that they made sure that there were no creepy-crawlies in it first.

Mam said that I have to write a letter to tell you about my haxident and I am very sorry about the nose on your white pot dog. It looks alright though now since we stuck the aniseed ball into the hole. My best friend, Amy, had a big nail sticking out at the front of her clogs that she didn't know about and it stuck in the coalman's horse when she was pinching a ride on its back and it jumped a bit and some sacks fell off. The coalman wasn't very pleased so I borrowed your hammer and that shoe thing to knock it back in. When I hit the nail her clog went up in the air and knocked the dog off the mantelpiece but it wasn't my fault because it just jumped up and the nail could have stuck in Amy if we didn't try to knock it back in.

I told Grandma and she said that she would swap it for her dog but Mam said I had to tell you anyway, so I am sorry because I know that you liked it.

I don't think that there is a 'h' in front of haxident but I couldn't find axident in your dictionary and our Edward said that is how to spell it and Mam keeps telling me to hurry up because she hasn't got all day to be waiting. Our Edward has been cleaning his delivery bike from the greengrocers all morning because he says that it will go faster but he can hardly hold it up.

Mam let me help her to whitewash the backyard yesterday so that it will look nice for when you get back. She just let me do the bottom bits so that I wouldn't get splashed. I was being very careful and didn't mean to get it on the cat but anyway it looked better with white patches on it like a cow.

I hope that you will be safe when you go to another country because in our books at school there seems to be a lot of fierce people with knives and spears. Be careful if you go to the pub with Mr Murphy when you get there.

I'm going now because our Mary is getting on my nerves crying all the time even when I push her dummy back in.

Love

Laura

They had been still going through their intensive training and drilling when they had heard on the 5th September that they were to be sent to Egypt.

Boarding their train for Southampton on the 9th September their worries and concerns for the families left at home were overwhelmed, for the moment, by the scale of the operation. It took forty trains to move the 15,500 men, their horses and guns and all the support equipment down to the south coast. The next day they boarded HMT 'Neuralia' at Southampton and at midnight they crept out of the harbour under a dark sky and a total blackout. As they looked back their last view of England was of a multitude of searchlights stabbing the blackness of the night.

Staring out into the darkness at the receding columns of light, Edward felt more profoundly than ever the trauma of the separation from the family that he had abandoned in Myrtle Street. Laura would have put little Mary in bed with her by now whilst the other kids would be in the next room, topping and tailing in the one big bed. The widening gap of the black sea was the final act in the separation. It denied him the right to walk back if his family cried out. Would the community around Myrtle Street embrace and protect its own in the same way that those who surrounded him as a child had? There was a different feel to the area where he now lived. It had grown dramatically in the last twenty years with the opening of the Docks and the upsurge in industrial development in Trafford Park. New shops and offices had been springing up everywhere and there was generally a greater sense of scheduled urgency.

But the old Salford above the railway line where he had grown up still had a much more traditional village feel about it. It was dominated by the large cattle market and the public houses that had been built to serve it but dotted around the area there was a selection of factories, cotton mills, stables, a variety theatre and the new Picture House. He had taken Laura there a couple of times to see the cinematograph shows.

He had been born in this top village in 1882, eight years after his parents had moved from Hulme pushing a borrowed handcart piled high with their personal possessions and their two young sons. His father, James, had had a trade as a wood turner but their life in Manchester had been tough as for most working class families. Utilitarian back-to-back housing with flooding drains from privies shared between a number of homes and the crushing poverty of unemployment meant disease was rife but treatment was poor. There they had had few rights and little property but the growing industry of Salford had offered many of them a beacon of hope. Arriving in their new house they had been given a hand to move in their meagre furnishings by the neighbours who also supplied cups of tea, sandwiches for lunch, food for tea, a minding service for the children and an introduction into the social framework of the street.

The Craigies' dream of a secure environment for their young family had, however, been cruelly shattered when, only two years after Edward's birth, his father James had died. In a desperate plight, his widowed mother, Martha, and her five young children had moved a hundred yards up Ellor Street into her mother's house in Turner Street. There she had been only a ten minute walk from some of the large houses around Langworthy Road where, to make ends meet, she had taken a job as a charwoman.

Edward gripped the rail and spread his feet to brace himself against the gentle swaying. He stared down into the inky blackness of the sea edged by the white frond as it lapped against the side of the ship. He hadn't felt deprived by the hardship or even aware of it. Only the families of the shopkeepers had some extra luxuries and that was their right. Fortunately, however, where the state failed the community cared. Neighbours would look out for the children, they would frequent the streets and they would spare the time to talk and, without being intrusive, they understood and cared about each other's needs. Shop proprietors stood behind their counters and they knew the customers and their families. They exchanged news and gossip, and formed an essential element of a mutually supportive social structure. They were aware of problems that families might have and were prepared to help when and where they could.

Edward had grown up in this tough but caring environment of late Victorian Salford without a father to provide a guiding hand and dependent on his big brothers for both sustenance and support. At home he had had his sister, Sarah, to share both his dreams and his troubles with, but it was the streets of Salford that had given him a deep insight into social and economic interactions. Streets where the neighbours were a watchful and guiding extension of his family. He felt sure that the people in Myrtle Street would provide the same support if it was needed in his absence but for how long before the sustaining bond was stretched too thin?

He knew from the dark night stillness on board the ships that there were 15,000 Salford men sharing the same pain and the same thoughts. There was only the distant rumble of the engines accompanied by the faint swish of the waves against the bows of the ships. The silence of the soldiers lay oppressively over the vessels.

Out of the darkness, Edward heard the lone but familiar voice of Liam as he started to sing '*Shine on Harvest Moon*' – one of the popular music hall numbers of the day. Shortly, the robust tones of Big Charlie joined in followed by others who were grouped around him. Edward looked up to see his two friends standing at the rail of the deck above. Very soon, the popular song was being taken up by troops on the neighbouring ships and within moments the whole convoy was singing.

The tension was broken and the bond of comrades-in-arms was sealed. During the next day they resumed training and, after being joined by other troop ships, including the battleship 'Ocean' and the cruiser 'Minerva', the first fleet to leave British shores since the Napoleonic wars headed out into open waters.

England
9th September 1914

Dear Pippin,

Thank you for your letter and for telling me about the Staffordshire dog. Your Mam was quite right to say that you should write to me and tell me about your accident because it is better to be honest about something and not to try to be sneaky. Don't worry about it. Accidents do happen sometimes and it is better that the clog injured the pot dog than it injured you. By the way, I don't think that axident will be in my dictionary because that is probably a very old way of spelling it from when people used to hurt themselves whilst chopping wood with their axes. I think that accident probably has a similar sort of meaning so I think that we could use this word instead. Maybe the aniseed ball will look alright if we paint it so we will try that when I come home.

We are on the train going down to Southampton at the moment. We are going to get the boat there and sail all the way to Egypt. We thought that the train had gone without Billy Murphy's Dad after we had stopped at one of the stations but then we found him at the next one. He had been in another carriage collecting the names of anybody who plays rugby and the train had started to move. I don't know how he thinks that we will be able to play rugby on sand, or whether we will ever have the time, so we will just have to see.

Thank you for helping your Mam to whitewash the backyard. It will probably be nearly Christmas by the time that I get back home and the weather will not be very nice by then, so I am glad that you have managed to do that for me.

I know that seems a long time to wait but just remember that I love you all to pieces and that you are all very precious to me. Hopefully the time will pass quickly and then I will be back with you again.

Love
Dad

Chapter 2

Egypt, Winter 1914

For the first three days the weather was bad and the journey was unpleasant – especially so for the Salford boys for whom the nearest contact with the sea had been a distant view from Trafford Road of the ships on the Manchester Ship Canal. The HMT 'Neuralia' was a 9000 ton passenger cargo vessel built in Glasgow and launched just two years previously. Its sleek 500 foot length and its two modern quadruple expansion steam engines were designed for mastery of the high seas but, unfortunately, its passengers on this voyage were not quite so well equipped. The transit of the Bay of Biscay proved a desperate trial for the Lancashire men who spent some days as almost permanent fixtures in their hammocks. Edward said his prayers and starved as a result of his total inability to face food, whilst Liam tried to remember his Hail Marys and struggled to climb back into his unfairly high hammock.

Big Charlie discovered, to his misfortune, that the open mesh metal stairs linking the decks together carried an additional hazard on this heaving ship when vomit from suffering soldiers on the higher levels dripped through the flights on to any unfortunates at a lower level.

For a while, Edward extracted some minimal pleasure listening to the desperate men prostrated around the deck who, believing that death was only moments away, were pleading forgiveness for a variety of intriguing sins. His own health, however, soon reached a nadir and even the entertaining diversion of the confessions failed to penetrate his consciousness. For days, he suffered the agony of the excruciating stomach contractions that ripped through them as he tried to eject the contents of an already empty stomach. The ship pitched and rolled, raised high into the air, sank gut-wrenchingly down into another monstrous abyss and the pale faces of the Salford soldiers grew greyer and their troubled eyes receded into dark sockets.

Finally, already some days beyond the point when they were convinced that death was inevitable, they passed Gibralter and the conditions improved. Now they were sailing across a sunlit, flat blue plain and white crested waves lapped gently on to the distant shoreline. Dramatic, almost white, mountains covered in splashes of green vegetation rose up from golden glowing beaches and communities of dazzling white buildings were scattered around the hillsides. Suddenly the journey seemed more tolerable.

They were especially lifted when, just after passing Malta, they saw a large fleet of ships sailing to the West. The Lancashire soldiers discovered that the vessels were carrying the Lahore Division bound for Marseilles. These troops were war-hardened Sikhs, Ghurkhas, Dogras, Punjabis, Pathans and Rajputs all anxious to take on the might of the German army. Edward and his mates, lifted by the thought of these famous warriors fighting on their side, cheered and shouted as the ships passed. Liam told them that there was an old soldier who drank in the Railway and that he had served in India. He had said that these fellas were great when they were on your side but, if they weren't, they would chop you into bits and leave you drying out in the sun for the birds to pick at. They then felt even more comforted to know that these fearsome soldiers were their allies.

A few days later, early on the morning of the 25 September, land was again spotted and everybody rushed to the ship's rail to watch as Egypt slowly emerged out of the mist. Edward was amazed to see this thin strip of surf-lined sand with occasional clumps of palm trees clinging to it. It was just like the pictures that he had seen in the books at school. The 'Neuralia' pushed effortlessly through the still, blue water and, slowly, more features of this North African landscape began to emerge. Eventually, they managed to pick out some gleaming white buildings scattered like a child's toy blocks along the thin strip of land. Soon they could see plumes of white smoke rising from the funnels of ships moored in the bay.

As the troopships slowly entered the harbour at Alexandria they passed an American battle cruiser on which the military band stood and played 'God Save the King'. The band of the 8th Manchesters responded with a rendering of 'Marching Through Georgia' which, they later realised, depending on the make-up of the cruiser's complement, might have been a slightly insensitive choice. However, everybody involved appeared delighted by the musical exchange and the Salford lads were buoyed by this unexpected reception.

Edward's battalion was one of the first to disembark on to the dusty, bustling dockside. They were given no time, however, to wonder at this alien land as they helped to unload their equipment. Along with the Yeomanry, the Signal Company and the Transport and Supply column, they quickly boarded the train to Cairo then headed for the main barracks at Abbasia.

The heat in Cairo during the day was stifling and the British soldiers found it difficult to acclimatise. Although they were soon issued with khaki helmets for protection they still had to wear, initially, the heavy serge uniforms that they had been issued with in England. All the tropical gear had been put into the hold of just one ship in Southampton and it took some days before the lightweight uniforms finally arrived in Egypt.

Perhaps the most serious setback that they had, however, was the loss of many of the horses. The ships that had transported them were not designed for carrying large animals, nor were there enough trained men to look after them, and many of the horses had died during the trip from

England. As they were the main way of moving men and equipment around, the death of so many was a severe hindrance to their operations.

He remembered how they had met as young teenagers when her family had moved into a house further down the street from where he lived. She had rebuked him for chasing a ball over her newly cleaned front steps. Her Irish born father had been a cloth fuller in Morley in Yorkshire but had lost his job. He had then made the fortuitous move to Salford and had found work there as a camel hair belt weaver.

The gentle, but tough, twelve year old that he used to taunt about her funny accent when she had first come to live in their street, had always seemed to him to be busy. She was the eldest, by five years, of six children and to Edward, who was the youngest of six, she seemed like a second mother in her family. She would often run errands to the shops on Ellor Street, using the opportunity for a quick kickabout with the boys. In the evenings she had looked after her younger siblings whilst her Mam prepared the tea before her Dad came home from the mill, but she had always been there with the lads when there was a bit of trouble with the gang from two streets away. On Saturday mornings he used to see Laura donkey stoning the front steps with dark cream in the centre and white stripes on the edges. She had thrown the cloth at him once when he had told her the lines weren't straight. Sometimes on Saturday afternoons, she would come with a few of her mates to join the rest of them for a bit of fishing in the Cut Canal. He'd tried to sneak a kiss off her on one occasion and she'd told him it was like kissing a fish.

She had always been there throughout his early teenage years, joining them as part of their group. As he had grown older he had walked out with a few of the other girls from around the Ellor Street area but it had somehow seemed inevitable that it would be the quiet but confident Laura from down the street that he would start courting.

Lying on his bed in the barracks, he was feeling the pain of separation from his wife more profoundly than that in his limbs from the afternoon's rugby match. He ached to be near her. He remembered when her family had moved down to Myrtle Street and he hadn't seen her for two weeks. He was shocked to find how many empty spaces were created in his life by her departure. He could still recall how nervous he had felt when he had finally plucked up the courage to knock on the door at her new house and ask her out.

He heard the springs on a nearby bed protesting loudly as Big Charlie lunged at a large insect buzzing near his head. 'Sod off, will you, and go and mither somebody else,' he yelled at the offending creature.

By the time that he was twenty, Edward's life had taken on a new pattern. Six mornings a week, he would walk down past the gas works to his job at the saw mills but each Sunday morning he would get up, polish his boots, put on his suit and best cap and take the short walk down Cross Lane to Laura's. She would be dressed in her Sunday frock and bonnet and in the summer they would walk hand-in-hand over Windsor Bridge and into Peel Park for an afternoon of strolling, talking, laughing or just sitting quietly on the grass listening to the brass band playing. He smiled as he remembered the day that Laura and Liam's girlfriend, Brigid, had linked arms and danced down the steps at the side of the museum singing 'Burlington Bertie.' They blushed and giggled with embarrassment when their efforts were loudly applauded by the crowd sitting on the hill at the side. On another occasion the girls had stepped into a group of brawling youths and, sternly waving their brollies at them, had instructed the boys to show proper respect for Sundays.

At other times, he and Laura would walk the big loop along Eccles New Road and up Langworthy Road, sneaking in at the back door of the Muirs' house. There Sarah would treat them to a scone and a cup of tea. Afterwards, they would carry on up to the Height, where the toffs lived, before returning along Broad Street to Cross Lane. They would spend hours dreaming about living in one of those big houses and of even owning one of the strange motorised carriages that they used to see.

'I can cope with those alright,' Liam mused as he lay back on the thin mattress that covered the taut springs of his iron frame bed, watching a lizard scuttling up the white wall of the dormitory. It stopped briefly to check around before proceeding up to the crevice where the red tiled roof met the wall. 'They do nobody any harm and they keep the flies down. Those beetles and scorpions though, they're vicious little sods. They weigh you up to see how tasty you might be.'

'Aye. It's a bit of a shock when you find them in your kitbag eating your last bit of cake,' Edward said, aiming a boot at a large unidentified creature that was progressing down the centre of the room.

'I wouldn't fancy waking up and finding one of those lizard things in my bed, though,' reflected Big Charlie, lounging in a large wicker chair as he polished his equipment. 'Never know where they might finish up.'

'There's no chance of that, Charlie,' Edward reassured him. 'That's why the legs of our beds are standing in those cans of water; so that no nasties can ravage us during the night. Unless they can swim, of course.'

'Well, I knew that,' said the slightly mollified Big Charlie. 'I didn't think they were for peeing in. But they could soon jump down off the top of the wall.'

Liam inclined his head towards the empty bed opposite. 'Jimmy Hargreaves didn't turn up for the game this afternoon and it looks as though he's still missing.'

'I heard that he's been taken to the Citadel hospital for a spot of treatment,' Edward offered, lowering his voice and directing his eyes towards his crotch.

'Oh, I see. What a piecan,' Liam said, grimacing. 'He obviously got more than he bargained for when he visited those exotic dancers.'

'What? Do you mean down there?' queried Big Charlie, crossing his legs protectively as he pondered Jimmy's misfortune.

Liam nodded in confirmation. 'Poor fella will be going through hell. I've been told that they stick an umbrella up your donker and then open it up to scrape all the VD out.'

'An umbrella? God help us.' Big Charlie's eyes were staring disbelievingly at Liam. 'They sound like maniacs, these Army doctors'

'It's probably just a bit of propaganda that the Army puts out to keep the lads away from those sorts of women,' Edward suggested helpfully.

'Well, it's worked for me,' Liam confirmed.

'And for me as well,' Big Charlie agreed, nodding vigorously whilst arching his body protectively forward.

'I'll start closing these shutters,' Edward said raising himself painfully off the bed. 'It's nearly five o'clock and it will be dark in a few minutes.'

'Aye, and freezing the balls off us to boot,' added Liam.

'You're lucky that you've still got any to freeze off after Chopper Hennessy trod on them in the match this afternoon,' chuckled Big Charlie. 'You're face was a picture.'

'I'm glad that you find it entertaining. I'll be bruised up to my armpits tomorrow and having to do a twenty mile route march through the desert and all you can do is laugh. Bloody Chopper Hennessy. He should stick to playing football. At least then it's only ankles he's bruising.'

Edward stood gazing through the window at the rapidly darkening sky. He was amazed by the speed with which it came light in the morning and by how it then went dark again at night within the space of about ten minutes. It also changed quickly from an almost unbearable heat to penetrating cold. In front of him was the huge expanse of the sandy parade square set on all four sides with the accommodation blocks, the offices, the equipment storage rooms, the Chapel and the extensive stables. The arched entrances of Abassia Barracks had heavy, fortified doors and a colonnaded arcade stretched all the way round the inside of the parade ground buildings. Elegant, slender columns standing on square plinths supported the upper levels along which ran the castellated walled walkways from which the guards kept their constant watch.

Reveille would be sounded in the morning at five o'clock and they would be on their first parade an hour after that. By seven o'clock the sun would be coming up and within minutes it would be uncomfortably hot. They would then have an intensive day of training and drill which, tomorrow, was to include the route march through the desert that Liam was dreading.

The training sessions, that had become a routine part of their Army life in Egypt, were divided between instructions in the techniques of desert warfare and familiarisation with the background to why they were there in the first place. They had been told that the main task of the British Army in Egypt was the defence of the Suez Canal as this was a vitally important supply route for the British Empire. Troops and equipment of the Australian, New Zealand and Indian forces passed this way en route for the Western Front, along with millions of tons of foodstuffs, minerals and other provisions bound for Britain and her Allies. It was explained that, because the strategic importance of the Canal had been recognised for a considerable time, Egypt had been occupied by British troops long before the Great War had started. For centuries before the Canal was built, however, this land had been part of the Turkish Ottoman Empire and the Turks bitterly resented this Western presence.

Edward was fascinated to hear the explanation of the significance of Egypt and the Suez Canal. None of them had really understood how the various countries had come to be involved and what the relationship was between them.

They were told that Germany had for many years before the war assiduously developed Turkey as an ally, which it saw as an important part of the Drang nach Osten – the Thrust towards the East. They wanted new markets, new territory. They wanted power and influence to match that of some of their European neighbours and they saw Turkey as a means of getting this. Their influence was already felt in the Turkish trade and commerce and the Turkish army was led by German military advisers. The Germans were also encouraging Turkey to declare a Jihad – a Muslim Holy War – against the British forces and they had put many Turkish agitators in the area to stir up hatred for the Allies.

The Arabs had thereby become an important part in the developing war. Some of the tribes responded to this rallying call from Muslim brethren but many, fearing a return to the dominating presence of the Turks, chose instead to fight with the British.

As he moved around the room closing the shutters, Edward could see hundreds of bats swooping over the parade ground. He watched the Arab labourers sweeping the dusty walkway outside the window. When they saw him they shouted a greeting, smiling broadly as they demonstrated their interesting, although limited and often robust, English vocabulary. 'Heh. Good bloody rugby man. You have good bloody win today,' one of them shouted when he saw Edward through the window.

'Aye. It was a hard game but we're well pleased with the win,' he said, smiling as the Arab waved his brush in the air. It had been a good game. They had played against the 7th Lancashires in front of a crowd of around eight hundred that had included a sprinkling of tourists and locals amongst the troops from both Battalions. The heat had been stifling but they had all suffered equally. They had made the 7th defend in their own half for most of the game and had come out eventual winners by 9 points to nil. Liam's constant probing attacks from scrum half had bemused the opposition and given Edward the space and the platform to operate in his position at stand off. Big Charlie's powerful runs from prop, particularly on balls fed to him by Liam, had been devastating and even the semi professional players in the 7th team had found him difficult to handle.

'Well, you might feel like knacker horses that have just finished their shift,' Edward said as he closed the last set of shutters, 'but let's go and get a couple of beers. We can celebrate and kill the pain at the same time.'

The Battalion found that, apart from training, drilling and desert marches, much of their time was spent in strengthening the defences around the Suez Canal and improving the communication facilities. What had become clear at an early stage was that they also had a special role in cultivating suitable relationships with the Arabs. They had a strict code of conduct to adhere to whenever they were in contact with local people but the good natured geniality of the northern soldiers broke down many barriers.

At first, they had found that the cultural differences and the unfathomable language created a large gulf, but the natural affinity and respect between working class men of any race soon helped to bridge it.

Edward was intrigued by the contrast between the Spartan and often shoddy clothes that the men wore and the brightly coloured clothes and glittery sandals of the women. Their contact was invariably with either the men or the boys as they were the ones who filled the jobs in the barracks and served in the bars, the cafes and the shops.

Off the main thoroughfares, the back streets of Cairo were a riot of exciting and vivid experiences. Plain, pale brown buildings with erratic windows and protruding upper floors supported by bracing, wooden jambs leaned together conspiratorially over narrow alleys. Broken render revealed the mud bricks of the structure. The streets had an amazing vigour, with heady aromas of exotic spices and cooking hanging sharply against the pungent and often putrid smells of cloth dying and leather tanning. Front rooms of the houses were given over to the pursuit of the family business with blacksmiths, pan makers, cobblers, leather workers and tailors, shops selling fruit and vegetables and stalls laden with colourful seeds, peppers and spices. The cries of the tradesmen, the sound of the carts and the babble of neighbourly exchanges and customer negotiations, created an atmosphere that thrilled the three Salford men as they walked around.

Liam was quick to pick up some Arabic words and enjoyed the rapport that he soon established. His technique was a combination of facial expressions, gesticulating and pointing, and a disarming willingness to laugh at his own difficulties. The Arabs responded warmly to him and tried to use the few English words that they, in turn, had managed to acquire.

Initially, Edward felt a natural reticence, fearing the embarrassment of using words in the wrong context, but Liam's determined and good humoured approach reinforced him and he quickly acquired a limited but useful vocabulary. Big Charlie, however, relied on his repertoire of expressive grunts reinforced by the nodding or shaking of his head, in order to get by. The Arabs were, anyway, generally just pleased to find that this large, somewhat intimidating, Englishman was actually quite affable.

The Salford Battalion, with their friendly and patient approach, and the Arabs, with their creative and articulate gestures, soon established a level of communication. Gradually, the soldiers managed to gain the trust and friendship of the natives and this helped to overcome the Turkish efforts to turn the conflict into a religious war.

During their time off the troops organized a variety of sports and social activities. Some of them discovered hidden talents as they took part in performances by the concert party whilst many, despite the stifling heat during the day, nurtured their talents in football, rugby, cricket and lacrosse.

On the odd occasions that they had a free evening, the three friends would take the opportunity to see a little more of Cairo, wandering around the busy streets, sitting in the cafes or in the bars. Their sense of adventure, or their yearning for a decent pint of beer, often induced them to sample a range of locally produced drinks with, sometimes, unfortunate consequences.

'Do you have a dominant leg when you've had a few, Eddie?' Liam asked, suddenly breaking the raw silence that hung over their breakfast cups.

Edward looked up, his bloodshot eyes and the untouched breakfast betraying the excesses of the previous night's visit to a bar suggested by another group of soldiers with a recommendation that they should try the Camel whisky. Mistaking the name for a famous Scottish clan and being surprised by the reasonable price, they had ignored the dubious taste, which the Egyptian barman had told them was because of the heat, and had drunk a few too many of them.

'Sorry, mate, what are you saying about legs?'

'Do you have one that takes over when you are a bit drunk?' said Liam, his voice sounding like two sheet of sandpaper rubbing together. 'I always find that my right leg goes off and takes my right arm with it. Then my left leg makes a bloody feeble attempt to catch up but my left arm gets no signal at all and just hangs there. Just when I'm trying to get my left side sorted out, my right leg takes off again and makes a right bugger's muddle of things.'

'Can't say that I've ever really thought about it,' Edward replied, frowning with the strain of having to address such a demanding issue. 'But I know that last night my left leg had a mind of its own.'

'Have you ever noticed Big Charlie? The signals seem to take a bit of time to get down to his legs. His body takes off first but his feet stay where they are, and then he has to do a bit of a run to catch up with himself.'

'Talking about Charlie,' Edward said, suddenly remembering his big friend's whereabouts, 'We'd better go and give him a shake. We're due on parade in ten minutes.'

When the morning parade was finished, and being much in need of some fresh air and exercise to purge the evil Camel whisky spirits, they decided on a trip to the pyramids.

'I wonder how many navvies they needed to build this lot,' the slowly recovering Big Charlie observed phlegmatically.

'Well, they would have had plenty to go at if Cairo had been anything like it is today,' Liam observed helpfully. 'And if they ran a bit short they could always nip up the Nile into Africa and grab another boatload. They controlled everything round here in those days.'

'But it sets you wondering, doesn't it, as to how they got those big blocks up there?' said Edward thoughtfully. 'They must weigh a few tons apiece some of those.'

'Aye. It'd take a fair bit of effort to lift them to the top of there,' observed Big Charlie, his brow furrowing as he concentrated on the heights of the mighty constructions.

'Hmm. I think that they would have had some kind of crane that they would have kept moving up to the different levels,' suggested Liam.

'Bit of a problem when you got to the pointed bit on the top though,' Big Charlie countered.

'Well, it's probably hollow inside so that they could pull the stones up round it,' Liam said impatiently. 'If you opened it up you would probably find a crane still inside it.'

Leaving the awe inspiring constructions they retreated to the welcoming shade of a palm tree and shared a much needed billy-can of water. They watched as a British Army officer marched down the line of a long queue and stood in front of a group of camels carrying soldiers from the ranks of the 1/8 Lancashires. The sandy moustached, slightly rotund Major, monocle stuck imperiously in his right eye, held up his hand to stop the procession.

'You there. Get off that animal and rejoin the queue. I will be taking this one over,' he commanded.

The man looked impassively down at him but didn't move and the Arab minder urged the camel forward.

'Do you hear me? I am ordering you to get off that camel. I am your superior officer and you will do what I say immediately,' the officer shouted angrily.

'Well, sir,' the soldier eventually said, "Appen there might be a bit of a problem there. I'm a bit high up like. You'll have to have a chat with the Gyppo there. It's his camel.'

The officer's already crimson face became like a glowing beacon. He pointed his stick angrily at the Arab. 'You. Get him down off there immediately.'

The camel's minder began to jabber incomeprehensibly, his thin brown arms flailing like a demented windmill as he pointed his long, almost black, finger firstly at the officer and the camel, then generally in the area. 'Perhaps, sir, he's explaining that officers only travel by first class camel,' a soldier seated on the animal behind suggested helpfully. 'These for the ranks do tend to whiff a bit.'

The men around began to laugh, adding their own less-than-helpful contributions to the rapidly expanding debate. The officer, trembling with anger, waved his stick threateningly at the Arab.

A European dressed in a pale linen suit and white trilby stepped forward from the waiting crowd. 'Excuse me. If I may be of assistance.' He smiled placatingly at the irate British officer. 'I think that the minder is pointing out that there is a queue and that you might like to join it along with the rest of us who are waiting for a ride.' He smiled again and nodded his head towards the back of the line.

The officer, eyes bulging and fists clenching and unclenching, erupted into a pneumatic, sweating frenzy. 'I am a Major in his Majesty's British Army and I will not have some filthy native telling me what to do,' he fumed. 'I am not queuing with this working class rabble. I have important duties at Headquarters to get back to.'

The Arab tried to ignore the bawling Englishman but the camel, clearly discomfited by the antics of this sweaty, twitching object jumping around in front of him, felt less generously disposed. It turned its massive head, curled back its thick, rubbery lips to reveal great, slab like, brown teeth and spat in the Major's face.

The soldier on the camel managed to keep his face fairly straight but others in the queue were less restrained. One man, seeing the officer attempting to wipe his face with the cuff of his sleeve, was heard to shout that it was nice to see the Major doing a bit of spit and polish, another informed him that the camel must have taken the hump with him, whilst a third suggested that the concert party, of which the

Major was a woefully inadequate director, should be renamed as Fosdyke's Follies.

'It's a pity it didn't bite the little bastard's head off his stupid fat shoulders,' Liam muttered almost inaudibly. Edward turned and was surprised to see the burning hate in his friend's face.

'Why, who is it?' he enquired. 'Can't say I have come across him before.'

'No you won't have. The only action he gets involved in is emptying whisky bottles.'

The officer, now turning from crimson into an unpleasant puce, was retreating down the dusty road and threatening to put everybody on a charge. His spluttering progress was accompanied by raucous jibes and loud laughter.

'Where do you know him from?'

'His name's Fforbes-Fosdyke. His dad was a General and now owns a lot of property round Salford and Hulme. That little sod thinks that's what entitles him to behave like an absolute dog's dick.'

Edward heard a rumbling growl and saw Big Charlie lumbering to his feet. For a moment he stood frowning at the comic figure before turning away and finding a seat under a palm tree a few yards away. His chin rested on his knees, his arms grasping round his calfs as he stared fixedly at the retreating figure.

'What is it with this Fforbes-Fosdyke, Liam?' Edward asked. 'He's obviously an unpleasant character but you and Big Charlie both seem really put out by seeing him.'

'Aye, he's the sort that would make rats seem like nice company. Anyway, least said soonest mended.'

29 Myrtle Street
Cross Lane
Salford 5
Great Britain

4th January 1915

Dear Dad,
Thank you for the Bible that you sent me for Christmas. It was very nice. I took it to Sunday School to show Miss Howard but I think that she was going to cry. I heard Mrs Jones telling Mrs Willoughby that Miss Howard has a sweetheart in somewhere called Flanders.

I asked Mam if Miss Howard is sad because you are in Egypt because I am sad when I think about you.

Me and our Edward went to the gas works yesterday for some coke. It's a bit cold now. The horses were slipping on the ice on Cross Lane which made us laugh. We took our Mary's pram out of the back yard.

Do you still love us in Egypt or do you get very sad?

Uncle James came round yesterday with a rabbit that he caught on Dorney Hills but it didn't look like my Floppy. Mam hung it on the rack in the kitchen with a piece of string. It smelt a bit funny.

Who does your washing in Egypt? Mam was darning our Edward's socks yesterday and she said that you will be having to darn your own socks now. Has the Army given you one of those mushroom things like Mam has?

I will finish now because we are going to get your wages and buy something to go with the rabbit.

Dad, will you bring us some of that sand home so that we can play in the backyard with it. Mam said that you are in a great big desert so it should be alright.

Love,

Laura – age nearly 8

Ps. Mam said to put ps to say something else and to tell you that we are all well and we all send our love. Mam said to hurry up because I have taken all morning to do this but I forgot to tell you that I got a nice doll for Christmas made out of wood. I have called her Dorothy because she is pretty like Miss Howard and I heard Mrs Willoughby call her Dorothy. But the bible is the best thing ever.

Ps2 Will you be coming home soon?

Chapter 3

Suez, 1915

Egypt was becoming, for the soldiers from Lancashire, a tediously hot and ultimately frustrating experience. Their capacity to take on board liquid was not met by the Army's willingness to supply it and Big Charlie's pleas that he did not have the build to be a Gyppie fell on largely unsympathetic ears.

Liam spent two days in detention on a charge contrived by Major Fforbes-Fosdyke who had emerged from the theatre tent in a haze of whisky fumes. Liam, unfortunately passing by at the time, had been ordered to run down at double-quick time to the officers' mess to get another bottle of whisky to use as a stage prop as it was essential to the plot and the smooth progress of the rehearsal. Liam had taken the liberty of suggesting that, as all the Arabs took things at a very slow pace in order to conserve their energy 'in this sodding heat' then, particularly as he was now off duty, he had no intention of running anywhere. He would, however, oblige the Major but would only walk down to the officers' mess.

The cell, apparently, did have the merit of being cooler during the day than the desert but he had yearned for his greatcoat during the night.

Although for much of the time the contact with the enemy had been restricted to minor skirmishes, the Army remained unshakeably keen to develop their abilities as soldiers. In the early months of 1915 they were increasingly taken out on route marches in the desert where, throughout the day, they suffered with the extreme heat, the dust and the flies. Even worse were the sandstorms which made breathing difficult and drove sand deep into their clothes.

At the end of the day the plummeting temperatures meant that any nights spent out in the desert in bivouac became long, sleepless, freezing hours waiting for the sun to come up.

There had been intelligence received, in October of the previous year, that the Turkish army were about to mount an attack. The Allied troops had been quickly put into position, the threat had petered out, and life had settled back into the normal dusty, perspiring routine.

By mid January 1915, however, the Turks were ready to advance again, having now assembled a force of two divisions, with another one in reserve, plus assorted camel and horse units. This was a relatively small army for supporting their ambitious plan to seize the Canal and, ultimately, to remove the Allied troops from Egypt, but they had many problems to overcome and a larger force might have made the task impossible.

The Turkish army had to march across two hundred miles of desert and this had needed careful timing in order that they could complete it during the short rainy season. They had taken the central route across the Sinai, enduring a hard, exhausting ten day march. Their objective was to capture Ismailia and therefore the critical drinking water supplies.

As the Allies prepared themselves for the attack, Edward and his battalion were moved back to the barracks at Alexandria and artillery was put into place alongside the west bank of the Canal. The guns were mostly concealed by the pines that were growing within a hundred yards of the Canal.

British aircraft tracked the progress of the Turks and, on 28 January 1915, observers identified a large column of troops on the central route. British and French ships entered the Canal and opened fire on the tired and exhausted army whilst the infantry manned defensive positions. Allied patrols initially clashed with the Turks on 2 February, but a sandstorm eventually halted the action.

At 3.00am the following morning a force of around twelve thousand Turkish and German troops made an attempt to cross the Canal. Being happily unaware of the close presence of the Allied artillery, and gleefully congratulating themselves on their success in reaching the Canal, they were carelessly loud in their attempts to launch their steel pontoons. The echoing metallic clangs, the loud splashes and the excited chatter gave the grateful British gunner commanders the opportunity to find an accurate range and position in the dark.

When it started, the thunderous onslaught from the British artillery came as a complete surprise to the shocked and startled Turks and they quite sensibly responded with an early retreat.

Elsewhere, the Indians also inflicted a serious defeat on the Turkish and German troops and captured many prisoners. The enemy soldiers, hopelessly beaten, turned and fled. For the next two days the British and Allied soldiers followed the retreating army and, in total, 1,600 prisoners were taken.

Various units of the East Lancashire Division had been engaged in defending against this Turkish attack but, once this first threat had subsided, life in the Canal Zone for Edward's regiment returned to its previous pattern. The officers resumed their training programmes with a renewed enthusiasm and the soldiers looked forward to any opportunity they could find to explore Cairo and its facilities.

The Turkish army, much to the irritation of Liam who accused them of deliberately trying to mess up the rugby matches that he had arranged, did make another attempt to take the Suez Canal on the 22 March. Once again they were routed fairly expediently by the Allied soldiers and the fixtures were only minimally affected.

Mustapha Barracks,
Alexandria,
Egypt.

20 February 1915

Dear Pippin,

I do still love you all just as much and miss you all the time. I get very sad as well, Darling, but hope that this job will be finished soon and then we can all come home.

It is very hot here during the day but then it gets very cold at night and we have to put our coats on top of our blankets.

Some parts of this country are very old and are just like it was when Jesus was alive. We have seen the men lifting the water out of the river with buckets that are tied to wooden poles with ropes. Then they tip the buckets and pour the water onto the fields to grow their vegetables.

I think that Miss Howard is mostly sad because her boyfriend is away in Flanders but she is probably also a little bit sad, as well, for all of you children if your Dads are away from home. Tell Miss Howard that we have seen lots of camels and they carry very big parcels and they don't need much to drink in the desert. If you get close to them they are very smelly and they spit at you if they are angry.

Your writing is very good now so keep trying hard at school. Are you good at sums as well?

Don't forget to help your Mam with Sadie and Mary and make sure that Ben doesn't get into any mischief.

I sometimes do my washing but mostly it is done by the Arabs that work in the barracks. They are also pretty good at darning socks.

I am pleased that you liked your bible and I know that you will look after it. I bet that you were really excited when you opened the parcel from Father Christmas and found a doll.

Love
Dad

Increasingly, the war seemed very distant for Edward and his colleagues and the Egyptians themselves seemed to be fairly unmoved by their presence. The training marches were becoming a feat of endurance. The wind was oppressively hot and the sun beat down mercilessly as the soldiers marched through the desert in full marching order. Even when they rested, the only respite for them was to shelter behind a blanket stretched over a couple of rifles. The feeling amongst the soldiers was that the main purpose of the army was to get you as fed up as possible so that you welcomed any change. More and more they felt a little bit cheated. This was not what they had trained for and what they had volunteered for. They wanted the chance to show what Salford men were made of. They wanted to give the Hun that bloody nose.

Such was the tedium that, when they were ordered at the beginning of May, to reinforce the beleaguered garrison on Gallipoli in Turkey, they all sang lustily in the cattle trucks which took them from Abbassia to Alexandria, regulating the beat of the song to the clip of the wheels. It was cold and dark as the train rumbled through the night but their spirits were high.

On the quayside, the early morning mist lay like a cold embrace over the sea and clung around the buildings that housed the offices of the great shipping companies. British names stood out reassuringly over many of the doors. Leaning out of the train window Edward watched the large, flat bottomed Arab dhows emerging out of the mist then disappearing again, wrapped by the slight breeze into the damp, white folds. Incomprehensible shouted greetings, warnings and instructions between the Arabs echoed over the slowing rhythm of the carriage wheels.

Approaching the looming presence of the Royal Naval vessels the sounds from the mists changed. Anguished voices, crying out from desperate pain, began to colour the spectrum of noise; scraping on Edward's suddenly taut nerves. When the shrouds of the morning fog parted he saw the rows of stretchers lined up on the dusty dockside between London bound crates of dates and figs and bales of cotton destined for Blackburn and Bolton.

He watched the sailors and medical orderlies unloading these ships that had come in from Gallipoli with the injured on board. The seemingly endless stream of heavily bandaged, agonised men flowed down the gangplanks and slowly covered the quayside. A cargo of pain and suffering waiting for whatever transport could be made available. Nurses moved amongst them dispensing strong painkillers and the stimulating medicine of firmly, but gently, delivered feminine kindness. They held cigarettes in the blistered lips of men with useless, or no, hands. For some of them, the kind eyes and the soothing nicotine became their last living memory.

Edward tried to suppress the shudder as he looked out over the wasted acres of the dying and the dead. His mind struggled to embrace the size and severity of it. There had been many Turkish soldiers injured in Egypt but what he was witnessing now, on this harbour side, was maiming on a massive scale. So many men with legs and arms missing or with major head injuries, the blood stained bandages binding the stumps of arms that had once driven the industry of Lancashire. The crying and groaning hovered in the air like wailing gulls and chilled the waiting soldiers. The singing had long since stopped.

Recognising the face of a man whose leg had been blown off, his thoughts were driven back to Laura and the kids waiting in Myrtle Street. He realized that some of these men had also taken that walk down Cross Lane to the Drill Hall. What would happen to their wives and families when they got home? Or to the wives woken by a knock on the door to read the few words of the telegram that would cleave through their lives?

Suddenly, chillingly, this war was not about football and rugby, about chattering Arabs and spitting camels. This was about death and destruction on a level that was hard to comprehend.

The officers had told them that they were about to enter a new theatre of war. 'Some show this is going to be' thought Edward with bitter irony. He stood at the rail of the ship, the HMT 'Karoa', numbed by the evidence of the awful carnage that was spread out below him, and thought about the kids in Salford, playing happily around home made maypoles; innocents on the streets who would now never see their dads again.

Chapter 4

Gallipoli, May 1915

The Lancashire Fusiliers boarded the troopship 'Karoa' at lunchtime on the 1 May 1915 and the activity in loading and securing all the weaponry and equipment that followed was a welcome distraction. They had been elated to be escaping from the stifling Egyptian summer and excited at the prospect of direct confrontation with the enemy. Only when they had been sitting on the quayside at Alexandria had they got a glimpse of the Hell's cauldron that they were about to be thrust into and their mood had become more sombre.

The following day they brought on board food, blankets, clothing, tents and medical equipment. They stacked crates of sacks ready to be filled with sand, tarpaulins for the construction of shelters and mail for the soldiers already out there. Finally they loaded the mules which they had brought over from the Reserve Park in Alexandria.

On the 3 May the ship nosed its way out of Alexandria harbour and the battalion diarist wrote '6 am 3.5.15 Saild'(sic). Edward and the now much sobered 1/8 Battalion headed out for the Dardanelles and the bloody fields of Gallipoli.

On board the ship, they then spent two days in intensive training. This was a new battle, they were told, a new type of warfare and a totally different terrain that they were heading towards. They had instruction covering the use of the ship-to-shore barges, the offloading of equipment and animals, the dangers from the shellfire and about where they should aim to position themselves under the cliffs.

As they sailed through the idyllic waters and the beautiful islands of the Aegean Sea, the story of the grim battles that had taken place less than two weeks before on the Gallipoli Peninsula began to emerge. Bit by bit, through official edicts and unofficial gossip, the explanation of the strategy, and the dreadful consequences, was gradually built up.

The fighting on the Western Front in Europe, it seemed, had by now settled into the form of siege warfare that defied attempts by both sides to unlock the other's defences. Attention had turned to look for other opportunities to break the deadlock. Some British politicians, led by Winston Churchill, had become infatuated by the idea of attacking Germany 'by the back door.' Despite pre-war Naval planning that suggested a passage of the Dardanelles Straits was not possible, the lure of an easier route to the defeat of Germany became irresistible. One strong argument put forward had been the need of the Russians for support in their struggle with the Turks. The senior officers in the Army high command, who felt that the attack should be concentrated on the Western Front, were overruled by the politicians and eventually they acquiesced.

The Gallipoli Peninsula was a part of Turkey and formed, along its southerly edge, one land side of the Dardanelles Straits – a historic waterway that linked the Aegean Sea to the Black Sea. The Peninsula was only ten miles across at the widest point and about forty five miles long. Cape Helles lay at its southernmost tip. Much of the terrain was rocky scrubland with little water. The hills were steep-sided and were cut into deep gullies and ravines.

Among the hills that lay along the spine of the peninsula, there were numerous peaks and valleys. The most important heights were the summits of Achi Baba, which stood at 709 feet and overlooked all of Cape Helles, and Sari Bair at 971 feet. From this peak the sea could be seen on both sides.

At the southern point of Cape Helles, where the Aegean Sea met the Dardanelles Straits, there were, along the Western side, a number of small sandy bays. There were no such beaches on the eastern side where the hills dropped down into the Straits. To the North West there was a large flat area surrounding a salt lake.

The whole region seemed to have little strategic importance as there were no towns and only a relatively few sleepy, insignificant settlements. Krithia in the South and Bulair in the North were the most important. Churchill's plan, however, was to assemble a large Allied force here and sweep up the Peninsula and on to Constantinople.

On 25 April 1915, under the command of General Sir Ian Hamilton, an Allied army of British, Anzac and French forces had started to land on the Gallipoli Peninsula. However, a naval bombardment of the area had been carried out a month before the landings took place and this had given the Turks a good warning that the area was about to become a focus of Allied attention. Under an able German General, Liman von Sanders, they had prepared a comprehensive system of defensive barriers and had land mined the beaches that they thought might be used for landings. Well-defended gun emplacements were situated in the cliffs overlooking the beaches, secure from further naval attacks.

On the other side of the narrow Dardanelles Straits they had positioned a number of big artillery guns. The welcoming party was in place and ready for the invaders.

These initial landings had included some Battalions of the Lancashire Fusiliers as part of the 86th Brigade. Having thought that they were going to France they had had their spirits lifted when they had discovered that their new posting was taking them to Turkey. Their boat journey through the Mediterranean and the Aegean seas had seemed idyllic to these men. Their view of the World had been restricted before that to occasional glimpses of the hills around their homes in the drab cotton mill towns of Lancashire.

These first troops had gone ashore at 6.00am on 'W' Beach on and had fought heroically against unbelievable odds to gain a foothold on Turkish soil. But the operation had been a disaster and they had been cut down mercilessly by the Turkish defences.

They had disembarked from HMS 'Euryalus' into the cutters taking them ashore but, as they touched the beach, they had been pounded by the Turkish shore batteries from the far side of the Straits. When they had jumped from the cutters to wade ashore they had found themselves entangled in thick barbed wire that was laid under the water. As the soldiers had struggled to cut through the barrier a ferocious tirade of gunfire from emplacements on the shore had torn into them.

Within minutes, the sea had flowed red with the blood of British soldiers, gunned down as they struggled to free themselves from the clawing grip of the submerged wire barrier. Officers, standing in the water waving their men on, had been cut down by snipers.

In the neighbouring bay, at 'V' Beach, the HMS 'Clyde', shelled by the Turkish heavy artillery, was blown apart and lay crippled on its side in the water.

For those on 'W' Beach who had managed to reach the shore there had followed a desperate run across the land-mined sands and through the incessant machine gun fire to gain the shelter of the cliffs. Many had fallen on the way.

Elsewhere, other Allied troops had met with varying degrees of resistance in landing on the Peninsula but they had failed to pursue whatever advantage they had gained. They had made the fatal mistake of waiting for communication from other forces to order an advance but it never came and the Turks gained the time that they needed to send in reinforcements.

Over those first few days various attempts had been made to take Krithia but the heavy bombardment that was needed to give cover as they advanced towards the enemy lines had not materialised. Unfortunately, with so much weaponry now committed to the Western Front and because there was, anyway, a belief in the higher echelons of the army that the Turks would not present a strong opposition, only three heavy guns and just a small supply of artillery had been landed.

The few remaining members of the Battalion who had survived the carnage of the beaches had fought bravely but had struggled against the odds. These Lancashire soldiers, at the end of April 1915, had been sent to war like Trojans in a glass horse.

Their training in Tatton Park had taught them how to march in strict formation, how to dig trenches, how to attack and kill the enemy with their bayonets and, when enough guns could be found, how to shoot more accurately. How to climb a cliff, however, or walk across an open field under enfilading fire from secure and barely threatened enemy machine guns had barely been touched on.

By the 30 April the 1st Lancashire Fusiliers had lost a thousand men from the battalion strength of around one thousand four hundred.

The following day the Turks had launched a night attack and had continued the offensive until daylight. The Allied troops, although initially startled by the manic ferocity of these soldiers who had come hurtling at them screaming 'Allah, Allah' had fought hard and had retained the positions that had already cost them so many lives to gain.

Many Turkish prisoners had been taken during those first few days but this action marked the end of the open warfare on Cape Helles. The losses for the Allied forces had been so heavy that neither sufficient men nor weaponry remained to pursue the attack. Under the blazing sun of the day, the freezing nights and the frequent drenching rain the soldiers from both sides dug themselves in.

It had become clear by then that if there was to be any hope of further progress they would need significant reinforcements and hence the decision had been made to transfer the 42nd Division from Egypt. Edward and his mates from Salford would be sent to stand shoulder to shoulder with the pitifully few Lancashire men in Gallipoli who had managed to survive those first landings.

The plan, to link up with the regulars who were already there and to then advance up the peninsula and take the village of Krithia, was explained to them as they huddled together in the hold of the ship. They were also warned that they should avoid touching the bodies that they would encounter both in the water and on the beaches.

The final hours of darkness were receding from the skies on the morning of the 5 May as the 'Karoa' gently nosed her way forward towards the landing beach at Cape Helles. The men had been up and preparing themselves for hours and, with the tension mounting, the Lancashire humour was a fortifying carapace.

'It could have been a bit more fun if we had been pulling into Blackpool Central,' Liam suggested cheerily.

'Well, at least there wouldn't have been all the dead bodies in the water to wade through,' Big Charlie replied. 'They don't make it sound much like a holiday outing.'

'No, but the weather will be better here.'

'And there'd be no barbed wire ripping your legs to shreds in Blackpool.'

'But you won't have any fearsome landladies to make your life a misery.'

'Aye, but I'd rather have any of those than that sodding Major.'

Liam grew suddenly serious. 'He's not with us, is he? I haven't seen him on the boat.'

'He'll be somewhere plaguing us. Not too close to any action though.'

'It all seems a bit strange to me,' Edward intervened. 'Why are we trying to take a place like this? Nobody lives here and it is miles from anywhere.

'They said it is to go in by the back door of Germany,' Liam explained.

'It's more like Turkey's back yard. And what's the sense in taking them on in there? They didn't seem all that bothered in Egypt but they're going to be a lot keener about us invading their own country.'

The clanking of the anchor chain echoed like a command for silence round the hold of the ship where the soldiers were waiting. Minutes later, the throbbing engines were cut and an eerie silence descended over the ship. From somewhere in the distance they could hear the rolling boom of heavy guns.

There was half an hour to go before the 6.00 am landing time. The men smoked their pipes and cigarettes and gripped their rifles more tightly as the officers gave the final briefing. There was a heightened sense of anticipation, a feeling that they were finally going to be involved in the real action. They were part of a team that was going to be called upon to show their bravery in a fight. Death had not been a close companion in their service so far and it did not insinuate its sinister, paralysing presence now. The detritus of the carnage on the quayside at Alexandria had been sobering but now the Salford men joked and boasted about what they would do to give one back to those Turks.

Edward watched Big Charlie take a large cloth from his kitbag and carefully polish his Lee Enfield rifle. He checked it thoroughly, scrutinising the detail of the mechanism and the precision of the bar of light reflected down the barrel. Satisfied with his inspection, he gave it a final polish, folded the cloth into exact quarters and replaced it in the bag.

The seconds ticked away and they heard the metallic thud of the steam tugs being positioned alongside their boat. Then came the command to be up on deck and they were racing up the ladders and into the open air.

Liam performed a few quick, dribbling steps across the deck shouting to Edward 'I feel like Billy Meredith coming out of the tunnel at the Cup Final.'

'Aye, well let's hope that we don't score any own goals,' Big Charlie grumbled as he narrowly missed Edward's head with the kitbag that he was swinging on to his shoulder but succeeded instead in catching Liam in the crotch with the butt of his rifle.

On the deck they were instructed to load the small landing vessels with a part of the consignment of supplies and ammunition. They set about the task with vigorous impatience, keen to get the job done and to get on to the beach so that they could 'give those Turks a good hiding.'

Edward stood on the deck of the tug and watched as the sandy line of 'W' beach with the high cliff behind grew larger. He could hear the whine of the shells being directed at them from across the Dardanelles Straits and saw the spectacular plumes of water as they missed their targets and fell into the sea. The mules on the other boats whinnied and stirred restlessly, distressed by the rumbling explosions.

Approaching the beach he realised that the line of flotsam that fringed the sea was the bloated carcasses of men and beasts that had perished in the water. The tugs eased their way through the stinking remnants and moored alongside the barges that had been fixed against the beach to provide temporary docking. In the rapidly increasing heat of the sunny morning they unloaded the tug and moved the equipment and supplies up to a sheltered position under the cliff.

As they struggled with their loads under the searing sun they heard the crack of a rifle shot. Edward turned and saw that an officer, who had been standing on the beach urging on his men a few moments before, was now lying in the sand with blood spurting from his shoulder. The medical orderlies dropped their loads and ran over to him. He was still alive and he cursed loudly as he was carried over the rough terrain to the temporary first aid post.

The soldiers in the area had fallen to the ground and, with rifles at the ready, their eyes searched the cliffs for the attacker. No snipers could be seen and no more shots came. They returned to the job in hand with renewed urgency. A canteen was soon set up and they stopped for a welcome cup of tea.

That day, all the men, equipment and animals were safely brought ashore from the 'Karoa', despite the constant threat from the shelling. As the sun sank down into the Aegean the battalion knew that they had worked hard together as a team and had done the job well. They now looked forward to the bivouac on the cliffs and a good night's sleep without the throbbing of the ship's engines that had accompanied them for the last two nights.

Edward settled himself down and took out the mail that he had been given. It had crossed from Egypt with them but it had been on the ship that had landed at the adjacent 'V' beach.

29 Myrtle Street
Cross Lane
Salford 5
Great Britain

1st April 1915

Dear Dad,
       This morning we all ran down the stairs because our Edward said that you and Billy Murphy's Dad were coming down Cross Lane on some camels. When we went outside to see he locked us out with only our pyjamas on and shouted 'April Fools' through the letterbox. Mam shouted at him because it started raining and he let us back in. He's horrible sometimes. Our Ben found a dead mouse in the back yard and put it in our Edward's shoe and when he got ready to go to his job at the greengrocers he went mad. We were too scared to shout 'April Fool' at him and we hid in next door's lavatory.
       I read about camels in a book at school and it said they are called ships of the desert. Do you see them going down that canal that Mam said you are working on?
       Elsie Craddock has been chosen as May Queen at Central Mission and I am going to be a Lady in Waiting. They asked our Edward to be the head page boy but Elsie Craddock's Mam moaned because she said that our Edward had broken their window with a football so he can't do it now. He said he is not bothered anyway because Elsie Craddock looks like a haddock.
       Mam got a chicken from the market yesterday and I helped her to pluck it but it hurt my hands after a bit. Ben was pulling the stringy bit in the middle of its leg and making its claws move.
       After we had been to the market we went to see Aunty Mary and Uncle Jim and he said that he will get some wood from work and make me a cot for Dorothy when it's my birthday and I told him that is in 6 weeks

71

and 5 days but it's only 6 weeks and 4 days today in this letter.

When I went down for a drink of water last night Mam was sat with her knitting on her knee and just looking at the fire without moving. I thought she had gone to sleep. She is doing a cardigan for our Sadie out of one of your old jumpers. She's going to do some socks for our Ben with the rest.

Do you think you will be home for the summer holidays and we could go up to the park?

Love

Laura

As darkness fell the temperature dropped and the men were stunned by the penetrating cold. No matter what they did they could not get warm. They jumped up and down, they did exercises, they ran around and they huddled together on the ground but nothing could resist the fierce cold of the Turkish night and when the orders came to prepare to move they were glad of the distraction.

During the night the officers had been out to view the enemy positions to the left of their line and then at 3.30am, on the morning of the 6 May, the battalion moved from the shelter of the cliffs and headed up to Gully Beach. They marched through the rest of the coldly lit night and, as the morning sun tinted the ground with colourful hues, they arrived at their position above the beach in Gully Ravine. There the Territorials linked up with the regulars who had fought their way up the Ravine a week earlier and were now holding a line there.

When Edward's battalion arrived they found a force of tired and demoralised soldiers. The drawn faces and the sunken eyes of the men still manning these front line trenches expressed more vividly than words the horrors and hardships of the past week. They had lost many men, including a lot of their officers, and they now needed both sleep and leadership.

These tattered remnants of what a week ago had been a proud battalion of fighting men, were very bitter as they recounted the details of the poorly prepared landings. They described the way that they were fired on from unseen positions whilst they had been stuck on the underwater barbed wire defences; how they had been mown down with ridiculous ease as they tried to take the almost impregnable positions that were held by the Turks. Only a mile of land had been gained at the expense of a huge loss of lives.

Edward's battalion was quickly organized into groups to establish the base camp at the entrance to Gully Ravine and to clear the lines of the corpses. After they had buried the dead they strengthened the lines and readied themselves for an attack.

They came across a Turkish prisoner of war with his face, arms and hands painted green and wearing a green uniform. He had been shot down out of his gun nest in a tree, from where he had accounted for many officers with his accurate sniping. He had told his captors how the officers were easily identified targets because they only had pistols and they wore different uniforms.

A sergeant with the Regulars, a Liverpudlian named Frank Williams, suggested to Edward that the officers would be better wearing kilts. 'The Turks never fire at the Jocks' he said 'because they think that they are all women and their principles won't allow them to kill women.'

Edward laughed. They should issue the kilts to all of us, he thought, then at least we would have a better chance. But he knew that the uniform was just another way of differentiating the officer class. The majority of them had no social, economic or educational common point of contact with the rank and file soldier who generally came from a working class background. Many of the officers were the sons of wealthier families for whom there was no clear career path other than the army. That offered them the chance of adventure and excitement and afterwards they would gain access to the best clubs, marry into the right circles and perhaps be given a safe seat in Parliament.

They were, however, professional and trained soldiers who provided leadership and guidance. It was clear that the number that were being killed or injured by the selective and accurate shooting of this strange looking Turk and his colleagues would leave them with a severe problem.

Nevertheless, the lads from Salford regarded the injured sniper not with hatred but with the sort of pity that is given to an injured carthorse. They had not yet acquired the callousness of war veterans.

74

By 7.30 in the evening, Edward and his Salford pals were positioned in the front line in Gully Ravine and stretching eastwards up the hill known as Fir Tree Spur. The complete Allied line reached from the Aegean Sea on the left, over Gully Spur and down into Gully Ravine, up over Fir Tree Spur and then across the Peninsula to the Dardanelles Straits on the right. The plan for the next two days was to advance the whole of the front line up the Peninsula and to capture Krithia and Achi Baba.

The evening breeze coming in from the sea was beginning to clear the sickly sweet veils of death from the trenches. Edward sucked in the comfort of another cigarette and tried to work out the time in England. He decided that Laura and the kids should be safely tucked up in bed by now. Would the same bright moon that was lighting up his trench be lighting up their bedrooms and pointing those bright silvery fingers through the slits in the curtain and on to their sleeping faces?

Thank God she wouldn't know that in a few hours time he would be leaving the safety of his trench and running up this ravine into enemy fire. Whilst she was giving Sadie and Mary a sugar butty he would be trying to kill the Turkish soldiers before they killed him. Turkish soldiers who at this moment were further up the valley, gazing up at these same stars and thinking about their own wives and families in their homes. Please God he would make it and Laura would not be getting that knock on the front door from the telegram boy.

Edward looked around him at the high sides of the valley that were capped with a covering of fir trees. The stream near where he lay ran down from the enemy positions about five hundred yards away and the land between was a rocky scrub land that would provide only limited cover for them behind the small hillocks and gorse bushes. Running off from the sides of the valley were a number of smaller gullies – each with its own surprises. Throughout the night the whine of exchanged shellfire continued with odd bursts of rifle fire between as the trench watches on both sides shot nervously at imaginary enemies in the shadows of no-man's land.

The small stream that ran down the ravine was full of slime and was blood-coloured in patches around the unreachable corpses. It was also home to hundreds of frogs that eventually added their loud croaking to the chorus of noise of Gallipoli. From nearby he heard a strained, mournful animal sound. He looked round and saw Liam, hands cupped around his mouth, croaking in counterpoint to the frogs.

The following morning, shortly before 11.00am, there was a brief and barely noticed artillery attack on the Turkish positions. They had earlier had a briefing from Major Fforbes-Fosdyke who had given them a theatrical, almost comic, address on the need for discipline under fire, showing courage in the face of adversity and for setting aside personal safety when fighting in this noble war. They were told that they should feel honoured to have been given this opportunity to pay the ultimate price for the glory of the King and the British Empire. The Major had come to Gallipoli only two days before, landing on 'V' Beach, but spoke the role of a heroic survivor of the first landings in April. He took a perverse delight in talking about the men who had died and how they must be prepared to meet death themselves to avenge the loss of their comrades.

Edward stared at the taut, white skin of his knuckles as his hands gripped round his rifle and wondered whether the King would look after his wife and kids if he was called on to pay this ultimate price. The NCO's had been calling out the five minute time signals for twenty minutes now. 10.50am – only ten minutes left.

Big Charlie carefully wiped his Lee Enfield with his polishing cloth and Liam, slumped on the firing step, muttered prayers for safe deliverance.

Around him he could see the tense bodies of his mates, rifles held in front of them, eyes staring into the ground. He looked at the soldier on his left. He was younger than Edward and came from near the gas works but he was the type who never said that much. Kept himself to himself really. Edward had played football with the lad's older brother, the aptly named Chopper Hennessy, and had had a more recent bruising encounter with him on a rugby field in Egypt. Young Hennessy had only recently joined the Terriers, having been brought along by Chopper 'to get him out a bit.' Edward noticed that the lad had taken off his glasses. Lines of shining dried salt traced down his cheeks. The tension was showing in the tight ridged muscles of the young man's neck and Edward asked him if he was OK. He got no reply. The eyes never flickered and the only sign of life was the huge throbbing blood vessel on the side of his head. 10.55am.

Edward turned away. The younger man was paralysed by an intense fear and Edward was already struggling to cope with his own. Acrid smelling smoke was beginning to drift down into the trenches.

At 11.00am the synchronized whistles of the officers sounded along the whole of the line and the trench erupted in a frenzy of shouting and movement as the soldiers went up the ladders. As Edward waited to go up he heard a furious shouting at the side of him. He looked round and saw Major Fforbes-Fosdyke screaming at the frightened soldier who was still sitting bolt upright on the fire step. The petrified young Hennessy didn't move and the Major, shouting at him to stand up and get over the top, grabbed at him and tried to lift him. The lad's body and mind, however, had completely shut down and he was rigid with fear. The officer took out his pistol and shot the young soldier from near the gas works through the head. The tense muscles in the boy's neck relaxed as the blood pumped from the wound above his eye. Slowly, but with increasing velocity, his body tumbled sideways, crumbling into a lifeless heap on the floor. Edward stared in disbelief and tried to grab the Major's hand but he pushed him back. They had already had their tot of rum but the smell of whisky on the officer's breath was overpowering. His sandy moustache was flecked with spittle and snot from his nose. The white, sweating face and staring blue eyes betrayed the demeanour of an unbalanced mind. 'Get on with it soldier' he snarled, waving the pistol threateningly at Edward's head. 'If we had left him there then next time we would have had more actors than the Hippodrome.'

Still reeling from the shock of what he had witnessed, Edward grabbed the ladder and went over the parapet. He followed the others as they strode off in a line, their bodies released from the coiled spring tension by the piercing whistles in the trenches but contained by the numbingly slow pace at which they had been trained to proceed. They tried to keep the formation that they had been instructed to hold but the Turkish machine guns swept their lines with enfilading fire and the Turkish infantrymen picked off their targets with ease. The enemy soldiers had established themselves in vantage points higher up the ravine and they could watch every movement of the Allied troops. Some men bent down and tried to help injured comrades but then they themselves were gunned down mercilessly. The officers yelled at them to keep going, waving their pistols in frantic encouragement.

The Turkish machine gun bullets were slicing through the Salford lads as though they were tissue paper. Edward saw men in front whose heads suddenly seemed to explode and others whose bodies arched impossibly backwards then collapsed on the ground. He could hear the bullets whistling past as they sought another victim and black smoke was starting to drift down into the valley from the hill on his left.

He jumped over the twisted bodies of friends, stumbled then raced forward again to catch up. They were running now, being driven by instinct in a blind rush into mayhem.

From behind him he heard an officer shout 'Get Down. Find Shelter and Get Down.' To his right he saw a small gully but the uphill struggle in intense heat and over rough ground had weakened him. The bullets flew around but the strength had drained out of his legs. The sweat was running inside his heavy uniform and the blood throbbed in his ears. He screamed at his failing body to keep going for the gully. He tripped on another rock, his unsteady legs collapsed and he fell to the ground. He lay there confused by the noise, the heat, the body that would not respond, and he waited for the bullet that would finish him. His blood raced and his lungs hunted for more air. He gasped huge mouthfuls of dust laden oxygen and from somewhere deep inside his body came a moment of stillness. He heard Laura's words 'Keep Safe Love' and he felt that last soft kiss on his cheek like an angel's touch.

A warm surge of strength flowed through his body and he was on his feet again. He drove himself forward through the scrub and flung himself into the shelter of the gully.

As his breathing became calmer and his heartbeat slowed, he felt a fountain of fury building up inside him. They had been told to attack and take the machine gun redoubts that were five hundred yards away and yet they only had their rifles with fixed bayonets to do it. They had not even been spared the shells for supporting artillery to give them cover. Ten days before, the regulars had failed to achieve those targets and now, after the enemy had been given more chance to consolidate their positions, they were being ordered to repeat the performance. Whoever had planned this attack in some remote office had gambled with the lives of the soldiers in these fields in a cynical attempt to retrieve what had been a poorly planned and badly organized strategy from the outset.

Edward looked around him at the dead and dying. If an injured man moved he would be shot at by a distant Turkish rifle. Sergeant Williams shouted instructions to re-group and they slowly made their way forward, inching along the ravine by erratic, darting runs. The rocks around them splintered with the enemy bullets and they returned the fire whenever they had a view of the Turkish trenches, but it was to no avail. They made little impression on the enemy and the officers realized that the goal that they had been set was an impossible one.

At nightfall they made their way back to their trenches bringing back all the injured that they could retrieve. Edward felt an overwhelming tiredness but couldn't sleep. He drew heavily on one cigarette after another then said a little prayer that he would be spared to return to Cross Lane and to see Laura and the kids again.

Edward told Liam and Big Charlie about the execution of Young Hennessy by the Major. Their stunned silence was eventually broken by Liam who asked 'Where's Chopper at the moment, then?'

'He's up on the hill with the 7th'

'He'll be out for blood when he hears about this.'

'Aye,' Edward said, 'but he'll have to watch himself or he'll finish up in a load of trouble.'

'Have a word with Frank Williams. See what he has to say.'

During the night they again cleared away the dead and then deepened the trenches. They were told that Gully Ravine was a weak point in the Allied line because it was low down and vulnerable. Up on Gully Spur, the hill to their left that lay between them and the Aegean Sea, the 6th and 7th Lancashire Fusiliers, along with a company from Edward's battalion, had that day made an advance of 400 yards and that had been held.

The next morning they again attacked the enemy line but this time they had been spared the diatribe by the manic Major. Edward watched as the first groups went over, knowing that shortly it would be his turn. It was the same, disciplined precision of the count down, the same words of command and the same mechanical response from the soldiers. The officers and NCO's ran around, shouting and waving rifles and pistols, the men went over the parapet and then, for too many, their lives were blasted out of their bodies. Some did not even make it over the top – they fell back off the ladders and the support groups cleared them away.

The last five minutes of the countdown began for Edward's group. He could hear the bullets thudding into the sandbags above his head. Hopefully, the first runners would have made some progress up the valley and would be threatening the enemy lines. They had their bayonets fixed, and they had been trained to use them, but the five hundred yards of scrubland that had to be crossed first meant that there would be little chance of close combat fighting.

Edward had been told that this time they would be going at intervals and running in small groups. That way they presented a smaller target to the Turkish machine guns. He knew, though, that the terrain in the valley and the fifty foot cliffs at the sides gave them little chance of crossing this no-man's land.

He heard the loud explosions as the ships in the sea beyond Gully Spur began firing on the Turkish positions but the chattering of the machine guns kept on. He saw pictures in his mind of the family room when he was a small boy. His brothers were nowhere to be seen but his mother was scrubbing the back of a man sitting in a zinc bath in front of the fire. He tried to focus on the picture but it was gone. The seconds ticked away, he said a prayer to be spared to see his wife and family again, and the shreaking whistles pierced his thoughts.

This time Edward followed closely behind the Liverpool Sergeant, Frank Williams. He seemed to know what he was doing as he ran purposefully along, ducking low so that he gained shelter from a low ridge which Edward had not seen on his first run. Clouds of acrid, dusty smoke rolled down the valley accompanied by the rumbling thunder of the bombardment higher up. They dashed quickly over an exposed section and then they were amongst the rocks below the cliffs. The sergeant directed the group as to where they should position themselves and then they sat back to recover their breath. One man stood up to stretch his back and as his head came above the rock the top of his skull flew off. His soft hat offered no protection.

'They do stop you getting bird shit in your hair, though,' said the sergeant seeing Edward's anguished face staring at the tattered regimental cap. 'It's the first in our group today so that's not too bad' he added 'but keep your heads down or he won't be the last.'

They crawled from one sun dappled rock to another for thirty minutes, progressing with painstaking slowness up the ravine, until they found themselves crouching behind a shaded hillock just below the Turkish lines. Across the valley they could see that various groups held positions which also gave them a view of the enemy. Down the valley they had a clear sight of their own lines and of the bed of the stream clogged with the bodies of British soldiers. Some had become gruesomely distended as they baked in the hot sun. On the top of Gully Spur, over the far side of the ravine, they watched the exploding shells from the Royal Navy vessels out at sea as they tried to dislodge the Turkish machine guns. Edward could see that, although they had done a lot of damage to the enemy trenches, they would never stop the machine guns as they had been securely sheltered in the mouth of a cave.

When Williams was satisfied that he had all the men positioned correctly he told them to ready themselves and to open fire if Turkish soldiers showed themselves. 'Remember that they have killed your mates and they will kill you if you give them half a chance' he said. When the soldiers in the trench above them fired on the Lancashire Fusiliers below, the sergeant's group responded. Eventually, they were spotted by the machine gunners and were forced by the furious onslaught of bullets to shelter below the rocks. Their Lee Enfields with their shiny bayonets felt puny and inept against this tornado of fire power.

It soon became clear that they could make no more progress and Williams guided them back down to their own trenches. They smoked, drank tea and cut off chunks of bully beef for their lunch. They talked about the events of the morning, exaggerated the number of Turkish soldiers they had seen fall, and quietly congratulated themselves on surviving.

That afternoon they went over again. The sergeant led them on a different course, heading this time for one of the side gullies. Their route took them through an area of dogwood scrubland and the Turkish gunners spotted them. By the time that they reached the shelter, one man had been killed and another had a splintered arm. The sergeant fixed the arm in the best way that he could with his field dressing pack but the man needed more expert treatment. He was screaming in agony and shouting for his mother. 'Will you bloody shut up,' Liam said irritably, cupping his hands to be heard above the racket. 'Every sodding sniper in Turkey will know where we are hiding with that row.' Turning to Big Charlie he confided 'His Dad's that Italian joiner from behind the Church, you know. They can't do anything quietly.'

'Aye, I know. Used to be like that when he got the cane at school.'

It was clear that they could not go forward because of the enemy gun fire and the only option was to crawl towards the cliffs and then to tack back down to their trenches.

In the safety of the trench, they took the injured man to the first aid post for treatment and then gratefully sipped at the hot tea that had been poured for them. Food had been brought up from the canteen on the beach by the newly landed soldiers who were now gradually filling up the trenches. Although they were hungry they were too tense to eat and they were still sat in the communication trench smoking and exchanging the small details of the battle, the scraps of success that members of a beaten team use to rebuild each other's morale, when the Captain arrived.

He told them that they were to be relieved from the line and were to bivouac at 'W' beach. He said that it was still being shelled and fired upon by the Turks but they might get the opportunity for a game of soccer and a swim in the sea. 'It'll be just like Blackpool on bonfire night,' muttered Liam as he picked up his enamel cup. 'I'll see if I can find my bucket and spade.'

Chapter 5

The Trenches at Krithia

The battalion spent three busy days on 'W' beach. Edward
and his friends helped the sappers, who had now arrived, to
strengthen roads, dig ditches and to sink wells in the search
for vital supplies of fresh water. They unloaded, under fire,
the ships that came in and they helped the men of no.2 Transport to load the pack mules that took the supplies to dumps
on the front lines. These transport men showed great
initiative in finding mules, usually grazing in the fields where
they had been left by the farmers, to replace those that had
been killed.

The soldiers managed to have the promised swim but
the shells dropping in the sea around them took the edge off
the enjoyment. Rifle fire from snipers hidden in the woods
meant the games of football were short and very fast. Any
movement around the area was hazardous. The casualties
mostly arose, though, when they were relaxed. They lay in
shallow trenches or squeezed into crevices and the snipers
watched for heads to appear over the edge of the shelter.

On the evening of the 11 May the order came through
that they were to take over the front line trenches on the
Krithia Nullah and the Krithia road. The nullah was another
of the ravines that ran down the Peninsula from the village of
Krithia and normally, unless there had been a heavy
downpour, only a trickle of water flowed down it.
Unfortunately, before it reached the Allied front line, the
water had passed through the Turkish line and was dirty and
contaminated. Although there was a deep pool which
provided a decent bathing facility the water could not be used
for drinking or cooking and there was a constant search for
suitable supplies.

The battalion moved into their new positions during the night accompanied by the incessant rifle fire, the constant shelling and a heavy downpour of rain. Within a very short time the trickle of water had turned into a torrent which raged through the narrow channel carrying the debris of the higher valley – broken trees, uprooted bushes and the corpses of British and Turkish soldiers.

The bottom of the nullah rapidly turned into a quagmire and movement became increasingly difficult. Men took to the higher ground to avoid the mud but found that they were exposed to the Turkish riflemen. On the way up they passed dressing posts set up by the RAMC. Tarpaulins had been stretched over metal drums and a flag with a red cross hung damply from a pole. They saw the transport company, who were on their way down the gully, trying desperately to drive their mules through the thick, clinging mud.

By the next morning, the Salford soldiers, a few less than there had been the day before, were established in the trench and enjoying a welcome cup of tea and a bacon breakfast in the warming sun. The landscape here was different with a few disused smallholdings and the occasional small vineyard. There were some lines of trees and bushes but generally the area was more open and was splashed intermittently with vivid red patches of poppies.

As they ate their breakfasts they were joined by the flies that swarmed in their millions around them and then stayed all that day and every subsequent day. The food became rapidly covered with the insects, they clustered on every forkful en route to the mouth and were often eaten. Mugs of tea became full of them and they landed on every exposed part of the body. Some of the men sacrificed their piece of greasy bacon as a decoy for the flies in an endeavour to buy time to soak their hard biscuits in their mugs of tea. Corpses soon became a buzzing, heaving mass of flies and the injured would be plagued by them swarming on their open wounds. The only relief that they would ever get from this omnipresent nightmare was in the cold of the nights or during the misery of the heavy downpours of rain.

Crouched in their shallow trenches they heard an increased level of firing from various points along the lines and some heavy artillery fire to their left. The captain told them they would be involved later in these moves which were a distraction to support a big action that was planned.

The sun dried off their clothes that were still sodden from the previous night. They fired their limited ration of ammunition at the enemy lines, producing a heavy and disproportionate response from the Turks. A meal of bully beef and vegetables was brought up to them from the canteens on the beach by the struggling transport company and their hard pressed mules. Heavy fighting could be heard throughout the afternoon from the direction of Gully Spur to the west. The afternoon sun burned on their backs as they stood on the firing step watching through the sandbag parapet. Later in the day, they heard the wailing call to prayer from the enemy line and as darkness closed in they were gripped by the biting cold.

Sleep did not come readily or pleasantly to the tense, nervous soldiers waiting in the spartan trenches. When the gold fingers of the morning sun began to feel their way through the night sky the men stretched their aching bodies in the restricted space. They straightened their kit and their uniforms and enjoyed delicious freshly baked bread from the newly constructed bakery on the beach. The bacon breakfast was transformed by it. They smoked, drank tea, swatted flies and listened to the constant whine of the shells grumbling under the raucous chattering of the rifle fire and speculated on the action that the captain had told them about the previous day. Frank Williams, the sergeant that Edward had followed over the top that long week ago, told them that the

Ghurkhas had pulled off a brilliant attack on the hill above Gully Ravine. In a well planned move they had scrambled up the cliffs on the far side and had taken the hill with the Turkish trenches and the machine gun redoubts that had caused so much trouble. The Turks had been taken by surprise and most had fled terrified when they saw the Ghurkhas coming.

'Don't wonder,' concluded the thoughtful Liam. 'Fierce looking barmpots that lot. I told you what the old fella in the Railway said. They'd cut your throat as soon as shake your hand.'

Gallipoli
Turkey
16th May 1915

Dear Pippin,

Happy Birthday Darling. Today is your 8th birthday and I am so sorry that I can't be there to share it with you but I have been thinking about you all day. Your Mam wrote to me and told me that she had got some flour and she was going to bake a cake for you whilst you were all at school. She said that she had made some little coats and dresses for Dorothy so that would give you a nice surprise. I hope that Uncle Jim managed to make the cot for you. He is very clever at making furniture.

Pippin, now that you are growing up you will have to help to look after your Mam and the others for me because I can't be there to help. If you see your Mam looking tired or sad then you give her a big squeeze and a kiss and say that Dad has sent it especially for her.

I'm sorry but I don't think that I will be home for the summer holidays. I know that this will upset you but things are a bit tricky out here at the moment. We are doing a lot of digging to find water and to make places where we can stay. We sometimes catch chickens to cook but often we have difficulty finding enough firewood to cook things. It makes my fingers ache as well plucking the feathers off.

I told Billy Murphy's Dad about Edward saying that we were coming down Cross Lane on camels and he laughed. He said that he would bring one home with him but the backyard would not be big enough to keep it in.

Keep on working hard at school, Laura, because it will be important for you when you get older.

Sending big hugs and kisses for all of you,
Love
Dad

By the end of May the Salford battalion had settled into a routine and a pattern of manning the lines. They would firstly spend three days in the front line from which attacks could be mounted and which provided the first line of defence in the event of enemy attack. This would be followed by three days in the support trench, from where troops could be fed into the front line assault, and from where they moved equipment and supplies into the front line. Finally they would spend the last three days of the cycle in reserve where, despite the commitments of engineering work and other duties, they were able to relax a little more.

Like all his pals, Edward enjoyed the reserve trench phase the most. They got more exercise, played a little football, had a yarn with their mates and attended to their personal hygiene. There were often casualties, as the Turkish snipers watched for men who were momentarily off their guard, but now they were more careful. The unfortunates who were hit were helped or taken away and those that were left got on with whatever they were doing.

Edward knew that the situation in Gallipoli, after a month of futile warfare and over 38,000 casualties for the Mediterranean Expeditionary Force, had not improved in any way. They had failed to achieve any of the initial targets that had been defined and the blood stained few miles of Turkish fields that they now occupied was only a tenuous toehold onto the Peninsula. Now, because of the collapse of the Russian campaign further north, freed up Turkish troops were pouring into Gallipoli as reinforcements.

Edward and his friends only saw what was happening in the area that they were operating in but they heard a lot of both news and gossip through the daily exchanges with the transport company. He heard about the failure to take any more ground, about the casualties, about the lack of supplies and the small number of replacement troops coming in. From the sailors on the supply ships they heard that the campaign on the Western Front was not going well, either, and that there had been a huge loss of lives.

Edward had already seen so many of his Salford mates go down that his mind now refused to contemplate the horror of it. The whine of the shells followed by the explosions and the crack of the rifle fire had become a background noise that went on night and day. His brain had built a protective barrier that insulated his mind against the claustrophobic din of warfare along with the need to think about the deaths and the mutilations.

They moved away the bodies of their friends and played their game of football.

Chapter 6

A New Strategy

On the 1 June 1915 the battalion was warned that they should be prepared to move and two days later the orders for the attack were issued. This time the strategy had been more thoughtfully prepared and the target – to move the line forward by half a mile – was more achievable. Edward's division was in the centre of the Peninsula on the road that came down from Krithia and beyond the valley, or nullah, to their left would be the 88th Brigade. Beyond them, on the other side of Gully Ravine and down to the Aegean Sea, would be the Indian Brigade. To Edward's right there would be the Royal Naval Division and to their right, and reaching out to the Dardanelles Straits, would be the French Colonial troops.

The Turks had realized that an attack was threatened and they spent the night shooting even more nervously at shadows in the darkness of no-man's land. For Edward and his pals it was another long, cold, almost sleepless night spent smoking and occasionally chatting but mostly they were lost deep in their own thoughts.

'Do you remember that coalman, Joe, who had a yard on Ellor Street?' Big Charlie's question broke into their thoughts. 'Bit of an odd name for a coalman, wasn't it? Joseph Coke Wood.'

'Aye, you're not wrong there,' Liam chuckled. 'I don't know whether it was his real name or not but we managed to earn a few coppers through him. Do you remember when Dirty Lil gave us that pram and asked us to go to Joe's and get it filled up with coal because his horse had taken bad.'

'I remember that,' Edward said. 'We finished up with the pram and went round all the houses to see who else needed any.'

'And it was me that did all the lugging while you two ponced around knocking on doors,' grumbled Big Charlie.

'Well, it was a good job that we did,' Liam answered. 'You wanted to do it all for nothing. That Joe would have thought that he was on a right good number there. Us running around the streets, working our goolies off while he sat there drinking his pints of tea.'

'It might have been a bit more than tea. He always seemed a bit jolly at the end of the day,' Edward added.

'He might well have felt a bit jolly,' Liam retorted. 'Three skivvies running round while he sat there with his feet up.'

'There was that place next door, what was it called? Made shoes for the posh people up Langworthy Road,' Edward said.

'Well, that would leave me out,' Liam snorted. 'I was only ever sent to that Kettley's for a pair of clogs. And then I only ever had one new pair. The rest of the time they were hand-me-downs from our kid.'

'It was called Thomas Preston's. They were right good shoes. Mine lasted for ages.'

Edward and Liam stared incredulously at Big Charlie. 'Just listen to the Duke of Salford over there. What were you doing patronising a place like that? Humble peasants like me and Eddie were never allowed to cross the threshold.'

'Me Grandad treated me once. Said that I had to have a change from wearing clogs at Whit Week. Got me a size too big because I was growing too quick.'

'I remember the shop near there that used to sell ladies' underwear,' Liam enthused. 'That was an important part of my sexual education – sneaking up there with the other spotty faced youths when it was going dark to have a quick snigger.'

'There wasn't that much to look at,' Big Charlie pointed out. 'They were all corsets. All whalebone and wobble me Mam used to say.'

'There was the occasional glimpse of some rather large pantaloons,' Edward said helpfully.

'It's all right you mocking but we weren't even allowed to think about such things at the catholic school. Looking in that shop window was the nearest that I could get to a bit of sin.'

'It's the nearest that we got as well. Do you remember that we used to hang around hoping that we would see actresses from the Hippodrome?' Edward asked.

'Eh, I remember that sign that she used to have up. *Ann Meredith – Staymaker to the Stars.*' Big Charlie said, a big smile spreading across his face. 'That would have been a right good job, fitting Daisy Dormer out with a corset.' He began to sing one of the music hall star's popular songs. '*After the Ball is over...*'

'You'd probably have got Florrie Forde and she'd have been singing *Take Your Hand Out You Naughty Boy...*' Edward chided.

'With my luck,' Liam complained, 'I'd have probably got Widow Twanky.'

A hissing whine broke through their reveries and they instinctively ducked their heads as a shell exploded with a deafening, body shaking roar just thirty yards from their trench.

'Bloody wars,' Liam shouted in surprise. 'Couldn't these sodding Turks have a bit more respect for our national institutions like Daisy Dormer?'

'Aye, especially in the middle of the night,' Edward added.

Big Charlie, bending almost double to ensure that he stayed below the parapet, dusted down his uniform before reseating himself and extracting his cleaning cloth.

'You can't have five minutes peace in this stinking pit,' Liam muttered. Then more loudly, 'Right, come on lads, we'll have a bit of a party. I'm going to have one of tomorrow's Woodbines. And this should help us sleep a bit.' He extracted from his kit bag a flask that he had liberated from a dying orderly during their last attack. It was still partly filled with the rum ration that the unfortunate soldier had been distributing when the bullet had gone through his head.

There wasn't now the same degree of fear that had gripped them before the first engagement but there wasn't, either, the same sense of awareness. There was a reluctant and unspoken acceptance, a conditioning to the inevitability. Edward didn't notice the cold as much at night. He didn't become so irritated by the swarming flies throughout the day and he didn't grieve so deeply for his mates who had been slaughtered.

There had been so many dead and dying, so many exuberant flames extinguished, that he no longer felt the shock or the pain of the loss. Now they grumbled when the meals didn't arrive or when the tea tasted of chemicals, they complained when the mail from home was delayed for more than a week and they felt let down if the RAMC didn't have supplies to replace the field dressing packs that they carried. They were trapped into this big machine of war, and they could not escape from it, so they turned their anger on to the machine itself when it failed them in the detail.

Throughout the night they sat in their trenches, huddled together for warmth. Occasionally they could hear the strange excited shouts from the Turkish sentries when they spotted another suspicious shadow. They watched the moon tracking slowly through the clear sky. Edward felt a stab of pain as he thought, once more, that Laura might be watching that same moon at that same moment in time. That bright orb, with its cold light, seemed to provide a bridge back to his other life. 'Please God keep me safe for her' he whispered. He checked his watch again. Only two minutes since the last time. Slow minute after slow minute.

He felt a deep unease that disturbed him, that he was unable to rationalise, somehow separated from reality. In a tortured world where Peel Park and the brass bands playing on sunny Sunday afternoons was an alien, evil thought. An anonymous pain in his left foot travelled to his left knee, his ribs ached from a bruising football tackle and his right ear lobe itched incessantly. He scoured ineffectively under his tunic to resist the pricking persistence of unidentified insects. Liam snored gently whilst Big Charlie intermittently relieved gaseous pressures. Nearby he could hear the clicking beads and monotone mumblings of a prayer for deliverance. The dark slow minutes of this surreal world.

The following morning at 8.00am the heavy guns and howitzers opened fire on selected strong Turkish positions. At 11.05am, there was an intense bombardment of the enemy trenches with every available gun on both land and sea firing. They sought to create as much damage as possible, particularly to the barbed wire defences. Within minutes the whole area became a mass of flames and smoke and it seemed impossible to believe that anyone could survive the bombardment. After a quarter of an hour, and working to the plan, all the guns ceased firing and the Allied infantry in the trenches cheered and shouted and waved their bayonets above the level of the trench. It was a deception intended to induce the Turkish infantrymen into believing that an attack was about to start, bringing them quickly into their trenches. The ruse worked and, whilst the Allied soldiers stayed hidden, a hail of bullets tore into the sandbags that formed a parapet along the trenches. Meanwhile, another fierce bombardment was launched at the enemy lines.

The countdown in the Allied trenches was proceeding and at precisely 12 noon the attack troops went over the top and advanced, without firing, towards the enemy front line. Edward's battalion, in Division Reserve, were able to see some of the action from their position in the rear. To their left the artillery cover had been lifted and was now directed at the Turkish second line. Behind this the men of the 88th Brigade were advancing steadily. Edward's view was slightly restricted but he could just about see the Manchester lads in the front line attack making their way towards the enemy lines.

In this central section the initial artillery bombardment had not been so heavy. It had now been lifted to focus on the Turkish support lines. The Manchester men advancing across the no-man's land were falling at an alarming rate, cut down by the hail of bullets from the enemy trenches. It soon became clear that the damage from the artillery bombardment had, once again, been insufficient and the Turks were still manning their trenches in force. The ploy had failed. The line moved steadily, without firing, over the two hundred yards of scrubland that separated them from the enemy front line and still they fell, unprotected from the bullets that ripped into them. Time seemed to stand still as Edward watched this painful progress. Every step they took was another life prematurely extracted in exchange for a yard of Turkish soil.

He was pulled back into a conscious realisation of his own situation by the shouted commands for them to move. He ran down the communication trench into their second line trench which had now been vacated. The support troops had been moved forward into the front line and were waiting for their signal to go over the top. He could see, through the drifting smoke, that some of their front line soldiers had now reached the wire. Unfortunately, the Allied artillery bombardment had failed to destroy this barrier and the Manchester soldiers died with the wire cutters in their hands.

Eventually he heard the shouts and screams from the Turkish front line and he knew that at least some of the men from his neighbouring town had got through and were engaged in fierce hand to hand combat.

Exactly fifteen minutes after the first line had gone over, the signal sounded and the support troops followed them. Their target was to move through the front line troops, who should by now have secured the Turkish front line trenches, and to attack and take the Turkish second lines. Edward's battalion took over the Allied front line trenches and watched the British soldiers drop into the Turkish support line. It was like watching a drama being played out on some far-off stage, peering through the smoke and clouds of dust that were blown into the air by the high explosive shells from the French 75's pounding the area to the rear of the enemy lines. Sometimes it seemed that, for minutes on end, nothing was happening. Only the barely discernible shouted commands bore evidence of the continuing struggle. No movement could be detected, but the dead and injured who lay scattered like discarded rags over the two hundred yards of scrubland in front of them were grim evidence of the passing tide. The cacophony of battle was unremitting. The sounds of dying men screaming against a background of exploding artillery and incessant gunfire turned the stomach muscles of the onlookers into tight knots.

After half an hour of fierce fighting the noise level began to subside, the turbulent air cleared and Edward caught glimpses of British soldiers advancing well behind the Turkish lines.

To his right though, on the other side of the valley that ran up towards Krithia, things were not going quite so well. The Royal Naval Division, having earlier made good progress, was now in retreat. It was reported that the French colonial division on the extreme right had begun the attack with great enthusiasm but a determined counter-attack by the

Turks had driven them back leaving a weakened flank for the Naval division. The troops of the Royal Navy were then, in turn, subjected to a ferocious machine gun attack from the Turks on their right and they themselves were forced to retreat having suffered a huge loss of lives. Edward learned later that one brigade alone had lost sixty officers. Unfortunately, this left an exposed gap of around three hundred yards up the line of the small valley between Edward's group in the Allied front line and the first Turkish trench now occupied by the Manchester troops. The Turkish troops were pouring through this undefended flank and assaulting the British with devastating machine gun fire.

The 1/8 Lancashires were readied and within minutes they were moving forward along the line of the valley to reinforce the line up to the Krithia vineyard. After a morning of watching this distant drama unfolding they had suddenly become key players in the plot. They progressed quickly over the first stretch of open ground and were half way towards the vineyard when they were met with heavy fire from the Turks. Edward fell flat to the ground behind Sergeant Williams and following his directions, they crawled on their stomachs protected by an almost imperceptible rise in the ground.

The final few yards were over open ground beyond which the Turks lay in sheltered positions. The only way to engage them was by a final charge into their line of fire. As they rose to go they saw that the Turks were armed with small, strange looking hand bombs that they carried around their waists. They hurled these at the British soldiers with devastating effect but some of the bombs failed to explode immediately and the Lancashire men picked them up and threw them back into the Turkish lines. The fighting was fierce and bloody but eventually the Turks were pushed back and the Allied defensive line was held.

The respite was short lived, however. By the late afternoon it could be seen that huge numbers of Turkish troops were being massed on the other side of the valley known as Krithia Nullah but further up towards the village of Krithia. The Manchester regiments had made good progress up this central zone, overrunning the Turkish lines, and the foremost of these, the 6th Manchesters, were now a thousand yards in front. But, because the Allied attack up the right hand side had failed, the Manchesters were now exposed all along that flank. The decision was eventually taken to withdraw these soldiers back to what had been the Turkish front lines but the soldiers had to be almost forced out. They could not bring themselves to concede the ground that had only been won by the sacrifice of so many of their comrades.

But the Manchesters, isolated at the front of the attack, were in severe difficulties and were being enfiladed with heavy machine gun fire from the surrounding high ground. Their commander, Captain Pilkington, though mortally wounded in the head, instructed the men to prop him in a sitting position in the trench whilst he continued to direct the withdrawal.

The final gain of a quarter of a mile that day had demanded a high price. Of the 770 men of the 6th Manchesters that had gone over the top at noon, only 160 answered the roll call that night. Out of a 200 strong company of the 8th Manchesters only 18 could be mustered by nightfall. Similar reports came from most of the other units and Edward's battalion, who had lost their much respected Captain Humphrey along with many of the other ranks, settled to a sleepless night in their newly gained, but exposed, positions.

The relative calm of the night seemed unreal. The stretcher bearers continued their endless quest for the injured, carrying them silently through the crowded and damaged trenches to the Regimental Aid Post, and the Medical Officers gave whatever treatment was possible before getting them down to the Medical Centre on 'W' beach. The minds of the soldiers in the trenches were numbed by the noise, the stress and the physical exertions of the warfare of that day and the clear moonlit sky was not peaceful. They could feel the static tension of the unfinished battle.

The next day, the 5 June, was a strange day of calm in the midst of battle. It was as if an unspoken agreement had been reached by both sides that this should be a day for the licking of wounds and for the assessment of damage. The 1/8 Lancashires moved their headquarters up to near the Krithia Nullah and worked tirelessly on strengthening their defences in anticipation of another attack. Two of their officers were temporarily assigned to the decimated Manchester regiments and then, after nightfall, two of their companies were moved up to the front line.

The attack began at 3.45am the next morning with the Turks shelling the British lines and, soon after, large numbers of their soldiers were seen working their way down the nullahs. They succeeded in gaining access to the British trenches at various points but, after fierce hand-to-hand fighting, they were repulsed by the soldiers from Lancashire. The Turkish soldiers were brave, resourceful and determined and they continued throughout the morning with their bombing attacks and bayonet charges. They came in wave after wave, first taking the trenches and then being pushed back again by the heroic Allied troops. As soldiers fell from both sides their places were taken by others moved up from the reserves. By late morning the Divisional reserve was down to only sixty and men from the Chatham battalion of the Royal Navy were brought in to support them.

Once more, the battle extracted a heavy toll in the lives of the soldiers and Edward's battalion lost its two senior officers. Both Lt Colonel Fallows and his second-in-command, the 44 year old Major Baddeley, were killed in the relentless fighting that morning.

By the afternoon the situation had eased and the number of Turkish troops in the area had diminished. The tired men from Salford, though, were called on to battle their exhaustion and to launch a counter-attack. By the end of the afternoon the redoubt that had been captured by the Turks that morning had been retaken and they began the task of strengthening the defences along the line.

Nightfall was a relief to all of the soldiers but sleep was an elusive friend to those who had looked into the eyes of another man for that brief moment before thrusting the cold steel of their bayonet into his body.

The next day the Lancashire soldiers again moved their headquarters forward to a point near the pool in Krithia Nullah and later joined forces with the Manchesters to launch an attack further up the nullah. They fought hard but the Turks had established themselves in a strong position and the British soldiers failed to take their objective. Frustrated and further depleted, they retreated back to the redoubt and there they spent the night.

The following morning, the 8 June, they succeeded in operating some new trench mortars for which the shells had only recently arrived. These were lighter than the big artillery guns and could be carried into the trenches. From there they lobbed high explosive shells into the enemy lines. Artillery shells fired from a distance came in at an angle so, at best, hit only the parapets around the trenches, whereas the mortar shells fell almost vertically into the trench and maximized the damage. In addition, they were close enough to be able to see how accurate they were so that adjustments could be made.

The day was marked by a series of minor skirmishes during which the battalion gained some ground and straightened up their firing line to give them a stronger position. The weary men pushed against the numbing tiredness, dug the trenches deeper along the line and repaired the sandbag parapets along the tops. Over the course of four days the men had worked and fought themselves to a virtual standstill but they knew that the Turkish soldiers had done the same.

The water in the nullah pool had been bracingly chilly as he swam and splashed around in the freshness of the early morning. Its piercing cold had been cathartic and he had emerged feeling cleansed in his body though his head still felt as though it belonged to a stranger. For the first few days after the main battle had finished the water had been stained with the blood of those who had died in it. Now, since the scavenging parties had been out and removed the corpses to identify and then bury them, the water had run itself clear.

Edward sat on the sloping rock at the side of the pool, enjoying the revitalizing feel of the warm sun on his back, and watched the water dripping off his hair and forming a small pool between his feet. In the first week since taking the Turkish lines there had only been a few minor skirmishes and they had been kept busy during the day deepening the trenches, filling sandbags and renewing supplies. The nights, though, were long and difficult and especially so when on sentry duty. Standing on the firing step and staring out through the small slits between the sandbags at the luminescent moonlit landscape, with the dark shadows scurrying across the ground, had kept the memories of his mates who had died out there fresh and troubling. He would try to focus his mind on his family at home, to remember the faces of his children and his lovely Laura, but he couldn't fit them into the background of the rolling thunder of the battle that was still being fiercely fought over to his left in Gully Ravine. He had tried to think about the times that he had had as a kid in Salford but the memory of the cattle being driven down Liverpool Street to the abattoir transformed into the vision of the hordes of soldiers going over the top to an almost certain death only to be replaced in their trench by the next group to be sacrificed.

He had been slowly managing to push these memories into some vault deep in his mind but then, the day before, they had poured back like bats out of a dark tower. Their Company had been assigned to provide covering fire for an operation by a small group of volunteers from the 7th Lancashire Fusiliers. The six men led by an officer – Lt Burleigh – had crawled up an old communications trench and bombed a redoubt held by Turkish snipers. They had timed the operation for 11.00 in the morning and, as hoped for, they caught the Turkish soldiers sleeping. The job was done quickly and the raiding party returned without a scratch but Edward's group had suffered several casualties. One of them had been a school mate from Turner Street.

Now he sat staring down at the glistening rock and thinking for the thousandth time what on earth was going on. After only five minutes of this campaign in the Krithia Nullah they had gained control of the front line Turkish trenches. Now, almost two weeks later and after the further loss of hundreds of lives, they were still occupying the same trenches.

Edward was surprised out of his contemplations by the appearance of Sergeant Frank Williams who sat down beside him. Williams was a similar age to Edward but he had been a regular soldier since his teens and had seen service in Africa and India as well as many places that Edward had never heard of. He had been transferred to the 1/8 Lancashires when his own battalion, part of the original landings on the 28 April, had been virtually destroyed by the Turkish onslaught.

'You look deep in thought, Eddie,' he said. 'Not bad news from Blighty I hope?'

Edward shook his head. 'Hi Sarge. It's the bad news that's going to Blighty, I suppose.' He told Williams how he felt this anger and frustration in seeing so many British soldiers – some that he had roamed the streets of Salford with when they were kids – being killed and maimed and for so little in return.

'My head feels all over the place. Especially since that bastard Fforbes-Fosdyke shot young Hennessy.'

'It wasn't your fault, Eddie.'

'I should have done something about it. I had seen that he was petrified and I should have tried to get him round. Or at least I should have shot that snivelling, drunken sod of an officer for doing it.'

'That wouldn't have solved anything. You would probably have finished up in front of a firing squad.'

'Well, at least the miserable little runt would have got his dues.'

'I hear that he's upset a few people one way or the other. He's been moved on to non-operational duties now.'

'Now isn't that just his luck. Our lads are going down like flies in this hell hole and he gets some soft job sitting on his fat backside.'

'Aye, you're right. But it won't impress his old man when he hears his war record.'

'Well, sod that for a game of soldiers. I'm not bothered about what his dad thinks. I'm bothered about all the good blokes who are rotting away in the fields out there. One of the Transport lads told me that our Division has lost 4,000 men since we arrived over here. That's a hundred men a day. '

'But they're not all killed. Some of them were wounded and have been shipped back to Blighty.'

'It's still a lot of telegrams and a lot of families that are going to have no breadwinner. And the worst of it is that none us really know what we are supposed to be fighting for over here. At least the Turks know that their blood is being spilled in defence of Turkish soil.'

'It's war, Eddie. People do get killed. Another generation and they're almost forgotten about.'

'They're my mates, Sarge. They're the kids I played with and grew up with. There's four already out of our class that have been killed. And that's only what I know of. It's stupid and pointless. A waste of lives and something needs to be done about it.'

'There's always going to be casualties,' the sergeant said. 'We will just have to hope that we can turn things round a bit.'

'There needn't be so many casualties though. What is the point in us all jumping over the top of the trench at the same time and then marching along as though we are on parade? The Turks just sweep along the line with their machine guns and that's it. They can't miss.'

'It's British Army battle tactics that we've used for about the last fifty years,' the sergeant said, 'We soften the enemy front line up first with the heavy artillery fire. After that we send our front line skirmishers across to disrupt the other side and then the support line goes in to finish things off – mainly with the bayonet.'

'Well, that's as maybe,' Edward protested. 'But it seems stupid to me that we walk along as though we are going for a Sunday afternoon stroll.'

'Aye. It's so that nothing is up to the individual, who might just panic if left to their own devices,' Williams countered. 'They also believe that it intimidates the enemy after the artillery fire has frightened the life out of them. What hasn't been recognised, though, is the effect that the machine guns are having these days.'

'But we're hardly getting any artillery cover,' Edward protested, 'We're going like lambs to the slaughter. What's the point in that?'

Sergeant Williams glanced around himself before replying. 'It's how the General fights his wars. That's all he knows. They retired him off once but they brought him back to run this show. There has been talk about trying different ways but he saw the Japs give the Russians a thrashing about ten years ago by advancing in a line, so that just confirmed it for him. That's how he'd been told to fight and it still worked so he was sticking with it. From what I heard, though, the Russians were bloody useless but he wouldn't want to know that, would he.'

'Surely he can see that it isn't working? The only time that we've got anywhere without being chopped down is on the second day. We went over the top but we ran like rabbits to find cover. We were all in small groups as well, so we weren't such easy targets,' Edward reasoned.

'Well, that was a bit of local initiative, shall we say,' Williams replied, looking around uneasily, 'We're not supposed to make decisions on tactics without authorisation from HQ. And no, he can't really see what is happening because he is sitting in Imbros and that's a good boat ride away. I personally think that is the main reason they like the slow moving lines. They can see them better through the binoculars from two or three miles away.'

'They should come down here to the trenches and see what it is really like. The junior officers see the reality of it but they are going down like fairground ducks,' Edward grumbled.

'Aye, I suppose you're right. It's like the other night, when we were being pounded by the Turks chucking tons of metal at us followed by a few thousand screaming madmen jumping on us. While all that was going on the General and his cronies were having a dinner in Imbros to celebrate the centenary of the Battle of Waterloo. He's probably only just getting the reports about what happened here.'

'How can you run a war when you are sitting miles away and don't know what's going on?'

'You tell me,' Williams said bitterly. 'When the first landings were made on the 25 April, the soldiers on S and Y beaches were almost unopposed. But they just sat there all day. They didn't know that, only a couple of miles away, our lads on V and W beaches were being wiped out. If they had turned south and attacked the Turks we would have been in Constantinople by now. Where was the General that day? He was sitting on the Queen Elizabeth miles out to sea.'

'Well, at least he could do something about getting some more heavy stuff over here now. The Turks have got more steel than Dorman's up there yet we're even on a daily ration for bullets.'

'He's tried, but no luck. It's all going into France and Belgium. I think that they thought that we would have an easy run through Turkey.' Williams checked around again as though fearful of being overheard. 'The problem will probably go worse, anyway, because so many of the experienced fighting officers on the ground are getting themselves shot. What we'll finish up with will be all these young accountants and lawyers who are being pushed through the Officer Training School. They come out to the front line but they are still wet behind the ears.'

'That's why they stand on top of the trenches waving their swords and pistols around when they are still three hundred yards from the Turks.'

'Yeh. And the Turkish snipers say 'thank you very much' and bam – they're gone. But listen Eddie, watch what you're saying and who to. If any of the toffs hear, they'll have you.'

'Right. Thanks Sarge,' said Edward, putting his clothes back on. 'Enjoy your swim.'

29 Myrtle Street
Cross Lane
Salford 5
Great Britain
10th June 1915

Dear Dad,
Thank you for your letter and for Happy Birthdaying me. I got a smashing cot off Uncle Jim and loads of clothes that Mam had made for Dorothy.

I don't know when we will be going to see Grandma again. Last time we went, there was a crowd of women outside a shop in Ellor Street and they were throwing stones at the windows and shouting. The man from the shop was there but he was dead scared. And he tried to stop them pinching stuff.

They just pushed him away and then I saw Aggie Sidebottom who's the sister of that snotty nosed kid who lives next door to Aunty Ada running off with a big piece of meat. Mam said to Grandma that this is all since that Lucy Taynier went down but I don't know who she is. She said that the women had come from the factory where they work in their dinner break because the shopkeeper's Dad had come from Germany and we are against the Germans in the war. She said that you are in the war Dad, and she prays to God that you'll be alright. I told her that Miss Howard prays for all the soldiers in Sunday School so you will be included in that as well.

Mam says that she comes from Yorkshire so I hope that the women don't start getting mad at them. Dad, can't you come home and be one of the soldiers that watch the men from the docks when they are doing their marches. The soldiers here have come up from London and are staying in the army houses down Regent Road. You would be able to stay at home and they could go to Turkey instead of you. Sometimes the men off the docks start fighting with the soldiers so they mustn't be very friendly. That's why it would be better if you came to do it because you know a lot of them.

I have been helping Mam as much as I can and she has shown me how to make jam tarts. I made some toast with dripping for our dinner before but our Sadie wouldn't eat it because it had too much salt on. Our Edward ate hers as well.

I did the front door steps yesterday because the donkey stone man had been round but our Ben came home after playing football and made a right mess of them. I told him that he can do them next time and he went and stoned all down the front pavement so Mam told him he hadn't got to touch them again. He just did it on purpose to get out of it.

I am trying hard at school, Dad, and my best ever class is English and then Geography. I don't like Arithmetic much but when I told Mam that the times tables were boring and I couldn't remember them she made me sit down for a whole hour after Sunday School and keep saying them to her. By the time that I went out to play Edith Hardcastle had picked every single daisy in the street and made a daisy chain for round her neck and there was none left for me. That makes times tables even worse.

Love

Laura

Ps if you come home you could mend the grid because the postman fell down it last week (I think that these ps's are a good idea because I always think of something else to say after I have finished.)

PS2 I don't think that we will be attacked like the man in the shop because on my birth certificate it says that I was made in Myrtle Street.

Chapter 7

Battle of Krithia Vineyard

The battles of May and June had taken a heavy toll on the 42nd Division, not only because of the casualties but also because of the mental and physical strain on those that were left. The haunted, empty faces of the soldiers, sitting up during the night and smoking, were those of men nearing breaking point. They all struggled with the realization that their lives were thought to be so cheap.

The British governing classes seemed to be locked into the economic and military system that had been put into place for ruling their empire. The soldiers like Edward were just numbers that were totalled up at the end of the day. An assessment of the resources available to be thrown into the next battle. If you didn't acknowledge your name in the evening roll call you were deducted from the total – dead, wounded or missing. The forms were filled in and the payroll records adjusted.

Edward knew that it wasn't just a class problem because they sent their own sons into the mayhem and they themselves became victims of the ritualized slaughter. Perhaps it was the remoteness from the action that prevented the decision makers from really thinking about how to fight a modern war with death dealing weapons like the machine guns. He felt, like all his pals, a growing and burning resentment about the price that they were paying in pursuit of this global game. A game about which they understood so little and in which they were the pawns that were sacrificed for some small strategic gain.

The morale of the soldiers in the trenches was reaching breaking point and it was decided that the battalions in the Division should be given a break from the front line. In the second week of July, the 1/8 Lancashire Fusiliers were taken over on trawlers from 'V' beach to the island of Imbros where they spent a welcome four days encamped at the Kephalos Rest Camp.

Given the opportunity to choose, they would probably not have elected to spend their days on Imbros in further, seemingly irrelevant, training. The high command had, however, deemed this to be an appropriate way to relieve the stress of the suffering soldiers.

'Digging bloody trenches,' Liam grumbled as they made their way to the bar after another tedious day of instruction. 'We've been living in sodding trenches for the last three months. What do we want to know about digging trenches for? We'd be better off having lectures on how to turn Big Charlie into a giant fly paper.'

'Hey. Don't start getting plans like that for me,' Big Charlie said, suddenly alarmed by the prospect of being enlisted into such a sticky and unpleasant role. He knew from bitter experience that Liam's spontaneous ideas often led to hurried actions that were later much regretted.

'It did seem a waste of time, all that trench stuff,' agreed Edward. 'But that bit about the tunnelling under the Turkish lines could be a good idea.'

The atmosphere in the bar was heavy with cigarette smoke, barely disturbed by the slowly turning fan. Loud laughter from the officers' table in the corner rose stridently over the hubbub of chatter from the soldiers crowded round the bar. A drunkenly barking voice, nauseatingly familiar, silenced the bar.

'It's the rabble from Salford come to join us,' Fforbes-Fosdyke shouted. 'I hope that the steward has enough barrels of beer in.' His fellow officers smiled weakly whilst he appeared to find the remark hilarious. 'Hey, bogman,' he bellowed addressing himself directly to Liam. 'Fetch us another bottle of whisky. I know that's one thing you're good at.' His sweating red face erupted into a cloud of flying spittle as he laughed uproariously at his belittling humour.

The crowd in the bar, suddenly tense, turned to look at Liam whose face was white and taut with anger. He muttered something inaudible but didn't move.

'Come on, you miserable little Irishman,' the drink crazed Major shouted. 'A bottle of whisky over here and be quick about it.' Liam's fists clenched and hate burned in his eyes but he didn't move.

'What's the matter, you pathetic paddy? Don't you understand the King's English? Obey an order when you're given one by a superior officer... else you and that good-for-nothing Irish tart that you're married to will be back where you belong... cutting peat.'

Big Charlie hmmphed loudly. 'I'll just go and squash the little runt,' he said, stepping forward.

'Leave it, Charlie' Liam instructed, restraining him. 'That way you'll just finish up on a charge.'

'It'd be worth it,' Big Charlie growled. 'The little fat sod deserves a good thumping.'

'It's ok. I'll sort it.' Liam swallowed hard then moved across the room, pausing to speak to a small group amongst the soldiers thronging round the bar drinking from pint pots. Edward and Big Charlie followed closely, concerned about their friend's intentions. The men huddled round and one of them reached into his pocket, extracted a canvas wallet and passed a small packet discreetly to Liam.

After a brief conversation with the barman, Liam carried the bottle of whisky over to the officers' table where the gloating Major cackled with delight, bouncing in his chair with the thrill of his power. His fellow officers, relieved at this peaceful resolution of a potentially nasty situation, guffawed and snorted their approval.

'Hope that you gentlemen enjoy your drink,' Liam said placidly, before adding in an affected broad Irish accent,

'It was actually my Granda' that came over in the potato famine… sir. Although I do believe that your family have done quite well out of starving Irish folk since then.'

The officers laughed uncomfortably at this riposte but the Major, bulging eyes swivelling as he struggled to grasp the significance of the comment, spluttered feebly and poured a large whisky.

'Well, all I can say is that that was getting a bit personal. He seems to have some vendetta going against you.' Edward drew on his cigarette and looked at the flies going round the paraffin lamp. They were lying on their beds in the dormitory tent having decided to forego the beers that they had planned. The bar had still been buzzing with appreciation for Liam when they had turned and walked out. 'I mean, bringing your Brig into it like that,' he continued. 'He was really out of order with that.'

'He needs a big fist shoving down his throat,' Big Charlie suggested, waving his own threateningly in front of him to demonstrate his intention. 'That'd shut his stupid mouth up for a bit.'

'You can't shut somebody like that up unless you shoot him,' Liam observed bitterly. 'He's been raised as a spoilt little brat and he still thinks that everybody is there at his beck and call.'

'Perhaps some Turk or German will do us all a favour then and snuff out the miserable little bugger.'

'They'll never get near enough to him to do that,' Edward said. 'If there is any action going, he's never to be seen.'

'They'd just have to go three miles behind our lines and look for the nearest bar,' Liam observed curtly, inhaling deeply on his Woodbine and sending circles of smoke curling up towards the canvas apex.

'He was right out of order saying things about Brig,' Big Charlie said, rolling over in his bed and thumping the floor. 'The dirty little, snot-faced pervert.'

'Leave it, Charlie,' Liam chided. 'Thumping him will sort nothing out. He'll like as not be a bit out of sorts for the next few days anyway.'

'Would that by any chance have anything to do with the packet that you had off the fella in the bar?' Edward enquired.

'Aye, it might just have been,' Liam agreed, permitting himself a weak smile.

'What was it? Hopefully arsenic. That would be a lot more painful than just shooting him,' Edward said.

'Not quite that bad. That was Billy Carter I was talking to. Used to work with the mules at Clifton Colliery. He's with the Transport Company now. I borrowed one of those powders that they give the horses when they are bound up. Slipped it in the whisky bottle.'

'But that means all the officers will have the runs,' Edward said, now feeling slightly alarmed.

'It won't be too bad. The barman said that, apart from Major Gobshite, they are mostly drinking beer with just the occasional chaser.'

'You know, I'm beginning to like that,' Big Charlie said, calming down slightly as he warmed to Liam's solution. 'I'm beginning to like that a lot. With a bit of luck the little sod might just shit himself away to nothing. Yes, I like that. Here, have another Woodie you two.'

They lay quietly for a while listening to the hissing paraffin lamp, the chattering cicadas in the fields and the prattling soldiers in the bar. Occasional rumbling explosions reminded them of the hostilities on the mainland.

'Big Charlie's right in a way,' Edward broke into the contemplative quiet. 'You know, having a go at the likes of us is one thing but bringing our wives into it the way he just did is right out of line. Has he come across your Brig before or something? I mean, how does he know that she is Irish anyway?'

'It goes back a long time,' Liam said after a long pause. 'When she was at home. There's a lot of houses round Hulme and Salford that were owned by Gobshite's Dad and he used to send that little bastard out to collect the rent. One day, Brig came home during her dinner break at the mill because her Mam had been taken bad. She found that slimebag in the scullery groping her thirteen year old kid sister. Poor little sod was too terrified to scream, especially with her Mam ill upstairs in bed.'

'That is evil' Edward said. 'What did Brig have to say about that?'

'Well, you know what she was like when she was sixteen. Never a one for wasting words when action was possible. She fetched him one with a cast iron frying pan round the back of the head.'

'Bloody good for her,' Big Charlie enthused, emphasising his point by thumping the side of his bed which twanged loudly. 'She always packed quite a punch, your Brig,' he added ruefully, remembering his own encounters with the beautiful but intimidating girl.

'It just seemed a good idea at the time but next day he sent his stooges down and they were put out on the street. Her dad was already dead so there they were, four kids with a sick mother sat out on the flagstones on a suitcase in the middle of winter. They spent the next five nights in next door's coal shed. Her mam just got worse and died. They buried her in a paupers' grave in Weaste cemetery. Brig found somewhere to stay in the cellar of a house that was rented by another Irish family. Trouble was, the drains used to flood and the crap would come up from the communal toilet. Her three year old sister got sick and died. Brig just didn't know what to do but she found out where the Fforbes-Fosdykes lived in Prestwich and went round there and smashed his front windows. Some of the blokes who worked there grabbed her and took her inside to see the old man. She told him what had happened and he got the son in and flogged him in front of everybody. Bit humiliating, I suppose, for a twenty year old fella. Had to take it though when his old man is holding the purse strings. But it didn't get her mam and the little girl back. And she was still homeless.'

The three friends were silent for a moment before Edward spoke. 'I knew Brig had had it tough, mate, but I didn't realise how tough. He deserved that flogging. It should have been done in the middle of Cross Lane market.'

As the detail of Brig's childhood ordeal had unfolded, Big Charlie had become less animated but smoked incessantly. He lay staring rigidly up at the roof of the tent. 'Aye, it should. It didn't change the slimy little bastard, though,' he said finally.

The trenches in Krithia Nullah were suddenly bursting with activity. The Division had been strengthened with the arrival of 1500 men and 47 officers from England on the 23 July though these had not been enough to make up the losses that had already been suffered. The troops, along with large quantities of supplies and ammunition, had been brought in by British ships adapted to give protection against enemy torpedoes and artillery fire. The Turkish army had, at the same time and with greater effect, been building their own reserves with the introduction of new troops, guns and ammunition. They had continued to pound the British positions relentlessly and, in just one morning, seven hundred shells had hit 'W' Beach – now known as Lancashire Landings.

It was the 6 August and it was extremely hot. Sweat was running in rivulets down Edward's back as he sat on the fire step next to Liam whilst they cleaned and checked their rifles. There was a dedication to the detail of the activity, screwing the corner of the cloth into a little spiral so they could pick out small particles of dust from every corner of the weapon. Their devoted attention, though, was cursory compared to the passionate care given by Big Charlie. He went into an almost trance-like state as he bent over the rifle, cleaning and polishing it with his special cloths. All the soldiers cared deeply for their rifles, not cynically as a weapon of destruction, but respectfully as a friend who saved their lives. For Big Charlie, though, his rifle was not just life preserving, it was life enhancing, and he loved it.

They had been told that a big landing of Allied troops was to take place at Suvla Bay a few miles to the North. The troops already on Gallipoli were going to mount an attack on the Turks to keep them pinned down in the south so that the landing troops could have a clear run into Suvla Bay. From there they would be able to swing round and attack the Turks from the rear.

The Salford men had known that something special was being planned. For the last two days they had been making jam tin bombs in earnest. They had scoured the area and collected thousands of spent bullets and any other odd bits of metal that they could find. Empty one-pound jam tins were brought up from the kitchens on 'W' beach, where they had been carefully cleaned and stored, and these were packed with the bits of shrapnel. A piece of gelignite with a fuse in it was then pushed into the centre of each tin and the lid was soldered back into place with the fuse protruding. The design was simple but effective. It had been developed by the ever-inventive Tommies whose official supply of hand bombs was sparse in comparison with the plentiful supply that the Turks had available.

Whilst relatively safe to use – light the fuse, count to five and then throw – when Liam mischievously announced on one occasion that he had forgotten where he had counted up to, the trench cleared within seconds.

That morning they had been introduced to a new weapon of war that had been brought up to the front lines. There had been general disbelief, and no shortage of pointed comments, when they had seen the four foot wooden catapults but it was explained that these would project grenades over a much greater distance. They had been reassured to see that they also had a supply of a new grenade that was being specially made for them in Malta.

They had practised with the catapults for a while, lobbing large stones towards the watching lines of bemused Turks. The exercise had resulted in clearing the agitated bird life out of the trees but they had managed to get a reasonable feel for the positioning of the catapult and the pull needed.

Shelling of the Turkish trenches had started earlier in the afternoon, signalling that an attack had now been launched in another part of the line. It would be another long night of waiting in the Salford trenches. They would be going over the top in the morning but already the tension was mounting.

'Do you remember those pork sausages from that butcher's on Ellor Street?' Liam asked. 'Were they not the most exquisite things that you had ever tasted?'

'Was that the one with all the white tiles? I think it was called Robert Lloyd's,' Edward said. 'We used to have them for our tea every Saturday night.'

Big Charlie, now distracted by the discussion of food, folded his cloths and put them in his rucksack. 'My Dad preferred belly pork so we usually had that.'

'Well, right now a plateful of that with a couple of sliced eggs and two rounds of Brig's bread would suit me fine.'

'We had it on Wednesday nights as well. Then on Tuesdays and Fridays my Mam used to go to Mary Deakin's for some tripe.'

'My Mam used to get her tripe from Frank Dawson's,' Liam said thoughtfully. 'Looking at the size of you though, perhaps she should have gone to Mary Deakin's sometimes. She must have been putting something in her cowheel.'

'I remember the clothes exchange place near the tripe shops,' Edward said. 'George Hughes it was called. Had to go in there if you took the backside out of your pants or if the family hand-me-downs didn't fit.'

'My Mam bought me a stupid, poncey jumper from there once,' Big Charlie recalled glumly.

'I remember it,' Liam shouted, slapping his big friend on the shoulder. 'A massive bright green thing with a big gold pattern down each sleeve.'

'Aye, that was the one.'

'You looked like a tree with two giant caterpillars stuck on it when you came down the street in that,' Liam taunted.

'It wasn't as bad as that overcoat that your Mam got you that was down to your ankles,' Big Charlie retorted.

'Oh yes. I remember that one,' Edward said. 'I borrowed it once and it was so long that it got stuck in the wheels of my bogey going down Rabbit Hill. Our kid overheard me telling our Sarah what had happened and within minutes all the neighbours had come round to have a good laugh. Fat lot of sympathy I got for all my cuts and bruises.'

Edward gazed out over the heavily scarred but still beautiful landscape of Cape Helles and watched as the warm August sun gradually cleared away the early morning mist. In the far distance he could make out a Turkish farmer and his wife working in a field whilst, in another, a young boy chased a yelping, excited dog through the long grass. A few hundred yards away he could see the barbed wire collar of the enemy trenches that were their targets for the action today. In front of them splashes of glowing colours of the wild flowers sat uncomfortably amongst the brown scars of the craters. Swirling, screeching birds marked the positions of unclaimed corpses.

Soon, this comparative peace would be shattered by the ear-splitting, mind-numbing roar of the high explosive shells then, exactly an hour and a half afterwards, it would be their turn.

Edward no longer felt the paralysing fear of going over the top. He had now seen so many of his friends blown apart or shot that the idea of death had become like an unwelcome companion on his elbow. Like his fellow soldiers, he weighed the odds. Although a good proportion of them would be hit, many of those would be non-fatal. The problem for the injured, however, was getting back safely to their own lines. Being hit in no-man's land invariably meant waiting until nightfall in order to make a move as doing so in sight of the Turks would probably attract a sniper's bullet. Unfortunately, after a battle, the men in the firing line remained tense and nervous and shot at anything that moved in the dark towards them. Many an injured man, having suffered the agony of remaining still for hours in the baking sun, was then killed by one of his own soldiers as he tried to gain the sanctuary of the trench.

Despite this, for Edward and his friends, the long exposure to the carnage had taken some of the fear out of being injured. If he was going to be hit he just hoped it would be a 'blighty' – an injury serious enough to justify a posting home – rather than one that would see him buried under Turkish soil.

Edward knew that a few of his mates got quite excited at the idea of going into attack. They got a special thrill from the direct combat, from the gladiatorial pursuit of the enemy with bayonets fixed. But for the majority of the soldiers the battle was for survival and the only pleasure was the relief in finding themselves still available at the evening roll call.

At 8.10am the shelling of the Turkish trenches by the British and French artillery started and the intensity was increased when, at 9.00am, the naval guns joined in. As they waited in their trenches they could see that the bombardment was much heavier and more accurate to the right but the area directly in front, where the two nullahs met, was hardly being touched.

They had their tot of rum and fixed the metal markers on their backs so that they could be seen by their own artillery spotters. The whine of the shells and the thunderous roar of the high explosive merged into a continuous wall of sound, the smoke and the clouds of dust that were thrown up into the air spread like a blanket over the area as it drifted down towards them. The trees and the shrubs, the flowers and the mounds of earth, the grassy fields, all became suffused in an orange glow as the brown dust clouds filtered the strong Turkish sunlight.

Their senses were assaulted by the surreal environment and the rum spread warmly in their stomachs. The countdown continued and Edward focused his mind with a little prayer. For the fourth time that morning, he removed the contents of his left breast pocket. He opened his service book, extracted a small piece of folded paper and read the verse that Laura had written when they had become engaged. Pressed into the paper were two buttercups from Peel Park that she had picked when he had proposed. He replaced the note carefully then put the book back behind the tobacco tin in his pocket. He then took out, once again, the contents of his right hand breast pocket which he checked through and ensured that they were in the correct sequence. At the front was the narrow embossed birthday card, printed with a rose, that Laura had sent him. Behind it was a crayon drawing of a steam locomotive done by a then six year old

Edward, and after it was a paper with a poem entitled 'My Dada' that young Laura had written. Behind that there was a drawing from Ben showing his Dad with a big, black moustache and his Mam with orange hair. Wrapped up inside the drawing was a baby tooth from Sadie and a lock of hair from Mary. Satisfied that everything was there, he replaced them hesitantly in his pocket. There was always a brief moment of uncertainty as he thought whether he should check them again, then he buttoned down the flap.

He checked his right hand tunic pocket to make sure that the lucky stone that he had found in a boyhood escapade on Dorney Hills was there alongside the rabbit's tail. Then he checked both trouser pockets to ensure that there was a handkerchief in each one. As a child, his mother had always chastised him if he didn't, at all times, carry a hankie to blow his nose and so now he carried two. Completing his checks, he straightened his hat and picked up his rifle.

To his left Sergeant Williams was giving some instructions and some final words of reassurance and to his right he saw Liam, fingers crossed on both hands, glance up and give Edward a quick wink. Beyond Liam, he could see Big Charlie going through his preparation routine. Edward was now quite familiar with the stages of this and saw that his friend was just completing the oiled cloth step of cleaning his rifle which was followed by a new cloth for buffing it. After this he would draw the weapon slowly under his nose to savour its sharp cleanness followed by a check on his rounds of ammunition. He would then fix and remove his bayonet a couple of times before taking out a further cloth and polishing his boots.

Edward turned away and tried to concentrate on the task that faced them but, as always in these last few minutes, he found that his mind was a jumble of thoughts from his past. Some were pleasant but many were small regrets about things that he wished that he had handled differently.

At 9.40am the whistles were blown and they went over the top. Their progress was steady across the open ground towards the first line of the Turkish trenches. They were met with little enemy fire. The soldiers headed for one of the gaps in the barbed wire that had been cut through by the earlier artillery fire. The shelling had been lifted now to the rear Turkish trenches and the British soldiers poured through and jumped into the front line trench. Edward noticed the Sergeant hesitate for a moment when he saw that the trench was not only empty but was surprisingly shallow. Then the fierce cracking of machine gun fire started, bullets whistling as they flew and then the strange dull thud as they hit their targets. The officers and men who had already jumped into the trench were falling everywhere.

Edward saw their captain go down with his sword and pistol still raised and heard Sergeant Williams shouting for them to go with him. He turned back through the wire and the platoon headed up to the right. The sergeant had spotted some of the cleverly positioned machine gun nests that had escaped the Allied shelling and he was working his way up to them. As the platoon approached they could see, across the Turkish trenches, that some of the 6th and 7th Lancashires had now broken through the first line and were approaching the second trench.

Within minutes Edward's platoon was attacking the machine gun positions and, after some amazingly accurate long distance throwing of the jam tin bombs by Big Charlie, followed by intense hand-to-hand fighting, they took out the enemy positions. The Salford soldiers then headed down the trenches through the sickly sweet smell of the dead to attack the Turks who were holding the flanks. By mid-morning they were occupying the trench and other soldiers from the Lancashire Battalions had taken over parts of the vineyard. Soon after 11.00am, however, the Turks launched a counter attack. Despite the fierce onslaught, the British soldiers managed to hold on to parts of their trench and to the vineyard. Losses were heavy on both sides but the Lancashires began to consolidate their gains and to set up machine gun positions.

At 1.30pm the Turks attacked again but this was brought to a standstill by the British guns. Later in the afternoon they came again with another ferocious assault. By now, Edward's battalion – the 1/8 Lancashires – had lost ten officers and a huge number of other ranks either killed or injured. They had only seven officers and seventy three men left in the firing line and the depleted forces were eventually forced to concede the trench to the Turks.

That evening Captain Goodfellow was buried near the 3rd East Lancashire dressing station and the 42nd Division counted its losses. Over just two days of action they had lost more than one thousand six hundred men and Edward, battered and strained, dressed his minor wounds and wondered why he was still there.

Gallipoli
Turkey
2nd August 1915

Dear Pippin,

Thanks for your lovely letter and I am very glad that you had a nice birthday. I'm looking forward to seeing the cot that Uncle Jim has made when I come home. I don't know when that will be just yet because we are still very busy here and things are getting in a bit of a pickle.

I think that what your Mam was talking about was a ship called the Lusitania that was sunk by the Germans and lots of people were killed. They shouldn't take it out on the shopkeeper, though, because it's not his fault and, anyway, he is not really a German now.

The trouble is that the women are a bit angry and upset because their men are away from home and it is very difficult for them. You have to try and remember, though, that it is a bit like when you get mad with our Edward when he teases you. Sometimes when you feel upset and angry it is better to dry your eyes and blow your nose and have a good think. Sometimes the kind thought fairy will show you a better way than you jumping on him and pulling his hair.

I can't wait to try the jam tarts that you are making. We have lots of jam tarts here but they are not as good as those that your Mam makes.

I'm sorry but I don't think that they would let us come home just yet. The men who are marching up Trafford Road are asking the dock owners to give them a fair day's pay. It is very difficult for some of them because they are keeping a few families going whilst the men are away and I think that I would be on their side.

The weather here is very hot at the moment and there are lots of beautiful flowers. In the morning we see big families of rabbits like your Floppy getting their breakfasts before it gets too hot. *After that we get masses of horrible flies. They even come into your cup when you are having a drink of tea.*

Darling, try to be a bit extra kind to Edith Hardcastle because her Dad has had an accident here and he won't be coming home again. Don't say anything about it unless she says something to you but, if she does, tell her that he was very brave and that we all said a prayer for him.

I am very pleased that you are doing well at school, Laura, because it is very important for you as you get older. I'm sure that your Mam knows what is right for you with the times tables so keep practising them and we will be very proud of our little girl.

Love

Dad

PS. Yes, ps's are very useful.

PPS. I have sent a letter to your Mam with this one but will you tell the others that I will send letters to them next week because the boat is leaving soon.

Chapter 8

Christmas 1915

The battle, in August, for small areas of Turkish soil around Krithia vineyard had continued for some days but there were no further gains by the Allied troops. The lives of thousands of soldiers had been sacrificed but the operation was a failure because of what seemed, for the soldiers in the trenches, to be the mesmerizing incompetence of those who were directing it. The Allied landings at Suvla Bay had been achieved with virtually no enemy resistance but the landing parties, instead of sweeping across and round to the rear of the Turks, encamped in the bay and did nothing.

Elsewhere, a combined force of four hundred from the Ghurkhas and the 6th South Lancashires had stormed the cliffs at Chunuk Bair and had driven the Turks before them. They had raced down the slopes after the fleeing Turkish soldiers, intent on achieving the major strategic gains of Maidos and the control of The Narrows in the straits. Suddenly, and with deadly accuracy, they had been hit by a salvo of heavy artillery fire and the band of heroes had been wiped out. The shells that had destroyed them had been British.

Since August, although the skirmishing had continued, there had been no major battles and both sides had entrenched in the positions that they held. Many of the sick and injured, along with new reinforcements, had joined them from Alexandria and life for the Salford soldiers had settled into a desultory routine.

They had spent four months in the line and in reserve in a variety of trenches around Gully Ravine. The landscape had taken on a new kind of beauty where the once green, but now straw coloured, grass was slashed and torn by the scars of the artillery shelling. The sometimes ethereal and tranquil appearance of the no-man's-land, however, had belied its deadly secrets. The whole of the area was littered with the unburied corpses of soldiers from both sides, the air was heavy with the stench of rotting flesh, and disease had become the new enemy.

The flies were like a plague. They got everywhere, and, no matter how many were killed, there were millions more to replace them. The British soldiers tried to cover their food and drink but the flies were creative and persistent and they quickly spread diseases around their luckless victims. 'Bloody big families these flies have,' a miserable Liam had observed, 'You kill one of the little sods and five thousand come to the funeral.'

The wells were drying up or becoming contaminated and access to clean water became a major problem. Special desalination vessels were brought in but many men were apprehensive about drinking the water in which they had seen the bloated carcasses of dead horses floating alongside the bodies of their fallen comrades.

Edward and Liam and their Salford mates had had their share of the jaundice and the epidemic of septic sores that had been so widespread, but it was the debilitating dysentery that had wreaked the most havoc. The disease, fuelled by the irrepressible flies that swarmed over the unburied corpses, had spread throughout the soldiers in Gallipoli without deference to rank or age.

Edward had watched pitifully weak men, stripped of their dignity and their soiled clothes, and mortified by their failing bodies, crawling on their hands and knees to the plank of the latrine. Some had been so ill that they had slipped off into the slimy filth of the ditch and, without the strength to lift their bodies, had drowned in the fetid excrement.

Many men had died from disease during this period and many others had been taken off to recovery units, but the options for natural clean drinking water were virtually non-existent.

In October, after a prolonged spell of hot, dry weather, there had been some frightening rain storms that had caused widespread damage. Tents had collapsed, blankets had become sodden and the trenches, acting like drainage channels, had become running streams. The Salford lads were, however, quick to turn adversity into an advantage. They collected every empty vessel that they could find and set them up to collect the rainwater. They pleated the tops of semi collapsed tents so that the water ran, as if from a spout, into empty petrol cans and they arranged spare capes to funnel it into waiting cooking vessels. For a while, the drinking water crisis had been averted and the men enjoyed a more frequent supply of tea, albeit slightly petrol flavoured. Liam promoted it as 'Ben's Ole Juice.'

The weather had improved slightly, for a while, but then in November it had changed again. From the 15th to the 17th there had been a violent storm that had driven the sea up the beach submerging the bivouacs that were set up there. The heavy downpours of rain had raised the level of water in the gullies and dead mules, bales of hay and huge amounts of debris had been scoured out of the ravines and then washed out to sea.

The soldiers barely had time to recover before being hit by an even more violent storm on the 26th November. In parts of the Peninsula the waist-deep water had poured like a mill race down the trenches taking with it rations and equipment and, sometimes, even men. To escape the water the soldiers had stood on top of the trenches where they were in full view of the Turkish snipers. A quick glance at the enemy lines, however, had shown that they were themselves trying to escape the devastating effects of the weather. An unspoken truce had been established between the two sides as both struggled to survive against this new, common enemy.

The gales had turned into hurricanes and, on the beaches, piers and landing stages had been swept away. The flashing lightning and rolling thunder had turned the Helles Peninsula into a theatre of war where nature was demonstrating her own awesome powers to the human bit players. The heavy deluges, combined with freezing cold, had made conditions for the soldiers almost unbearable for two days then nature had delivered her coup de grace. On the 27th November the winds had changed to northerlies and the ice cold air had caused a fearsome blizzard. The Allied troops, with their sodden clothes freezing to their bodies, had struggled to find enough dry wood to light the fires that they needed for warmth and for cooking food. When the blizzard had stopped, the soldiers had been confronted with a calm and hauntingly beautiful, snow covered landscape but, before their numbed minds and frozen bodies could respond to it, there had been a rapid and devastating thaw.

Within minutes the gullies had been filled with raging torrents and many soldiers had drowned or were frozen to death. Many men had lost limbs and some had lost their reason. The casualties on the British side had been 15,000 men killed or injured. This was 10% of their total force and it had probably been a similar number for the Turkish army. More than 10,000 sick men from the Allied forces had had to be taken off the Peninsula to receive treatment.

Action between the two opposing forces over the recent months had ground itself into local, and largely unsuccessful, skirmishes although there was rarely a break in the shelling and sniper fire.

The Salford lads had been invited, in October, to volunteer for mining duties which was, in some ways, a relief from manning the trenches and it gave them a useful pay increase. The strategy had been simple, if exhausting and dangerous. They had dug tunnels underground to a position underneath the enemy trenches and then laid a large charge of

131

explosive before retiring to the safety of their own trenches. There they had exploded the charge and watched as the spectacular clouds of dust and debris plumed up into the air.

Unfortunately, the Turkish soldiers had been practising the same mining techniques against the British lines and both sides had employed listeners to try to determine what their opponents were doing. Sometimes the two sets of tunnels ran dangerously close together and, at the end of October, the Turks had exploded a mine in a British tunnel in which soldiers from the 5th Manchesters had been working. Edward and Liam had been involved in the rescue party, digging out tons of fallen earth, and they had eventually pulled out three men alive and two dead. Another three that were known to be part of the mining party had been given up for lost.

Three days later Liam had come bouncing down the trench and told them excitedly that he had just heard that the three missing men had just been brought from the shaft. Although they had had no food and only one bottle of water between them, one of the soldiers, a young Manchester lad called Grimes, had had a penknife and a lot of determination. Over three days they had dug their way through twelve feet of fallen earth, clawing at the debris and pulling away the large rocks. When they had finally broken through, on the point of collapse, two of them had had to be carried on stretchers from the mine shaft but the third – Private Grimes – had determinedly fought through his exhaustion and walked out.

The news had spread rapidly throughout the Allied forces around the Peninsula. They had seen many of their comrades die but to have three of them come back from the dead was like a small miracle for them.

In the middle of November they had received a visit from Lord Kitchener who had come to see for himself the situation on the Helles Peninsula. All the early misgivings that he had expressed, he now saw, had been borne out but there was no triumphalism as he inspected the desperate stalemate of the opposing sides. Instead, there was an enormous sadness as he saw the evidence of the catastrophic failure of the Gallipoli campaign and counted the cost that his soldiers had paid for so little gain. The strategic objective of sweeping up through Turkey and attacking the Germans from the south could, clearly, never be achieved. On his return to England the decision had been made to pull out of the Peninsula and orders were issued to the local command.

29 Myrtle Street
Cross Lane
Salford 5
Great Britain

15th November 1915

Dear Dad,

I knew already about Edith Hardcastle's Dad because her mother was running round the street one day and she was screaming and crying. Then she was lying on the floor and banging on the flags with her hands. Mam said 'Oh My God. She's had the telegram' Mam and some of the other women went over and picked her up and brought her back to our house for a cup of tea. Mam gave her one of your cigarettes out of the sideboard but she coughed a lot because she didn't smoke so Mrs Potter smoked it for her. Mam told me to go and call for Edith but she had gone to her Aunty Lily's so I took our Mary down the street on our Edward's bogey instead.

Edith told me that her Dad is dead now but he was a hero and he will get lots of medals. But I think that she'd rather have her Dad because he was teaching her to play the piano and she doesn't know what she will do now. She broke her glasses at school yesterday so that's another problem for her.

I am working hard at school and the best lesson is when we all get dictionaries and it's who finds the words first and I usually win. And this week I have written three letters for girls at school to send to their Dads because they are not very good at them. One of them was Trudie Thompson who pulled my hair really hard when it was my birthday so I made some spelling mistakes on purpose.

Do you remember when you used to take us down to Ordsall Park and past where that big pond was? Well the teacher told us in the history lesson that there is a big old hall that is supposed to be haunted and that is where Guy Fawkes went to make the plan to blow up the King in London. She said that it is a bit of a mess now but children shouldn't go on their own because there is the ghost of a lady in white that wanders round at night and gets any kids that climb over the wall. Will you take us, Dad, when you come home because I don't think that she will grab a soldier?

We are having a Christmas fair at the Mission next week and I have made some jam tarts. Mam has made some toffee and our Edward brought some apples from the greengrocer's where he works so that she could make some toffee apples as well. Mam said they were cookers and wouldn't do so she made some pies instead.

Uncle Jim said that he will send you some rolls of fly paper over so then you can enjoy your cup of tea better.

I don't know whether to put a note up the chimney for Father Christmas this year. Mam says that there won't be many toys because there is a war on and all his helpers are in the army. Perhaps they are making things so that you can have a good Christmas in Turkey. Our Edward said that the man in his shop told him that there was no such thing as Father Christmas. That's probably because he never gets any presents anyway because his nose is always dripping and he smells funny.

I think that perhaps I had better do a little note anyway, just in case.

Love

Laura

The Christmas dinner of 1915, eaten on the beach below Gully Ravine, was a welcome treat for the British soldiers. They had roast beef and potatoes followed by plum pudding and rum sauce accompanied by the band playing Christmas carols. Now Edward, Liam and Big Charlie sat in the crispy clear sunshine and enjoyed their special issue pint of beer. They talked about their families at home in Salford, what sort of Christmas they were having, whether it was snowing so that the kids would be out making ice slides on the pavement and where they might finish up if the rumours were true that they were about to move off the Peninsula.

They all had mixed feelings about the idea of withdrawing from the area. They had come to do a job and it hadn't been finished. They would be leaving hundreds of their friends with whom they had played football and marbles in the streets around the market, lads that they had walked up Broad Street with shouting suggestive remarks to the posh birds from Pendleton, mates that they had drunk with and played crib with in the pubs along Cross Lane and who had later joined up with them as Terriers. Now they lay scattered and rotting around the fields of Krithia and Gully Ravine.

'Our Laura wrote and told me about Bill Hardcastle's missus,' said Edward, trying to formulate words to put into shape the turmoil that he and his friends were feeling, 'She was lay on the floor in the street, screaming her head off, after she got the telegram.'

'Aye,' Liam said reflectively, 'He was a good bloke. Poor sod will be turning in his grave if he sees us sailing off and leaving him to get covered in Turkish horse shit.'

'It's to be hoped that some good comes out of all this. It's hard to know what, but just something for the sake of all the Bill Hardcastles.'

'We're sneaking off leaving the dead bodies of thousands of fellas from Britain, India, Australia and New

Zealand,' Liam said reproachfully. 'That's all we've finished up with – corpses. What's the good of all that?'

'You've got to be fair to the Turks, though,' said Edward. 'They have always respected the dead and injured. They never fired at any of the first aid posts even though they could see them clearly.'

'No. Not until some stupid sod put a Union Jack up at the side of the Red Cross flag. Then they started firing.'

'Yes. But they stopped again as soon as the shells had taken out the Union Jack flagpole.'

'It's a funny thing, though, with the Turks,' continued Edward. 'You go out there and fight them and kill them but you can't really hate them. You just feel as though they are all decent lads who are just fighting for their patch of soil.'

'Aye. We'd be a bit bloody mad ourselves if we heard that there was an army of their lot coming up Regent Road. Mind you, they might do a better job of running things than those Mary Anns that we have down in London.'

'It's been a complete farce from beginning to end. Eight months here and we've got nowhere.'

'They couldn't run a piss up in a brewery,' Liam said bitterly.

'I hope that the Turks respect the blokes that we're leaving behind.'

'There'll be a lot of their own laid there with them.'

'It seems wrong, going without them.'

'We might not make it ourselves. With those bloody Germans running things, they're not going to stand on the cliff tops waving us off when they see us packing our bags.'

'It would be handy if we could get a posting home for a bit,' Big Charlie said. He had been sitting quietly for a while, staring thoughtfully into his glass, seeing distant memories in the amber fluid.

'That's true,' Edward said. 'It's been over a year now.'

'It's the second Christmas that we have missed spending with our wives and kids,' Liam said, wincing.

'Not in my case though,' Big Charlie said despondently.

'What's not in your case though?'

'The kids.'

'Oh, sorry mate. I wasn't thinking,' Liam said in a placating tone before adding, 'But why don't you just get on with it. Your Dot needs something to keep her occupied.'

'It's not always that easy,' Big Charlie said reddening slightly. 'Dot gets a bit nervy like sometimes.'

'Well, you are a bit on the big side compared to her,' Liam observed. 'And let's be honest, you do look a bit scary bollock naked.'

Big Charlie ran his finger round his collar. It was beginning to feel uncomfortable. 'Aye, that's as maybe. But she's more scared being on her own and I should be with her at Christmas.'

'Have you noticed that they haven't chucked anything at us all day today?' asked Edward, diverting the direction of the conversation. 'It's nothing special for them but they must know that it's Christmas so they are giving us a bit of peace.'

'They'll have a bloody shock after, then, when we start throwing some steel at their lines,' Liam replied. 'I've heard that we are going up to Eski later so we'll be putting some Mills over with those catapults. Could do with another pint of this stuff to steady my hand. I always throw a better dart when I've had a few.'

The men continued to share their thoughts on the possibility of a withdrawal from the Peninsula and the dilemma that it caused them. Clearly the situation was hopeless but the idea of going without finishing the job, the thought that so many of their friends had been sacrificed to achieve nothing, left a bitter taste in their mouths. They had seen some amazing acts of courage from all the ranks out there in the field and they had shared moments of selfless bravery with mates that they had been to school with. They had, also, all felt the strange detachment as their minds struggled to cope with the noise of battle and the killing for survival and how, for some, this had exposed a darker side to their natures as they had gloried in the mayhem.

Sarpi Camp
Mudros West
Lemnos
29th December 1915

Dear Pippin,

Happy Christmas to you and let's hope that it will be a really good New Year for all of us. I hope that Father Christmas did manage to come and see you even though most of his helpers are away in the army. I think that Uncle Jim could be a good helper for Father Christmas because he is very clever at making things from wood. Have you been helping your Mam with her work at the Assembly Hall? She told me that she was going to be busy with functions and Christmas parties so I'm sure that she would have been glad of your help. Do you still have the milk crate to stand on to wash the pots or are you tall enough to reach now?

Don't forget about feeding Floppy when the weather gets very cold and make sure that he has plenty of shavings from Uncle Jim.

I am sorry to hear that Mrs Hardcastle was so upset. I was hoping that your Mam might have been able to tell her before the telegram boy got there but my letter mustn't have arrived in time. Things have been a bit bad out here and most of us have had bad stomachs for a long time. We are packing up now and, hopefully, things will soon be a bit better. I am stationed for the moment on a little island called Imbros and then we will move somewhere else. I will write to your Mam and give her my new address.

I have really missed being with you all preparing for Christmas but on Christmas Day I had an especially strong think to wish you Happy Christmas at dinnertime. I made it a really strong think hoping that perhaps you could feel it come to you in Salford.

The weather here has not been so good recently. A few weeks ago it snowed very hard and we were freezing cold. When it stopped, though, it looked really beautiful and we expected Father Christmas to come riding round the corner with his big sacks on his sledge. The trouble was that the snow all melted in the sun and it made a terrible mess everywhere.

I know the place that you mean on the other side of Ordsall Park. It's a nice old building but it is getting a bit derelict now. I didn't know that Guy Fawkes had been making his plans there. We will go and look at it when I come home and we'll keep our fingers crossed to keep the ghosts away.

Take care of yourself, Darling, and look after your Mam for me.

Love

Dad

Chapter 9

Shallufa, Egypt March 1916

When Edward arrived at the hospital tent, Liam was already in the recovery unit. He was lying on his stomach with his lower torso loosely covered by a sheet suspended over a wire frame to prevent contact with his skin. He had a grim expression on his face and averted his eyes when he saw Edward standing in front of him with an asinine smile fixating his face. 'Just thought that I had best come and get to the bottom of this story myself,' Edward grinned.

'Sod off, Eddie,' Liam replied through his clenched teeth, 'I've got near fatal burns to my back end and it is not funny.'

'What had you been eating? You've not been trying one of Ahmed's famous red hot chilli goat dishes again, have you?' asked Edward, determined not to let it go.

'Listen, I've just had sodding Big Charlie in here almost wetting himself. Is this the support that you get from your friends when you are in agony?'

Edward's face suddenly grew serious. 'No. Sorry mate. I just came to tell you that there is a delegation of officers coming down to see you. I heard that they were thinking of developing you as a secret weapon to use against the Turks.' Tears were now wetting the edges of Edward's eyes as he struggled to present a straight face to his agonised, and pathologically unsmiling, friend.

'Look, it's no joke,' Liam said, elevating himself then wincing at the pain from his blisters. 'I take my responsibilities as captain seriously. You don't realise what sacrifices I make to get a decent team together.'

'Well, it looks as though it has backfired on you this time,' Edward said, now failing woefully in his attempts to suppress his glee. 'What were you doing in the toilet that's got anything to do with the rugby team anyway?'

'I was trying to find a replacement prop for Big Charlie. He's out for three weeks and we've got the 5th Manchesters on Saturday.'

'It's not the most obvious place to go recruiting.'

'I saw Cyril Shitehouse going down there,' Liam said, feeling slightly irked by his friend's clear lack of sympathy for his painful plight. 'You know him, that big brickie from Ellor Street.'

'Oh, you mean big Cyril Whitehouse, drinks in the Craven Heifer? Breaks chairs over policemen's heads?'

'Yeah. That's him. Well he's built like one, anyway. Someone had told me that he'd played at Swinton Park until his wife put a stop to it, so I thought I'd try and get him to turn out for us.'

Edward struggled to contain himself. 'It must have been an explosive discussion. Did it all blow up in your face?'

'No it bloody didn't. It's those stupid sods on Latrine Duty. They had poured petrol in the middens ready to burn it out, then they'd gone off and left it when they heard Parade Call,' Liam said, grimacing as he tried to shout. 'I sat down next to Cyril and gave him a cig, you know, just being a bit friendly to smooth the way. But the big daft bugger threw the match down the bog. There was a terrific flash and a bang and all five of us flew up in the air.'

Eventually, Edward rose up from his knees where he had collapsed in a fit of giggling, prostrated by the vision of the five soldiers, trousers round their ankles, flying through the air with their exposed bottoms blistering even as they flew. He wiped the tears away from his eyes with his shirt cuff. 'Anyway, did he say that he'd play for us or not?'

'You can ask him yourself. He's over there having his backside painted with calamine,' growled Liam 'There's no chance now, though. The bloody RSM said that we have got to clean up the mess afterwards ourselves – even if we have to do it just wearing our shirts.'

Edward glanced over at the big, hairy man lying uncomfortably on his stomach, his ruddy face full of apprehension and fear as he submitted himself to the attentions of the male orderly that he had always had his doubts about. 'Maybe it's not a good time just at the moment. You ask him yourself later,' Edward said as he reached into his bag and took out the two dresses – one large and one small – that he had borrowed from the theatre company's props wardrobe. 'Thought that you might both be needing these. You could play a hooker instead of scrum half.'

He turned and left quickly.

The withdrawal from Gallipoli had gone smoothly and without casualties. The expectation had been that the Allies might lose up to half their soldiers as they withdrew but the plans had been carefully thought out and the men thoroughly prepared. Various tactics had been employed to create the impression with the Turks that the Allied soldiers were still manning the trenches, including home-made devices that fired off unmanned rifles at the Turkish lines. Similar devices, with small candles in tins that would ignite a trail of oil and waste as they burned down, were set to ignite the dumps of ammunition and equipment that were left behind after the last soldiers had left.

Edward and his battalion had boarded HMT 'Ermin' at Lancashire Landing on the 27th December 1915 and headed for Mudros on the Greek island of Lemnos. They were tired and traumatized, they were distressed to be leaving unfinished the job that they had come to do and they were grieving for their dead comrades who they felt they were letting down by withdrawing from the Peninsula. But they also felt an overwhelming sense of relief to be escaping from this nightmare of the Dardanelles. As the ship pulled away from shore and the rolling mists of the Straits wrapped up the spirits of 100,000 lost souls, it was hard not to feel bitter about what might have been if only things had been done differently. So many had been lost and so little achieved.

They had had two weeks of rest, rehabilitation and training in Sarpi Camp at Mudros West and then on the 14th January 1916 they had boarded the HMT 'Egra' for the three day trip to Alexandria in Egypt. Of the 14,000 men of the 42nd Division that had embarked there only eight months before over 8,500 had been listed as killed, wounded or missing.

There had been no song this time on the lips of the weary Salford men as they travelled by train to Cairo and then by road to the Mena Camp near the pyramids of Gizeh. The few days that they spent at Mena, though, had helped to revive some happier memories from their previous stay in Egypt. They had walked around the narrow alleyways and passages of the old town, exchanged greetings with the locals in the few words of the language that they had acquired during their previous stay and they had visited Groppi's for French teas and ices. As their bodies had warmed so their minds had, by slow degrees, healed.

After a week of recuperation they had moved again and eventually they had arrived at Shallufa, just to the north of Suez. The camp was out in the desert to the east of the Canal, strategically positioned to deal with the attacks that would come from this direction. It had been decided that the enemy must be prevented from launching an artillery attack from within a seven mile zone to the east of the canal so a series of defensive works were being constructed down that side.

Edward was impressed by the new camp. They had been supplied with new first-line transport vehicles that were making their lives a bit easier and they had new, fully equipped field kitchens giving them a few interesting variations on the stews and shepherd's pies. They had occasional visits from the Divisional Band who entertained the soldiers with music that was more normally heard in the music halls and dance halls back home in Britain. The nostalgia was revitalizing to these men who had locked out of their minds the happy memories of their families back in Salford as they had struggled to cope with the brutalizing reality of war in Gallipoli. Many a hardened soldier left the concerts early to go for a smoke and to shed a quiet tear in the sand dunes.

The men had quickly re-established a pattern of activities for themselves, much as they had done more than a year before. The concert party had been re-formed and delighted in putting on revues that took a barely concealed swipe at the commanding officers and politicians of the day. One of these depicted a portly officer wearing a ginger wig and stumbling drunkenly round the stage whilst trying to grab the buttocks of a soldier in a flowered dress. It produced loud laughter and wild applause from most of the audience though there was a steady trickle of the less enamoured that got up from their seats and left.

Although the sand was still warm on their backs there was already a bracing chill in the air as they escaped the sickening reminders of the hated officer. They opened the bottles of beer that they had bought from the camp bar and drank the first mouthfuls quickly.

'There was a bloke who lived on Unwin Street who used to be like that,' Big Charlie said eventually.

'Be like what?' asked Edward, unable to make the connection.

'Be like the fella in that show. He used to dress up in his wife's clothes on Tuesday nights when she was out at work.'

'Perhaps she had left him to do the washing and he had nothing to change into.'

'No. The whole lot, you know, knickers and brassieres. Looked a bit of a rum sod. He was tall and built like a beanpole, she was short and fat.'

'Must have looked like a standard lamp,' Liam suggested. He was lying on his stomach to keep the pressure off the raw flesh on his back but had to twist uncomfortably to have a mouthful of beer.

'And it was every Tuesday.'

'Oh come on, Charlie. You're pulling my leg now,' Liam said becoming exasperated. 'You're surely not expecting us to believe that there was a married man, living on Unwin Street, who dressed up in his wife's clothes while she was out? How do you know that anyway?'

'I knew the lad who lived in the house opposite. We used to go upstairs and watch from behind the curtains.'

'Well, that's a bit bloody nosey, that's all I can say.'

'It does seem a bit odd, though,' Edward said. 'You can understand him, perhaps, looking at them if things weren't too good between them in that direction. But why hide himself away in the bedroom and put her clothes on?'

'He used to come and stand at the window sometimes but if he saw anybody coming down the street he'd scarper quick.'

The three men were silent for a while as they considered the implications of such alien practises in their neighbourhood. Edward and Liam were stunned by the revelations and struggled to grasp the significance of such activities. Finally, Liam took a triumphant swig out of his bottle of beer and turned to his friends. 'I know,' he shouted.

'I'll bet he was a pantomime dame. He probably rehearsed his part while his wife was out.'

'I've never seen a pantomime with the dame doing what he was doing. They'd have closed it down,' Big Charlie said. 'I just think he was weird. Liked the feel of her underwear and all that.'

'Well, there's not much wrong with that is there?' Liam put his bottle back down in the deep hole that he had made in the sand.

'Doesn't seem right to me,' Big Charlie mumbled, slightly disconcerted by Liam's challenge. He felt uncomfortable in finding that his views on such an essentially private matter perhaps differed from those of his friends but felt the need to explore it. 'Dot used to do the ironing sometimes then ask me to take her stuff upstairs and put it away. I used to leave it where it was. Not for me to do it.'

'Perhaps she was trying to say something, Charlie,' Liam suggested.

'Oh aye, like what?'

'Maybe it's her way of getting you to relax a bit and enjoy sharing these little intimacies,' Edward said.

'Maybe she is trying to get you roused so that you will give her one,' Liam added more directly.

Big Charlie took a large gulp of his beer and ran his hand over the back of his neck. He felt that already he had gone too far. He couldn't mention the tension that he often felt was gripping her and he was fearful of their response if he shared with them his constant apprehension about the unpredictable and vitriolic rages that his wife would be seized by.

'Aye, well. You have to tread a bit carefully sometimes with Dot.'

29 Myrtle Street
Cross Lane
Salford 5
Great Britain

4th February 1916

Dear Dad,

<u>Floppy is gone and I'll never see him again, ever.</u>
<u>We had him for Christmas and I didn't know because</u>
<u>Mam said we were having something that was a bit like</u>
<u>chicken.</u> Our Edward had tried to grab Floppy when it
was escaping under the back yard door and its tail came
off in his hand. He told me that Mam had said it was no
use now without a tail so he took it to the greengrocer
and he saw to it. I was sick for three whole weeks and I
might have died but then our Edward and our Ben were
eating all Mam's angel cakes so I had to force myself or
there would have been none left by the time that I got
better. I will have another cry after because I am writing
this down and it has reminded me about lovely Floppy.

Blacky won't go near our Edward now even
though he told it that nobody wants to eat a cat anyway
but I told Blacky not to trust him. Dad, don't you think
that that is really, really disgusting and especially when
Floppy was so beautiful?

I am sure that your very strong think did come
through to us on Christmas Day because our Sadie found
Mam crying in the kitchen and she said that she was
thinking about your poor Dad and then we all started
crying. We went to the service at the Mission afterwards
and said prayers to God to let you come home soon and
to keep you safe. Nobody must have ever said a prayer
to keep Floppy safe because he was already dead by
then and I didn't know.

I hope that these people in this place that you are
in now are a bit more friendly than those people at the
last place. Out teacher said that they were Turks and
they used to own lots of countries called the Ottoman
Empire and they don't like us because we are making

them give some of them back to the natives. But if they are natives then perhaps Turkey was just making them great like we do with the countries that we own. I told our teacher that but she just said 'I don't know what will become of you, child,' and then she said 'Who threw the blotting paper ink bomb at Sarah Greenacres who already has enough sadness in her life?'

Mam told us that you have gone back to work in Egypt now so you will have somebody to do your washing. She said that everybody feels a bit better when they have clean underwear to put on but I think that she was saying that for our Edward. Sometimes he forgets to change his on Saturday morning and Mam finds out on Monday when she does the washing. She shouts at our Edward but she has finished the washing by then. He tries, as well, to get out of having a bath on Saturday because he says the tin bath is too cold and a draught comes under the door in the scullery.

Edith Hardcastle has started having piano lessons for nothing from Mrs Jones because she felt sorry for her. Edith said that Mrs Jones always says that we all have to rally round and play our part. She said that she also keeps saying 'Chin up, my dear' but when she does that she can't see what she is playing.

Please try and hurry up in Egypt because we are all missing you.

Love

Laura

Edward lay back in the sand, inhaled deeply on his cigarette, and gazed up into the clear Egyptian night sky. It always amazed him how every corner of the visible sky was filled with these bright, twinkling stars. Somebody had told him once that there were more stars up there than there were grains of sand on Blackpool beach. You couldn't say that about this beach that we are on now, though, he thought. You'd need a big sky to fit that lot in.

They had just played the 5th Manchesters, who were the in-form rugby team at the moment, and had been soundly beaten. Unfortunately, a few key players had been missing. Their regular full back, who could tackle a camel to a standstill, was injured. Their arch schemer, Liam, at scrum half, and the mighty Cyril, who could have made quite a difference at prop, were also out. They were all unavailable because of severely blistered bottoms.

Liam's woes in the hospital tent had been exacerbated when he had mistakenly passed the still fuming, but unfortunately illiterate, Cyril a bottle of Sloan's Liniment instead of the calamine lotion that he had needed to dress his wounds. The mighty roar that had erupted from the mountainous bricklayer had galvanised Liam into a hasty, though very painful, departure from his comforting bed. The sight of the large, shrieking, red-faced man, his shirt tails flapping over his glowing nether regions and a trenching spade waving in his huge hand, stumbling painfully after the tortured but panic stricken Liam round the camp on his mission of revenge had raised the spirits of the whole battalion.

After the latrine incident, Liam and Cyril, still seriously impaired in their movements, had been assigned to the chain gang that hauled the pontoon stage across the Canal during the day. It was hard work that nobody liked but they had been told that it would keep them fit at the same time as teaching them to have greater respect for army property. Liam had sworn never to hold selection meetings on the privy again and Cyril had said many unkind things about Liam's parentage in asserting that he would never even consider playing for a team that was captained by him.

It was generally agreed in the battalion that Liam's recruiting drive had not been a very successful tactic. The 5th Manchesters had revelled in the opportunities for ribald jokes and gestures that had been presented to them by the Salford lads' misfortunes and they had exploited it on the field by running in ten unopposed tries.

Edward now sought solace in the cool of the desert just outside the camp and wondered once again whether he was sharing this view of the moon with his wife, Laura. The thought warmed him even though he knew that it was unlikely because of the time difference. Most of the time he tried to push away the thoughts of Laura and the kids because it felt as though somebody was trying to drag chunks out of his insides when he did. It pained him to think about them, to picture what they might be doing at that moment in time, when he couldn't see any end to this separation. Originally, he had come away thinking that it would just be for a few months, but now it seemed as though a huge physical barrier had been built between them and he felt helpless in the face of it.

There had been many times, though, in Gallipoli when he felt that he had been sustained by that gentle voice, by that last, whispered entreaty 'Keep safe, Love.' When he had been scared almost to the point of rigidity as he went over the parapet he heard her voice. When he had felt that his mind was being pulped by the noise of battle and his senses paralysed by sights and the smells of the ritualised slaughter, it was then that she reached through and touched his consciousness. When, later, he had lain desperately ill in a hospital bed, he had heard her voice and relived the soft, parting kiss on his cheek. He knew that he had to fight; he had to cope with everything that was thrown at him, so that, when the time came, he could go back.

He picked up handfuls of the desert sand and then let them dribble back slowly through his fingers to rejoin the endless billions of their brothers that lay beneath him. He saw in much sharper focus now the importance of his family. Things that had become routine and commonplace when he was at home in Salford had crystallized into a desperate need, the endearing gentleness of his wife had become a yearning that he cried out for.

He had always loved her voice. It wasn't loud and shrill like some women's. It had a soft, warm timbre that gently embraced and calmed you. Even when they were kids and she had played in their football team, or when they played 'Which Direction?' round the streets, she never screamed like some of the girls. Her voice had befriended him. He wondered if young Laura would grow up like her. She was a lot like her now. She had the same slight mischief in her face, the spark in her eyes. She shared her mother's determined spirit that challenged things, a drive that made her keep going at difficulties until she found a way round them in her own quiet little way. Perhaps it was the red hair that they both had. Her Grandma had said that it was the Irish blood in her. That's probably where she gets her spirit from.

She clearly wouldn't let young Edward push her about like big brothers try to do. He'll be getting his comeuppance there when he gets older if he doesn't watch himself. Edward lit another cigarette and drew the relaxing smoke deep into his lungs. He tried to stifle the resulting cough because he didn't want to be joined by any of his mates. Young Edward would have been eleven on his last birthday. He's probably changed a lot by now. He'll have grown bigger and stronger with that job he's got at the greengrocers. It's to be hoped he's behaving himself for his mother. He's always been quite sensible, especially seeing as now he didn't have his dad there, but sometimes the tricks that he would get up to would land him in trouble. Just like me as a lad, though.

Edward suddenly felt a cold shiver running down his back. The way this lot was going young Edward might soon be left without a Dad altogether and he'd have to shoulder the burdens of the eldest male in the family. His own Dad had died when he was only two years old so he knew what it was like to be without a father. But the difference was that he had had his older brothers who gave both protection and guidance and he'd also had his sister, Sarah, with whom he shared all his secrets. For young Edward it would be tough and he would lose out on so much of his childhood. And then what about Laura? How would she cope on her own? There would be the widow's pension but that was barely enough to survive on.

In the distance he could see the setting sun burning red behind the black line of the desert. On the right, hills rose uncomfortably out of the flat horizon. He threw his cigarette away and stood up, brushing the sand off his clothes. It needed some hills on the left.

'Who the Hell cares about how many stars there are, anyway?' he raged at the cold Egyptian moon.

Shalufa Camp
Suez
Egypt

8th April 1916

Dear Pippin,

    First of all let me wish you a big Happy Birthday because it will almost be your birthday when you get this and then you will be a whole nine years old. I wish that I could be there to give you a nice birthday hug and kiss but, unfortunately, I am stuck out here in the desert.

    We have been helping to build a new camp for the extra soldiers that are coming here and it is now like a small town.

    I am enclosing a little present from Egypt so I hope that you like it. I bought it from a village near here when we had a bit of leave. It is a headband and we watched the women making them. They are very clever doing the tiny little stitches. I chose one that is mostly green because I thought that this will go with the colour of your hair. Perhaps you will be able to wear it for school.

    I was very sorry to hear about Floppy but I'm sure that your Mam knows what is best. Tails are very important for rabbits so he would probably have found it very difficult not to have one. Some of the soldiers here have really strange pets that they keep in boxes. One man had a scorpion but it bit him when he was trying to teach it to do tricks so he squashed it. Billy Murphy's Dad has a pet rat which he races against other rats. They're not very good, though, because they never go straight. Mr Murphy says that he would have had a camel but they spit at you and that's not very nice.

    It's starting to get extremely hot here during the day and it makes it very difficult to work. We get up really early in the morning and then have a break in the middle of the day. In the evening, when it gets a bit cooler, we might have a game of rugby or football or, occasionally, some of the lads put on a bit of a show

155

in the 'Theatre Royal.' It's quite a laugh, especially seeing them trying to do the ladies' parts.

Sometimes in the afternoons we have horrible sandstorms and the wind blows the sand into your food and your clothes. It gets everywhere and there seems to be no escaping from it. You even find it inside your kitbag.

Last week we spent three days digging a big trench then a sandstorm started and within a few hours it was all filled up again. We were a bit upset but you just have to knuckle down and get on with it.

You can tell your Uncle Jim that we have been working with a lot of native carpenters and they are very clever. They have some very strange tools which I am sure must be the same as those that Jesus and his father used to use. It's funny to watch them because they have no shoes on but they climb all over the place.

Tell your Mam thank you for the lovely fruit cake that she sent. She told me that you helped her to bake it so a big hug and thank you to you as well. There were eight of us that shared it and I told them that it was your early birthday cake. They all shouted out 'Happy Birthday Laura.' I shouted loudest of all.

Help your Mam with looking after everybody, won't you.

Take care of yourself, Darling.

Love

Dad
X X X X X X X X X – kisses for your birthday

Chapter 10

Kantara, Egypt – July/August 1916

On the 22 July 1916 the 1/8 Lancashire Fusiliers found themselves on a train heading for Kantara in the north of Egypt and Edward's carriage buzzed with excitement as the soldiers faced the prospect of a scrap with the enemy during the next few days. It had been seven months since they had returned from Gallipoli and they had worked hard to get back their fitness and enthusiasm. Their memories were still vividly with them but they felt that out here they could have a proper battle in territory that they had grown familiar with. At least this time they would be there honourably and legitimately defending this country against an invading army.

Edward and Liam gazed through the train window at the endless miles of desert sand, the distant hills transformed to shimmering brightness by the midday sun. 'Wonder what sort of show this will be?' Edward ruminated, 'They reckon there's about twenty thousand of them heading for Kantara.'

The fearsome Cyril Whitehouse, having unwittingly found himself in the same carriage as his tormentor, Liam, and then having been drawn into a discussion on the merits of Swinton's pack, now made his contribution to this new debate. 'That makes twenty thousand daft sods then, if they've spent the last two weeks marching over here in this heat.' Cyril, pleased with his contribution to the debate, replaced the cooling, wet handkerchief over his head. He had struggled all day trying to decide whether to use his water ration to drink or to assist in this head cooling procedure. Eventually, after an offer by Liam to let him share his own water ration – a move which had enabled the profusely sweating Cyril to see a slightly more endearing side to the nature of 'the stupid little bog bomber' – he had finally settled on the head cooling option plus a few mouthfuls in between.

'The CO reckons that the Turks have been told that they will be given holy protection because it's Ramadan and they will sweep all the infidels out of Egypt,' offered Liam, anxious to lift the debate to a plane where he thought Cyril might be slightly less willing to offer his contribution.

'Aye, and an eternal after life in paradise if anything goes wrong,' grunted Edward, returning his gaze to the window as he spotted a small group of trees on the approaching horizon.

'At least it gives us chance to do something for all those poor sods who turned their toes up in Gallipoli to get no bloody where,' rejoined Liam clenching his fist.

'That's it. Give 'em a bloody good hiding. That'll make those lads rest a bit better,' muttered Big Charlie from the corner, succinctly summarising the feelings of all of them.

They would have the chance to do something for the memories of their mates whose bodies now lay abandoned in Turkish fields and, at the same time, they might just do their bit to move this horrific war out of the territorial stalemate that had developed.

In the middle of July, information had been received that a large Turkish army, led by German officers, was advancing across the northern desert. Once again, the Lancashire soldiers were forced to admire and respect the courage and determination of their Turkish counterparts. They had made the long march across the desert in extreme heat and with only occasional water supplies. Now the British forces were being reorganised into a mobile column to counteract this new threat.

Over the next few days, in camp at Kantara, preparations for the coming confrontation were hectic. Equipment was stripped down to a minimum and wheeled carriages, which were useless in desert conditions, were replaced with vehicles fitted with pedrails to allow them to be hauled across the sand. Additional drilling tools, troughs and pumps were brought in to sink wells and improve the water supply. The massive task of finding and organizing thousands of camels went ahead at pace. Many of the camels were equipped with fanatis – metal water tanks that were strapped on either side of the animal – whilst others were fitted out to carry the tons of other equipment.

Meanwhile, General Lawrence, the commanding officer for this newly created Brigade, was devising his strategy for tackling the approaching army. Spotter planes had been reporting on the progress of the Turkish army since the 21st July and Lawrence was deploying his troops in a pattern that would lure the Turks into a carefully laid trap.

On the morning of 4th August Edward awoke to the sounds of battle coming from the direction of Romani, to the north of where they were camped at Hill 70 in Kantara. The Turkish attack had begun. The soldiers of the 1/8 Lancashires rose quickly and prepared themselves. Carefully trained into exactly what was expected of them, they were eager for the affray and anxious to achieve a victory after the humiliating stalemate of Gallipoli.

On the train to Pelusium they settled in their seats, smoking and talking excitedly, shouting through the windows at soldiers hanging out of the windows of neighbouring carriages and joking like schoolboys off on a seaside trip.

The apprehension, that sharp edge of fear, was still there but it was more contained. This action had been carefully thought through by a man with a deep understanding of the country and a profound affinity and respect for the Arab. They also felt that in this confrontation they would have the chance to contribute to the result with personal skills, courage and judgement rather than going over the top like lemmings to an almost certain death in a hail of machine gun bullets.

Liam could barely contain himself. Every few minutes, he would jump out of his seat and clamber over the outstretched legs of his friends to get to the window. There he stared into the shimmering desert in front of him, listening attentively. 'They're still at it. I can hear some heavy stuff going in now so the Aussies must have pulled them into the trap. The jocks will be giving them a bloody good hiding now. Tough sods they are. Frighten the socks off a bloody donkey if one crossed 'em. Some of the Manchesters went up last night. Wonder if they're getting stuck in yet.' Liam addressed his commentary to anyone who would listen but, after a while, few did. Despite this, he seemed content still to pursue this agitated, but now one sided, discussion.

The train came slowly to a halt in Pelusium in a juddering diminuendo of steam whistles, screeching brakes and clunking buffers. The station was a scene of intense activity with Arab porters working alongside British soldiers to unload the masses of equipment that had been brought up on the train. Members of the Catering Corp darted fussily about amongst their equipment, arranging and sequencing the crates whilst keeping a watchful eye on their native assistants to ensure that nothing disappeared into any of the numerous dark alleys. The excited and noisy chatter of the Arabs belied the slow and methodical pace with which they approached their tasks and blended with the gruff curses of the sweating Lancashire tommies and the more cultured, barking instructions shouted by the officers.

Edward stepped from the train and into the wall of hot, damp air inside the station. He was assaulted at once by the symphony of sounds and smells that was the hallmark of the typical Egyptian town. The noisy voices of the locals now augmented by the clattering hooves of the sweating horses as they towed away the heavy gun carriages, the trains blowing clouds of steam into the air and the combustion engines in the lorries that were being coaxed, spluttering and coughing, into life. The heady mix of spicy aromas, cooking smells and the less hygienic vapours that resulted from poor sanitation, hung like a heavy cloud over the town.

Edward half smiled. It was noisy and vibrant but it was familiar and safe. He was part of a team and he understood clearly how he fitted into it. He knew that there was a big show going on nearby and he had been trained and rehearsed in the part that he had to play alongside his mates.

Moments later he was struggling to contain this good humour he felt as he spotted a woeful looking Liam emerging from one of the shadowy alleys opposite the station. His friend had set off on a mission of mercy hoping to find a home for his pet rat, which he had imaginatively named 'Ratty', as he was reluctant to expose it to the dangers of the anticipated battle with the marauding Turks. Sadly, the first Arab that he had offered it to for safekeeping had inquisitively lifted the sliding door of its wooden box home whilst Liam was still searching for some suitable words of explanation. His surprise on seeing the emerging whiskers and beady eyes of this hated vermin had been so great that he had slammed the door back down on the head of the unfortunate Ratty. The grieving Liam, relieved by this grim mischance of his rodent responsibilities, had buried the box and its now lifeless contents under a palm tree before hurrying back to his unsympathetic mates.

They worked tirelessly, despite the merciless heat, in transhipping the supplies and equipment over to the nearby camp.

A message had been received from the front line in the middle of the afternoon stating that the Anzac Brigade was in need of support against the Turkish attack near Mount Royston. This was south of Romani which was itself a good six miles march south east from Pelusium. Within three minutes of their detraining, the 5th, 7th and 8th Manchesters were marched off into the desert without the benefit of any transport. They didn't have time to try the stew that had been prepared for their lunch and they didn't even have the support supplies of water as the camel train that they were expecting had not yet arrived.

By 11.0 pm, however, the one thousand strong chain of camels had arrived and the soldiers who had remained in Pelusium set about the task of sorting them and loading them with supplies and ammunition. Despite a lack of understanding and knowledge of these big beasts, the work was performed with great enthusiasm and good humour. The convoy was soon on its way again carrying its precious load of water, blankets and ammunition and the 1/8 Lancashires prepared themselves for their own imminent departure.

They had heard that when the three Manchester battalions had arrived at the front, the sight of them, lining up with the mounted Anzac Brigade and preparing to attack, had proved sufficient to persuade the already weary Turks that perhaps this wasn't their chosen time for glory. They turned in their thousands and fled, chased by the determined Allied troops. The sight of this retreating army, however, was almost eclipsed during the night by the vision of a thousand camels, many carrying water in fanatis on their backs, trudging out of the desert night. The Manchester men had endured a long march through the blazing desert without food or water and now these huge animals were like angels bringing deliverance from their parched agony.

The next morning, having made a start in the early hours, Edward, Liam and Big Charlie found themselves in the front line of Allied troops marching in pursuit of the fleeing Turkish army. They were in high spirits and as they marched they laughed, joked, sang songs and smoked cigarettes and pipes. As they progressed they collected souvenirs of bayonets, belts, caps and badges from the bodies of dead Turkish soldiers that lay in the slowly embracing sand.

Their respect for the Turks, who had so recently made the long distance march across this vast, open desert, grew as the day wore on. The glaring sun rose higher in the cloudless sky and the heat became stifling. As they marched through the treeless landscape the heat radiated from the sides of the low hills and turned the valleys into ovens. Their bodies ran with the sweat that poured out of them but they were told to conserve their water supplies because the support units were so far behind. The yielding sand sapped the strength from their legs as they trudged wearily through this huge desert expanse towards the blinding heat haze of the horizon.

The Lancashire soldiers became increasingly affected by this relentless, oppressive heat. They discarded the souvenirs that they had collected earlier in the day and tried to focus on dragging one weary foot after the other. Some collapsed with sunstroke and were left under a temporary shade formed by a blanket draped over a rifle until they could, hopefully, be collected later by the support units.

Edward had become increasingly concerned for the sweating Big Charlie. When he had asked him how he was coping he had replied that he 'felt hotter than an iron caster's arse.'

Edward and Liam had shared their water supply with their desperately struggling friend and their efforts to keep him going had provided a temporary distraction from their own troubles. By the late afternoon, on the outer limits of their reserves of strength, they heard a shout from the front of the column. Looking up, they could see the looming bulk of Mount Meredith where they were to bivouac that night. Spurred by this welcoming sight, they drove themselves forward and, as the cooling, evening air provided welcoming relief from the heat of the day, they dragged their aching limbs up the slopes to the ridge.

The whole of the area was littered with the corpses of hundreds of dead Turkish soldiers and, as they achieved the vantage point of the ridge, they could see in the distance the cavalry pursuing the fleeing Turks. Out at sea an Allied ship was lobbing shells into the ranks of the retreating army, the explosions echoing with a dull clumping from the surrounding hills.

The stop brought only shallow relief for the British soldiers, however. As the sky darkened the night temperature plummeted. There had been very little food or water to sustain their weakened bodies and they had been told that the following day they were to march on to Qatia where the enemy had established a strong and determined defence. There was little hope of improving the situation regarding the food and water because many of the natives who were bringing the supplies had been stampeded by enemy shell fire. The prospect of a repeat of the day that they had just endured was profoundly depressing to these shattered, hungry men as they scooped out hollows in the sand and lay down, hoping to snatch a few hours sleep in the bitter cold of the Egyptian night.

At 3.00am the next morning, the tired, hungry soldiers were woken up and prepared for the agonies of another day's march through the desert. Liam, having vowed not to pee because he wasn't prepared to part unnecessarily with another drop of water out of his body, had gone for a walk to stretch his legs and to check on the condition of some of his mates. Edward tidied himself up the best that he could and, shivering in the bitter cold of the clear night, he wearily packed away his few belongings.

'Eddie, Eddie.' He could hear Liam shouting his name but couldn't see him. He stood up to get a better view and saw Liam running over the ridge and waving frantically. 'Come up here quick. They're here. We're saved. You'll never believe it. Bloody Norah. We're saved. Yeheeee.'

Edward struggled up towards his excited pal and followed his urgently pointing finger. Peering out into the eerily lit desert that they had so recently crossed he at first saw nothing. Then his eye caught a slight movement. He stared, trying to focus, not daring to believe what he was seeing. It couldn't be true. He had been told about mirages that appeared before you in the desert but that was only during the day. He held his breath and stared again. He could see the movement more clearly now and he jumped into the air, threw his arms around Liam, and they danced round and round like demented clockwork dolls, whooping and shouting.

Eventually, they stopped, breathless, and, for the benefit of the crowd that had now joined them, pointed down to the plain where the long line of camels snaking slowly towards them was more clearly visible. Many of them had fantasse – the large water tanks – strapped to their backs whilst others carried food and other precious supplies. When they approached closer, the cheering soldiers saw that some of the camels were carrying the casualties that had dropped out on the previous day's march.

Liam did a jig down the hill, hands in the air, and made a dash for the first, water-laden, camel. 'Just look at this lovely fella,' he shouted, pointing at the camel's native minder who was plodding morosely along holding a rope attached to the animals halter. 'Did you ever see such a thing of beauty? The man is an angel sent to save us.'

He lunged forward, intending to show his gratitude with a manly, welcoming hug. The Egyptian, slightly less certain about the apparent amorous intentions of this wild looking British soldier, ducked under the camel's head and Liam was left grasping the dusty neck of the big beast. Camels are renowned for being both bad tempered and unsociable, especially after a long trek through the desert, and Liam found himself inches away from two flaring black, cavernous, nostrils and large, thick lips furled back to reveal big, brown, slab teeth. From the depths of its body it emitted a low belching growl, accompanied by a noxious vapour, straight into Liam's startled face. He jumped away with alacrity.

'Bloody Hell. That smelt worse than the Grapes on a Sunday morning.'

The columns of troops eventually moved off at 4.00am. Alongside them were the cavalry and the heavy artillery guns being hauled along by large teams of horses. They were refreshed by the food and water although this was strictly limited. The ration was less than one pint of water per man and the order had been given that no one was to have a drink without the permission of a commanding officer. But as the sun rose in the sky, the day grew rapidly hotter. The conditions became as unbearable as the day before and the desperate soldiers forced themselves forward through the soft sand.

After eight hours of marching in the insufferable heat, during which many had gone down with heatstroke, they saw the green tops of the trees that heralded the approach to Qatia. Their spirits were lifted again, they pushed their weary bodies into covering the last, short distance to the beckoning oasis and their befuddled brains struggled to focus on the confrontation that awaited them.

They finally reached Qatia in the early afternoon and were almost disappointed to find that the Turkish army had already departed. The Turks, by now, had lost over half of their army and they had decided that the desert was a safer prospect than facing the formidable army that was approaching them.

The disappointment of the British soldiers was compounded when they discovered that, despite the clearly thriving trees growing in the area, there was no water. Rumours went round that an underground supply was available two feet below the surface and, over the next hour, holes started to appear all over the camp as frantic soldiers searched for the precious liquid. Fortunately, as they were reaching the point of desperation, a camel train arrived carrying supplies of food and water and, once again, these ugly beasts with their patchy, vermin ridden hides and their unpleasant habits were greeted with rapturous cheering by the Lancashire soldiers.

The men, so used at home to seeing excessive amounts of water falling freely and, often, inconveniently out of the skies, sipped at the now scarce liquid with a reverential relish. They rolled drops of it with sensuous delight around their mouths, experienced its pleasure as though it was nectar from the hands of some lustrous goddess, and then let it slide caressingly down their throats.

Their thirsts slaked for the moment, Edward and Liam went to root out Big Charlie who they found prostrated and gently snoring in his bivouac. They explained to him that they had volunteered the three of them for a scouring party to go out in the desert to find and bring back casualties. After a long succession of loudly repeated 'Sod Offs' from the big man they managed to persuade him to his feet and to adopt a minimum of a half-interested expression.

29 Myrtle Street
Cross Lane
Salford 5
Great Britain

15th July 1916

Dear Dad,
Something very sad has happened to Miss Howard because when I went to Sunday School at the Mission she was in the Church Hall by herself playing the piano and crying so much she was dripping on the keys. I stood near Mrs Willoughby whilst she was talking to Elsie Craddock's Mother and she told her that Miss Howard had had some bad news from the Somme (Mam told me how to spell Somme. She said it is foreign.) Mrs Willoughby said that Miss Howard had been sat there crying all day playing the same music called 'Jesu Joy of Man's Desirings' and she wouldn't talk to anyone.

I asked Mam how they would get the piano keys dry because you can't get a cloth down those little gaps between the keys and she said it is not important because her sweetheart must have been killed. She said that she should have got married when she wanted to but she didn't because her Mam was a widow and was pulling her face. Mam told Billy Murphy's Mam when she came round and said now she might never know. I asked her what she might never know but she just said that I was too young to understand and, anyway, I was supposed to be washing the pots. I heard Mrs Murphy telling Mam that he shouldn't have been in the army but some woman had given him a white feather. That must be some kind of secret code.

I told Mam that perhaps she had better go and get Miss Howard and give her a cigarette like she did with Edith Hardcastle's Mam or else she might stay there for ever. She said God will put his arm round her and comfort her and I told her that Reverend Williams was trying to do that when I left and he is God's spokesman but he wasn't having any luck.

Thank you for the headband that you sent for my birthday. I really like it and I saved it and wore it at Whit Week with my new dress that Mam had made. I told everyone that it was from Egypt and that you had bought it from near where Jesus came from. I told Uncle Jim about the carpenters and he said to ask you if you have come across any nice stables.

Our Mary has started in the beginners' class at Sunday School and I had to sit with her the first time because she was frightened of old Mr Hillman whose nose is always running. She was alright last week because Mrs Hillman was there and she told the story about Jesus feeding thousands of people with a bit of bread and some fish.

Mam said that I can help her tomorrow to make another fruit cake for you. She said that it depends a bit on what our Edward can fetch home but we should be alright although sometimes it might be handy if Jesus could come round here and do his trick with the bread and the fish.

Love

Laura

PS Mrs Murphy told Mam that she had had a letter from her Liam and he'd had an accident with the toilet. She used some naughty words about him but then asked God to forgive her so that it would be alright.

'This bloody, sodding war. Just when you think that you are coping something else comes along and kicks you in the balls.'

Hearing the agonized cry from his friend, Edward looked up from his letter to see Liam, his own post scattered on the sand in front of him, holding his bowed head with his clenched fists as his body was shaken by a deep, racking sob. A slight evening breeze blowing through the doorway of the bivouac fluttered the letters then left them still again at Liam's feet.

'What's the matter, mate? Is there anything I can do?' Edward searched for suitable words but felt inadequate in the face of this surprise show of naked grief. Liam, in all the thirty years that he had known him, had coped with any difficulty with a shrug of the shoulders, a laugh and a joke. They had been to infant school together, played football together, swum in the nude in the lake at Ordsall Park and shared the same bed when Liam's mother had been confined with his young sister. The close bond between them was never discussed or even thought about. It was just there. Now Edward felt slightly uncomfortable and totally unprepared as he witnessed the turmoil that his friend was trying to contain.

He needed to show concern but he was fearful of revealing his misgivings. So many of the lads had received letters from wives whose desperate search for survival for themselves and their young families had led them into new relationships, that he feared that the same destructive message might have been now delivered to Liam. It seemed impossible to believe that the staunchly Catholic, God-fearing Bridget could have strayed in this way but something had delivered Liam a profound body blow. He lit a cigarette and passed it over silently.

The cooling smoke seemed finally to settle Liam enough for him to salvage words from his inner pain.

170

'Eddie. We've changed, haven't we? You know. Like now, you hardly ever talk about your Laura and the kids and I don't talk about our Brig and the family.'

Edward's heart sank. She must have done it. What could he say to help? 'I suppose it's how we cope. They're still important. But when you're this far away and can't do anything about it, you just seem to lock it away.'

'It's like having some precious jewels and you lock them in a safe when you have to go away,' Liam said slowly. 'You think that when you get back they'll still be there to enjoy just as much as before. But then some bastard comes along and steals one from you.' His face contorted as the hurt pressed into his mind with renewed vigour.

Edward reached out and put his hand on Liam's back. 'What is it? Has something happened to Bridget?' Liam's shoulders drooped and his head fell forward as he shook it. He handed the screwed up letter to Edward as his body shook again with the great waves of anguish.

Edward took it, pressed it against his thigh to straighten it, checked the top right-hand corner for the address then looked at each page for the numbers to confirm the page sequence. He was reluctant to start, as if doing so would make him complicit in the words that had caused this grief, but he knew that he felt compelled to share the burden of the pain in any way that he could.

Finally, he slowly read the body of the letter. The writing was in pencil in a large, flowing feminine script that sometimes strayed from the ruled lines on the blue writing paper. Bridget had clearly struggled for control of her emotions as she had written it.

'My Dearest, Darling Lee,' he read. He felt an embarrassed flush of heat on his back. He had never thought of his pal as someone who shared the same touching intimacies with his wife as he did with his Laura. *'I don't know*

*how to find the words to tell you this but you need to know and I don't
know how else to do it.'*

*'I told you in my last letter that our Lizzie had the scarlet fever.
She was really poorly and her little body was on fire with it. I had the
doctor round to see her and he did what he could. Father Regan came
and blessed her on Sunday but on Monday morning she passed on into
the loving arms of Jesus our Saviour. God Bless her and keep her. She
struggled so hard, the poor little mite, but in the end she didn't have the
strength left to fight.'*

*'Laura had the kids whilst Lizzie was ill and she was round
here when she died. She has been a big help, as have all the neighbours.
We're putting Lizzie in with your Mam in Weaste Cemetery on Friday
morning.'*

*'Lee, I'm crying as I write this because I know that every word
I put down is like sticking a knife into you, the man I love more than
my own life. I want to put my arms round you and hold you tight and
take all the pain away. One day, please God, I will.'*

*'I know this will be hard for you when you are so far away but
please don't worry about us. We will be alright. I am proud of you for
fighting to keep us safe and you will always be my hero. Be strong for us
and keep safe, my Darling. All my love for ever. Bridget.'*

Edward stared at the creased pieces of blue paper in
his hand, hardly believing what he had just read. Lizzie would
have been just two and a half years old. She couldn't have
been taken just like that. He went over the words again,
willing them to change, to deliver a message that wasn't so
searingly corrosive. They were the same. He reached out and
put his arm round Liam's drooping shoulders. 'Christ, mate.
I'm so sorry. She was such a bonny little thing. I can't believe
it.'

'I never had the chance to get to know her,' Liam said
quietly. 'Working all week, like, then going to watch United
on Saturday afternoon. Used to take her out in her pram on
Sunday, though. Down to the park and then to see her

Granny. She was such a pretty little thing. I was proud as a button, showing her off, you know.'

'I know what you mean, Liam.' Edward struggled getting the words out. His mind seemed to be racing away to nothing. 'She was a beautiful little girl. A lovely smile. Black curls like her Mam. It's hard to believe.'

'She was crawling when we left. Since then, she'd started toddling and I never had the chance to walk down the street holding her hand. She'd learnt to say Dada and I wasn't there to say what a clever little girl she was. She'd learnt lots of words, could sing little songs, could sit there and feed herself. She played with dolls and toys and gave the others what for if they tried to take them off her. And where was I? I was crawling round a stinking rat-infested hell-hole in the arse end of Turkey thinking that I was making a better life for them.'

'But we don't have a choice. We've got to do what's right. The women understand.'

'Maybe. But little Lizzie didn't. If she fell and hurt herself, I couldn't bend down and pick her up and give her a cuddle. What I wanted, more than anything in the world, was to feel her little arms squeezing round my neck. I wanted to feel her wet tears on my face, to give her a kiss and take all her troubles away but now, all that'll be left by the time I get back will be a name on a gravestone.'

'But you've still got all the memories of when you did things like that with your lads. You'll have to try and build on those.'

'Aye. I know that I've done it with the lads but it's different with a daughter. You love all your kids the same, but you want the lads to be tough enough to take the knocks in life. If they fall you rub the bit that hurts and tousle their hair. You know it's different, Eddie. I've seen you with your Laura and your Sadie. There's a sort of… tenderness when it's your daughter. You want to protect them and be strong for them.'

Liam's words began to stir memories and emotions that Edward had long since buried deep inside him. He was right. They were like priceless jewels, those unique moments of innocent love between a parent and a child. He had locked them away to protect them from the murderous savagery of the life that he was now leading, just as Liam had done. But now fate had visited her cruel intentions on the little terraced house in Goodiers Lane and had snatched away the life of Liam's only daughter.

He looked out of the bivouac at the puffs of dry sand that were rolling down the dunes. A sea breeze was building up as the evening sun lowered slowly behind the palms at the rear of the camp. The summits of the sand hills glowed fiercely red as the dying sun picked them out. A native walked past leading a train of camels and soldiers wandered unhurriedly by. They were close but strangely distant. The two of them had been trapped in this silent capsule of sadness and those around them could not penetrate its invisible barrier.

Edward did know the special moments that Liam craved for. He was a little taken aback by this revelation that his bluff, wisecracking friend had actually noticed, and had been coveting, those fleeting intimacies, those sweet seconds, when solace is offered and accepted. These were those brief but important occasions that engrave the footsteps on the path of life that a man treads uniquely with his daughter. He thought of the scrapes that Laura, and later, Sadie, had got into as they tried to match their older brother in everything that he did. How, so many times, he had picked one or other of them up and hugged them and kissed their tears. Kissed tears that had formed like jewels on tiny eyelashes. Salty tears.

'I just thought' Liam said slowly, 'when all this started, that I'd be walking back in the house within six months. I could just see myself going home. She would hold two little hands up to me. I would bend down and pick her up and I'd be there… hugging my own little daughter.'

An electrifying bolt hit Edward's brain as another memory unleashed itself into his reluctant consciousness. His little Mary. She had been born just after Lizzie and his wife, Laura, had often told him in letters about the progress that she was making. But over the last two years he had increasingly sealed the snippets away in his memory, with only an occasional cursory review. Dwelling on the memories of his family brought the pain of longing to be with them, so he coped by not thinking. Liam's torment had exposed this rawness. He had not had the opportunity, yet, to enjoy with Mary those jewels of time and, if fate dealt him an unkind hand, he also might never have that chance.

He turned and kissed the top of Liam's head and rested his forehead against his. 'Eh. I'm so sorry, our kid. I'm so very, very sorry.'

The tears of both men merged and fell onto the dry sand.

Ballybunion Camp
North Suez
Egypt

23rd September 1916

Dear Pippin,

I was very sorry to hear about Miss Howard and how sad she was. She is a lovely lady and I hope that she is feeling better now. I was also very sorry to hear about Lizzie Murphy. She was a beautiful little girl but Mrs Murphy will know that she is safe with Jesus now. I hope and pray that you are all alright and that you are managing OK in these difficult times.

Since I last wrote to you we have had to do a long march across the desert and it was not very pleasant – mainly because it was so hot. We started off at a place called Pelusium which has been an important trading port since before Jesus was alive. Some of the buildings were very old and parts of the town were a little bit smelly. If you look at a map of Egypt at school, and you find the top bit near the coast, well that is where we are now. When the Romans occupied this area two thousand years ago, they built forts spaced out along the coast for their soldiers to stay in. So it is quite funny because we stayed in places where the Roman soldiers had lived all that time ago.

Our engineers have just found a good way of building roads in the desert. Do you remember those chickens that Uncle Joe had in his back yard and he kept them in with wire netting? Well, they found that by rolling that out, and pegging it down to the ground, it would stop the sand moving so much. They can run the motor lorries on it so that is really good.

We are seeing a lot more of those flying machines out here that the British Army have got. They are amazing when you see them, like big birds up in the sky. It's strange when you think that they have got men in them. They use them to see what the other side are doing. Mr Murphy said that he wouldn't mind *having a go in one of them but I told him that they are not for me. I want to keep solid ground under my feet as God intended.*

We have heard that next month they are going to start giving us a week's break in Alexandria which is still in the top bit of Egypt but further to the left. It is a big, old town but there are lots of nice beaches so, hopefully, we should be able to go swimming quite a lot. It will be a nice change not to be doing army work for a week. There are these horrible things called lice that get in your clothes and make you itch a lot when you are in camp, so going in the sea will give us a chance to clean up a bit. We said that we would prefer to come home for a week but that takes three weeks there and then three weeks back.

Your Mam wrote and told me that you had had a good school report this summer. Well done. I am really pleased about that. She said that you like reading and you are always hiding in a corner with your head in a book – especially when she wants you to do something. Where are you getting your books from?

I know that I have not seen you for two years now, and you will have changed a lot, but please remember me, my little Darling, and know that I love you all with all of my heart. I pray to God for your safekeeping and hope that it will not be too long before I can see you again.

Love

Dad

29 Myrtle Street
Cross Lane
Salford 5
Great Britain

1st December 1916

Dear Dad,

I am enclosing a Christmas card that I made at school in the art class. They are supposed to be the three Kings on camels in the picture but our Edward said that they look more like the mangy dogs from the Maltese café on Trafford Road. It's not my fault because we don't have any proper paints left at school so the teacher makes them out of plants and things. She says that they were good enough for the great Dutch artists but when we do it they go all over the place. Anyway, will you send it back when you have finished with it so I can use it next year because teacher said we can't get hold of good quality card now.

When I read your letter out our Ben started laughing because he thought that you had mice in your clothes. Mam told him they were lice but then he kept mithering asking what lice were until our Edward threw a cushion at him.

I get the books from Barney's Books on Regent Road. They cost a halfpenny but you get a farthing back if you return them. Sometimes I do errands for Barney and then he lets me borrow the books for nothing. I like to read in bed if I can but Mam shouts at me because she says that you don't know where they have been. She says that you can't be too careful with things like that.

I do remember you, Dad, and I love you as well. I say a prayer for you every night because I am a bit worried. Edith Hardcastle's Dad got killed in the war and Mr Kirkstall from round the corner has come back with no legs. If it's not raining he sits outside all day just staring at nothing and not talking. He nearly smiled a bit the other day but, when we started laughing because his

178

smile was only up one side, he started crying and Mrs Kirkstall shouted at us. Mam said we should try to understand and be kind to him. He has been badly injured and there will be lots more Dads who won't come back at all before all this lot is over with.

I am getting excited because we have got a Christmas party at Central Mission in two weeks time. We all get a present and I used to think that they came from Father Christmas but our Edward said there isn't one but not to tell the others. He said that the presents come from the posh people and from Americans. Our Edward said last year it was Mr Hillman dressed as Father Christmas because he kept wiping his nose on his sleeve.

Mam said not to expect too much in our stockings this Christmas and it might be just a bite of the cupboard knob for Christmas dinner. Our Edward told me that he's got a surprise for Mam but I mustn't open my mouth or else. If I tell you, though, I am only writing words so that should be alright. He has been saving money every week at the greengrocers where he works doing deliveries and he is going to bring a goose and some oranges home on Christmas Eve. I can't wait to see Mam's face. She will be really excited.

The best present of all, though, would be if you could come home Dad and then I wouldn't even go to the party at the Mission. Please, Dad. Can't you come? Is it not nearly finished yet?

Love

Laura

PS I told teacher about those bird machines and she said that she doesn't think that they are very safe, so you had better tell Mr Murphy.

Bir-el-Mazar
Egypt

25thDecember 1916

Dear Pippin,

Happy Christmas Darling and I hope that the New Year
will be a lot better for all of us. I received your letter and card
this morning and I thought that it was lovely. Our Edward is
not being very fair because I could tell straight away that it was
the three Kings with their camels. I also got the cake that you and
your Mam had baked and we shared it out after our Christmas
dinner. We all stood up with our mugs of beer and said 'A special
Happy Christmas to big Laura and little Laura.' We gave some
to the two Gyppies who cooked the dinner and they said 'More
please, Miss Laura.' They are smashing fellas and never stop
singing when they are working. I wish that we could all feel so
happy.

We have been clearing the area of Turkish soldiers whilst
our engineers are building a railway and water pipeline along the
coast. They have been using a lot of Arabs to help with this work.
They are like our cooks – they sing all the time. Now, the British
soldiers have started doing the same, so you can imagine, we hear
some very strange noises when they all get going. They are
frightened to death of the flying machines, though, and they run
like mad when they see one.

I hope that you all enjoyed your Christmas dinner. I have
told our Edward in his letter that I am very proud of him for
working so hard and saving up for that goose. I will take him to
watch United for a treat when I get back.

Please don't worry about me, my little Darling. I am
sure that your prayers will keep me safe and when I do get back
we will do lots of things to make up for the time that I have been
away. The main problem that I have at the moment is some big
sores that don't heal up properly. Nearly everybody has them.
We think that they are caused by the lice and dirty sand but
hopefully they will soon be gone.

I hope that you had a good time at the Christmas party. Mam told me that last year our Sadie cried when she sat on Father Christmas's knee and she tried to pull his beard off. I hope that she was better behaved this time.

I enjoyed the break that we had in Alexandria. I got leave at the same time as Mr Murphy so that was good. We did a lot of swimming and walking around the town. There are some lovely parks and lots of beautiful old buildings. We used to go down to the docks sometimes and watch all the ships coming and going. We couldn't believe the amount of railway line that they are still bringing in. We have already built about 80 miles of it but they say that they want to push it right along the coast and into Palestine.

I remember Barney's Books. He must be getting on a bit. Your Mam and me used to look in his window when we were courting. Your Mam always liked a good read but she says that she doesn't have much time now, what with one thing and another. I will buy her some brand new books when I come back so that she can have a nice long read and a good rest. She told me that you had been helping to darn the lads' socks. That was really nice. It's a big help for her if you can share some of the work like that.

'Bye for now my little Pippin. Take good care of yourself.

Love

Dad

Chapter 11

France March 1917

'By the left. I could have managed another ten minutes on parade with that one.'

Edward looked up from the corner of the train carriage where he sat huddled inside his greatcoat to see Liam leaning against the door with a slightly vague, beatific grin on his face. He looked like their cat had done after it had found Laura's carefully hoarded half block of chocolate.

'I've not had a kiss like that since I gave Beattie Bountiful that toffee apple,' said Liam sighing as he revelled in the rapturous memory of his more recent encounter.

'Whose Beattie Bountiful when she's at home, then?' queried Edward.

'You know. That girl with the er...' Liam gestured with his hands to indicate the ample curves of the girl in question. 'Lived off Ellor Street. Round the corner from the tripe shop.'

'Oh. You mean Beatrice Brown. What was you doing with her then? She was three years older than you.'

'She was a girl of a well known generous nature and I thought that she might appreciate my thoughtful gift' Liam replied, hurt by his friend's slightly hectoring tone. He sat back down next to Edward with the inane grin still fixed on his face. He looked up at the ceiling of the train and sighed.

'And did she?' Edward demanded.

'Did she what?' asked Liam, emerging briefly from his reverie.

'Did she appreciate the sodding toffee apple?' Edward was now beginning to feel a little exasperated by the whole conversation.

Liam seemed to be determined to fuel his friend's growing frustration. 'Mmmmm,' he said enraptured as his head sank down within the embracing collar of his greatcoat.

The train jerked as it moved out of the station and Edward pushed his hands deep inside his pockets and pulled the coat round him. It was bitterly cold now and he stared at the grey sky through the train window and wondered whether he really wanted to pursue this discussion any further. It was encouraging to see these small, familiar signs of the old Liam emerging. Since he'd had the letter from Bridget telling him that Lizzie had died, Liam had become withdrawn and reclusive. When they had gone on leave to Alexandria he had walked around the bazaars, swum in the sea and sat in the bars with the rest of them, but he had barely spoken. He had been offered compassionate leave but he had refused it saying that, by the time that he got there, it would be all over bar the shouting. Instead, he had immersed himself into the routine of the job, working hard, but mechanically, and barely communicating.

By the end of the year the railway along the Egyptian north coast had reached Bir-el-Mazar where Liam had remarked at the Christmas dinner that the only one good thing about the place was that they were not stopping there. They had eventually reached El Arish, having pushed the Turks back over the border into Palestine. There, the desert sands were the best that they had encountered for playing football and rugby. Challenges had been thrown out, training resumed and fixtures arranged. Apart from two nights that they had camped at El Burj – seven miles further east – they had stayed in El Arish for over two weeks. The 8th Lancashire's rugby team had struggled again against opposition that they should have defeated. Liam had seemed distracted and distant and failed to give his players the structure in their play or the possession that they needed from his position at scrum half. Playing outside him at stand off, Edward had tried cajoling, pleading and finally cursing but nothing had shaken his friend out of the rigid despondency that gripped him.

In early February they had started the journey back to Alexandria and there, on the 23rd, they had boarded HMT 'Transylvania.' For weeks there had been rumours that a posting was in the offing and finally it had been confirmed that they were heading for the Western Front. Despite the reports that they had heard about the heavy casualties suffered in the summer offensive, particularly around the Somme, they felt that this was not a bad option. The Salford soldiers were battle hardened and had given a good account of themselves when called upon to fight. They were keen to have a go at the Germans and to help to push them back to where they had come from. They were also going to be a lot nearer to home than they had been for the last two years.

There had been various items of news that had encouraged them to the belief that something different was about to happen, that they might be approaching something of a turning point. The brutal German commander von Falkenhayven had been replaced on the Western Front by Hindenburg and, at home, the Liberal leader, Asquith, had been replaced by Lloyd George heading up a coalition Government. It was known that Lloyd George was not particularly impressed by the unimaginative British Commander, Haig, and many believed that a change there could herald a breakthrough.

Liam, however, had failed to be enthused by all this and he had persisted in his dogged, grey gloom. Now, after two days on this cold and draughty train heading up through France, watching the weather outside getting progressively worse, the humour of all of them was wearing very thin. For men who had spent the last twelve months acclimatizing to the searing temperatures of Egypt, the sleet and snow of this French March weather felt like an Arctic wasteland. The glowing smile that was now fixed on Liam's face, therefore, was not only unexpected after his months of tortured misery, it was also totally at odds with the numbed faces that stared at him through narrowed eyes peering out of the slits between the pulled down hats and the elevated collars. Sitting in the V shape formed by the greatcoat lapels, the tips of the brightly coloured noses were like a string of baubles hung round the carriage.

Edward's irritation lay not only in his friend's enjoyment of this teasing game, which he was used to, anyway, after all these years, even though it was a surprise considering the mood he had been in for so long. It was this revelation of Liam's perfidy that had slightly shocked him. As fifteen year olds their focus had been on playing and watching football and rugby. Their wage packets were handed directly to their mothers and a small amount was given back as spends. If they got the chance to earn a bit of extra they might go and watch United or Salford and, if not, they would go fishing on the Cut Canal or go swimming at Regent Road baths. Apart from Laura, who lived down their street and was, when she could come out, really just one of the gang, girls were a different species that you rarely came into contact with. In moments of false bravado, and following the example of older mates, you sometimes shouted remarks to passing girls that were probably slightly improper but without really understanding the sense of what you were shouting.

Girls went to different schools, they went to the swimming baths on different days, they had cookery lessons whereas lads did woodwork and the only time that you came near them was at Church or at some mate's house if he had sisters. At fifteen, the frightening thought plagued you that you would soon have to find a way of bridging the gulf between yourself and this increasingly fascinating species and you created little stories of conquests to impress your pals. You were primed with an endless supply of usually less than helpful suggestions from workmates and older brothers about how you should approach girls. Then, just to make sure that you felt totally inadequate to the task anyway, they taunted you about your unimpressive facial hair.

Now Liam, who, Edward remembered, at the time of the toffee apple incident had excused himself because of an alleged bad stomach, was implying that his worldly education had taken a great leap forward at the hands of this older and, it was generally believed, more experienced girl. There had been no inference beforehand that he had been planning such an initiative, no sniggering discussions and, from what he could recall, no signs of nervous anticipation on the day. How had he managed to carry off the whole operation with such outward calm and then kept it a dark secret for almost twenty years? This escapade wasn't the serious and, essentially private, sort of relationship that you formed when you were older and that eventually led to marriage. No, this was more on a par to challenging the widely feared Crusher Hawkins from Tatton Street to a bare knuckle fight.

Liam's smug silence and inane smile was clearly inviting further probing both on the subject of the benevolent Beattie and also on his recent encounter on the station. Edward, however, was not going to be easily drawn. He knew his friend's mischievous humour could quickly pull you into a bewildering maze of repartee where the joke invariably finished being on you.

'I knew that Beattie Brown once,' rumbled Big Charlie's voice out of the large untidy pile of khaki material stacked in the corner of the carriage. He clearly wasn't in quite as deep a sleep as they had thought. 'She was a big lass, she was. How you managed to do owt with her I don't know.'

Liam was stung by this oblique reference to his stature. 'It's quality that counts, mate. Anyway, what was you doing chasing after her? You'd have got nowhere there, her being a Catholic and you being in the Honorary Order of Big Daft Sods.'

The large pile of material became animated and Big Charlie's face appeared above it. 'What's that got to do with it? Dot was brought up as a Catholic. Anyroad, I never said that I was chasing after her,' he retorted. 'And if I had been I'd have given her something better than a bloody sticky toffee apple.' Having assessed, wrongly, that his riposte couldn't be bettered, he withdrew into his coat.

'Well, she wouldn't have been chasing after you, mate. She used to call you Aniseed Balls because there was only your mangy dog that would come sniffing round you.'

Edward was beginning to feel a little alarmed by the way the conversation was turning. 'How come you knew her, Charlie?' he asked in a placatory tone, 'She lived up our end, so where did you bump into her?'

'Her old man worked at our place,' Big Charlie said, re-emerging from his greatcoat. 'He had a smashing pair of workboots that I used to borrow after we'd finished work on a Saturday morning.'

'Why?' Edward queried, 'You never worked in the afternoons.

'No. But her Dad was our rugby coach and I wasn't going to play in my bare feet, was I?'

Edward decided on a change of tactic and turned to Liam whose smile had now slightly faded. 'Where had you been anyway?' he asked.

'What? With the blessed Beattie?'

'No. Just now. When you got back on the train with that silly smile on your face.'

Liam detected another opportunity appearing. 'I'd just been down the station to the pissoir.'

'So that was enough to put that big, daft grin on your face?'

'I'd been waiting two hours so I was getting anxious.' Having regained the initiative, Liam was enjoying the manipulative twists that the conversation was now offering.

'So what has that got to do with having your wicked way with Beattie Brown, then?' Edward demanded.

'It was this beautiful, young French lady who had been lusting after me and she couldn't keep her hands off me.'

'Oh yes. Pull the other one. What did she do, drag you into the waiting room and ravish you on the floor?'

'Well, not quite,' Liam laughed. 'She grabbed me when I came out of the privvy. She was shouting something about 'Bag-a-Dad' and calling me 'Victoire'. She must have mistaken me for somebody else but she wouldn't stop kissing me so I wasn't complaining.'

'She's done a good job, I'd say. She has certainly perked you up a bit. I was beginning to get a bit worried about you.'

'I know. I'm sorry mate. I know I've been a miserable sod lately. I just felt so guilty about Lizzie. I couldn't stop thinking that it was my fault, not being there to do my bit,' Liam said, settling himself back in the seat next to Edward and suddenly becoming more serious.

'But you couldn't have done anything about it, could you? It was the scarlet fever that took her and you couldn't help that.'

'Aye. Maybe. But I could have perhaps got a few bob from somewhere and got the doctor out again. He might have done something.'

'There's nothing much they can do, though, with scarlet fever,' Edward reasoned with his troubled friend. 'There are a lot of kids who die with it.'

'Aye. Because our lasses are struggling to bring up the kids with next to nothing. I reckon they've a better chance if they belong to the posh people like those your Sarah worked for up Pendleton.'

'You might be right. But it's not your fault. We're doing a job that we have to do. Let's just hope that it's over soon.'

'Yeah. Let's hope.' Liam looked wistful and the pain showed in his distant eyes. Suddenly, he cheered himself up a little. 'Well, we're half way back now, so that's something. That mamselle's kiss made me think about our Brig. We've become so hardened by all this lot, Eddie, we forget what a nice kiss from the missus can do for you. You know what I mean, mate. From someone who really cares. It's something special, isn't it, their gentleness, the way they smooth the edges off you? You come in from work, all rough-arsed and hairy, and smelling like a mad dog, she gives you a kiss and, wham, you're in a different world.'

'I suppose with being out here we've shut it all out. It's how we survive. If you didn't, you'd go mad because you can't do anything about it.'

'Aye. You're right. There's not much room for love and kindness in a place where we're shooting the bloody heads off each other,' reflected Liam. 'I was just so wrapped up in my own misery I wasn't thinking about Brig and how she's coping. It must have been a bloody nightmare for her seeing that coffin go down and me nowhere in sight.'

'But she knows what the score is, mate. She knew that you was in Egypt and had no chance of being there.'

'No. I know. There's not an ounce of spite in her. When I go home she'll give me a kiss and treat me like a hero. There won't be a second of blaming me for what happened to Lizzie. She'll hurt for ever because of it but she'll just say 'It's God's will' and get on with it.'

The two friends settled back into their own thoughts. Liam's brief experience with the French girl on the station platform had triggered memories of home for both of them. Edward wondered how Laura and the kids were really coping. Liam's assertion was true. You did miss that tenderness that seemed so alien in this masculine world of bravado and butchery. Laura's letters were always reassuring about how they were managing and cheerfully encouraging about the children. She told him little stories about what they were doing and how they were developing but she never dwelt on the problems. He knew that she was tough and resourceful and that she would manage somehow. He felt sorry for young Edward, growing up without a father. He'd had to do the same thing, but when he was young he'd always had his older brothers there as breadwinners and to give a guiding hand or a sharp cuff round the ear. Young Edward would just be celebrating his twelfth birthday yet already he was the man of the house and his part time job as an errand boy was proving an invaluable support.

Edward stared at the carriage windows, now blinding white with the driving snow outside. What sort of a show was this going to be that they were heading towards? They had heard all sorts of stories about what was happening in France and Belgium. They knew about the horrific casualties on both sides and the stalemate that seemed to have developed after the mayhem on the Somme in the summer of 1916. After becoming acclimatized to the heat of Egypt, the weather that they were now passing through was bitingly cold. Memories of the Gallipoli winter, and the thought that this campaign could be even worse, depressed him.

The large bundle in the corner stirred. 'What were you just saying about bagging Beattie Brown's Dad?' queried Big Charlie.

'Oh it was nowt,' rejoined Liam, 'We were just philosophising, that's all.'

'That's a bit bloody daft in this weather.' Big Charlie retreated into his greatcoat.

Liam turned to Edward, smiling, and said quietly 'It wasn't what you think, you know.'

Edward looked puzzled. 'What wasn't what I think, then?'

'You know. The beautiful, busty Beattie. It all started quite – well, fairly – innocently. That Martha Jarvis – the girl from the tripe shop on Ellor Street – kept asking me to go for a walk round The Crescent. Well, I thought, I'm going to look a right Mary Ann here, you know, with the kissing and all that. You didn't get to learn much about that at our school, did you?'

'No. It certainly wasn't included in any lessons. The nearest we got to sex education was Miss Brown playing 'Sweet Lass from Richmond Hill.' The rest of the time it was 'Hearts of Oak' and all that stuff.'

'Well, anyway. I had heard that Beattie was a bit generous in that direction so I thought, her being older and that, she might be willing to give a bit of kissing practice to a needy person. Rather make a fool of myself with Beattie and have done with it than with Martha Jarvis.'

'Right. Did it work?'

'Oh aye. She was very helpful. She sat me on Nitty Norah's junk stall in the market and kissed me so hard I thought my eyes would pop out. They nearly did after the next kiss. She undid her cardigan right down the front.'

Edward was aghast. 'What, in the middle of the market?'

'Oh aye. It was closed though by then. Next thing, she's dragging my kex off.'

It was worse. 'She what...? You didn't er...? you didn't... you know? Did you?'

'Aye. I did. I grabbed my toffee apple and bloody scarpered.'

The march from the station at Pont Remy, near Abbeville, was through deep, icy slush with freezing sleet driving into their faces. The howling wind explored every opportunity to push frozen fingers down their collars and up their sleeves. The horses at the rear of the line skidded clumsily as their minders tried to calm them and encourage them forward. They whinnied loudly in complaint at the conditions and grew more fractious as the forlorn column of Salford soldiers progressed slowly up the French road.

These horses, like the men, had spent months in the blistering heat of the Egyptian deserts and were now traumatized by the dramatic change in the weather. The minders had worked with the same team of animals for a long time and, to them, they were like close friends. They hated having to subject the horses to such stressful conditions but all they could do was to cajole them and hope that they would not stray off the road and go down a ditch.

Eventually, the Battalion arrived at the village of Erondelle where they were split into groups and directed to the different buildings where they were to be billeted. Edward, Liam and Big Charlie were relieved to find that they were to stay in a fairly substantial barn. They had been sleeping in bivouacs since they had enlisted so this accommodation felt quite palatial. The straw was comfortable and infinitely more preferable than the icy mud outside.

During the next few days the Royal Engineers came and erected a large communal bath. The facility was a novelty for the Lancashire men whose bathing opportunities had been very restricted for the last two years and it was enjoyed with loud enthusiasm. A catering unit was established in the village and the improved rations made the appalling weather more tolerable.

The issue of steel helmets brought a mixed response from the soldiers whose experience, up to that point, had been limited to cloth hats. Liam, grumbling about wearing tin hats in freezing weather, stuffed it immediately with straw to improve the insulation. The respirators that they were given left many of them puzzled until it was explained that both sides were using gas, the effects of which were, at best, extremely uncomfortable and, at worst, lethal. When they were issued with short Lee Enfield rifles to replace the older, long rifles that they had used for so long the men were fascinated and keen to try them. Liam was quick to point out that they had been designed with him in mind but that Big Charlie should tuck his into his belt like a pistol 'to save him looking totally stupid.'

The addition of a number of motorized vehicles and some heavy trench mortars to the Division helped the transformation into a newer, better equipped fighting force. They were being made ready to face an enemy even more formidable than the Turkish soldiers that they had confronted in Gallipoli and Egypt. There could be no doubting the awesome, destructive power of the German army. The evidence was everywhere. As they progressed through the villages towards the front line, the Lancashire men were sickened and disgusted by the wanton destruction that had been wreaked by the Germans upon the French countryside and its inhabitants as they had retreated back to the Hindenburg Line.

Not satisfied with the enormous damage that had already been done by the heavy artillery fire from both sides – the roads and fields blown into a lunar landscape and the woods reduced to a few leafless, charred stumps – they had strived to make the countryside as useless as possible to the advancing Allies. They had destroyed orchards and crops in the ground, felled trees that lined the roads, booby-trapped buildings to make them unusable and had blown up bridges to make them impassable.

The most sickening, and most puzzling, sight for the Salford lads was the pointless desecration of the cemeteries. Smashed gravestones stood like broken teeth though a large marble cross had been allowed to survive. The broken remains of worthy peasants, who had died in peace but had now been exhumed by war, lay scattered and anonymous. The men had seen many dead soldiers over the past two years but seeing body parts of long-dead locals sticking out of destroyed graves filled them with shock and disgust. Liam, the death of his daughter Lizzie still fresh in his mind, collapsed to the floor weeping. Edward muttered a confused prayer to himself whilst Big Charlie, the pain flickering across his ruddy features, bent over Liam and scooped him up. He carried him from the cemetery like a loving father carrying an injured son.

29 Myrtle Street
Cross Lane
Salford 5
Great Britain

22 February 1917

Dear Dad,
Thank you for your Christmas letter and the bracelet that you sent me from Egypt. I can't believe that it is real gold and I don't think that I should wear it if it is very valuable. Mam said that perhaps I should save it until I am a bit older else people will think our rich uncle has died. I asked her who was the rich uncle and where did he live so that perhaps we could go and see him. Our Ben thought that he might have some cows. But it turned out that it was just one of those figure-of-speech things that grown ups use. Perhaps Mam just doesn't want to go and see him because we would all need new clothes.

I think that those flying machines do sound a bit scary. It's no wonder that the Arabs run away from them. One might fall out of the sky on top of you and then the Arabs would be laughing because they had been sensible.

Our teacher was telling us that they are making some things that look like massive iron slugs now and that they are sending them to France to help in the war. I hope that they work and that you can come home then. It has been freezing cold this winter because of the war. Our Edward and our Ben go out collecting coal from the railway sidings and sometimes we get coke from the gas works. They brought a back door home last week but Mam made them take it back. She said the people couldn't have finished with it if it was still hanging up on the hinges.

Our Sadie didn't pull Santa's beard again and she got a nice doll so she was very pleased. But I was more pleased because I got a set of pencils and a pad full of clean sheets of drawing paper which I don't like to use

195

because it spoils them. They are nice and thick and they are a lovely white colour. I think that new paper always smells special. Our Ben got some lead soldiers that Uncle Jim had made for him and he keeps dreaming that they have come to life and are waiting at the bottom of the stairs for him to play with.

Dad, why are you fighting against the Germans in this war? Teacher said that it started because some Prince from Austria got shot but why did you get dragged into it? She said that we are peacemakers because we run the most powerful Empire in the World so why don't you just go with your army and tell the Austrians and the others to stop arguing like Mam does with us kids? Mam tells our Edward to keep his nose out of it when other lads are fighting at school because it is nothing to do with him.

Mam is looking after Edith Hardcastle's little brother because Mrs Hardcastle has got to go to work now making big guns in Trafford Park. I heard her telling Mam that some of the girls at work write their names and addresses on the guns to see if any soldiers will send them a letter. Mam told Mrs Hardcastle that she had better not try it because she has enough worries as it is without adding to them and that she'd never been right since she'd had the telegram about Mr Hardcastle.

There is a man comes down our street every Sunday after Sunday School sitting on a bogey because he has got no legs. He sits in the middle of the road singing and then takes his cap round hoping for some money. Mam always gives him a cup of tea and a piece of cake and says 'There but for the Grace of God. It could be your Dad.' But it couldn't because he is the Dad of one of the kids at the Mission and he said that they've got no money because he can't get a job now.

If you do come home, don't bring any of those lice because they sound horrid.

Love

Laura

Erondelle
France

6th March 1917

Dear Pippin,

I'm glad that you liked your present from Egypt. The Arabs make some beautiful jewellery and I wasn't sure which to choose. You can wear it as a special treat for me when I do come home. It's a very complicated situation with this war, Darling, but I'm sure that people in the Government are trying very hard to sort it out. You will just have to believe that we are fighting because we want to make sure that our wives and children can be safe in their homes and because we want our country to be free. I am sorry that it is causing so much upset and difficulty. I just hope that it will be over before too long and then we can all come home.

I haven't seen any of these giant slugs yet but I have been told about them. They are called tanks and they have soldiers inside them so that they can't be shot at. They seem like a good idea but they have been having problems with them because they keep getting stuck in the mud. The weather here has been awful. We have had a lot of snow and it is bitterly cold. We complained about it being so hot in Egypt but I know which we would prefer.

Mam tells me that you are still doing well at school, particularly in English and Geography. She said that you keep checking in the atlas to see where I have been. You keep working hard, Darling, because your schooling is very important. We want a better future for all our children – both girls and boys. If you have a good education people can't take advantage of you as easily and you have more confidence. You want to be able to make something of yourself when you grow up. One day you might become a teacher and we will be really proud of you.

Hopefully, at least, when all this is over we won't have the same problems in Britain that they will have in France. All around here the villages have been virtually destroyed and people have to move in with others in the houses that are still standing. A lot of families are struggling because their men are away in the army and their houses have been hit by shells. They try to keep everything going as normal if they can. The baker still makes the bread if he can get to an oven and the little bars open and the old men sit outside having a coffee.

We are staying in a barn on a farm at the moment. The sappers have built us a special bath that can be used by 60 men in an hour. It's worse than being the last in line for a bath at home but at least that is your own family. They said that they are building quite a lot of these units because some of the soldiers here in France haven't had a bath for months. In the village the army have fitted out a cinematograph unit like one that I took your Mam to see once up Cross Lane. You would be amazed if you could see it. They have brought some films over from England and we saw our planes shooting down the German airships. We watched a few minutes of Manchester United playing when we went last night. We got very excited when Billy Meredith scored a goal.

Perhaps you and your Mam could knit me some more socks. Our feet are freezing all the time. I have cut finger holes in my old ones to use them for mittens.

Take care of yourself my little one.

Love

Dad

During the second half of March 1917, the men of the 1/8 Lancashire Fusiliers helped the Royal Engineers to patch up the small French communities and their heavily scarred countryside. They repaired roads and cleared them of debris; they repaired bridges and made houses habitable. Their hearts went out to the devastated families that were struggling to survive in the midst of this mad, destructive warfare, the innocent civilian bystanders who were trying desperately to keep some sanity as the shells thudded into their homes blowing their animals, their livelihoods and their loved ones to smithereens.

The continuing bad weather, however, began to take its toll on the horses. They struggled to acclimatize after spending so long in Egypt and many of them developed bronchial infections and died. The conditions also took their toll on the soldiers' equipment with the boots becoming a particular problem for the men working outside all day. They had been issued just before the Battalion had left Egypt but they fell apart in days when exposed to the bleak, wintry weather in France.

On the 5th April they arrived in Peronne where the Divisional Headquarters was to be established. Virtually every building in the town had been destroyed or badly damaged. The municipal building – L'Hotel de Ville – had survived with its ground floor almost intact, protected by the sturdy, arched colonnade that ran along its front. The five Grecian style columns rose aloofly out of piles of broken masonry and splintered timbers – sad relics of the first floor and roof. Above the colonnade, the departing Germans had fixed a sign with the mocking message 'Nicht ärgern, nur wundern' – 'Don't be angry, just be amazed.' Despite its attractions, it was immediately declared out of bounds by the suspicious officers. They knew that, as the most usable building in the town, it might have been packed with high explosive by the departing Germans.

Edward, Liam and Big Charlie stood in La Place and gazed gloomily around at the once beautiful buildings that now stood broken and humbled around the old square. Tall brick chimneys straddled roofless buildings and broken shutters flapped aimlessly over empty windows revealing the smoke blackened walls of the gaping holes behind. Elegantly arched windows of shop fronts pleaded for glass and beautiful clothes whilst broken cast iron lamp standards stood like pointless sentries in the piles of rubble.

Piled against the walls of many of them were stacks of bricks that had been sorted from the rubble by defiant old men, determined to show that the German explosives could not extinguish their community.

Some of these old men now sat on chairs outside the boarded-up bar enjoying a coffee and an extra cognac to celebrate the arrival of the British soldiers. Others had occupied the site of a demolished building on the other side of the square and were instructing some teenage boys in the strategy and skills of petanque. In one corner of the square a large group of women chattered excitedly around a cluster of horse drawn carts containing much needed provisions that had been halted in front of the badly damaged church.

'Let's go and see if we can buy some pommes off them' said Liam hopefully.

'Aye, alright' Eddie concurred. 'But look at the crowd from our mob over there. They're reading something on that board. Let's go and see what they've found to get excited about first.'

Pushing their way through the animated group, they discovered to their delighted amazement that they had been granted two weeks home leave.

Chapter 12

England 1917

Big Charlie walked jauntily down Broadway with his kitbag slung across his shoulder and his mind teeming with visions of the culinary delights that awaited him over the next two weeks of this unexpected leave. He had been deprived of his wife's expertise in the kitchen for almost three years now and his body ached with the eager anticipation of the delights that awaited him. He was already envisaging that big, brown cooking dish full of hot pot crowned by a thick, golden brown crust; juicy red cabbage with vinegar running out to accompany it. He was almost salivating at the thought of a steaming steak and kidney pudding being placed on the table in front of him.

He had just two small regrets. The first was that he had not sent his wife a note to say that he was coming home so that she could have had a nice suet pudding just reaching its point of maturity as he walked through the door. He didn't much like that writing business and he generally got Edward to write his letters home.

The second was that his wife would expect him to sit down and do all that catching up stuff, all that being nice and lovey-dovey and everything, before he could hope to sit down to a good solid meal. It was bad enough after he'd been out at work all day and, when all he wanted was his pint mug of strong, hot tea and a big plate of tasty food, she'd be wanting to know what he'd been doing all day and telling him what the neighbours had been up to. Then she'd start on wondering about why they'd had no kids yet and he'd tell her that he was trying and she'd say perhaps you're not trying often enough and why don't you try surprising me when you come home from work. He supposed that he could cope with that. It wouldn't be too bad and he could even enjoy the nightly routine of getting the zinc bath off the wall in the back yard for the ritual cleansing that she so desperately needed.

Big Charlie pushed the key in the lock thinking that a big plate of chips and black pudding with thick, rich gravy poured over them might not take too long to prepare. Opening the door he was quite surprised to hear the sounds of music emanating from the parlour and even more surprised to see a black, woollen gent's overcoat hanging up in the lobby. This was surmounted by a dark grey striped suit jacket and, on the floor below it, a leather case confirmed the presence of a male stranger in the house. Big Charlie's puzzled eyes followed up the lobby to the stairs where, on the side of each of the bottom two steps, stood a pair of polished black leather shoes whilst on the third a pair of leather slippers waited to welcome their own into domestic comfort. Big Charlie's discerning glance quickly perceived that the feet for which those shoes were intended were on the small side and so were clearly not his own.

He felt the hot blood surging up into his head as he slowly pushed open the door of the parlour. There was a small, dapper man at the piano with oily hair slicked back and shirt sleeves restrained by silver arm bands. Big Charlie's wife, Dot, was standing at the side of the Dapper Man and they gazed into each other's eyes as they sang together with obvious passion 'I Love You as I Never Loved Before.'

The only merit with Big Charlie's retribution was that, although lacking in planning and finesse, it was meted out swiftly. Grabbing the Dapper Man by the back of his collar, he hauled him off the piano stool, lifted him some distance off the ground then slammed him against the wall. The Dapper Man's watch jumped out of his waistcoat pocket, his carefully polished, but slightly oversized shoes, fell to the floor and his neatly trimmed moustache was smeared with the mucus that was forced out of his nose by the rapidly exhaled air from his deflated lungs.

The harmonious singing of only a few seconds before was now replaced by the loud screaming of Big Charlie's wife and the equally loud, grating moans from the Dapper Man as he struggled to drag air back into his pained chest.

With a quick jerk, Big Charlie scooped up the groaning Dapper Man, threw him onto his shoulder and strode out into the lobby where he grabbed the offending coats and the leather case. Moments later, he was out through the still open front door and striding purposefully down the street pursued closely by his shrieking wife who had thoughtfully collected the Dapper Man's rolled, black umbrella. She chased after Big Charlie, aiming repeated blows at his head with the furled umbrella but mostly missing, thereby only adding to the already severe discomfort of the Dapper Man. She surprised Big Charlie and the neighbours, who had now come out of their houses to watch the entertainment, with her, hitherto undisclosed, command of descriptive invective. The colourful harangue, whilst drawing just occasional murmurs of disapproval from the neighbours, had no obvious effect on her husband.

Big Charlie, aware of the fact that the people in the street had, in the past, witnessed various public, albeit minor, humiliations of him at the hands of his considerably more diminutive wife, felt reinforced by their vocally encouraging presence as they gathered in their doorways. The doubts that had started to creep in to his mind were dispelled as he demonstrated his masterfulness in handling his deceitful spouse and her snivelling suitor.

Despite the blows being rained on his head by his brolly wielding wife, and those to his back by the wretched Dapper Man, Big Charlie marched proudly forward, waving the suitcase occasionally to the cheerfully supportive audience. Emerging into Broadway like a gladiator entering the forum, he was joined by some young urchins skipping along in front of him. Followed closely now by an ever-growing throng of neighbours he stepped over to the horse trough where he dropped the suitcase and coats to the floor. Reaching up, he then grabbed hold of the terrified Dapper Man and held him suspended over the water for a few seconds before dropping him in with a mighty splash, followed immediately by the suitcase and coats.

Big Charlie smiled and waved briefly at the laughing crowds before pushing his way through them in order to pursue what now seemed to be the only course of action that was available to him and that was to go for a few pints of beer. Minutes later he was sitting gloomily staring into his pint in The Clowes Hotel and contemplating his now grim looking future and what it held in store for him. No longer stimulated to minor hero levels by the cheering neighbours and forced by the quiet loneliness of the bar to consider his situation more rationally, his mind seemed to have been enveloped in a cold, grey fog.

The thought of going home to face his wife, and of trying to further pursue this briefly held dominance as master in his own house, filled him with an untold dread. His determined response of only a quarter of an hour ago had somehow lost its momentum and become quickly enfeebled. Almost as bad was the thought of going to his Mam's and asking her for his old bed. That would almost certainly result in a clout round the ear – probably delivered, humiliatingly, whilst he remained standing on her doorstep.

Thoughts chased each other in a hopeless whirl round Big Charlie's head and came to nothing. He took a large gulp out of his pint glass and watched the barmaid mop limply round the line of empty ashtrays.

'I just heard about you dumping that oily little sod in the trough down Broadway,' she said. 'Should have held his head under for a bit longer. Mind you, that might have poisoned the horses.'

204

Big Charlie smiled bleakly. His dreams of nourishing days of good Lancashire meals had rapidly vanished to be replaced by the unpalatable prospect of a future without the woman that he needed so much. He had to admit that things had not always been quite right between them. Her sudden eruption into screaming rages, her capacity for rapacious derision and his bulky awkwardness in her slight presence made him almost fearful of physical contact. He had done his best to understand her torment but the memory of her in loving harmony with the dapper man made him now realise how badly he had failed.

A pat on the back and a cheery greeting 'You did well to give that bloody dandy-pants a good dousing, Charlie,' broke into his reverie. One of his neighbours joined him at the table whilst another went over to the bar to get them all a pint. Gentle probing was not a conversational art form that Big Charlie felt particularly familiar with so he was grateful for the subsequent willing disclosure by the two men of the story of his wife and the Dapper Man. It seemed that his wife, having endless lonely hours in the evenings to fill and not having the commitments that are the natural concomitant of a young family, had decided to take the first, faltering step in pursuit of an ambition that she had cherished since childhood. She had joined the Salford Glee Club that met every Tuesday and Friday evening at the Trafford Road Assembly Rooms. Her modest talent for singing, combined with a surprising gift for expressive drama, had soon resulted in her elevation to the ranks of the lead players.

From time to time the Salford Glee Club gave enthusiastic, if somewhat melodramatic, evenings of songs and sketches to parties of old people at the Regent Assembly Hall and to socials at a variety of churches. Their recent performance in front of an audience of injured soldiers at the wartime hospital in Langworthy Road School had been a triumph.

Occasionally, they went to the main hospitals to cheer up the patients with renditions of currently popular music hall songs and, only last Christmas, they had presented to a rapturously appreciative audience of four hundred inmates at the Salford Workhouse, a specially written version of Cinderella. Big Charlie's wife, Dorothy – billed exotically by the Glee Club as Dolly de Vine – had given a tear jerking performance as Cinders. She had touched the hearts of the wretchedly unfortunate inmates with her interpretation of the role as the beautiful, though often beaten and humbled, young girl who did all the chores whilst her privileged, but ugly, older sisters went off to the Ball at the Palace.

So sympathetic had they been to the plight of the unfortunate Cinders that members of the audience had shouted angrily at the ugly sisters when they had told Cinders to go and prepare their gowns and then to clean the kitchen. The two loathsome women had then told her that she wasn't allowed to go to the Ball and that she must stay behind and clear the cinders from the fireplace and scrub the floor. So moved were the socially disadvantaged inmates by this outrageous exploitation of the sobbing child that, when the brutish sisters took out a stick to thrash their desperate sibling, three unmarried mothers had jumped on the stage and attacked the startled bullies. A group of wardens had leapt forward to restrain the incensed women and a sword wielding Prince Charming – actually the Dapper Man, Sidney Snelgrove – had jumped in from behind the bed sheets that substituted for curtains at the side of the stage, having been forcibly propelled from there by the robust Chairwoman and director of the pantomime, Mrs Bollevant. Whilst the wardens grappled with the unmarried mothers, Prince Charming had stood trembling and waving his sword ineffectively at the restless audience. In a nervously high pitched voice he had pleaded with the crowd to remember that it was only a story and that it wasn't real life but that had proved to be the breaking point for one old man who had then jumped up, brandishing his stick fiercely at the now quaking Prince Charming. 'Don't you come here telling us that rubbish, you raving Jessie,' he had shouted. 'It is real life. Why do you think we've finished up in here? It's because people like you have put us in here.'

A portly Alderman in an expensive overcoat, who had unenthusiastically attended the pantomime only in order to show the concern that the city fathers felt for the welfare of their more unfortunate citizens, had then stood up and pushed the old man forcibly back into his seat. The old man's wife, furious at this rough response to her husband's rightful protest, responded with a surprisingly heavy blow to the Alderman's nose. This had provoked a screaming reaction from the Alderman's wife who, forgetting her carefully cultivated status and her Cashmere coat, had grabbed at the old woman's hair and threatened to punch her eyes out. Her attack on one of their number had proved too much for some of the inmates in the adjoining seats who jumped up and tried to pull her off. The wardens, however, worried about this assault on their VIP guests and the implications that this might have for their future employment, had then reacted with a much too heavy response and within minutes the room was in chaos.

Inmates, sensing an opportunity to vent some of their suppressed anger at the inequitable lot that life had handed them, turned on the shrieking Prince Charming, intent on stripping him of some of the ill-gotten benefits that his high status had clearly conferred on him. Two old crones, having been deprived of the comforts of a male companion for some years, took the opportunity that fate had so generously presented them with, of a further exploration of the desperately struggling Prince Charming. Some of the other inmates had rushed over to the assistance of Cinders who was by now screaming and weeping with genuine fear. Moved by her awful distress many had joined the unmarried mothers and berated the ugly sisters who, sensing that their reception was less than warm and that their continuing presence might put themselves in serious danger, had picked up their skirts and fled through the nearest door. Those of the audience who were able, persuaded that their moment of destiny had come, had taken up the pursuit, ragged clothes streaming out behind them, bony fists waving their walking sticks and the swords stolen from Prince Charming's courtiers.

After a frantic dash down the road, during which they had caused a horse to bolt leaving behind a very surprised coalman, the ugly sisters had sought refuge in the gent's toilet at the corner of Trafford Road. The noise of the pursuit had brought the customers pouring out of the Ship Hotel and the word had quickly spread round that this was some upper class scoundrel who had put his servant girl 'up the chuff' and had thrown her out onto the streets. Outraged by this, and fortified by the strong ale from the Ship, the worthy dockers had joined in the protest. When, eventually, the police had arrived to deal with the three hundred strong mob that was blocking the road and they had discovered that the two terrified women were actually men, the rumours were greatly embellished. After much licking of pencils and taking down of notes, the police had finally arrested the ugly sisters 'just to be on the safe side, like.'

Big Charlie listened with wonderment at these revelations of his wife's involvement at the centre of a riot. He'd heard her singing in the cellar as she pounded the washing in the dolly tub, and he had to admit that she had a fair voice. But it appeared that Dorothy had confided in the woman next door that she nurtured a secret plan. She wanted to be a great singer so that when her Charlie came home, she could take him to a concert and surprise him with a dazzling performance. She reasoned that, when he saw how the audience applauded her and enraptured men stood and cheered and shouted for more, then Charlie would see her in a new light. He would see that there was more to her than just a sloven in a pinny who did all his fetching and carrying and who mithered him when he came home because she wanted some company. She would still be his Dot but she would be somebody special and that might put a bit more spark in his fire, a bit more oil in his can, so to speak, and, hopefully that could resolve this problem of her not having any family.

Big Charlie winced with shining embarrassment at the revelation that his less than masterful performances in the marital bed had clearly been opened up for speculative assessment by the gossiping wives of the neighbourhood. When Dot had learned, just two weeks after his Prince Charming humiliation, that Sidney Snelgrove had suffered another misfortune when his mother had thrown him out because of his funny ways, she saw this as an opportunity to further her plan. Despite some strange traits in his character, he did have a talent for the piano and for interpreting and presenting a song. There was much that could be learnt from him and the chance for more frequent rehearsals could not be ignored. She offered Sidney the use of the spare room for a modest rent and on the strict understanding that she would need it just as soon as she and Charlie started their family.

Big Charlie 'Hmmmphed' a few times and drank several mouthfuls of beer. His mind struggled to form a link between the slightly frumpy wife that he was familiar with and the glamorous Miss Dolly de Vine that his neighbours were describing. He pointed out, however, that it was obvious to him that there was a lot more to it than they thought because he had seen with his own eyes how they were gazing longingly at each other and singing 'I Love You as I've Never Loved Before.' It was Big Charlie's opinion that what you had witnessed with your own eyes couldn't be argued with and he would bet that he had been made the laughing stock of the whole area by their antics.

The neighbours countered this by agreeing that, initially, there had been a bit of gossip. However, the truth about Sidney Snelgrove had soon started to emerge. There was the story about why his mother had thrown him out because she was so ashamed of him but they wouldn't go into all the detail now. There were the customers of the gent's outfitters on Regent Road who confirmed Sidney's enthusiasm for measuring up clients for suits, and the whole area knew that he had been turned down for army service because he would be bad for army morale. 'In other words,' the neighbours explained 'Your Dorothy was in no danger from Sidney Snelgrove because, as everybody knows, it's not women that he has a fancy for.'

Big Charlie's mind finally grasped the awful significance of what he had just done.

The train was crowded with servicemen making their way down to the South Coast for the ferry. The majority were grim faced, battle weary soldiers rejoining their regiments after a pitiably short leave. Despite the obvious dangers that they would face, most of them felt sordidly reassured to be going back rather than afraid. These were men who understood the part that they had to play in this death-dealing structure. They worked together, played together and suffered together. Decisions were all made for them and they had no responsibility other than to each other. They were a meld of different characters from similar backgrounds that had been moulded into a fighting unit with a shared common focus. Fears were dealt with by complaining about the officers, the politicians, the toffs, the quality of the tea and the bully beef, the weather, the vermin and the equipment. But they did what was asked of them, and more as well. And, as they sat on this train heading back towards France, they all knew that they had a big job still to do.

Amongst the group there were clusters of newly trained recruits, easily distinguished by their loud, nervous laughter, their fresh faces and their neat, unblemished uniforms. They pressed the older soldiers for information about the fighting and the conditions on the Front but the responses were guarded and mostly superficial. Liam had enjoyed an hour of mischievously explaining to some of the young listeners how the diet included horse meat, which was partly true anyway, frogs and snails. He warned them that the French women, having been denied the comforts of their own men, had voracious appetites for young Lancashire boys, some of whom had not been seen again. He explained that it wasn't wise to take on the old French men in the game of bowls which they play with metal balls on a croft. They always let you win a few to encourage you before they up the stakes and clean you out.

Now he had settled himself back into his seat and was thoughtfully watching Edward who had barely spoken throughout the journey. 'What's bugging you, Eddie?' he eventually asked. 'You've been a bit quiet, even for you. You certainly won't be talking the hind legs off any donkeys today.'

Edward looked at him and half smiled. 'Sorry mate. I've just been thinking. I seem to have really buggered things up at home over this last couple of weeks and now I've come away leaving things not sorted. I suppose Laura partly understands but I don't think the kids do.'

'What've you done – shot the cat thinking it was a trench rat?'

'No. Nothing so simple. At first it was just shock at seeing how much the kids have changed. Our Edward was about five inches taller and I felt a real sod seeing him going out on his job straight after school and at weekends. I don't know where they would have been without him because he's been bringing loads of end-of-the-day stuff home from the greengrocers where he works.'

'It's been very handy,' agreed Liam. 'Laura's been giving Brig quite a bit of it, which has helped. And your Edward has been taking our Billy over to the railway sidings collecting coal that has fallen off the wagons. There's a place near Oldfield Road that your Edward knows about where the trains always get stopped and it usually shakes a bit off. They take your Ben with them to dog out and watch for the nightwatchman or the police. I told our Billy, if he gets caught, to tell them that they are just tidying up.'

Edward laughed at the idea of a couple of little urchins, their faces, hands and clothes covered in coal dust, trying to convince a policeman that they were just keeping the place clean.

'It was young Laura as well,' he said, 'She'd grown into a little lady while I've been away. She's the spitting image of her mother at that age. She was just a little 'un when we left and now she's cleaning the house and cooking the meals. She wasn't yet seven when I last saw her and now she's ten going on twenty. And the young ones have changed so much. Even little Mary was running around and being a right little devil.'

Liam winced. 'Oh. Sorry mate' Edward said. 'That was a bit thoughtless.'

'It's ok,' Liam said quietly, 'I've got my head sorted now. It was hard at first. Our house seemed full of empty spaces where Lizzie should be, and it just broke me up. I couldn't cope with it. Everything was just going on as normal but she was missing.'

'That must have been tough, mate. Your family have had the time to get used to it, perhaps, but you expected things to be just the same as when you left.'

'Aye, I did. But it's a bit more than that. Brig is just so controlled and calm about everything. I wanted to shout my bloody head off and batter something – for her as well as me.

One night, the quiet was driving me mad. I started pounding the wall and yelling at Him upstairs.'

'You must have frightened the life out of Florrie Hardcastle next door.'

'Probably,' Liam smiled. 'It's a good job that Brig came down and stopped me. Gave me a big cuddle. Said she was sorry she'd not talked about Lizzie but she didn't know where to start. She told me how the poor little mite had suffered and that I wouldn't have been able to do anything for her. She said that it was God's will and that she is safe now with Him.'

'She has a lot of faith, Bridget,' Edward offered supportively. 'It must be a big help in times like these.'

'Yeh. She copes with things better than I ever could.'

'Have you had a walk up to Weaste cemetery yet?'

'Aye. Next morning,' Liam answered, shuddering slightly as the memory came back. 'Brig said that I had to go and see her – to put her to rest, like. It was hard, Eddie. When I saw her name on the stone I was wailing like an old widder woman.'

Edward tried to break the sombre mood of his friend. 'The gravediggers probably thought it was the Liverpool train going through.'

'Hmm. I perhaps should have gone down to the pub at the corner. They call it the 'Widow's Rest'.'

'I'd have been there with you,' said Edward morosely. 'I spent half my time standing at the rails on Trafford Road corner talking to the lads off the Docks.'

'Why?' Liam queried, 'Couldn't you settle? Have you started prowling around like Ninepence Nellie waiting for a customer? You must be missing all the excitement we've been having in France.'

'It's the change in diet, more likely,' retorted Edward. 'I've not had any bully beef for over two weeks now.'

'So why was you out resting the rails every day?'

'I don't know,' Edward said hesitantly. 'It was strange. I just didn't feel as though I belonged. Not that they weren't all welcoming and pleased to see me. I couldn't have asked for better. I just felt a bit like a lodger. Laura even had to tell our Edward to give up my chair because that's where he sits now.'

'You're right. But we've got to try to understand.' Liam spoke thoughtfully. 'It's nearly three years that we've been away and we've all changed. We think that we have been to Hell and back but so, in a different way, have they. They've had to manage on next to nowt and bring the kids up as best they can. They've had the worry of keeping a roof over their heads and taking stuff into 'three balls Isaac's' to pay the rent. The postman comes in the morning and they don't know if it's a letter from us telling them about sunny Egypt or if it's a 'KIA' from our CO telling them that we'd fought like heroes but we'd snuffed it instantly. They've had to take charge Eddie. We've not been there to whitewash the backyard and to sweep the chimney. And we've not even been there to tip up a wage packet.'

'Aye, you're right. I've been a bit of an inconsiderate sod. But I didn't know how to handle it.'

'I wouldn't have done either. But I was so messed up about Lizzie that it forced me and Brig together.'

The screeching brakes of the slowing train roused the pair from their torment. The first few signs announcing the name of the station passed in a blur before they had chance to read them but, as the speed reduced, they saw that they were easing their way slowly into Crewe station. Doors flew open then crashed to, people shouted and porters trundled trolleys stacked high with suitcases down the platform of the cavernous, steamy station. A rotund, red faced man with a black, peaked cap and a white, shiny patch on his waistcoat above the pocket that carried his fob-watch walked in a self-important gait down the platform. Liam established from him, after two consultations with the tightly embraced watch, that the train would not be departing for another thirty eight minutes.

He turned to Edward. 'Come on,' he said, 'If you think that you have made a cobblers of things at home, you can buy me a cup of tea and I will tell you about Big Charlie. He's already back in France but he's left a right bugger's muddle behind him in Salford.'

'Just give me ten minutes and I'll be with you,' Edward said as he walked towards the waiting room.

Liam told Edward that the police had generously waited whilst their friend finished his beer before removing him to the station to discuss things quietly. Next morning, the magistrate, showing only the faintest hint of a smile, had ordered that Big Charlie, in recognition of the circumstances of the case and the service that he, Big Charlie, had already rendered to the Country, should be put on the next available train and sent back to rejoin his battalion in France.

Railway Station
Crewe
18th April 1917

My Darling,

    I'm writing you a quick note before we carry on down to Folkestone for the boat because my head has been spinning all the way down here trying to think why things didn't seem right between us whilst I've been home on leave. I suppose the problem was with me so I want to say that I am truly sorry if I have hurt you in any way.

    Everything seemed so different even though it was basically just the same. It's difficult to put my finger on it but I felt sometimes as though I didn't belong any more. I felt as though there was a gulf between us and I couldn't get to you and share things with you the same way. Even the kids seemed to treat me as though I was a stranger at times. And there was that time when I was asking Laura about her schooling and she said that she was taking her tests for the High School next year. I thought that it was right to encourage her and tell her that it would be good for her to go and you turned round and told her not to be wasting her time getting fancy ideas like that. Don't we both want the best that we can for our kids?

    I'm sorry if this is sounding a bit stupid and I should have talked about it when I was there but I just didn't know, and still don't, what has gone wrong. It just seemed hard to talk about things. I think that you must think that I have been up to something because I didn't want to talk about where I've been and what I've been doing but it's nothing like that. There are things going on in this war that have no place in the home – not in ours, at least. I suppose that, perhaps, I am almost a bit ashamed of some of the stuff that goes on but it's nothing against you. When this is all over with, it's best to lock all these things away and throw the key in the bin.

I know that I kept going out a lot and that didn't help but I just couldn't settle. I felt like a lodger in my own house and at the same time it kept going round in my head that there was still a job to do out there that's not finished yet.

I'm worried sick that something has changed and that you don't want me in your life anymore. Now I am going away again and I should have got this sorted out before I left. But if that's the case then it's best that you just tell me so that I don't keep making a fool of myself. I pray to God that things will be alright between us.

I'm sorry if I have hurt you in some way. You'll have to forgive me for being just a clumsy soldier.

I love you so much I cannot tell you,

Eddie

Chapter 13

Epehy, France May 1917
Edward stared disconsolately out at the strangely beautiful landscape in front of him and pulled deeply and frequently on the cigarette that he held. The sun was now shining and the days were hot. The warm weather had raised the spirits of most of the soldiers, helping them to shake off the debilitating lethargy resulting from the long period of heavy rain. The fields were still fractured and the villages still crumbled but they had been able to carry out much essential repair work to roads, bridges and rail links and this was greatly appreciated by the locals.

The sun-baked earth around the rim of the shell craters was almost dazzlingly white and formed an exotic, sinewy pattern that snaked through the fields. Blossom was shining defiantly on the remaining half of a riven tree and vegetation was thrusting bravely through the battered ground all round the craters. Within the mouths of the gaping holes, tufts of weeds and previous crops made vivid splashes amidst the grey earth but Edward knew that this was a gross parody. From his position on the firing step he could see decaying limbs protruding from the soil. In one crater he could see a detached head, an eerie smile crossing its face as the hot sun dried the unnourished skin.

Across the fields, the trees in the woods had been stripped of their branches and stood in naked defiance, erect and proud, like darkened chimneys in a mill town landscape. A zig-zag trench cut into the ground in front of the woods hid the waiting and watching enemy soldiers.

On most nights they went out on patrols around this no-man's land to repair damage done to the wire barricades by enemy shelling and to gather information about the activities of the German troops. One night they had gone within yards of the opposition trenches and had lobbed in grenades in the hope of silencing a troublesome trench mortar. On other occasions small groups went out to attack a German trench position and to attempt to bring back some live prisoners. Many times, on these patrols, Edward had seen that these gaping holes carried the grim relics of this horrendous war. Lying in the mud at the bottom he had often seen the bodies of both British and German soldiers, grotesquely intertwined like executed lovers. His stomach had heaved when he had seen the rats tearing at the rotting flesh. On some trips they had managed to rescue wounded comrades who they had found lying helpless as rats chewed on their still living bodies. At other times the bayonet had been the only relief that they could offer.

He listened to a cuckoo calling in the shredded remains of the distant woods and wondered how it had managed to survive the bombardments that had devastated the area over the last couple of years.

He was still deeply troubled about his relationship with Laura and thought constantly about why things had suddenly seemed to go so wrong. He had now talked to a number of his friends who had also just come back from leave and they mostly had experienced similar difficulties. His anguish was deepened, however, by the fact that he had not yet had a reply to the note that he had eventually posted to her from Folkestone. Each day that went by without a letter confirmed even more deeply his worst fear. Laura's feelings for him had changed.

His mind had already started developing scenarios in which he could try to repair this damage, but the problem was that he still barely understood how it had occurred. Now he was also worrying about whether he had been right to accept the promotion to Lance Corporal that had been offered to him that morning. When he had been told to report to the headquarters office set up in a nearby chateau he had braced himself for bad news. That's all you ever got, bad news. There was never anything good to tell you when you went up to HQ. It was either that something had gone wrong at home or it was an army matter and that was never pleasant. He remembered how some soldiers from another Battalion had been called to the office only to be told that they were to form a firing squad for a deserter. It was a Northern lad who'd fought bravely for two years but after enduring the carnage of the Somme his nerve had finally cracked and he walked off to go home to his Mam. He was picked up three days later, half starved and delirious.

After his execution feelings had run high amongst the lower ranks of the British soldiers. There was overwhelming sympathy for the accused man and none at all for his accusers. The sentiments expressed were shared by all of them. These same people, who conducted the war from a very safe distance behind the front line, now also acted as the judge and jury. If that's what they wanted to do then they should fire the bullets themselves. Instead they were putting the shame and the guilt on to ordinary working class blokes. When it's their own kind that crack up they're looked after. Look at those who are drinking whisky from the minute they get up and you see nothing of them when there's any action. People like that bastard Fforbes-Fosdyke who, in a drunken state, had forgotten to take his foot out of the stirrup when he dismounted from his horse. They get a Blighty so they can go and convalesce in some posh hospital and have those toffee-nosed nurses wiping their brows and feeding them grapes. When it's one of ours that cracks we get ordered to shoot the poor sod.

Edward had been surprised, then, to find the Adjutant relaxed and friendly when he reported in. 'Sit down Craigie. Have a cigarette. Did you enjoy your leave? Not too much happened whilst you have been away. In support at Saulcourt, you know, but nothing too exciting.' There was a sharp knock on the door and the adjutant shouted for the newcomer to enter. Edward looked up and was surprised to see a grinning Sergeant Frank Williams standing there.

'All right, Eddie? Did you think you'd left me behind in Gallipoli?'

'There's going to be a few moves round, Craigie,' the Adjutant said, turning back to Edward. 'As you know, we are currently a bit short on our establishment strength because of losses and moves and whatever. Sergeant Williams is rejoining your platoon as Second Lieutenant and he has specifically asked that you should be made up to Lance Corporal, which we are more than happy to do if you agree. I know that you have already turned down promotion twice and I sympathise with your reasons. You don't want to be responsible for making decisions that might cost the lives of your friends, especially when you can't agree with the tactics that are being used.' Edward, surprised by the officer's directness, felt a sudden flush through his body.

The Adjutant paused for a moment and stared at the engraved silver letter opener that he was turning restlessly in his fingers. 'I will be honest with you, Craigie, and tell you that, for a lot of the time, most of us are not happy with the way things are being done and we do our best to influence it at local level. But there is a job to be done and if we don't stand up and be counted, the Germans will overwhelm us. Things seem to be in a bit of a stalemate at the moment but there could be another push soon and we need the right men to be able to do it. You have already shown courage and dedication in anything that you have tackled and the men respect you. You will only be called on to take over if your sergeant is taken out by the enemy but your experience could help you to make decisions that will save lives rather than lose them. I would like you to take it on and I know that Sergeant Williams does, so what do you say, Craigie? Do you accept this time?'

Edward had sat there, still slightly dazed by this unexpected turn in the interview, and had tried to collect his thoughts together. He had turned down promotion so firmly in the past that he had been sure that the subject would never be raised again. The Adjutant was a Major who had seen a lot of active service in the lines, and he was well liked by the men, but he had been so seriously injured that he had been taken back to England with only small hopes of survival. He had eventually recovered enough to be offered a position training new recruits near his home in Norfolk but this he had flatly refused. Instead he had demanded a posting as near to the front as possible so that he could be available for front line duties as soon as he felt able. Now he was coping with the administration work in Company Headquarters without much enthusiasm but in the knowledge, in his mind at least, that it was a temporary expedient.

Edward had felt reassured by the Major's comments and by the further, supportive encouragement of Sergeant Williams. He had thanked them for their confidence in him and said that he would do his best.

The cigarette cupped protectively in Edward's hand burnt his fingers as it faded down to a minute stub. He was skilful at taking them down to the last shreds of tobacco but this time he hadn't noticed. He threw it to the ground, cursing to himself, and crossed his arms on the sandbag in front of him in order to provide a cradle for his chin. He looked through the tiny gap in the barricade of bags over the haunting landscape. It was starting to acquire a burnished glow from the sun that was slowly setting behind them. If he had stood there at night and smoked he would probably have been shot at by German snipers who aimed at the glowing points of light but Edward knew that during the day they rarely bothered. There was almost an unwritten code of conduct between the serving ranks of soldiers lined up facing each other across this no-man's land. Mutual respect had given rise to a set of rules that were only broken by the orders from higher ranks.

The British soldiers also knew that during the day they would only hear the occasional whistling rush of air as shells were fired at them from behind the German lines. They would brace themselves knowing that they were the targets and it was always a relief to hear the heavy thud of a failed shell or the distant explosion of a successful one. They had escaped again the other possibility, the blinding, searing flash as your body was being ripped to pieces.

Edward felt in his tunic pocket and took out the cigarette packet. He stared at the last, neat, white cylinder that was in there and wondered whether to save it for later. He was trying to limit himself to the ten cigarettes that they were allowed each day as their official ration but he rarely succeeded. Usually they could supplement them with a local supply. He wasn't thrilled about the rich sweetness of the French cigarettes although he had to admit that they were a considerable improvement on those that they had in Egypt. He was sure that the Gyppies had made them from sun baked camel dung and grass. He'd meant to buy some more Woodbines on his way to the railway station in Salford but his mind had been a turbulent mess of doubts and insecurity as he pored time and again over every second of the strained farewell when he had left the house.

Lighting his last cigarette, Edward watched a fox emerging cautiously out of a copse of trees to the left. Its reddish brown coat shone in the rays of the fading sun. Under its chin and down to its chest it had a vivid stripe of white fur, like a clean bib, and another patch of white on its tail. It hesitated for a moment, standing rigid and staring over towards their line as if aware of their presence, before moving along the edge of the trees. He wondered what they did when the shelling started and thought that they must be immune to the noise. He drew heavily on the cigarette and enjoyed the soothing warmth flowing down into his lungs. When he had gone to young Edward to give him a hug, the lad had held out his hand awkwardly and with a 'Bye Dad' had disappeared out of the door. Young Laura had given him a poem that she had written at school, kissed him, and then sat down in the corner with her head buried in a book. The three youngest had just about managed a goodbye as they carried on playing noisily with some pans on the floor.

What troubled him most, though, was the parting from his wife, Laura. She had held him tightly for a minute, her body taut and unyielding, with the damp towel that she had just been using to wipe Ben's face clasped in her hand against his neck. Suddenly, she had pulled away, straightened the skirt of her long black dress, and rushed without a word into the scullery. He had lifted his kit bag on his shoulder and followed her in there. She had been standing with her back to him, her knuckles as white as the thick rim of the ceramic sink that she was gripping. 'I'll be getting off now love.' She had nodded imperceptibly. He had put his hand out and touched her shoulder. 'I'll be seeing you soon.' Her head had dropped forward. As he had turned away he had just about caught her whispered response. 'Aye. Happen.'

Perhaps he would get a letter tomorrow. The torment was driving him mad. Perhaps he'd rather not know. If something was wrong, what could he do about it? He was stuck out here in some remote part of rural France and they were up there in the North of England. There was no chance of leave. He'd only just come back after two weeks away. He pounded the sandbag with his clenched fist. 'Bloody, sodding, useless war,' he groaned.

Liam had been intently watching his troubled friend for some time. He was huddled with other soldiers round a group of upturned shell boxes that formed an all-purpose table in the trench. They were 'game hunting', huddled over short stubs of lighted candles, and running the seams of their clothes over the naked flame. In the trenches they were plagued by lice which lodged and bred in the seams of their clothing. They hated the lice with a passion but they couldn't escape from them. The lighted candle was the most effective way of fighting them but it only gave temporary respite. Nevertheless, they derived great pleasure from hearing the popping noise as the loathsome creatures burst and shouts of 'Yes!' heralded the destruction of a particularly large one.

'Right then, Eddie,' he announced. 'Let's celebrate your promotion. Better a barmy sod that we know than a barmy sod we've never heard of. That's what I say.' Liam blew his candle out and went over to his kitbag. 'Come on now. Gather round everybody and see what surprises Uncle Liam has got for you.'

Finally distracted and intrigued by his friend's summons, Edward walked over to where Liam was rummaging in the bottom of his bag, pulling out various items of clothing, two copies of the Salford Reporter and an assortment of various items of army equipment. Eventually, like a magician reaching the climax of his act, he stood up and waved a large parcel wrapped in brown paper above his head. He performed a brief, but clumsily executed pirouette, and danced slowly round the circle of now fascinated soldiers, waving the parcel under their noses and challenging them all to guess what the contents were.

'It's a slab of your Brig's parkin,' was a popular and enthusiastically received suggestion.

'A nice leg of lamb would be a pleasant change.'

'A leg of a camel would be a pleasant change after all this sodding bully beef'

'Have you brought a rugby ball so that we can start up a new league?'

'A barrel of Walker's would have been nice but it looks a bit small for that.'

225

'No. Come on. Think a bit harder,' Liam encouraged them. 'What gives you so much pleasure last thing at night? What sooths away your troubles and takes away your stress?'

'You haven't brought Gertie Grimshaw out of the Ship have you?'

'No, you daft sod,' Liam rebuked. 'Look. I'll show you. This is with the compliments of the Salford Comforts Committee.'

Accompanied by many questions as to the nature of this philanthropic group, Liam removed the wrapping from the parcel, watched carefully by eleven pairs of curious eyes. With a great flourish he threw away the brown paper cover and revealed to the fascinated audience around fifty neatly stacked packets of cigarettes.

'Where did this lot come from then?' enquired Big Charlie, so intrigued that he hadn't noticed the smoke curling up from the jerkin that he was holding over the candle.

'I've told you. They're from the Salford Comforts Committee.'

'That's nice of them. Who are they anyway?'

'It's a group of kind hearted, generous people who donated money to buy cigarettes for the injured soldiers in Salford hospitals.'

A frown crossed Big Charlie's brow. 'Hang on. We're not in a Salford hospital.'

'No,' replied Liam. 'But Brig's brother-in-law was. He'd been quite badly injured in France and he was in that military hospital up Langworthy Road. Didn't feel like smoking at first, but he didn't want to miss out, so he stashed them under the bed pan in his locker.'

'So has he decided to stop smoking now?'

'Well, I suppose you might say that. He's died.'

Edward smiled at his friend's skilful manipulations to pull him away from his troubled thoughts. Well, perhaps a letter will come tomorrow.

Sitting in an agitated state in Havrincourt Wood, Edward was battling to keep his nerves under control and to maintain at least an outward appearance of calm. He wasn't looking forward to the night ahead in the slightest. It was June 1917 and he was taking charge, for the first time, of his platoon and it now included some fairly inexperienced recruits. The Division was holding a recently captured sector which ran down from the Canal du Nord to just below Havrincourt. They had had orders to move the line ahead by three hundred yards and the engineers were trying to achieve this by digging sap trenches forward from the existing line. Unfortunately, the Germans appeared to have some good positions embedded in the woods and the Division had suffered heavy casualties.

The patrols that would be going out soon were targeted to remove these. For some weeks now, they had been on trench rota in various positions along this line and the night patrols were fairly commonplace. They had then been led by a sergeant but he had recently been moved to another section whose own sergeant had been seriously wounded.

Edward called his section together. 'We'll go out from half way up the new sap trench – number 3a – where it runs alongside the large crater. The bottom of the crater should be fairly dry by now but watch out for any nasties. When you come up the other side of it you will find that you are in a small gully. It's not very deep but it should be enough to give cover if you stay down low. At the end of the gully we will have cover for about fifty yards from some bushes that look like the remains of an old hedge. After that we have to cross about one hundred yards of open ground to reach the east side of the woods. If they start firing machine guns at us don't drop to the ground looking for cover. They aim them at the ground in front of your feet so, if you drop, you will probably be killed. If you do get hit and go down look for any dips or hollows. Otherwise make sure that you keep your helmet on and lie with your head pointing towards the Germans. The helmet will give you some limited protection. Then dig yourself in as quickly as you can. We'll have a weigh-up of the situation when we get into the woods. We will leave in twenty five minutes from now. Good luck.'

'Aye, we'll need it,' Liam grumbled. 'Bloody daft day to be going out on a show if you ask me.'

Edward looked quizzically at his friend. 'Why's that? What's so different about today?'

'It's Friday isn't it. You know that they say it's bloody unlucky if you get killed on a Friday.'

Big Charlie looked over at Liam. His raised eyebrows quivered in synchronised harmony with his twitching lips as unformed words emerged in meaningless grunts. Finally, his face settled into resignation as he gave up trying to grasp his friend's convoluted logic. 'Aye, right' he muttered as he turned away and gave his rifle a final polish.

Before they left, Edward went out to check, for the fourth time that day, if any post had arrived. There was nothing. They had been almost constantly on the move now for the last three weeks and during that time nobody had had any post. The strain of waiting, of wondering if or why he and Laura had drifted apart, was proving a depressing burden. It was especially bad if he was on night watch. After a while, you almost didn't notice the noise of the nightly barrage that the Germans sent over and the strange contrast that it made with the melodious, undaunted nightingales. For hour after hour, Edward would pick over every detail of what they had said and done during the two weeks of his leave but understanding eluded him. The logical explanation for one situation did not stand scrutiny under another. One moment he was sure that it was only his imagination playing tricks, which if he was there with her would all be shown to be the falsehoods of his anguished mind, but then the next he remembered how she had stood with her back to him when he left. At least a letter would settle it.

Leaving the sap trench they made their way carefully round some bodies lying huddled in the bottom of the crater. A British soldier lay with his arm outstretched over the rotting corpse of a German in ironic reconciliation. They ran quietly forward, grateful for the shelter of the old hedge, and stood in a nervous group at the edge of the open ground. Edward felt as though his heart was pounding so loud that the attention of the enemy would be drawn towards them. He put his fingers to his lips then pointed upwards towards the moon. It was shining brightly but a small bank of cloud was moving quickly towards it. He held two fingers up then raised his eyebrows questioningly to the others. They all nodded their understanding.

Minutes later, they were tracking quickly across the open fields and they reached the safety of the woods as the moon re-emerged from behind the cloud. The area was bathed again in its silvery glow as Edward waved the others deeper into the shelter of the trees. In one of those brief moments of silence that hangs like a spectre over the landscape between the rounds of shell fire, there was a loud crack followed by a louder curse as Big Charlie, bringing up the rear of the column, ran into a low branch. The nervous German gunners were alerted immediately and yellow tongues of flame spouted out of the undergrowth some distance ahead of them.

Bullets splintered branches and pinged off the trees as the machine guns poured endless rounds into the area where the British soldiers crouched. Edward returned to where Big Charlie lay in an untidy heap. His nose, which had taken the full impact of the branch, was split and bleeding but otherwise there seemed to be no serious damage. Big Charlie was, however, clearly in another realm of consciousness at that moment and Edward knew that it would be impossible to move him by himself. He got three others to help and, when the moon again went behind a cloud, they each took a corner of the big man and carried him to safety in a shell hole.

As they part carried, part rolled Big Charlie over the rim of the crater they heard a series of explosions coming from the wood and the four of them, looking for a better view, dropped their recumbent colleague who continued his sliding descent into the bottom of the shell hole. Edward stood up and looked into the woods where flames were now starting to lick into the air. For the moment, the machine gun fire and the shelling had both stopped and the only sound was the crackling of the burning woods. Edward checked the time and smiled to himself. It was ten o'clock. The German artillery in this area always stopped at the same time each evening for half an hour. Unless there was a show going on they stuck to their routine. They weren't sure whether it was a shift change or a schnapps break but they could be relied on.

'Stay under cover and do what you can for Charlie. I'm going to see what's going on up there. Where's Liam?'

'He went off with Jim,' one of the others offered. 'I think he's gone looking for a stretcher bearer. He said they'd have to get something sorted so we could get Big Charlie back.'

'Right. You two come with me, then. The rest of you stay down. If we're not back in twenty minutes start working your way back with Charlie before they start chucking their iron work over again. Make a break for it when the moon is covered.'

They tracked carefully through the woods towards the distant glow. The slight breeze was carrying burning shreds of timber towards them and the smell conjured up comforting memories for Edward of bonfire night back home in Salford. In the swirling smoke ahead he saw a slight movement and he pulled the other two behind some tangled bushes. They cocked their Lee Enfields as they saw German uniforms emerging from the direction of the fire. Edward's heart pounded and he tightened his grip on his rifle but he realized that something was not quite right. The German soldiers wore scared looks on their blackened faces. They were not hurrying and they were not armed. In a moment his grip relaxed and he stood up as he saw Liam and Jim come through the smoke with their rifles pointed at the backs of their three prisoners.

Liam's face erupted into a huge grin when he saw his friend's surprised look. 'You alright then, Eddie? You look as though you've just seen a ghost. Your Dad hasn't been round to have a chat, has he?'

Edward's lips moved silently as he struggled to overcome his surprise. He waved his rifle in the direction of the prisoners. 'Where've they come from? In fact, where have you come from? I've just been told that you'd gone looking for a stretcher so that we could get Charlie back.'

'Well, not quite. When I saw the big fella on the ground looking in a bad way, I thought there's no chance of getting him back to the line without a few of us copping one off these trigger happy Germans. So I told the lads to tell you that we were going to see what we could sort out so that we could get Big Charlie back for some treatment. Me and Jim went for a bit of a walk and followed where the bullets were coming from. We found them easy enough. They had their machine gun set up in a trench and they were only a few yards away from their dump. So we chucked a couple of feet warmers in and they were out of there like scalded cocks.'

'You've done a good job there, mate. Perhaps we could get them to carry Charlie back for us.'

'I'm sure that they'd be glad to oblige. To be honest, I think that they were quite glad to be caught. They've had enough. They're looking forward to a stay in Hotel Blighty.'

When they got back to the crater, Big Charlie was sitting up with a sheepish grin on his face.

'Bloody wars,' Liam whooped on seeing him. 'I'd put you down as at least a fractured skull. You must have a head like pre-cast concrete.'

He sat down at the side of Big Charlie and put his arm round his shoulder. 'I'm glad you're ok mate. I was getting a bit worried about you,' he said consolingly, before adding 'We've got a big match against that lot from Leeds next week.'

He ducked the poorly aimed cuff to his head then bent down to help his ailing prop forward to his feet.

When they returned to their front line, they delivered the hapless prisoners to the dugout occupied by the Company Captain. They took the tot of rum that was offered them by way of thanks then collected together the few personal possessions that they had with them in the front line trench. Their tour had finished and they were due to be relieved. The Captain told them that they could escort the Germans back to the reserve trenches where there was a holding compound.

It had been a long night and the prospect of a two mile walk before they could get some sleep was not appealing. They knew, however, that at least they would be able to get some decent food and a good bed so they hurried their charges along with enthusiasm. The Germans seemed to relax more as they moved away from the line and, by the time that they had reached Battalion Headquarters, they had managed, with the help of much gesturing, to tell the British soldiers their names. Liam was disappointed to learn that none of them were called Fritz – the only German name known to most of the Tommies.

The pale rosy glow of daylight was just easing its way into the sky as they shook hands with their prisoners and wished them good luck. They made their way over to the canteen knowing that it would still be too early for anybody to be about. Liam had assured them that he knew where everything was and that he would brew them the best cup of tea that they had ever had.

The tables were littered with grease proof paper and chunks of cake with green mould thriving on them. Packs of cards, crib boards and sets of dominoes were scattered untidily around and English newspapers were left open as if waiting for their readers to return.

Whilst Liam stood frowning at the array of knobs that held the key to success on the blackened stove, Edward collected some enamel mugs and carried them over to where the rest of the group had organised sufficient of the metal framed, plywood seated, chairs around a table. Two of the men were now searching through the oddments of the newspapers for the latest sports news. Another was fixing a crudely applied plaster to the wound on Big Charlie's nose.

Over the general hubbub of shifting chairs, shouts of delight at the news of a Manchester United win, hoots of derision at the appearance of Big Charlie's blooded brow and the banging of enamel mugs there was a triumphant whoop as Liam succeeded in lighting the temperamental stove.

In the gloomy far corner of the otherwise deserted mess a young officer was slumped in a chair, an empty whisky bottle on the table in front of him, and a crumpled letter written on blue note paper clutched in his hand. On his head flies congregated on a dark red stain of blood that was matting his fair hair and congealing round the hole where he had shot himself.

The mail from home had finally caught up with them.

29 Myrtle Street
Cross Lane
Salford 5
Great Britain

25th April 1917

My Dearest,

I cried so much when I read your letter and thought of the pain that you are suffering because perhaps I was a bit insensitive. I am sorry if I hurt you by being so thoughtless and I can only ask you to try to understand that it was also difficult for me and I don't even know whether I can begin to explain it. I suppose that I was a bit surprised when I saw you because your appearance has changed quite a bit. Since you first joined the army and went away I have kept an image of you locked away in my heart, to preserve you for ever and keep you safe. It has given me the strength to get up every day and look after us all, and to brace myself against the possibility, that I dread every minute of every day, that someone will come and say that you have been taken away from us. There's not a day gone by in nearly three years that I haven't thought about you back with us and yearned to hold you. But when you came through the door you looked, for a minute, like a different man. You are thinner and browner and, I'm sorry if this hurts you Sweetheart, but you look older and careworn. When I looked in your eyes they were full of dark shadows. I felt almost guilty for a moment, as though I was embracing another man. But then, I suppose, you are another man. You have been through things that I cannot even begin to understand and when I tried to share them with you, you just closed up.

There's something inside me that I don't really understand that stops me letting go of this memory even though you were standing there in front of me. I felt as though somebody was teasing me by just sending you back for a few days and then taking you off us again and that might be the last time that I ever saw you. (Please God forgive me for writing these words and tempting fate but I am trying to make you understand).I know that things have changed whilst you have been away, with the kids growing up and me having to make do the best that I could, but that can't be helped and can't be changed in a few days. When you get back for good, we will do what has to be done then to make things right. We have both got to face up to the fact that it will never be the same again for any of us but we will pull together, just like we always did, and we will make things work for our family.

Eddie, I'm sorry if any of this hurts you because it is not meant to. I have had to change in some ways in order to manage without you being there for the time being, but you are still as dear to me as ever. I love you just as much as when you first put the ring on my finger in Stowell's Church and I won't change till I breathe my last.

When I said that about our Laura going to High School I wasn't meaning to push you out. It was just that I didn't want her getting her hopes up too much. I want the best for her as well, even though she is a girl, but things are a bit tight now, Eddie, and that would be very expensive with the uniforms and books and everything. Just let's see what happens when you get back.

By the way, our Laura doesn't know why you got up suddenly and went into the parlour when she asked you how many Germans you had shot. I didn't tell her that you were crying in there because she wouldn't really understand. She thought that you were annoyed with her when you went out so quickly but I told her that you had just gone for a cigarette out of the way because of our Mary having a bad chest. She was only asking you that because, the other day, Edith from next door to your Jim's was in their house breaking her heart. She had just heard that her Frank had been killed in France and our Laura heard your Jim saying that he hoped that you would kill a few of those 'Bs' and get this mess over and done with. You know what she is like for listening in when you don't know. She doesn't mean any harm.

Take care, my Precious, and come back home safe to me just as soon as you can.

Laura

29 Myrtle Street
Cross Lane
Salford 5
Great Britain

19th May 1917

Dear Dad,

It was nice to see you home again on leave and I hope that you have got back safely. I have finished that book that you brought for my birthday. I'm ten now but I just feel the same as before. It was a really good book and it sounds very nice in Yorkshire. Mam said that it is God's county and that's where she was born. Perhaps when you have finished in France we could go for a holiday in Yorkshire because Mam would really like that.

They have cancelled the Whit Week Walks now from the Mission but Mam has made us some new clothes anyway so if we're lucky we might still get a penny in our pockets from Uncle Jim. There are hardly any people left in the brass band that leads us because they are all in the army and the big drummer has come back with only one arm. I heard Mrs Willoughby telling Mrs Jones that he was slow enough at the best of times and if we were to go at only half the pace we would never get round.

Our Ben has asked me to tell you that he has just won his third class certificate for swimming at Regent Road Baths. Mam told him to write himself but he's gone down to Ordsall Park playing football. He is going to do his second class in the summer holidays and, if he passes, he will win a free season at the baths.

I'm sorry that I haven't finished your socks yet but it is hard to do knitting round four needles and Mam keeps making me undo it even for the tiniest little mistake. I don't think that I will have enough of the green wool because it was only one of our Mary's cardigans that I've undone. I might just put some stripes round the feet because we have a bonnet that she doesn't need now. I might decide to keep them for me to wear in bed this winter because they might stop those horrible chilblains and I don't mind just little mistakes.

Dad, you would have been alright if you had been injured because the King has just been to Salford and he went talking to the injured soldiers in Salford Royal. We went to watch on Chapel Street and there were loads of carriages and all the horses had been polished and plaited. The King waved to us but he was nothing special and he didn't have his crown on. The Queen was very beautiful but she was waving at the Catholics outside the Cathedral so we didn't see her properly. The policemen had to stop some men with buckets who were nearly having a fight. They were arguing about the horse muck that they wanted for their allotments and one nearly hit the other with his shovel. Mam said it is Lloyd George's fault because there isn't enough food to keep your family. We have meat coupons but there is never much in the butcher's anyway. The police started the coupons to stop the big queues but the butcher runs out of stuff. Mam was telling Mrs Murphy that he favours those who favour him and she'd rather send our Eddie up to Rabbit Hills with his Uncle Jim.

Our Mary is starting school next year and I have been teaching her to read but she doesn't like it very much. We played school with our Ben and our Sadie last week but then our Edward came in and said that he was the headmaster and he was going to cane them for being naughty children and they all finished up crying. Mam said that I should stop being so bossy but our Ben said that it was our Edward so she sent him up to the greengrocer's where he works to see what they had that might be on the turn.

Love

Laura

Gomiecourt
France

15th July 1917

Darling Pippin,

It was lovely to see you all again when I was home. I was so surprised to see how much you had all changed. You are the image of your Mam when she was your age. Ask her about when she used to play football with the lads.

That must have been very special, going to see the King. It's a shame that you didn't get a proper look at the Queen as well. I'm told that she is very nice but I have never seen her.

Tell Ben that I am very proud of him for doing his swimming certificate. Don't you go to the baths with him? I heard that they were talking about having mixed bathing for children. When I get out I will take you all swimming and playing football. Perhaps we might get the chance to go to Blackpool for a holiday. I was talking to another soldier the other day and he was saying that the sands there are lovely and they stretch for miles. It would be lovely to sit in a deckchair and get a nice jug of tea for the sands.

I am sorry that I seemed to be a bit strange when you talked about killing the Germans. I wasn't annoyed with you. It's just a bit upsetting because the ordinary German soldiers are just the same as us and lots of them are getting killed as well. They have wives and families at home and they would rather be there with them – just like we would. The fault is with the people at the top who are running things. They seem to lose their proper sense of values when they get power and it's the rest of us that have to suffer for it. That's why it's good for you all to get a proper schooling and then you can make your way in life without being at the bidding of these people who've never done an honest day's work in their lives.

Don't worry about the socks, Darling. I don't think that I would notice the little mistakes but your Mam would want you to get them right, which is good. If you would like to use them for

239

yourself to stop the chilblains then that would make me very happy.

We went to help a local farmer last week for a few days. His daughter spoke a little English and she taught us a few words in French. They say 'Bonjour' for 'Hello' and 'Merci' for 'Thank you.' She was telling us that things are very difficult because when the Germans left they slaughtered their animals and burnt their crops and they had to hide anything of any value. Her Dad was trying to repair the roof where it had been damaged by the shelling so we gave him a hand. The girl cooked some nice meals with produce from the farm. It will be very hard for them when the war is finished because they have already lost so many of the young men from the village.

We see lots of interesting wildlife around here that we never see in Salford. There are some beautiful birds. They have one called a chaffinch that has lots of different colours on it and they come down in the trenches to see if we have any bits for them. We sometimes hear one called a nightingale that sits in the woods singing its head off. There is a big bird flying over us at the moment and I think that it might be called a buzzard. It is soaring in the air looking for any little animals on the ground that it can have for its dinner. Sometimes we see a family of foxes. The little ones wait near to where they live for their Dad to come home with something for them to eat. We're just hoping that they will take a fancy to all these rats that are running around because we are fed up with them.

Look after yourself and take care of your Mam for me.

Love

Dad

Chapter 14

Frezenberg September 1917

Big Charlie had been persuaded to write a letter home to Dorothy and Edward had agreed to pen it for him. The mood of the soldiers, as well as the weather, had changed since they had moved North into Belgium. When they had marched into Ypres a few days before, they had been profoundly disturbed by the sight of the mutilated buildings that littered the streets with the debris of their downfall. Medieval structures stood roofless and gashed. Towers that had been built five hundred years before, when craftsmen devoted years of their lives to just one project, had been ripped apart as if by the hand of some petulant child sick of the sandcastle that he was building.

They had approached up the Menin Road, which was subject to almost round-the-clock enemy shell fire from the Germans and repairs by the British, and now they were in the front line at Frezenberg. Big Charlie had been prompted many times to try and put things right at home but he had firmly resisted. Now, suddenly appearing aware of his own mortality, he had decided that it should be done. The air of gloom, that had weighed so heavily on him since his April folly, had increased daily with the lack of any forgiving or loving words from his beloved Dot and now the scarred images of Ypres faced him with the cold and deadly reality of this war. There had just been another major action in the area, the third in as many years, and although thousands had died there had been no strategic advantage of any consequence gained by either side.

This whole battlefield area was pock marked with water and slime filled shell holes that claimed many victims from those who had the misfortune to slip off the duck boards. The front line trenches were a series of joined-up craters whose shape was changed constantly by the incessant barrage.

The three pals sat huddled over a makeshift table trying to think of the elusive words that might soften the implacable resistance that Dorothy had developed. The thunderous roar of high explosive, shrapnel-filled shells rocked the ground and shook their table. Big Charlie was avoiding the idea of anything that might sound personal or affectionate having convinced himself that there was no possibility of his wife harbouring any shred of feeling, other than loathing, towards him. He had dismissed 'My Darling Dot' as an opening line, feeling that 'Dear Madam' might be safer, but had settled in the end for 'Dear Dorothy.'

He wanted to make his wife understand that he had reacted as a gallant yet outraged lover and that he still cared very deeply for her, but he dreaded inviting a sarcastic and scathing response. The three friends sat with their elbows resting on the table, their hands cupped round their chins, and stared distantly ahead waiting for inspiration to strike. They each had their view on how the wording of the letter should be approached, although Liam and Edward both agreed that it should have been done a long time ago.

They watched as stretcher bearers, mud-spattered, heavy eyed and grey faced, their heads bent forward with resigned weariness, trudged past them. The first of their charges had a large, bloody pad pressed to his shoulder and a cigarette propped in his mouth. The second had a large gash in his side and a ripped and bloody leg. His white face lacked evidence of life. The bearers probably knew that there was little hope but at least they would know where he was buried.

'Why don't you just tell her that you know that you've been a bloody fool, but this might be the last letter that you can send and you want her to know how sorry you are,' proffered Liam. 'Tell her there is a show coming off and you don't want to risk getting killed without having got this sorted out between you.'

'Aye, and if I didn't oblige by getting my head blown off, she'd just turn round and say I've let her down again,' replied the terminally gloomy Big Charlie.

'Surely the best thing is just to tell her how much you love her and you can't live without her,' suggested Edward.

'Hmhh. Maybe. But I haven't said owt like that for ten years. She'd probably laugh herself silly.'

Eventually the letter evolved itself into a slightly pompous sounding apology that just avoided the distancing formality that Big Charlie preferred but it fell miserably short of the intimate plea for reconciliation that Liam had hoped for.

Big Charlie felt safer with the slightly legalistic sound of 'righteous indignation' and 'personal feelings' suggested by Edward but recoiled away from 'deep felt and abiding love' proposed by Liam. He thought that 'the unfortunate victim' was a safer way to refer to the Dapper Man, Sidney Snelgrove, than the 'scheming little scumbag' offered by Liam. He conceded that just putting 'Yours truly, Charlie', but without adding his surname and regimental number, as he was keen to do, could manage to give the letter a personal touch without risking the burning fury of his wife's acerbic tongue.

Finally, the letter was sealed and given to the runner, accompanied by a threat from Big Charlie as to what he would do to him if he was careless enough to get himself killed whilst he had this important document in his safekeeping.

Edward pursed his lips as he watched with morbid fascination the toe cap of a boot that was gradually emerging from the wall of the trench opposite. He adjusted his feet to avoid the muddy water that was beginning to creep over the lip of the flunk hole where he sat huddled at the side of Liam and screwed his eyes to focus through the rain onto the shiny, rounded leather. He had originally thought that it was another rock in the gradually eroding façade of the gleaming mud but now he could see the clean line where the sole met the upper.

The hissing rain had been falling incessantly through the night and was now stifling the morning light. Rivulets, carrying floundering insects, small twigs and dead leaves, were flowing down the sides of the trench, accumulating into a thick slurry at the bottom. Along some stretches of the trench the mud was already over the level of the duckboards making any form of movement hazardous. The leaden grey sky was discharging its excessive load with unrelenting vigour, splashing noisily into the deepening water in front of them. Thunder rolled around the neighbouring hills and vivid, jagged lightning flashes slashed into the ground in a mocking, storming response to the humbler efforts of the warring factions on the ground. A sharp dank death smell, pounded out of the earth by the hammering rain, was pocketed in the flunk holes.

Stretcher bearers clad in shiny oilskin capes struggled past, plodding mechanically through the mire with their groaning, often hopeless, burdens lying like a pile of sodden rags in their cradle. Runners, red and shiny with their exertions, occasionally splashed by on their way to the officers' dugout further up the trench before returning, a few minutes later, to struggle their way back to Company headquarters. Their capacity for inventive cursing of the weather, the Germans and their own officers was an interesting, if fleeting, distraction. Distractions were always welcome in these numbing hours before the whistles would blow and they would be hurled into the oblivion of another attack.

Liam, rifle propped on the seat at the side of him and his elbows resting on his knees, pulled his head back quickly as a stretcher party pressed into their flunk hole to allow two soldiers, swearing viciously at the trench mortar that they were relocating, to pass by. Liam stared at the inert body for a few seconds then peered under the rim of the helmet that was balanced protectively over the head of the injured man. 'Well, blow me. It's Billy Perkins from down Brindle Heath isn't it?' he asked, poking the waterproof cape that covered the still form.

The sick man opened his eyes slowly and smiled weakly on recognition. 'Alright Liam. Not seen you around much lately.'

'No, well, we're down on Goodiers Lane now. I still see your Elsie sometimes on Broad Street.'

'Aye. She lives just off Frederick Road,' the injured man replied feebly.

'She married that Arnold with the red hair and a hair lip from behind St James' Church, didn't she?'

'Aye. Daft sod put her up the chuff but she seems ok with him,' Perkins said, coughing with the effort.

'What happened to that mate of hers, Dreamy Doreen? Used to really fancy her when I was a lad.'

'Our Elsie said you used to follow them everywhere like a lapdog. She's done alright for herself. Has a greengrocer's in Irlam now.'

'She'll be well admired for her big caulies then. How've you been, anyway, Billy? Must say you're not looking too perky for a Perkins.'

'Not too bad, I don't suppose. It's the arm. Shrapnel. Might have to lose it.'

'Well, look on the bright side. That's a sure fire Blighty. I wish we'd have known earlier. You could have taken a letter for Big Charlie's missus that we have just posted. You might have been able to put a good word in for him.'

'Postman. I suppose that's a job you could do single handed,' Billy said wryly as the stretcher party moved off.

Liam returned to staring morosely at the wall of water falling in front of him.

'He used to play on the wing at Swinton,' Edward said. 'Quite fast too.'

'I know. It's a bloody shame. We're short of a winger since Frankie Hopkins got himself shot last week. Then you think that you've come across a good replacement only to find that he's dying on you. You just can't win for losing.'

More of the toe cap of the boot had now emerged and its shape was quite distinct.

'What do you reckon to that, then?' Edward asked, nudging Liam into a grudging response.

'Reckon to what? This bloody awful weather or that poor sod Billy Perkins.'

'No, I mean over there,' Edward said, directing his friend's attention through the curtain of the torrential downpour.

Liam peered through the flickering, shiny screen at the wall of running water.

'It's mud,' he concluded loudly. 'The same slimy, sodding mud that's getting into every crevice in my body.'

'I know that but look, there,' Edward cajoled, pointing across the trench.

'Oh, that. I can see it now. It's a German boot.'

'German? Why do you think it's German? I was thinking that it's English.'

'Well, it's obvious isn't it? It's probably some poor Fritz who copped one the last time that our lads were in these parts,' Liam asserted.

'But if that was the case then where's the other? I reckon that it's one of ours. It was probably in a store that got blown up when we were here before.'

'It's German,' the booming voice of Big Charlie interrupted decisively. Their large friend was sitting by himself in a flunk hole about four feet away. Nobody else was small enough to share the narrow seat with him.

'So how do you know that, then?' queried Edward. 'There's only a couple of inches of it showing.'

'You wait and see,' Big Charlie replied, giving them an irritatingly knowing wink. 'But I'll put tomorrow's Woodbines on it.'

'Right. You're on,' Edward said rising to the challenge. He patted his jerkin to ensure that he still had some of those sickly French cigarettes left. Better those than none at all, he thought, slightly disconcerted by Big Charlie's apparent confidence.

Edward stared at the boot that was emerging slowly from the mud in front of him. Two or three inches of the toe cap were showing now and the front was being washed clean by the heavy rain. There were no scuff marks so it could hardly have been used, if at all.

Supporting planks had been fitted at intervals along the walls of the trench in the sections that were vulnerable to erosion, but these had only served to concentrate the flow of the water into the exposed areas. Edward looked up at the grey sky, streaked with the trails of the thousands of shells that were flying over from the British artillery guns packed into their muddy beds behind them. The screaming whistle of this barrage formed an orchestrated background to the rolling thunder of the German response. High explosive shells crashed into the already tormented countryside throwing huge plumes of soil into the air and scattering the slimy debris over the soldiers huddled in the trenches.

'There's my ten,' said Big Charlie, proffering a small green packet. 'Who's going to hold the stake, then?'

'Hang on a minute,' interrupted Liam. 'I want a slice of this action. It was me that said that it was German in the first place. And there's only two choices between three of us.'

'Right then. We'll make it a combination bet so that we can all have a go,' Edward decided. 'You and Charlie think that it's a German boot and I say it's English. The question is, when the mud has cleared away, will there be a person still inside it?'

'A person? How can it be a person?' Liam was incredulous. 'If there was a person there would be two boots. The only thing that's anywhere near it is a tree stump. What did he have, a wooden leg? No wonder he got killed, trying to run away in this mud.'

'Well, I think that it is a German boot and there will be a foot inside it because he had his leg blown off,' Big Charlie said decisively. 'And there's my ten Woodies to back it up.'

'You know, since you've not heard from your Dorothy, you've become a right morbid sod,' Liam observed with a sudden profundity. 'I agree that it's a German boot but Eddie's right. There's only one of them and it is completely and utterly empty. It is full of absolutely nothing, not one shred of human flesh. It has never, in its total existence, been occupied by a German foot. And there's my ten that says so.'

'I think that you're both wrong,' Edward said thoughtfully. 'I don't think it has ever been used because there are no marks on it. So I think that it is an English boot and nobody is inside it. Look at the angle and the fact that it is by itself. There are roots round it so it has been here quite a while. We were round here for longer than the Germans so the chances are it is one of ours. I suppose that I may as well put my ten in even though I will be taking them back again in about an hour.'

A shell exploded just above the ground about thirty yards in front of them flinging deadly shrapnel across the top of their trench. The sandbags above their heads, on the lintel of the flunk hole, were pierced by the flying metal and spilled the contents across the legs of Edward and Liam. Water began to drip through the exposed section and tapped noisily on their helmets.

The rain had now washed the relatively new sole clean and he could see from the inscription that it was German Army issue. He reckoned that at the present rate of erosion, and provided that the rain kept falling with the same intensity, it would take about half an hour to reveal whether the boot still contained its owner's foot.

'Well it's German anyway,' Edward said, more than slightly irked. 'So that means that I'm out and it's down to you two.'

'I told you that didn't I?' Big Charlie was being unbearably smug. 'Do you want to pass those cigs over to me now, Eddie? There's no point in waiting any longer.'

'Well, you're right so far,' Edward conceded. 'But why were you so sure that it was a German boot?'

'It's easy really. Look at the stud patterns. They're different than ours. You could see it as soon as they started showing through.'

Liam leaned out of the flunk hole in order to direct a fierce glare at the smirking big man but its intensity was diffused by the rain pouring off the front of his helmet. 'Bloody wait, you sycophantic sod. Eddie might be out but there's still a bet on between us two.'

The water flowing down the trench wall had cleared more of the boot and Edward could now see the tightly bowed lace on the German boot. The foot was probably still in there. He pulled Liam back into the recess. 'What's this sycophantic got to do with anything? Where've you got that one from?'

'Well, I don't know. But it sounded alright and it's shut him up for a bit.'

'Aye. But I don't think that it will be for long. Look at the boot now. The laces are tied and there's some sock starting to show. Somebody must have been wearing it.'

'Oh, sod it,' Liam groaned. 'That's it then. Have you got any of those bloody awful French smokes left?'

'Aye. I suppose we might as well have one of these each now. We'll save today's Woodbines so that we can treat ourselves when this show's finished.'

Edward passed Liam a French cigarette and they lit them gingerly.

Liam grimaced. 'It's going to be a long day tomorrow if we've got to depend on these things.'

'I'll have to play on Charlie's good nature,' Edward said, without much conviction. 'Make him feel indebted to us for helping him with that letter to Dorothy.'

'Good idea. And in the morning, all being well, I'll be having a walk down to the hospital tent,' Liam said thoughtfully.

'Why? What's wrong with you?'

'Do you mean other than that I am soaking wet, being bitten to death by sodding lice, I've got itchy arse and foot rot, I might get killed later and now I've got no cigarettes for tomorrow? All because bloody know-all Big Charlie knows how they put the studs in German boots. He should try talking a bit more, like any normal person does, then he wouldn't notice so much.'

'So which of those things are you going to have seen to at the hospital tent?'

'I'm going to have a chat with those orderlies. They always have a private stock of cigarettes stashed away. Surplus to requirements, I suppose you could say. At least, they are for the poor sods that they took them off. Mind you, I don't suppose anybody is gasping for a cigarette once they've handed over their ID tags and popped their clogs.'

Occasionally, a shell would fall into the trench, wreaking destructive havoc as their deadly loads of shrapnel flew down the section, tearing into the bodies of the crouching men. Soldiers from the next section would then dash round the zigzag of the trench to do what they could for their injured comrades until the medical support arrived.

'You know, the man who designed these trenches must have just finished saying his prayers,' Liam suddenly observed, kicking out at a rat that was trying to scramble from the water into their flunk hole.

'What? You think that he had divine inspiration?' Edward asked.

'No. Just put your hands together as if you're praying. Not like that. That's the girl's way. Lock your fingers together like this,' Liam said, clasping his wet hands together. 'Right, now look inside your hands where your fingers come together. There it is. That's the exact plan of a trench system.'

Edward stared at the water that was dripping into his palms. 'While we've got our hands like this, perhaps we should ask Him to turn this rain off for a bit. It drives you mad.'

'That's a good idea. Or even ask him just to drop it on the Germans.'

The barrage had increased in intensity as the time approached for their attack and now it created a wall of deafening noise. The Battalion was in support for an attack that was to be launched on a strong German position on a farm just outside Frezenberg. In the last few days, there had been two attempts to take these positions and both had failed with massive losses. The feeling amongst the Salford soldiers was that, whilst a victory would be a feather in their caps, the chances of them succeeding in a mission where the dour but highly respected warriors of the Black Watch and the Gordon Highlanders had already been ignominiously defeated, had virtually no chance. But, as Major Fforbes-Fosdyke was so

251

fond of telling them, it was not for them to question the decisions of their superiors. Liam had suggested to the Major the previous day that it wasn't them who were getting killed but the Major had become apoplectic and threatened to put him on a charge. Liam had said that they had better wait to see if he got back in one piece or not before doing the paperwork.

'I could just murder one of those billy cans from The Cattle Market,' Liam shouted above the din whilst bravely consoling himself with another French cigarette. Edward smiled as he remembered how, as young lads, they had both used to get up at five o'clock on cold winter's mornings and carry a long pole between them threaded through the handles of steaming billy cans. The hot coffee, with a bracing tot of rum added, was a service provided by The Cattle Market Hotel. The shivering cattle drovers, who warmed their frozen hands on the hot cans before enjoying the steaming contents, generally showed their gratitude to the boys with at least a farthing. Despite the cold and the early hours, he used to enjoy the lively, exciting atmosphere of the market. Sometimes there were around three thousand beasts herded into the pens, steam rising in clouds above them, and they grunted and grumbled and moaned complainingly as they pushed and shoved each other in the confined and alien pens.

Edward had been fascinated by the brash and confident auctioneers, gold fob watches stuck in their wide waistcoat pockets and their thumbs hooked protectively over them, as they strutted around the market ground disposing of groups of unhappy animals in a strange, incomprehensible language. They had been the star performers in that great, open-air theatre but he had, at the same time, been intrigued by the stoic buyers who assessed the cows and sheep with uncommunicative, steely eyes and bought with the merest of nods. He also used to enjoy the generous, boisterous friendliness of the drovers. Their varied accents fascinated him although he often found himself baffled by the Irish. It was a busy, noisy, thrilling experience filled with heady smells and bellowing men and animals but it was ultimately safe and unthreatening for the young lads.

Liam interrupted his reverie. 'Eh up. Here's General Gobshite to give us his pep talk before disappearing into his hidey-hole.' Major Fforbes-Fosdyke was, indeed, preening himself near the dugout and starting his 'Alright you chaps. Pay attention now' routine.

Behind the Major, Edward could see Big Charlie, who had frequently suffered the biting sarcasm of the Major's sneering humour, sidling rather ungainly away and disappearing round the corner of the trench. 'We all have a difficult job to do and we must do it with courage and determination,' continued the plummy voice. 'When the signal is given you will go over the top and keep a line formation. Do not start running. There should be little opposition. We are destroying the Bosche positions with our overwhelming firepower. We will show them what the British soldier is made of.'

'Will tha be joining us today then?' asked a mud spattered Salford soldier with a scar along his cheek and part of his ear missing. 'Sir,' he added after a momentary but meaningful pause. 'Just by way of a change, like.'

'Don't be so impertinent to a senior officer,' the Major barked. 'I am needed at HQ for making important decisions.'

'Sorry… sir' the Salford lad responded. 'Just thought as how you might have been fancying a run out with the lads to enjoy a bit of this nice weather.'

A bright, boiled beetroot red started to rise above the Major's cape as he angrily sought for some appropriately scathing words. As he lifted his hand to point an accusing finger at the soldier there was a loud explosion just a few yards to the rear of the trench where he was standing. A huge black mass of mud rose into the air and covered the men in stinking slime. The Major's gold braided authority was buried by wet earth and mud and only his deathly white face could be seen peering under the dripping peak of his hat. He was a man whose bullying demeanour hid a deep, abiding fear of the horror and reality of war. The Salford soldiers watched, mesmerized, as the spluttering, humiliated officer looked round with fearful staring eyes then turned quickly and ran as fast as his shaking legs and the clinging mud would allow back down the communications trench. Within minutes he was on his horse and galloping towards the safe haven of Battalion Headquarters.

'Nice of him to lay on a bit of entertainment, like,' observed one soldier, shaking the mud off his oilskin.

'Aye. First time in three years that he's been that close to any action,' said another.

Liam spotted Big Charlie coming slowly round the corner of the trench, checking carefully to see if the coast was clear. He knew immediately, from the smile on his large friend's face, what had happened.

'Well, you've made a bloody mess of us all, but we'll let you off this time,' he said, reaching up and cuffing Big Charlie under the chin.

By the time that the signal went for the support troops to go over, the torrential rain running down the wall of the trench had washed the earth from around the boot and Edward could now see the sock covering the leg that it contained. For a time, he had watched the first attack going in and had become increasingly depressed. The men from Manchester, who had done all that they had been asked, were mown down by the German machine gunners. Once again, the optimism of the commanding officers had been misplaced. The German trenches were well established and their soldiers simply hid in their underground bunkers until the actual attack started. When it did they emerged to man their machine gun posts and the British soldiers were treated to the usual destructive response. Were the decision makers unable to see this or was it that they placed such a low value on the lives of the rank and file soldiers that they were of little consequence in their blind pursuit of small successes? Edward knew that this was not for him to answer or change. He was trapped in this war machine and all he could do was to hope desperately that it would soon be over.

The possibility of being killed was something that they tried not to think about and rarely discussed. Most of them now took the approach that, with a bit of luck, it might only be an injury and, if you were really fortunate, it might be a Blighty – an injury that earned you a discharge and a return to England.

He sat back into his flunk hole with the tension rising in his body. The constricting feeling that always came into his throat and chest had started. His heart was pounding and he tried to focus his mind on what they should do. He wasn't leading the section this time, as 2nd Lieutenant Frank Williams had been assigned to join them, and Edward focused on listening to the explanation that was being given about the new tactics that the Germans had been employing. Williams was telling them that they might encounter break-out groups of highly trained and heavily armed troops who would try and circle round the back of them and mount an attack from the rear.

They were fearless and ruthless, he told them, and they could create chaos by breaking up the pattern of the attack. Liam observed that that should blow the minds of some of our officers who were still trying to work out how to cope with the previous tactics. Edward marvelled at his friend's ability to produce a quip in a situation when his own communicative abilities seemed to be restricted to grunts and nods.

A soldier emerged from the dug out carrying the rum allocation. They drank it back quickly and enjoyed its comforting warmth as it slipped into their stomachs. It did seem to help. Or was it just part of the routine that they went through? Liam always wiped his boots on the back of his trousers and then crossed himself before they went into action. Edward checked his pockets and said the names of each of his children and then his wife before saying his little prayer. Big Charlie polished and re-polished the barrel of his Lee Enfield three times with an oily cloth that he carried in his pocket. Frank Williams always took a wallet out of his left side breast pocket, removed a carefully folded piece of paper, and read its contents slowly to himself, before kissing it and replacing it with careful precision. He had told Edward once that it was a poem that his wife had written.

None of them thought that the others' routines were strange. They had to do them.

They were their talismans.

They gave them luck.

'Please God, keep us safe in thy…'

The shrill whistle blast sounded above the battle noise and the trench erupted into a frenzy of action. Edward dragged himself up the ladder and he was out into no-man's land, bayonet fixed and head bowed. Smoke from the high explosive barrage was curling around the stubby trees and dipping into the shell craters. It provided a limited degree of cover as they headed for the protection of the trees and the low shrubbery. When Edward looked up to get a view of where they were heading, he was almost blinded by the driving rain. He dropped his head again to get the protection of the rim of his helmet and fixed his eyes on the boots of Frank Williams stepping confidently in front of him. The claggy mud stuck to his boots and made running difficult.

Rain was forcing itself up his wrists and down his neck and, defying logic, up inside his helmet. They stepped carefully round the slippery edges of the great hollows in the ground fearful of slipping into the thick, clinging, deep mud at the bottom.

He was getting hot inside his oilskin cape and his breathing was becoming more laboured as he struggled to drive his increasingly heavy boots through the clay, He could hear the thudding boots and the rasping breath of his friends as they strove to reach the deeper cover of the trees. Machine gun fire had started up from a position near the perimeter wall of the farmhouse. Hopefully, the weather conditions would hinder them.

The breathing at the side of him seemed to be getting heavier and the pained wheezing told him that Big Charlie was suffering. He glanced under the side of his helmet and was surprised to see the bottom of two grey trousered legs plodding wearily along at the side of him. His shout, as he realized that this was not his large friend, but a dirty, mud-spattered, very wet and unhappy German, attracted the attention of the others.

Liam stopped, his hanging jaw betraying his total surprise, and grabbed hold of the panting German. 'What the...' he exclaimed. 'You're not one of those bloody shock troopers are you?' he shouted as he suddenly perceived the possible explanation for the man's presence.

The soldier stopped and, bending almost double, took a few moments to regain his breath. 'Nein. Not shock' he finally managed to get out.

'Well you certainly gave me a bloody surprise' Liam gasped.

The German's drawn face was grey and his pink-rimmed eyes showed pain and fear. His fair hair was plastered to his bare head by the rain and his unprotected uniform was soaked and the water dripped off the edge of his jacket. Liam took his hands off him and his voice calmed as the others gathered round. 'Look you daft sod. We're British. What are you doing here? You're supposed to be over there with them.'

'Nein. Here good.'

'Hang on a minute,' Frank Williams joined in, speaking loudly to make himself understood. 'You German, we British. We attack German line. You not with us. You with them.' He waved dramatically to emphasise the point.

'Nein. I stay here.'

Edward, impressed by the man's obvious understanding of the English language, offered a different approach. 'Are you ok mate? You don't look too good. Do you feel ill?'

'Ya. No food three days. We are wet und very cold.'

'So are you lost?' Edward enquired. 'Where is your unit?'

'Not lost. I with you. I am prisoner.'

'You know, I must be going a bit bloody barmy,' Liam rejoined. 'You suddenly appear out of nowhere and say you're a prisoner. Where have you come from? Have you escaped from the camp?'

'Nein. I am your prisoner now.' The German was now shivering violently and Liam put his arm round him. 'Look mate. You seem to have cocked things up a bit. You can't come with us. We're going this way to attack the German line. We don't want to but that's our orders.'

'War is bad,' the quaking man replied. 'Ich habe eine Frau und junge Kinder. Viele gute Männer sind gestorben.'

The Salford lads looked at each other, puzzled by the explanation and at a loss to suggest a solution to this deepening dilemma.

'He said that he's got a wife and young kids and something about good men. I think he's had enough.'

They looked round in amazement at Big Charlie, the source of the explanation, who now stood there looking rather sheepish as if he had been caught out playing with dolls.

'How the bloody hell do you know that?' challenged the astonished Liam

'It's our Dot's Uncle Arthur. He works for the German butchers on Trafford Road. I go in and hump for him at weekends, now he's getting a bit older like.'

Frank Williams, realizing that decisive action needed to be taken, took the German's rifle and threw it into a mud filled hole where it quickly disappeared. He pointed to the sickly man and then at a sheltering clump of trees with a low wall behind. 'You. Stay there. We come back for you. Take you to camp for food and doctor.'

'Danke. I wait.'

The British soldiers fished around in their pockets and produced a bar of chocolate, some dry biscuits and a couple of cigarettes which they handed over to the grateful German.

'Bloody rum do this is,' observed Liam. 'It would be handy if the rest of those shockers were starving.'

The Salford soldiers saw the drenched man settled and continued on their mission. As they emerged on the far side of the trees, with a view of the badly damaged farm buildings, the machine gun fire restarted. To their left they could see various companies of British soldiers tracking their way carefully across the heavily shelled fields. The landscape was littered with the bodies of the dead and wounded and smoke was billowing defiantly up into the heavy grey sky from a point just beyond the buildings where a dump had been hit. The still smouldering tops of trees bore witness to the recent shelling from the British artillery.

The German defensive positions were clearly well embedded and there was no evidence of any British troops having established positions within a hundred and fifty yards of the German lines although the scattering of bodies suggested that some had tried. Edward could see that a unit of the Manchesters was gradually advancing up the right flank and Frank Williams decided to support them. They moved quickly and made good ground across open fields. The British artillery battery had now lifted to a point beyond the farm where the German support trenches had been plotted by the Allied aircraft. The heavy rain hindered the German marksmen but it also inhibited the progress of the British soldiers. They picked their way carefully through the mud, trying desperately to avoid a potentially fatal fall into the deep mud of the craters.

They dragged their feet through the heavy, clinging clay, forced into single file by the restricted thread of firm ground, and slithered down slopes of flowing water. Machine gun fire ripped into the ground around them and splintered the wood of the sparse trees. Liam yelped as a bullet pinged loudly off his helmet and lowered his head even further. One of the men shouted as he felt a sharp stinging at the top of his leg and looked down to see a neat hole cut through his oilskin cape. Frank Williams assigned one of the men to assist him to fix a pad over the wound and then to make their way back to their own lines.

The forward unit of the Manchesters had stopped and were gathered in a group when the Salford men approached them. Their soldiers were standing round some casualties being treated on the floor. One of them was clearly beyond treatment. Blood was still flowing from the wound in his chest and diffusing into the rain that was washing over him. A red stream was running down the slope at the side of him.

'Oh, Jesus,' Edward heard Big Charlie groan behind him, 'That's our Ada's lad. He's only seventeen.'

'Poor thing. She'll be demented when she hears about this,' Edward said. 'Her husband's over here isn't he? You'll have to get your Dot to go round and see her.'

'I can't do that when she's not even speaking to me. She hasn't sent me a letter back, so that's it.'

'Well, just write to her and tell her about this. She'll be upset if she hears from somebody else,' Edward suggested.

Frank Williams was in discussion with the Captain of the Manchesters who was explaining that his battalion had suffered heavy losses that morning. He said that there was a well embedded machine gun position in the trench at the front of the farm and that there was a sap trench with an observation post running directly from the main trench. It was from there that they were feeding back the movements of the British troops and it was almost impossible to make progress without being seen.

He told Williams to take his unit to try to take out the sap and he would, at the same time, attack the MG position with the Manchesters. They discussed a few more points then rejoined their respective units. The rain had eased by the time that they set off but the ground was still a quagmire. They made slow but steady progress enjoying the cover for a while of some low lying hillocks. The gun fire seemed to be concentrated across to the North for the moment and the German artillery was intermittently firing towards the Allied lines half a mile to the West.

They were within fifty yards of the sap trench when the shattering explosions flung them to the ground. As they painfully picked themselves up from the muddy earth they looked around for the cause and to check for any casualties. The cause soon became clear. The Germans had obviously seen them and were putting mortar shells over from the sap. Another came over from the main trench but fell short. They found two of the recent recruits from England lying in a crater, unable to crawl up its slippery sides. Another shell came from the sap and exploded with terrifying ferocity in a nearby shell hole. The tons of mud that roared up into the air cushioned the blast but covered the British soldiers in its filthy slime. Williams shouted at the men to keep low and help to get the two injured men out of the crater.

He took four men and the Lewis gunners with him and traversed in a wide arc towards the head of the sap trench. After various attempts to rescue the men, which failed because of the depth of the hole, Liam took off his belt and fastened it round his ankle and Big Charlie's wrist. Then, with two men anchoring Big Charlie's legs, Liam was lowered gently into the hole where he reached down and pulled the men up the muddy wall. One had a broken arm and the other slight concussion.

As they strapped the man's arm, Frank Williams returned, his face grim and taut. He had got near enough to lob a couple of grenades at the observation post but the mortars in both German trenches were peppering the area so heavily that further progress was impossible. There were no other British units in the area. They had all been driven back by the fierce, and seemingly unbreachable, German defences. The Captain of the Manchesters had already signalled that he had failed and was heading back. Williams told them that their present position was untenable and they had no alternative but to try to get back to their lines safely.

Mortar shells continued to fall but without too much accuracy. The grenades thrown at the OP had done their job and the operators in the trenches clearly couldn't get a fix on their positions. The soldiers made their stumbling way out of the vicinity of the shell fire, sharing the burden of their injured comrades as they slithered perilously along the narrow tracks. There were stretches where they were visible to the German gunners but the fire was spasmodic. They had lost interest in their now retreating foes.

Eventually, they reached the edge of the woods where they had left the ailing German soldier. There were now five miserable, wet men in grey uniforms huddled together for warmth. They had thrown their own rifles into the mud. 'I don't know about shock troops,' Liam mused, 'but it will give them a big surprise at the office when we take this lot in.'

Four of the German soldiers rose unsteadily to their feet but the fifth remained prostrate under the trees. 'Er ist sehr krank,' the original prisoner said, pointing towards the man on the floor. 'Not good.'

The Germans tried to lift their weakened comrade but their own enfeebled condition meant that they could barely raise themselves. The face of the fair haired young man sprawling limply on the ground had, already, a deathly pallor. Big Charlie stepped forward, checked to make sure that there were no broken limbs then poked the dying young man in the ribs. The German's lips moved slightly. 'It's ok. Ich trage ihn,' Big Charlie told the group of Germans, 'I will carry him.' Bending down, he gently picked up the dying man.

The original prisoner, struggling with his emotions, put his hand on Big Charlie's arm. 'Er ist mein Bruder,' he said. 'My brother.'

29 Myrtle Street
Cross Lane
Salford 5
Great Britain

25 September 1917

Dear Dad,

We are back at school now but it is a bit boring because we might have to have all our hair cut off. The nit nurse has been round and Freda Higginbottom is full of them and they said that we might all have to be treated. Mam has got a special comb and she said that none of us have got nits because she makes sure that we are looked after properly. The teacher said that they are called head lice and I told her that you get rid of them over a lighted candle. She said that I know too much for my own good sometimes but I told her that that is what my Dad does.

We don't have any wild animals around here so you are very lucky being able to see all those. I have been looking them up in a book at school and you should be careful of those foxes because they can be a bit sly. I wish we could have some of those chaffinches though. We only have sparrows. We hardly ever see any pigeons now because people trap them.

Our Edward has told our Ben that he has got a girlfriend at a house he delivers to and he gave her a kiss in Buile Hill Park. Our Sadie wants to know if she wears clogs like us or is she posh. Mam said that there is nothing wrong with clogs and they are no better than we are just because they don't wear them.

We had a ceremony in the street last week for the opening of the roll of honour. The Mayor came down and made a speech and Billy Murphy said that it was the same speech that he had made in their street the day before. We all had to put on our best clothes and then we took them off again an hour later because the Mayor had gone home. They left horse muck and straw all over the street after we had spent all morning cleaning the road ready for them coming. Mr Kirkstall with no legs from round the corner, sat in his chair and cried all the way through. Then somebody brought him a big glass of that whisky stuff that Uncle Jim likes and afterwards he started singing and then Mrs Kirkstall started crying. Old Mr Cooper took his pipe out of his mouth, which he doesn't do very often, and sang a song for his son because they didn't know where he was, and Mrs Cooper was singing and crying at the same time. Mr MacFarlane came out of the pub and marched down the street playing his bagpipes then Mr Simmons went in his house and came out with a big piano accordian that he pumped up strapped round his neck. He was marching behind Mr MacFarlane and then some more people came out of the pub and one had a mouth organ. They all stood singing near the new roll of honour. Mr Simmons took one of the flowers out of a wreath that we had made – well it was one that Billy Murphy brought round from their street because they had finished with it and we put a new card on it – and he sang one called 'Will Ye No Come Back Again.' Mam said it is Scottish, which it probably is because Mr MacFarlane knew it, and Mrs Cooper started crying again then nearly everybody was singing and crying at the same time. It was getting a right miserable do but Mam brought out a tray of treacle toffee so that was better for all the kids.

Dad, I hope that you don't mind but I have decided to keep those socks because I forgot to put a heel in one of them until I had gone past it and I don't want chilblains again when it gets cold..

Our Ben has passed his second class certificate for swimming so he can go to the baths for a year without paying.

Love

Laura

Oblinghem
France
11th December 1917

Darling Pippin,

I so enjoyed your letter about the ceremony to dedicate the Roll of Honour in the street. I told Mr Murphy and some of the others about it and we had a good laugh. We needed something to cheer us up and that was a real good tonic. We were in a place called Nieuport at the time on the coast of Belgium and it was a pretty depressing place. The destruction to the villages and towns is beginning to get us all down but it must be worse for the locals. In Nieuport there is a large canal that runs through and it has three bridges that cross it. The Germans have positions on high ground outside the town and every night they shelled the bridges and every day we rebuilt them. They think that it is some kind of game but it was not very funny for us in this awful weather.

The whole of the area is very flat and miserably muddy. Sometimes we spend all day on little islands in the river hiding behind low shelters and hardly daring to move because you would be seen by the Germans. Fortunately, there are still parts of the town which are largely undamaged where life goes on more or less as normal. We go into town when we have got time off and have a beer in the bars.

They speak a very funny language here. I have been told that it is a mixture of Dutch and French but it could be Double Dutch for all I can understand it. It makes you very homesick, sometimes, when you sit in a cafe and you don't understand a thing of what is being said. I would give anything for one of your Mam's hot pots with a thick pastry crust on the top. With some nice pickled red cabbage, of course.

Our Edward is getting quite a young man now if he has a girlfriend. I won't ask him about her, though, or else he will guess that you have told me so it will have to be our secret. I sneaked a kiss once off your Mam when we were fishing on the cut canal. She said that it was like sucking a stickleback. I was very hurt so I didn't try again for quite a few years. So that's another secret that we have.

Your Mam told me that you have been reading a book called 'Little Women' and she says that you hide away in the corner and ignore everyone. I used to enjoy reading when I was young but it was difficult to get hold of books then. Our entertainment was mostly found out in the street and down at Peel Park. We used to help out round the market whenever we could, to earn a bit of extra money. Sometimes we got paid in kind by the stallholders who gave us some of the stuff that hadn't sold. It was good fun but it wasn't great schooling. Knowledge gives you strength, Darling, so keep enjoying it. Maybe one day you will be another Emily Pankhurst. You might not have heard of her but she is the lady that has been fighting for women's rights, especially for their right to vote. She is a Manchester girl, born in Moss Side, and her Dad owned Goulden's Calico Printers in Salford. We all have to be willing to fight for our rights and to be respected for who we are so I admire Mrs Pankhurst for devoting so much of her life to this. Her daughters are very keen supporters and I read in the Reporter that there are a number of ladies in Salford who are in the Women's Movement. I hope that they succeed. They deserve to. There are too many of us in Britain who are treated as second or even third class citizens.

I have sent a little parcel with some bits and pieces for everybody for Christmas. It's not much, but it is difficult to get hold of things when you're doing a job like this.

Happy Christmas my little one. I can't tell you how much I would like to be there to share it with you all.

Love

Dad

Chapter 15

Vaudricourt, March 1918

'Vous voudrez le meilleur?' the young woman enquired. She was pretty, with long dark hair, but her eyes were tired and her smile more fixed than welcoming. She was the daughter of le patron and, although they came to this bar quite often when they were on free time, they found that she distanced herself from the visiting soldiers with her quiet, but powerful, authority.

The room had cheerfully painted walls and a smoky ceiling. A local artist had, at some time, decorated the top half of the walls with sensual, though clearly agricultural, females. The tables were heavy cast iron with marble tops but the chairs were a motley mix of styles and quality. The bar was popular with the British troops who welcomed the draught beer and enjoyed the local wines, and they savoured its authentic charm. It was also frequented by the older locals and the British soldiers delighted in the small exchanges that they were able to make with the few French words that they had acquired.

Big Charlie shifted uncomfortably under the searching gaze of the young French waitress. He never felt at ease in the presence of attractive females and the minimal contact that he had enjoyed with any member of that sex during the last three years had only served to erode his confidence further. Her dark eyes stayed on Big Charlie as she waited for a reply but the words were nowhere near forming in his brain. He wasn't certain, even, whether she had been addressing him in English but he did know for sure that he hadn't understood a single word.

He had always felt discomfited when young women spoke to him. He was usually the butt of their jokes. He was a chance for them to sharpen their humour and then to walk off arm-in-arm, laughing as they enjoyed their minor intellectual conquest. He sometimes thought of suitable responses but they were always too late. Even the day after. When his Dorothy had come along and seen in him qualities that others had missed, he couldn't believe his good fortune. She was bright and funny but not at his expense. She saw in him a gentle, caring and protective temperament and she understood his dark moods of frustration.

Big Charlie had never been able to totally accept her commitment to him because he never understood it. She was a thing of beauty that had come into his life but he had always believed that the day would come when she would be snatched away again. He was in awe of her and fearful of doing something that might hasten her departure. His physical contact with her was hesitant and guarded, dominated by his constant worry that his size and clumsiness might in some way harm her.

But he did know that Dorothy accepted him for what he was and she took care of him with a good humoured tenderness. He, on the other hand, responded to her sudden bouts of shrieking fury with silent resignation. Now, as he sat glowing uncomfortably under the mocking stare of the French girl's big dark eyes, he felt the familiar sense of panic and the rushing blur of words and thoughts in his head.

'What's she on about the Mayor for?' he eventually asked Edward and Liam. His two companions, who clearly didn't share his aversion to the obvious charms of the young waitress, dragged their attentions away for a moment to address this difficult problem.

'You're not in trouble about something, are you Charlie?' asked Edward.

'You haven't been daubing slogans on the wall of the Town Hall, have you?' Liam pursued. 'Or perhaps Farmer Pierre has complained about you nicking his cow.'

'I didn't nick his cow,' protested Big Charlie.

'No. But he could see you was weighing up how many steak pies you could get out of it,' retorted Liam.

'Just ask her,' suggested Edward. 'She might understand a bit of English.'

'I'll ask,' Liam said. He cleared his throat and said loudly and precisely, in the way that the English believe somehow converts the words to the recipient's language, 'What... you... say... about... Mayor.'

'Non, non, c'etait le meilleur,' she affirmed patiently.

'Hope that you don't mind me interrupting, mate.' The voice came from an adjoining table in the bar. It was a teacher from Bolton who had just been assigned to their regiment. He had gone through the Officer Training Corps before coming to France where he had been for the last two years. 'I think that she is asking you if you want the best.'

'The best what?' queried Edward.

'I would think that she means the wine. They usually have some decent quality stuff in the cellar that they keep for their favoured customers.'

'Well, this stuff isn't too bad,' reflected Liam, taking another mouthful and letting it roll gently down his throat.

'I suppose that we could always try some of the good stuff for a change,' Edward said encouragingly.

'Good idea,' Liam said. 'We'll order some. It's about time we spoiled ourselves a bit. Tell her we'll give it a try,' he instructed Big Charlie.

A look of alarm started to spread across the already flustered face of the Salford soldier and he started to splutter. He fingered his collar and glanced briefly at the lovely face. 'Aye. Right,' he said, nodding.

'Bien. Venez,' she said, beckoning Big Charlie with an elegant finger.

Accompanied by much barracking from around the bar, Big Charlie rose uncertainly to his feet and followed as if mesmerised by the gently swaying hips of the waitress. The neat black skirt was his preferred option for somewhere to rest his gaze rather than meet the eyes of his fellow soldiers who were offering their own helpful observations on the nature of his mission. Heat raged up through his body, his tight collar constricted his breathing and sweat dripped into his unseeing eyes. Chairs, and sometimes their occupants, fell as he followed the French woman clumsily towards the door marked 'Privee.'

Liam poured some more wine from the carafe and fished in his pocket for the few francs that he needed as his contribution. 'We might as well finish this so that we can compare it with good stuff.'

There was a hushed moment in the bar as all its occupants watched the graceful hips in the long black skirt, surmounted by the elegantly curved white blouse, go through to the back of the bar. This was a confused silence of envy and incomprehension. It was not within the scope of the average Tommy's thinking to believe that this beautiful lady might be available, and to see her disappearing through this door, beckoning the reluctant Salford lad, was a mental challenge with which they could not cope. They listened in total silence to the heavy tread of Big Charlie's boots ascending the stairs accompanied by the constant prompting of the French woman.

Edward and Liam clinked their glasses together. 'Here's to a good show – when it arrives,' they wished, alluding to the rumours that were rife that the Germans might be planning something big. There had been reports that they had been moving divisions in from the Eastern Front to support their French operation.

'Let's hope that it's a short one and that the whole thing's over with soon.'

Whilst the occupants of the bar remained staring in open mouthed amazement at the door into the back there was a thunderous thudding noise on the stairs, the door burst open and Big Charlie came crashing through. He was muttering something about 'getting in bed with a scabby old tart' as he dashed past them and out through the front door.

Moments later, le patron's daughter appeared, bending forward and holding her stomach as she struggled to suppress the violent laughter that was, in that peculiarly feminine way, applying pressure to her bladder. She struggled over to the corner of the bar where the locals were gathered and in seconds they were shrieking. The French woman gesticulated dramatically as a substitute for the words that she couldn't get out and the old men spluttered through their cigarettes. One held his hand to his chest as his excitement mounted and another failed to hold his buttocks tightly enough to restrain the gases that his uncontrollable laughter had promoted. Hands were slapped on the bar and large, and sometimes dubious, handkerchiefs were wiped over their eyes as the waitress's recounting of her story was accompanied by gales of laughter from the locals. The British soldiers stared at them, totally bemused.

The Bolton teacher had moved closer to the bar and was listening attentively to the discussion. Presently, he came over to Edward and Liam and explained that, apparently, the best wine had been hidden under the Grandma's bed since the German army had arrived. Le patron's daughter had needed assistance to lift her invalid Grandma from her bed so, in the absence of le patron, she had selected Big Charlie because of his obvious power. Unfortunately, the obliging Salford man had misunderstood the nature of his assignment when the French woman had pulled the sheets back and pointed first at Big Charlie and then at the bed. The situation had not been clarified when the occupant had given him a toothless smile and held her arms up in a welcoming gesture. He had taken one look at the wrinkled old crone smiling invitingly up at him and fled.

They had a brief discussion and concluded that Big Charlie might prefer to have a little time to recover before the situation was explained. There was the carafe of wine to finish anyway and it was improving as the evening progressed. They took their wine and joined a group from their platoon on the adjoining table. They discussed the football match planned for the next day and the shooting competition that was due to be held later in the week.

In the training sessions, heavy emphasis was now being placed on the platoon as a unit and much of the sporting activity was organized as inter-platoon competitions. After more than three years of fighting, many painful and expensive lessons had been learnt by both sides and the training was now focused on responsibility being taken at a more local, and even personal, level. The rigid patterns of battalion warfare were giving way to a more flexible approach at platoon level and the army was encouraging them in the recognition of the significance of this by arranging these inter-platoon activities.

The soldiers enjoyed the rivalry that was engendered and they thrived in the team environment. They became more mutually supportive of other members of the platoon and developed a greater recognition of the strengths and weaknesses of their colleagues. They would often send non-players out to watch other matches to assess their better performers and their tactics, and many off-duty hours would be enjoyably passed discussing forthcoming fixtures.

When the light faded outside small guttering candles were placed on the tables and the debates continued. More wine was ordered and games were analysed, tactics were discussed and le patron's daughter was admired.

Eventually, they decided to make their way back to their billets and they fished under their seats for their boots. It had been made clear to them, when they had first started using the bar, that their studded boots were not welcome on the tiled floor so they politely removed them whilst standing on a small square of carpet near the door.

Liam had carried his boots over to the door, and was bending carefully to replace them, when that strange sensation that occurs as an intoxicated head becomes enshrouded by the night's cold fresh air, began to overtake him. He put out a steadying hand on to the bench at the side of him and was surprised to feel the warm comfort of a female breast. Two large hands came up and clamped his wrist, pressing his hand firmly into position on the recumbent woman. Liam looked down to find that he was attached like a limpet to the ample breast of Camille. His heart sank. Deep despair quickly engulfed him. The British soldiers didn't know Camille's real name but they called her that because she reminded them, with her rolling gait, her bad breath and her unsociable habits, of the beasts that they had become so familiar with in Egypt.

She lived on a farm out in the country and came into the village once a week on market day. She was large and powerful, with a pronounced moustache and an abundance of warts, and she was frighteningly predatory. She had been known to clear the bar of British soldiers in less than two minutes when she began hunting. She had been drinking all afternoon and now Liam had clearly become integrated into her lascivious dreams.

His head was clearing rapidly as the gravity of his situation settled over him like a cold shroud. He tried carefully to withdraw his hand but Camille's hands clasped more firmly round his throbbing wrist. Her prey was trapped and now she was going to devour it slowly and with relish. There was not even the tiniest corner of Liam's mind that could contemplate a sexual contact with this snoring woman and panic started to overwhelm him like a creeping paralysis. He tried again to free his hand but the grip tightened. A cold, clammy sweat settled over his body. He could feel the muscles in his stomach twisting into tight knots and his bowels erupted into gaseous action. He wanted to shout Edward, who had gone outside and was threatening to walk off, but all that came out was a strangulated squeaking sound.

He contemplated lashing out at the recumbent Camille but the consequences of doing so were almost as frightening as the prospects of the encounter that she seemed to be currently dreaming about. He waved his free hand and emitted more formless squeaks but he failed to attract the attention of his friend. Desperate now for a solution before the control of his groin muscles let him down totally, he played his do-or-die card and flung his boot through the door where it rattled and bounced down the pavement. The noise attracted the attention of the parting soldiers and the group turned back.

Liam's frantic yelping reached fever pitch as he tried to communicate with his puzzled friend. Edward stared, bewildered, into the half light of the bar. He could see Liam's frightened eyes pleading for help but the nature of his discomfort eluded him. A few paces more, however, revealed the depth of Liam's plight and Edward searched round for a solution. Liam's hand was now being moved in a rotating motion around the breast of Camille, who was smiling blissfully. He was arching his fingers backwards in an effort to minimize contact with the coarse, woollen jumper, as if he was trying to avoid touching a hot metal surface.

A rapid solution was required but it had to be discreet; anything else could produce a response of cataclysmic proportions from the fearsome Camille. Finally his eyes settled on le patron's cat that was curled up and sleeping peacefully on a chair near the door. Bending down, he carefully picked up the cat and placed it gently across the repulsive face. Within seconds she was struggling for breath through the seemingly contented animal. She instinctively opened her mouth to take in air but filled it instead with fur.

Her hands reached up to remove the offending animal and Liam was free. He grabbed his other boot and rushed out hauling Edward behind him.

'Let's scarper quick, before she sees me,' Liam gasped. 'If she sets eyes on me I won't dare come in here again.'

When they got back to their billets they decided that, at least, they would avoid going in on market days. Big Charlie asked for a return of his contribution towards the wine and told them that the Germans had opened up a massive artillery bombardment over a 50 mile front to the south and they were moving out during the next few days.

Their bodies ached with tiredness and their minds were numbed by the deafening thunder of the high explosive shells. They stumbled around in the trench, gas masks fixed to their faces and inhibiting their vision, and they struggled to free the bodies of their comrades from the cloying mud. They slithered on the blood laced slime as they heaved on the inert bodies and tried to sort out those with any flickering evidence of life from the obvious corpses. The hopefuls were carried over to the first aid posts. There the medical teams fought the overwhelming urge to sleep in order to render whatever assistance they could give that might help the injured survive until more comprehensive treatment could be administered. The corpses were moved to a processing area where their details could be recorded and their burials arranged.

The artillery bombardment by the Germans had been intense since it had opened at 5.00am. Gas had been used freely and veiled the British trenches in Bucquoy. It was now 5 April 1918 and two companies of the 1/8 Lancashire Fusiliers had been almost wiped out on the left flank that morning. Edward's group had moved down to sort through the casualties. The incessant rain over the last few days had turned the bottom of the trench into a quagmire and the bodies of the injured lay amongst the blasted corpses and disembodied limbs of the dead. Edward had again inhaled some gas that morning before he had fixed his mask into place and now, as he coughed, the glass steamed up and blurred his vision. He tried to adjust the mask to make the seal more effective but suspected that it was designed for a less noble nose than his.

He had been on scavenging duties like this numerous times during the last three years but these conditions were as bad as any he could remember. The lower half of his body was chilled by the freezing slime that plastered his trousers where he had slipped and fallen as he wrenched at the interlocked forms of the casualties. He had recognized a few of his mates from Salford amongst the dead bodies. He felt the clutching pain in his lower throat as he thought of the devastated families receiving the dreaded letters.

For the moment Edward was working by himself. The soldier that he had been working with had just gone into the dugout for a short break. Minutes before, they had pulled out the mutilated body of the other man's older brother.

As lads they had lived two streets away from Edward and he knew that the two brothers had been inseparable. The older lad had taken the younger sibling to school, taught him to swim and to play football. He had shown him how to make fishing nets with a bamboo cane and a piece of old muslin. He had taken him with him to help in his job as an errand boy then got him a job as an apprentice typesetter at Heywood's printing works. When their father had died at the age of forty, the two brothers had worked hard to feed and clothe their younger sisters and their mother and to pay the rent on their little two up and two down terraced property.

The older brother had guided the other through the minefield of relationships with girls and had encouraged him to accompany him to join the Territorial Army. The Battalion had benefited greatly both from their courage and determination and from their sporting prowess. The older brother had been an outstanding cricketer and a talented chess player; the younger had shown himself to be an extremely skilful footballer and rugby player.

They were flesh and bone and blood of the same mould and the same pattern. And the younger brother had turned over an anonymous corpse, with a large hole ripped into its back by scrap metal from a German engineering works inserted into a high explosive shell, and found his brother's sightless eyes staring out of the lifeless face.

He would now be posted home to break the news to his family and he would feel like a coward for surviving. He would feel guilt and shame as he walked down the street to deliver the news, to thrust knives into the hearts of three women whose innocent, trusting love would now be rewarded with a raging pain that could never be healed. And they would never know, and would never understand, the searing intensity of his own hurt. The red stain that had been blending into the French mud was his lifeblood and it could never be replaced. They would never know that his being was now a total void. There would never, now, be anything that would be worth doing.

They found his body later that day with gunshot wounds to his head, lying alongside his brother. The two of them were processed together as casualties of the same action, their names listed one below the other and their names bracketed together to ensure that the officer writing the 'sorry to have to tell you' letters could avoid duplication.

Edward replaced the mask on the face of an injured soldier and struggled to get him to higher ground. One soldier dies and many lives are lost, he thought, as he heaved the man on to the collection cart. He watched Liam and Big Charlie lifting a man further down the trench. Liam, unnaturally silenced by the constraining gas mask, tackled the legs whilst his large friend looped his hands under the arms. They gestured and mouthed in the mode of communication that had been developed by the soldiers to cope with the incessant noise of artillery bombardments.

For ten days now the fighting had been intense. The Germans had launched a major attack in what seemed to be a do-or-die attempt to break the deadlock. After the devastating onslaught of shell fire from the heavy artillery, the Germans had thrust a hundred Divisions – many moved from the Eastern Front, now quiet after the collapse of the Russian effort – against only fifty Divisions of the defending Allied forces. They had concentrated their troops into narrow fronts where they thought the Alllies would be most vulnerable. The German storm troops attacked the British lines and, when they were exhausted, a second wave was thrust into the line followed shortly by a third wave heavily armed with machine guns. They sought to destroy anything that lay in their pathway, to get round the flanks of the defending armies and then attack them from the rear.

Just three days after Big Charlie's embarrassing misunderstanding in the village bar, the 42nd Division had been moved out in hundreds of buses and trucks and had headed down towards Bapaume. They had passed hordes of weary refugees carrying their pitifully few possessions as they fled the oncoming Germans. Their eyes were dead and their faces grim after over three years of the fighting that had destroyed their homes and harvested most of their young men. As the day had passed, the journey had become increasingly difficult for the British soldiers as the traffic had become more and more congested. Troops were converging from all over the region and they were facing massed ranks of hapless refugees heading in the opposite direction.

They had finally arrived at Adinfer at 7.00pm and the Battalion had moved up to Adinfer Wood where they had set up their bivouac for the night. There had been a strong sense of anticipation amongst the Salford soldiers. Suddenly the arena had changed. They were out of the trenches and the enemy would be engaged in a combat that could change the direction of the war. After months spent in training and manning the trenches they would now face the Germans and have the chance to move the war towards a conclusion.

The night in the woods had been bitterly cold and the soldiers had hardly slept. The clear, starry sky had been spectacular but the frost was numbing and they had tried to keep warm by walking around the woods. Edward had made a brief attempt at writing some letters home but he had found that his fingers had gone numb within minutes. They had suffered a brief visit from Major Fforbes-Fosdyke who had regaled them with the usual series of platitudes about facing the enemy with courage and determination and fighting for the King and the greatness of the British Empire. He had then put two men, who had enquired how many blankets the officers had, on a charge for insubordination before disappearing to some safe haven well behind the lines. Liam was forthright in the fullness of his descriptive analysis of the Major's war involvement with the phrase 'two faced sod' being one of the kinder references he used.

Edward had suggested that the Major appeared to be slightly the worse for drink, although that wasn't unusual, and that the view of him disappearing was perhaps his best angle. They had both agreed that Big Charlie's ploy with the hand grenade, placed in close quarters to the Major's rear, had been equally as entertaining as the Christmas concert but that it wouldn't be wise to repeat it too often as it might arouse suspicion. Maybe they could persuade Big Charlie to do it just once more but this time with something more spectacular.

No fires had been allowed in order that their position would not be revealed and the men paced around like restless tigers, smoking cigarettes cupped inside their hands, and huddled together in groups for some shared warmth.

The next morning Second Lieutenant Frank Williams had addressed their Company on the situation in the area and had explained the different tactics that were now being employed by the Germans. He had told them that the enemy would just appear in small, running groups without an obvious pattern, but that soon there would be huge numbers in close proximity. He had advised them that many of the German soldiers were highly trained and battle hardened veterans of the fighting in Russia and that their secret weapon was unpredictability. He had also said that the Germans were now occupying the town of Bapaume to the south and that shortly the 42nd Division would be moving out to relieve the 40th Division which was holding the villages of Sapignies and Behagnies to the north of Bapaume.

Williams had explained that the positions being held were changing constantly because of the fierce fighting and that some villages had been captured by the Germans only to be retaken by the British. He said, however, that the Germans had made a lot of territorial gains because of the weight of their attack.

Later that day they had moved out of their positions at Adinfer into a temporary placement at Logeast Wood ready for a transfer up to the front line where the fierce fighting was continuing. The whole area was like a transhipment zone. Heavy artillery was being moved back from Bapaume into new positions and there was a constant procession of wounded men in vehicles or on foot. At 6.00pm the 1/8 Lancashires had gone forward into positions on the right flank of the front line.

This part of France was familiar to the Salford soldiers. They had been in camp here during the previous summer but the war ravaged countryside of 1918 bore little resemblance to the place that they had become so familiar with. The fields and woods where they had trained and played were now scarred and ravaged by the artillery shells and the bar where they had drunk the local wine was a battered wreck.

Edward had looked in dismay at Le Mairie in Behagnies. He had seen so much damage to fine buildings in recent years that he had almost become hardened to it. At first, he had felt violated by the seemingly wanton destruction of the skilful work of the medieval craftsmen. He understood the skill and loving devotion that had gone into creating these beautiful buildings. When he stood inside the old churches, he didn't just see the finished whole and appreciate its worth as a balanced and symmetrical unit, he saw a space that was gradually being enclosed, he saw large, rough rocks being hewn from the quarry and brought to the site on horse drawn carts before being crafted into elegant and mechanically perfect shapes and he saw the artisans with primitive equipment lifting the one ton stones hundreds of feet into the air. He felt awe and wonderment when he thought of the achievements of these unsophisticated but hugely talented and creative men working with the most basic of tools.

He sensed the spirit of community that dwelt in every corner of these dusty edifices; he breathed the cells of the town's forefathers that hung in the still air; he saw the bustling, busy men, women and children who had worshipped there, who had held markets within its walls, who had had their lives, from baptism to burial, dominated by the embracing structure of their church.

Here in France and Belgium, however, he had witnessed barbaric destruction of cathedrals, churches and merchants' houses on a massive and unforgivable scale. War, though, dehumanises the individual, neutralises sensitivity and degrades the caring, so that they might survive.

But his feeling of loss when he saw the Mayor's office in this tiny village had been more personal. It wasn't just the damage to the 19th century building that had left him with the grief of the bereaved. It was the death and destruction of this little community that was represented by this once grand structure standing starkly damaged against the grey skyline. Half of its roof and most of one side had been blasted away; just like so many of his friends. A force only of noise and rushing air, yet so powerful it could tear apart structures of stone and cement; and man.

Le Mairie had stood proudly dominant in the small square of Behagnies. The sturdy sandstone quoins and the carved Doric columns and moulded lintel of the elegant doorway had given the building a stately authority as it presided over the affairs of the community. Each Tuesday, in a tradition that had lasted for centuries and had survived various wars and deprivations, a market had been held in the square under the watchful eye of the mayor. In the last three years the farmers had braved the weather and the loss of so many of their young men, to defiantly bring into the village whatever produce they could gather.

Edward had recalled the colourful fruit and vegetables that he had seen on the stalls, the farmer's wives chattering incoherently, the children who came to help their mothers then chased each other round the donkey carts. He had thought about the times that he had sat on the bench and watched the villagers weaving their busy patterns of social interactions and business transactions in the square. He had remembered the frequency of the visits that the locals made to Le Mairie and wondered on their nature. But mostly, and most personally, he had remembered the Mayor, Jacques Planche, who had farmed a smallholding adjacent to where they had camped. He had been a man of huge energy, despite his years, and he had used a very limited knowledge of English to make the British soldiers feel very welcome in his village. The Mayor had frequented the small bar in the square and had willingly spent time with the visiting troops to teach them how to count in French, to exchange greetings or to order drinks.

Edward had got to know him quite well, the previous year, when they had been based in nearby Gomiecourt for six weeks. He had been detailed to go and assist Jacques in harvesting one of the fields in exchange for which they were allowed its use for some of their sports fixtures. After an arduous afternoon in the fields, Edward had been invited back to the farm for a glass of wine and, on the way, he had been delighted to come across a small sawmill. In no time, he had been reminiscing about his job in the Salford sawmill and the two men had then spent a relaxed hour discussing and gesticulating their way through the relative merits of English and French oak, the best cuts for pine and the advantages of sycamore in kitchen furniture. After that, they had become firm friends and Edward had spent as much time as he could in the company of Jacques and his welcoming family. His parting from them, when the Division had moved up to Belgium, had been painful and sad.

When, just a few days before, he had arrived back in Behagnies with his Battalion he had been barely able to recognise it. He had looked up and down the main street and around the square at the broken buildings and had felt a penetrating cold down his back as he realised that there was not a single villager in sight. Had they all fled or had some been killed? There was an eerie silence hanging over the village but the thunder of the artillery rumbled on from the direction of Bapaume. There was a feeling of death hanging over the broken buildings; the gaping mouths of their wounds open to the skies like the bodies of so many of his dead comrades had been, laid in the mud.

Apart from two dogs rummaging in a semi-demolished house further up the street and a cat watching them guardedly from the top of a wall in the square, there had been no signs of the busy village life that he had known.

There had been no chimney smoking, no garlic laden smells of cooking, no cries of children or their mothers. The German war machine had purged the village of human spirit and left behind lifeless rubble.

The Battalion had checked through all the buildings before taking up its defensive positions around the village. Unfortunately, because of the heavy volume of traffic on the roads, the British soldiers were still without the support of horses and vehicles, and communications between the Divisions had remained difficult. Reports had been coming through of the disposition of the enemy troops although many had proved inaccurate.

The Germans had attacked at dawn the following day along the whole of the front that the Division was holding. To the north, the 10th Manchesters had brought three companies through and had encountered men from the 40th Division in one of the trenches. These soldiers had been fighting for four days and, despite being totally exhausted, they joined with the Manchester men in taking the battle to the enemy.

It had been an uncanny experience for the soldiers moving up into the line. Behind them, the early morning sun had been bathing the relatively calm countryside and the birds had been singing their welcome to the day. Ahead of them a furious storm had raged as the German artillery spewed out its destructive power. Clouds of belching smoke from the guns, and the huge eruptions of debris, had rolled across the skies, blending with that from the fiercely burning landscape, and had cast great, night-black shadows over the approaching army.

That day the Germans had proved themselves to be a formidable fighting force but the training that the Salford Battalion had received had helped them to resist the attacks. The enemy soldiers had appeared, as expected, in very small groups on the skyline and had drifted down into the hollow, running and walking in different directions, but in a short time the British soldiers had been faced by a mass of Germans. Fortunately, the Battalion's machine gun crews had finally arrived after carrying their equipment for seven or eight miles because the transport had not been able to get through the chaos on the roads.

The British had been able to meet the German assault with rifle and machine gun fire but the open order approach that they had adopted had made them a difficult target. It was at close quarters that the bayonets of the Salford soldiers had finally repelled them. Elsewhere, some British battalions had started to fall back but an order was received from Divisional Command that the line had to be held and they had regrouped and resisted.

During the morning, the Germans had succeeded in breaking through further up the line and had taken the village of Sapignies. A company of the 7th Lancashire Fusiliers, another Battalion from Salford, and men from the 5th had been fighting valiantly to check their advance but the Germans had massed machine gun units in the area and the Lancashire soldiers were being decimated.

Edward and his company had then been transferred down to Sapignies at about 10.00 am and, after a bravely fought and cleverly devised battle, they had regained control of the village. As they had approached down a narrow, winding alley towards the square, they had been spotted by a German machine gun emplacement on the roof of a building flanking the square. Unfortunately for the enemy, Big Charlie, the Divisional potato lobbing champion and deadly accurate with a hand grenade, had been in another platoon that had skirted round and was coming down a different alley. It had been a mighty throw but the machine gun post was taken out with one grenade.

The noise had alerted the rest of the enemy troops, however, and the British soldiers had heard loud commands being shouted from a position to the south of the square. Almost instantly, hundreds of men had stumbled out of the bar, shouting loudly and tripping over their rifles. The German army had been a long time without food and even longer without alcoholic drink and they had found the large casks of vin rouge irresistible.

The inebriated soldiers had fought bravely but foolishly and, by the time their support arrived, the Salford men had gained an advantage. Shortly afterwards, the Germans had counterattacked and pushed, once again, through Sapignies only to be met on the other side by the 5th Manchesters who had driven them back into the village.

To the west of Sapignies, the small country roads had been growing increasingly congested as the day went on and, by midday, there was total gridlock. Nothing was moving anywhere and an artillery attack by the Germans would have been devastating. A solution had been needed urgently. The British army filled in ditches and cut down barbed wire and vehicles were sent across open fields. By the late afternoon, the traffic was on the move once more and the crisis had been averted.

All of that day the battle had raged over a wide front and villages had been lost and retaken only to be lost again. Artillery units had moved from one position to another and some had been wiped out. British planes had flown only feet above the ground and poured bullets into the German lines. In the afternoon, the British had brought tanks into the line with dramatic effect.

The casualties on both sides, particularly for the Germans, had been enormous but the British had been fighting against overwhelming odds and, gradually, their line had fallen back. That evening, the Salford soldiers of the 1/8 Lancashires had withdrawn reluctantly back to the Gomiecourt Ridge. During the course of the next two days, they had fallen back, step-by-step, to Ablainzeville and then Essarts.

No ground had been given easily or cheaply. Sometimes it had been conceded in order to lure the enemy into a trap of enfilading machine gun fire and on occasions they had retreated to higher ground to enfold the German soldiers into a welcoming and visible valley. As they had withdrawn, groups had held back and maintained a level of fire on the Germans, slowing down their advance and inflicting severe casualties. In one area the Allied soldiers had been ably assisted by the German artillery who had mistakenly poured shells down onto their own troops. The number of deaths had been very high.

The British soldiers had not wanted to give an inch, but they much preferred this open, intuitive style of warfare to the rigid posturing formations of the earlier years. They had suffered losses but they had dealt bloody and fatal blows to the enemy.

The policy of slow withdrawal by the Allies, fighting against such overwhelming odds, had created major problems for the Germans. Their armies had already been severely weakened by the heavy casualties, that were mounting rapidly, and now they had found that the scorched earth policy that they had practised as they had withdrawn the previous year to the Hindenburg Line was starving their own soldiers. Their men were seriously fatigued and demoralised and they needed rest and food. But the German supply lines were failing and there were no crops in the fields and no livestock in the barns, the locals had been driven from their homes and their villages destroyed, so there were no stores to loot. Their soldiers were going hungry whilst the British soldiers, even in the front line, were getting at least some hot meals.

As the German front had become stretched and weakened, the British troops had occupied trenches that had not been used for a year and the line was eventually established and held. During the following two days the Germans had launched eight attacks on the British lines but only once had they succeeded in entering the trenches. On that occasion, they had met with a fierce bayonet response from the Lancashire soldiers and most of the enemy were killed or captured.

Edward's battalion had finally gone into reserve at Gommecourt on the 29 March 1918 and the men, desperately tired after five days of almost continuous fighting, had enjoyed the few days' opportunity to catch up with some restless sleep and their restricted personal hygiene. They had eaten good meals, burnt the lice from the seams of their clothing, cleaned their equipment with Big Charlie's special cloths and collected their letters and parcels from home.

They had had the usual influx of new recruits into the ranks to replace the casualties; the fresh-faced and sparkling boys who had just come over from England with pristine uniforms and bursting enthusiasm and the grey faced, dead eyed men transferred from other battalions with stitched up uniforms supplemented by souvenirs collected from both British and German soldiers who now no longer had need of them. Each new batch had to be absorbed into the existing group and their skills understood and their style adapted. Each replacement brought something new but it was never enough to fill the gap left by the man who had gone. He didn't have the steel ties that strapped his fear; he didn't have the instinctive response to the tiniest facial movement that was the battlefield communication between long-serving soldiers and he didn't have the evolving understanding of strategy that experience provides. Most importantly, few of them had the grit of Salford coursing through their veins.

For three days the 1/8 Lancashires had enjoyed this chance to relax, to tend their wounded and bury their dead and then, on the 2 April, they had moved into the front line at Bucquoy. That night, they had launched an attack on some new German constructions and then at 2.00am they had combined with the 32nd Division and had made a successful attack on Ayette, captured two hundred prisoners and established a new line to the east of Ayette.

The next two days had been relatively quiet and the soldiers had done their best to improve the old trench that they now occupied. They had reinforced the parapets, repaired the dugouts, strengthened old flunk holes and built new ones, replaced the firing step where it had been washed away by the rain, reinstated the latrines and tried to build some drainage to help to clear the foot deep mud at the bottom of the trench. In parts, it had been difficult to follow the line of the trench because heavy shell fire had caused it to collapse and the men had had a major task to excavate it.

Then at 5 o'clock that morning, the 5 April 1918, in the dark before the light of the day began to streak the clouds, the tenuous calm had been pierced by the shriek of heavy artillery. Screaming shells had shredded the air above their trenches and thudded mercilessly into the distressed ground. They listened to the emerging drone of destruction, sensing its ultimate proximity by the arcing intensity of the sound. Their bodies were rocked by the thunderous roar as high explosive and gas shells blasted earth and men into the air. For hour after hour, the Germans had sustained this destructive downpour and the British troops had pressed back into their dugouts seeking the limited shelter that they could give.

The heavy, cold night air had pushed the gas immediately into the trenches and Edward had felt the burning throat and smarting eyes even as he was pulling on his mask. They were uncomfortable and restricting but they offered the only chance of protection against the poisonous vapours. The men had stumbled around in the dark and slipped on the water-logged duckboards as they had struggled to their watch positions or to help their injured friends.

The sky had become a symphony of flashing lights and glowing clouds, traced through by the fiery trails of the arcing shells. As the hours had passed, the stretcher bearers had trudged up the communications trench carrying their bloody burdens with increasing frequency. Progress through the deep mud became increasingly difficult and the soldiers' uniforms were coated with the stinking slime.

The light of day had revealed the grey gloom of gas and explosive clouds hanging only feet from the ground and the plumes of earth rising into the air as the shells rained down. Mud fell around them as they peered into the desolate landscape for signs of the inevitable attack and they listened keenly to the whistle of the shells to judge where they would land. It was always a comfort to hear the thud as it landed

Edward had coughed and spluttered inside his mask then lifted it briefly to sip some water. The deafening noise had numbed his senses; an iron band had tightened round his head.

The Germans had come at 8.00am. The mask had blurred Edward's vision. He had desperately wanted to remove it and wipe his face and his eyes. When he could see more clearly, he had picked out the grey uniforms emerging through the copse of trees. He had been struggling to regain control of his mind and focus on the fight for survival when he saw them swarming forward, rifles at the ready, grenades strapped to their bodies, knives sheathed at their sides. As they approached, he had seen the cold determination in their desperate faces and he knew then that these soldiers were playing their final card. The muscles in his neck and chest had tightened and a vein in the side of his head was thudding as he had lifted his rifle to prepare for the onslaught.

The machine guns were pouring bullets into the oncoming army and his mind was closing down when he had heard the familiar voice whispering in the depths of his body.

291

'Keep safe, Love' he had heard as the cataclysm had · descended.

The fighting had been ferocious and the German attack had been executed like a mindless machine. Their soldiers were men crazed by hunger, by fierce alcohol poured into empty stomachs and by a fear of the consequences of failure. They had been demented and inflamed. The Salford men had responded with a courage and pride that words would only humble. They had met steel with steel and they had overcome, they had responded to bullet with bullet and their enemy had fallen, and they had faced murderous insanity with determined and unflinching bravery. The blur of the battle, the frenetic fighting against hurling humanity, the shouted warnings, the screams of attackers and the cries of the dying had lasted for over an hour. They had stood shoulder to shoulder with their fellow Salfordians of the 1/7 Lancashires and looked into the staring, fanatical eyes and the spitting mouths, and the Lancashire bayonets had prevailed.

They had begun to push their way northwards up the trench but had, eventually, been forced back. The 1/8 Lancashires and the 10th Manchesters had suffered severe casualties on their left flank and these positions were now surrounded by the Germans.

The rest of the Lancashire men had withdrawn to the line which they now held and yearned for the cigarette that they couldn't smoke because of their masks. They had paired off and begun to sort through the casualties.

They were still processing the dead and attending to the injured in the deep mud of the trenches when the order came through that they had to clear the enemy out of the lines immediately. The two brothers were listed as 'KIA', their identity cards were filed and their bodies were laid side-by-side on the cart ready for burial. The men who had shared so much in their lives would now be embraced into eternity by the same piece of war ravaged French soil.

It was 11.40am and the men were weary and hungry but their determination was strong. They sensed that a corner had been turned and they felt a powerful need to press home their advantage. A wind had now lifted the gas away from the trenches and they gratefully removed their masks. They strapped on their rounds of ammunition and their grenades, shouldered their packs, cleaned the mud off their rifles and within minutes they were on their way.

By midday they had pushed through to the crossroads in the centre of Bucquoy where the Germans held a strong position. A pole carrying the power lines hovered like a crucifix over the tattered remnants of what had been a large gate guarding the entrance to a farm. Two huge stone gate posts with a plank slung perilously between them now flanked the littered entrance through the crumbled remains of a farm wall. Facing it on the adjacent corner stood the shattered remains of a French family's home. Half the house had been blown away revealing dusty, muslin drapes hanging listlessly over where the bed had stood. Splintered floorboards and the rubble of the walls were scattered around the garden alongside oil lamps, cushions and battered pots and pans. A large oak table and two spindle back chairs stood in the remains of the kitchen where a peeling, green wooden shelf swung on one retaining screw.

Down the street a solitary chair stood outside a door, its occupant long since gone, and across the road a ladder, serving a now forgotten purpose, leant into an upstairs window. Beyond the ladder, a German army motorbike stood against the house wall and the front of an armoured vehicle protruded out from a side street.

The Lancashire soldiers knew that, although there was no sign of them, the Germans were well embedded in the village and it would need a major effort to remove them. But the British army had gained enormous experience of fighting outside of the confining trenches and they also felt that they were fighting an increasingly demoralised enemy. The Germans had suffered massive losses in the last two weeks since they had launched their major attack to break the stalemate. Their assault had now faltered and their troops were being repelled. Most importantly, the Germans also knew that the Americans were moving troops into the Western Front giving the Allies a huge reserve of manpower to face a nation whose stock was being rapidly depleted.

The Lancashire men were deployed and the attack was launched but the response from the Germans was fierce. They inflicted heavy damage on the Salford Batallion with their strategically placed machine gun posts but the Lancashire soldiers slowly ground away their advantage with ferocious hand-to-hand fighting. Two platoons of the 5th Lancashires were brought up to lend support and yard-by-yard the village was repossessed.

For eight hours the fighting continued relentlessly and by the evening of the 5 April a line was gained and held and the fighting gradually came to a halt. With the red glow of the setting sun behind them mockingly turning the whole area into a semblance of a dying furnace, the smoke from still burning houses lending their grudging support to the illusion, the British soldiers collected the dead and wounded. They gave the same respect to the German corpses as they did to their own, except to occasionally relieve them of their unwanted boots, daggers and badges.

The German campaign had started to weaken. Under mounting pressure at home and growing unrest in their army, they had launched a massive attack to break the Allied resistance. Their Commanders had dreamt of marching triumphantly into Paris and subjugating the French nation and its colonies. They had failed.

Edward and Big Charlie hobbled back into the village giving each other mutual support. They were returning from the advanced dressings station after having their wounds treated. Big Charlie was shouldering Edward's rucksack as well as his own because Edward had a sprained shoulder and a cut forearm. Big Charlie was using Edward's other shoulder as a support because he had a badly gashed calf muscle.

Big Charlie was muttering about the 'bleeding iodine' and his conviction that the medics applied it so liberally just for a laugh. Edward's eyes were darting everywhere as he sought the whereabouts of Liam. He had seen his friend earlier whilst he had been waiting with Big Charlie in the minor wounds queue. Liam had been having a head wound attended to but he had since disappeared.

They asked many people if they had seen him until eventually somebody remembered 'the little fella with his head bandaged up' and pointed in the direction of the crossroads. Edward found Liam huddled down in the kitchen of the derelict house, his rifle propped between his legs, the clean bandage on his head contrasting starkly with his dishevelled and torn uniform, now covered in dried mud and dust. He had pushed his helmet back and was picking dried blood off the hair that was protruding from beneath the bandage. A tear had scoured a clean path down his dusty cheek and he stared fixedly at a photograph of the family that had lived there, still hanging on a nail on the opposite wall.

The two men sat down at either side of him and Edward looked at the photograph. There were three generations of the family posing in their best outfits. Grandma and Grandad sat proudly in the centre with a grandchild on each knee. At their side was a young teenage girl and behind the grandparents were the Mother, holding a baby, and the Father – both in their late thirties. The sepia coloured print showed a family who were proud of their standing in the village and enjoyed some minor affluence as the owners of the village shop that they now posed in front of. Staring at the photograph, Edward realised that the building in the picture was the one that they were now sitting in but the whole of the front had been blown away by a shell.

In a shaft of the fading sunlight a dust cloud hovered in wraiths over the three men like the fretful spirits of past owners. A small bird bounced inquisitively along the shelf of an oak dresser. Edward shuddered as he saw a green chenille tablecloth, like the one that they had at home, discarded carelessly in the corner.

He tried to interpret his friend's distant thoughts as they stared at the photograph. 'I expect that they managed to escape before the Germans came, but there won't be much left to come back to.'

'Aye,' Liam replied abruptly.

'He's probably in the army somewhere,' Edward tried again 'but the old man looks fit enough to have got things sorted out for the rest of the family.'

'Aye, maybe.'

'She looks a bit like your Brig,' Big Charlie said, cutting incisively to Liam's troubling thoughts. 'She looks tough enough to look after them all.'

Liam glanced up at his big friend. 'I'm not going back,' he said.

They looked at him, astonished. 'You're not going back where?' Edward finally asked.

'I'm not going back home, to Brig and the kids.' The words were eked painfully out of his strained throat.

Big Charlie's wide eyes quizzed the little man and his mouth opened and closed as he sought the words that would formulate his concern at this outrageous statement. Finally he spluttered, 'Are you going barmy or summat? Has that cut damaged your brain?'

'No, it bloody hasn't.'

'Then why are you coming out with stupid bloody remarks like that then?'

Liam's lips clamped tightly together. Big Charlie's insensitive approach had driven him back into his hunched-up, glowering contemplation of the photograph.

'She needs you, mate,' Edward said quietly. 'That's what is keeping her going – waiting for you to come back.'

'She's waiting for the person that left four years ago. And I'm not him.'

'None of us are, Liam,' Edward said, reflecting the words that Liam had said to him a year before. 'We've all changed. But we've done what we've had to do and we've done it for them – to give them a proper life.'

Liam was incensed by Edward's glib assertion. 'What proper life is that? Scrimping and scraping to make ends meet so that people like that Major sodding Gobshite can live a life of luxury and Jimmy Pearce's widow will be skivvying for Gobshite's wife? Does that bastard care when your kids are ill and you can't afford to get the doctor? Will he be full of charity for the poor sods who've had their legs blown off when they can't afford their rent? No bloody chance.'

'Aye, you're right' Edward said appeasingly. 'There's a lot going to have to change after all this is over. But it's not going to solve anything just walking out on our families.'

Liam leant back on to the wall, his eyes closed. 'I'm sorry, Eddie. It's not what I was meaning. I'm not walking out on them. I just can't go back to Brig.'

'Well, I'm sorry, mate' Edward said, slightly exasperated. 'But I seem to be missing the point here. What else is that if it's not walking out on her?'

Liam was quiet for a long time before he pushed himself forward and got to his feet. He stood in front of his two friends and his hands clenched as he said fiercely, 'It's those bloody kids. Did you look in the eyes of those Germans today? Some of them were not much older than our kids at home. They were scared bloody stiff. They've got Mams at home who are fearing for their sons. Mams like Brig and Laura.'

A breeze was rustling the leaves of some old magazines that were on the floor and Edward felt a cold chill settle on him. 'It's the same as before though, Liam. Most of them don't want to be there but, now they are, they are out to kill us. It's dog eat dog in this situation.'

'I know that. But it's made me realise just how low I've sunk. We're worse than animals. You block it out so that you can get through but I feel dirty now. We're putting bayonets through fifteen and sixteen year old kids. That makes us worse than the rats in the trenches. I could never look Brig in the eye again. I could never bear to even touch her again for fear I would contaminate her. Do you think that she would respect me if I told her that we had been killing young boys, but I did it for her? She would despise me.'

Edward felt helpless to respond to his friend's arguments. Big Charlie sucked in his lips and frowned. 'I can't see that about the rats. Foxes maybe,' he said. 'Foxes just kill for the sake of it.'

The other two stared at him in astonishment. 'Since when did you become an expert on wildlife, then?' queried Edward.

'They used to come on my Grandad's allotment. They'd kill the chickens and then just leave them there,' Big Charlie responded.

'So I should say that I feel worse than the foxes in the field then?' Liam questioned, frustrated by this distraction.

'Well, maybe. The difference is that we are doing what we are just to survive but foxes don't. They do it because they are mischievous little sods and they'll keep at it until somebody shoots them.'

'Well it doesn't make any difference whether it's a fox or a rat,' Liam said, returning to his enveloping gloom. 'Brig wouldn't want either of them in her house, never mind in her bed.'

'Your Brig is not daft, you know. She knows what's going on and she's tougher than you think sometimes,' Big Charlie rejoined. 'I remember when she was a kid and she battered a lad in our street who was bullying her young brother. Clouted me once, as well, when I pinched some of her chips. She knows what's going on out here, like they all do. If she'd have been asked she would have been out here with the rest of us.'

He sat back suddenly, exhausted by his lengthy diatribe. A faint smile crept across Edward's face. He had not heard the big man speak for so long since Liam had knocked a crib board over in The Railway when Charlie had been holding two sevens and two eights and a seven had been turned up. He also remembered the fearsome punch that Bridget Gallagher had thrown at Big Charlie and it wasn't just her chips that he had been trying to pinch. Big Charlie had told his mother that it had been an Irish hooligan that had given him the black eye.

Liam shrugged, picked up his gear and walked out.

29 Myrtle Street
Cross Lane
Salford 5
Great Britain

24th March 1918

Dear Dad,
	Thank you for your 'Happy Christmas' but it wasn't so good this year. We had a chicken off Uncle Jim's allotment and we were lucky to get that because two of them had already been pinched by the time it came to Christmas. Mam said that geese are only for rich people these days. Uncle Jim has been growing lots of potatoes like the government has been asking you to do and Mam said that he is good at it because his grandad was Irish. I told our teacher and she said that it is not good to depend on one thing because a lot of Irish people starved to death when they had a potato famine and that was because the crops caught a blight. I think that Mr Harrison in the next street must have this disease because I heard Mrs Harrison telling the woman next door that her Ernie had blighted her life.
	A boy called Jimmy from the Mission was birched by the police last week for stealing from a shop. Mam said it is wrong to steal but the kids are starving and she bets that the magistrate is being fed well enough. Jimmy said that he was lucky because one of the other lads was put in the navy and sent to sea. I think, though, that he might at least get well fed and he will see lots of places around the World.
	Round here, you're alright if your Dad works on the docks because they didn't go in the army and the girls at school say that their Dads are always finding things lying around on the docks that they bring home. But for everybody else, you have to rely on granddads and older uncles else you've had it. I think that is why Jimmy was pinching stuff, because his Grandad is dead and his Dad has gone missing somewhere and now his Mam is ill.

Dad, when is this war going to finish? It's not fair.

I have heard of Mrs Pankhurst but Mam says that she is working with the government now to beat the Germans. Mam said that they've all got a shock coming to them when the war is over because the men will come home wanting their jobs back but the women won't want to be pushed down again. It's nearly all women conductors on the trams now and everybody says that they do a good job, so why should they be pushed out of them? At least they smile at you and they don't snot their noses on the floor like some of the men because the women take the trouble to carry handkerchiefs.

Our Sadie is good at reading now and she is helping our Mary. Our Ben got the cane at school last week for kicking a football through a window. He said that he hadn't been playing football and he was only hiding in the cupboard to stay out of the way.

I didn't really understand 'Little Women' but our teacher was pleased because I showed an interest. I am reading a book about the Romans at the moment but the people sound so boring. Why don't they have interesting books for children?

Those socks were blissful when the weather was really cold so I hope that you don't mind that I had them instead of you.

Love

Laura

Big Charlie's face was contorted by a series of deep furrows which ran from the screwed up contemplative forehead down to the pursed lips. He was staring at the letter that he had received that morning and at regular intervals his shoulders rose up and he emitted a deep thoughtful sigh. He sat on an empty ammunition container outside the dug out with his elbows resting on his broad knees. His brown hair was stuck up in unruly spikes where he kept ruffling it as if trying to stimulate some mental activity that was so far eluding him.

Edward and Liam watched their friend's agitation with increasing apprehension. Liam was clearly anxious to probe further and repeatedly made to start the questions that were burning him. It was clear, though, from Big Charlie's distant demeanour that he would not be subjected to interrogation and Liam's questions hung unspoken in the air.

Eventually he stuffed the letter into his top pocket and reached down for his rifle and his cleaning kit. He spent the next half hour meticulously cleaning and polishing the weapon whilst his friends indulged a favourite pastime of recounting childhood memories in the hope of gaining the interested participation of Big Charlie.

'Do you remember that time when Tommy Ten Pints came out of the Craven Heifer and he walked straight off the flags and into the cart road?' asked Edward.

'Do you mean when he didn't see that horse until it bumped into him and he turned round and smacked it on the nose?' Liam rejoined.

'Aye, that's it. And the carter tried to crack Tommy with his whip and instead he lashed the horse across its face.'

'Yeah. Next minute the horse was up on its back legs and all the crates came rolling off the cart,' Liam enthused.

'I've never seen so many oranges in my life before. All rolling down Cross Lane trying to escape' Edward recalled.

'Aye. You had to feel a bit sorry for the carter, though. The poor sod was trying to pick up his oranges and hold on to the reins at the same time.'

'It didn't turn out too bad though,' chuckled Edward. 'We had orange butties for our tea that night.'

The disinterested Big Charlie remained unmoved. Completing his cleaning, he placed the rifle on one side and folded his cloths. He took a sip of the tea that had been poured into his chipped enamel cup and resumed his contemplation of the letter.

Suddenly, he stood up and walked over to Liam, handing him the letter. 'Here. Have a look at that. Looks as though we're both going nowhere. Only difference is you've got a choice.'

Liam read the letter then passed it over to Edward without comment. Edward looked at the plain white sheet on which faint pencil lines had been ruled. Along these a neat, feminine script delivered a slightly confusing message with a fairly direct end.

> *Dear Charlie,*
> *You big, daft, stupid man. You make me the laughing stock of all the neighbours and then you have the nerve to send me a letter as though it's from a solicitor. It's not me that has done anything wrong – it's you who threw that poor Mr Snelgrove into the horse trough. Now I have had to leave the Glee Club because I couldn't bear the humiliation and I will never again be able to enjoy the humbling reward of the ripple of applause in appreciation of my small talents.*
> *I have never asked much of you, Charlie. I've fetched and carried for you and always made sure that you have had a hot meal on the table when you came in and clean underpants in the drawer. If that is not enough to show that I love you then what is?*

But what thanks do I get for that? What do I get in return? Somebody who comes barging in like a madman and, without a by your leave, assaults a paying guest, a man of great musical talent and a gentle disposition.

Now, after causing me so much embarrassment that I have had to move house twice because of the gossiping neighbours, you send me a letter that doesn't contain a sow's ear of sincerity in it. All this on top of that dreadful pantomime at the workhouse is almost too much to bear and sometimes I think you care more for your pigeons than you do me. Well I'm sorry to say that they have gone because I couldn't move house with those as well.

Perhaps now you'll put more of your attention on to me and understand that I have needs as well. It's not proving you're a man throwing around gentlemen of a generous nature who are so thin that you could spit through them without wetting them. I want you to show me you are a proper man, Charlie. Just come home and overwhelm me and give me babies like normal married couples. Now.

Love
Dot

Edward folded the letter thoughtfully and handed it back to Big Charlie. 'Well, she looks as though she might be happy to have you back, Charlie. Perhaps you should try and get a bit of compassionate leave. Say your Mam's been taken bad or something.'

'No,' said Big Charlie firmly. 'That would just be a waste of time.'

Edward was slightly taken aback by his friend's curtness. 'Why's that then?'

'Well, I'd need a long leave. There's no address on the letter.'

Vauchelles
France
9th April 1918

My Darling Little Pippin,

 I can't tell you how nice it was to receive your letter and those from the rest of the family. I have read them over and over again because they give me a lot of strength. We have just had a few very difficult days and reading about life at home helps me to get back to reality. Sometimes it seems a bit hard to think what normal life was like back in England so your letters are a big help. I know that you must be wondering sometimes what on Earth we are doing out here and, when you read about them in the paper, you must think that some of the things that we do are pretty terrible. But please believe me Darling when I say that we are doing what is necessary to defend our freedoms and keep you all safe at home. Our supposed betters have got us into this war and now we must see it through or else the Germans will take over Britain and our Empire and our country will be ruined.

 We are not heroes, Darling. We are just ordinary working class men doing what we have to do to build a better future for our children. Please don't let it be in vain. Try to make the most of your chances and your education. The world won't change overnight but, please God, the sacrifices being made will be worth something for you and for your children after you.

 I think that your Mam is right when she says that the women will not want to give up their jobs when the men come home. The men will have to remember that a lot of women are widows with young families and they will have to work to support themselves. We will all have to work together and then we will build a better future.

 I am sorry that you did not have a very good Christmas. We were quite lucky; our Christmas dinner was very nice although we didn't have it until Boxing Day because we were on duty. We also had a Christmas concert which was organised by a group of the soldiers. They asked me if I would do a song but I think that they might have been sorry if I had done. Some of the men were dressed as women and they were hilarious. They nearly all had moustaches and their voices were too deep but the funniest thing was their dancing. They were falling over their own feet.

I suppose size 10 boots don't help. We had a comedian who came over from England and he had appeared once at the Hippodrome on Cross Lane and he gave us a good laugh. There was a soldier from Newcastle called Our Willie who played an accordion. He was brilliant. We all enjoyed a good sing-song.

I know this war is not fair, Darling, as you say in your letter, but life does send a lot of challenges that we have to face up to and beat. When we overcome them we gain a new strength which helps us to face the next problems that arise and that makes us better human beings. People who are born with everything have nothing to gain and their lives are the emptier for it. Be brave, my little one, and hopefully soon things will start to get better.

I am really pleased that the socks stopped you getting chilblains. I think that it is really clever of you to knit them because your Mam has told me that it is very difficult to knit on four needles.

Pippin, I want you to do a little favour for me but this must be another little secret between us. Will you have a word with Billy Murphy and ask him if he ever writes a letter to his Dad. I don't think that he does, so suggest that he writes and tells his Dad the news and also how much he misses him. It could be very important but don't tell him that I suggested it.

Love

Dad

Liam's mood vacillations seemed to get more extreme. Any form of sporting competition would lift him to an irrepressible level. His wit was sharp and often acerbic and his voice reflected his fever pitch enthusiasm. His energy sparked from him and those around him either allowed themselves to be caught up in it or they wilted under its heat.

When the confrontation was with the enemy, however, whether in hand-to-hand fighting or the more normal artillery bombardment or even just manning the front line trenches, his mood became dark and withdrawn. It was as though some powerful force was pressing in on him, his skin became grey and his eyes flat and empty. For days on end, he would hardly speak to anybody and his friends opted to remain at a comfortable distance. When Major Fforbes-Fosdyke arrived one day so drunk that he could barely dismount from his horse and delivered a lecture full of meaningless platitudes on the need for courage in this noble warfare, Edward could see that Liam was shaking with barely contained anger.

Unfortunately, the Major, misjudging the feelings of deep antagonism felt by the men around him, told them, in a preening, self-congratulatory performance, that he had been mentioned in dispatches and recommended for a MC in recognition of the heroic way he had led the troops in the Battle for Bapaume.

The volcano inside Liam erupted and he waved an accusing finger at the Major as he raged at this injustice. 'You weren't even around at Bapaume. You had disappeared like you always do as soon as there is even a whiff of a German,' he roared. 'How could you be mentioned for anything when the only action that you ever see is in the bar?'

The red faced and seriously discomfited Major grabbed his batman's arm. 'Arrest him and have him charged with treason,' he ordered.

Liam's face was now taut with fury and his eyes stared with a dangerous madness. He waved his clenched fist at the Major and screamed in his rage. 'What about some recognition for the thousands of poor sods who've died fighting on the front line? The only decoration that they will get will be a wooden cross.'

Edward put his hand on Liam's shoulder to restrain him but he shook it off. 'Our men are having to stick bayonets into German boys with bum fluff on their chins,' he shouted, now waving both fists, 'but the only people that you ever killed were British soldiers. Have they mentioned the Hennessy kid in the dispatches? You shouldn't be decorated, you lily livered bastard, you should be shot for cowardice.'

A stunned silence hung in the air for a moment before others joined in the condemnation of the now twittering, slavering officer. The agitated major, panting like a cornered prey, suddenly took out his pistol and pointed it at Liam. He stepped forward but fortunately the batman's stray foot impeded his progress and he fell forward accompanied by much laughter and applause from the surrounding soldiers.

The next day the military police arrived and arrested Liam but the case against him collapsed when the only evidence that could be obtained was relating to the Major's obviously drunken condition.

Liam later went to see the chaplain to discuss his inner turmoil. The letter that he had received from young Billy had thrilled him but it had added to his confusion. The value that his son placed upon him as a father, a mentor and a friend only made him feel less worthy of that role. He felt inadequate to his son's expectations of a principled hero. He now felt a deep shame about what he perceived as his own complicity in the destruction of the moral framework that had structured his early life in the Catholic Salford Cathedral and school and that had informed his recent years as a husband and father.

The chaplain was sympathetic but had his own struggles as he tried to preserve a state of grace for vast numbers of British, and occasionally German, deaths. He told Liam that there had been many Christian martyrs who had fought for freedom and justice and they couldn't just walk away, especially as, at last, the war seemed to be turning in favour of the Allies. However, he reminded him of the importance that the Church placed on the family and the duty that he owed to his wife and children.

Liam had a wailing in his mind that could not escape. When, in his darkest moods, he tried to draw strength from thoughts of his wife he would see her loving grey eyes and he would look for repose in them but they would suddenly be the frightened blue eyes of German boys. Then faces would pass in front of him like the pages of a book. Dark brown faces with shining, passionate eyes; arrogant faces with snarling mouths; pale, white faces with burning hatred in their eyes; haughty, superior faces with steely, disdainful eyes. They had all wanted to kill him first.

29 Myrtle Street
Cross Lane
Salford 5
Great Britain

20th May 1918

Dear Dad,

Thank you for the birthday postcard and the present from you and Mam. I am eleven now and I don't feel much different but Mam said that I am allowed a more grown up dress because I am going to be a young lady soon. Well she actually says that I am a bit of a Madam sometimes, so I suppose that means the same thing.

Dad, what extra things was you allowed to do when you were eleven? Mam said that you were working on the cattle market when you were eleven. Apart from doing my scholarships there's nothing else that is any different for me because I still have to go downstairs on the tram, I still have to come in for seven o'clock and our Edward won't let me play cricket with them in Ordsall Park because he says that I'm too young. So what is the point of being more grown up when the only extra thing that I'm allowed to do is to take our Mary to Sunday School?

When I was playing tops in Billy Murphy's back yard there was a horrible, horrible crying noise from next door's yard. I was playing tops because you had asked me to go and see him and he has made a top with all patterns on that he has done with different colours of paint out of his shed. It's really brilliant because when you whip it really hard it goes nearly white. So we got a ladder and climbed up to look over the wall and the man next door was holding some little parcels wrapped in bits of cloth under water in a white bucket. When he saw us he said that he was doing some washing, but the parcels were squeaking and the cat was sat on the lavatory roof crying. Billy said that we should go and tell the police because he was murdering the kittens but his Mam said

310

that perhaps he was just seeing to some rats. I helped Billy write a letter to his Dad. He hadn't sent him one because he said his Mam wrote and told him everything.

I am good at keeping secrets because I never told anybody, apart from Mam. When I heard Mrs Willoughbyl telling Mrs Jones about the butcher and the woman who reads palms on Trafford Road, Mam said that I had to keep that a secret and I never told anybody apart from Amy, who is my best friend so that is alright, and you because you are my Dad and you are in France.

I am working hard at school, but we just want you to come back before anything happens to you. Some of the girls at school have Dads who have been killed and I feel a bit frightened when it happens. They stay off school for a bit, which isn't bad, but after a few days you know that something terrible has happened to them and one of the girls now has all sores on her hands. Mam is missing you as well, and sometimes I hear her crying at night. She says that she has had a bad dream but it's always more if your letters haven't arrived. My friend Amy says that we should write to the King and ask him to talk to their King and tell them to stop fighting because our Edward said they belong to the same family. I think it might be better to write to their mother so that she can boss them into stopping.

Our Edward has been chucked by his girlfriend because there was a butcher's boy from Weaste who had a nicer bike. There is a girl in the top class at Sunday School who told me that she likes him but our Edward said that she is too old because she is nearly sixteen. I think that he is frightened of her because he won't go down her street now.

Come back soon. Mam says that perhaps I can have another rabbit when you come home.

Love

Laura

Sailly
France
14th June 1918

My Darling Pippin,

It was so nice to get your letter this morning and it was just in time because we are moving out of this place tomorrow. We have been doing some training here for the last few days and some young lads have joined us from England. One of them comes from Turner Street where your Grandma lives. Things are looking a bit better over here now. The Germans had a big push at the end of March and took a lot of territory but now we are pushing them back. Everybody is feeling more hopeful now. The Germans seem to be getting a little bit weaker so maybe it won't be too long before it is all over.

Darling, if you and your Mam get the chance to make some cakes for the men over here they would be very much appreciated. The food is not too bad but it is mostly tins of bully beef and some potatoes or dried biscuits. Occasionally we have a stew or perhaps a bit of tripe. The Army can't buy anything locally because the land is so devastated by the shelling that there is not enough food for the local people.

It's very sad when you see the villages. There were lots of beautiful old buildings but now they have been so badly damaged that it will be impossible to restore most of them. I don't know how the people will go on when all this is finished because the heart is being ripped out of their communities. I am just glad that this hasn't spread to England. I know things are a bit hard in Salford but we have a better chance of building our futures than the poor people over here.

I was trying to remember what I did when I was eleven and I think that, like you, there was not much difference to when I was ten. I already had a little job on the cattle market and met lots of interesting people. I went to school and I played a lot of football. Your Aunty Sarah used to make me help her to do the washing on a Saturday morning. She used to light the boiler in the cellar and I would pound the clothes in the dolly tub. She

312

used to crack me round the ear if I did it too hard because she said that I would tear them and then I would have to learn how to do stitching. The trouble is that I was always in a hurry so that I could go and play football. I don't remember feeling any different either. When you are nine then eleven seems very old but when you get to eleven it doesn't seem much different. Because the change is so gradual you don't notice it yourself but I haven't seen you much in the last four years so I know that there has been a big change. I know, both from your letters and from the photo that your Mam sent me, that you are growing up to be a lovely young lady and I am very proud of all of you.

I was sorry to hear about the girls at school who have lost their Dads but I am trying very hard to stay safe and hope it will not be too long before I am home. If you see your Mam looking very sad then put your arms round her neck and give her a big kiss from me. Tell her that the kiss fairy has been with a special delivery from France. Please be brave, my little angel, and pray to God that this terrible war will be over soon so that we can all be together again.

Love

Dad

Chapter 16

Serre 22nd August 1918

The Lancashire Fusiliers had been involved in intense fighting for almost two days and they were tired to the point of dropping. The heat during the day had been oppressive and the Germans had responded to the Allied attacks with massive artillery bombardments, including thousands of gas shells. But the British and New Zealand troops in the area were enjoying a level of success in taking the fight to the larger German army that they had not seen for years and they were now anxious to drive home this advantage.

They were elated to see the enemy retreating slowly over the land that they had taken four months before and the Germans were paying a high price in casualties. It had taken almost three weeks for the Allies to push them back only four miles but their attack was gaining momentum and they were keen to maintain the impetus. They had waited so long for this moment to arrive that they did not want to let it go and desperate tiredness was held back by adrenaline.

The counter attacks from the Germans had been massive and destructive but the British soldiers were not to be denied. They had repulsed every assault and held all the line that they had gained apart from a patch of high ground known as Beauregard Dovecote. The building that had housed the doves had long since gone and all that remained were the mutilated trees that had once surrounded it.

The Dovecote had no aesthetic merit whatsoever but it had a great strategic importance. It stood on a hill overlooking Miraumont – a small town garrisoned by the Germans as a part of their line which followed the direction of the River Ancre down to Albert. The Allies needed to control Beauregard Dovecote so that they could push through to Miraumont but the Germans were determined to hold on to it.

In a heroic assault on the previous afternoon, the soldiers of the 1/7 Lancashires had taken the Dovecote as a part of the gains made along the whole line. At 2.30am that morning, however, the Germans had launched a thunderous artillery bombardment along the whole of the Allied front around Serre which lasted for almost two hours. In the ensuing counter attack, the British troops had been overwhelmed and the Dovecote was regained by the Germans.

At 8.30am there had been another massive counter attack launched by the Germans. They were trying to regain sections of the line but they had been repulsed with huge losses. Four machine gun posts had been placed in forward positions and, as the enemy troops attacked in waves, they were taken in enfilade fire by the Lancashire soldiers. Eventually, two hundred German troops were forced to give themselves up to a New Zealand Division.

Later that day, the Germans mounted another attack but once again they were thrown back. The enemy had suffered heavy losses during these counter attacks and the Allies had retained all the ground that they had gained with the exception of the Dovecote.

Now the British soldiers were reinforcing their lines, bringing up supplies and ammunition, and desperately hoping that they would get a few minutes to snatch some sleep. Later Frank Williams, now a Lieutenant, came and told them that they would be going with two companies of the 10th Manchesters, a Battalion formed in Oldham, to retake the Dovecote.

'What a team, eh,' Liam observed. 'Salford and the roughyeds. The Boche will soon be running down that hill.'

Williams went over the detail of the planned attack with great care and pointed out the routes that each platoon would take and the various places that they knew were being used by the Germans for machine gun emplacements. Over the last year, the approach to an attack had evolved to recognise the circumstances and weaponry of this current war. The British had also learnt some important lessons from the Germans including the concept of the storm troops and they had introduced them with devastating effect.

Now, the philosophy of attack was of small, responsive units which, whilst working within an overall plan, enjoyed a much greater degree of local control. The soldiers could react more quickly to situations as they developed on the ground and they worked effectively as part of a team.

Edward was to lead a platoon that would approach, with the other Salford groups, up the left side whilst the Oldham men would go up on the right. They were given the exact positions of their first and second objectives and zero hour was set at 2.30am the following morning.

Edward didn't get any sleep. He was coughing badly and it was worse when he lay down. The hot, still days had not allowed all the gas to clear and they had unwittingly come through pockets of it. He lit a cigarette and inhaled deeply. The warm smoke was soothing.

He felt apprehensive about the attack that they were about to launch because he knew that they would be approaching from a lower, exposed position. He did, however, feel confident in the team that he had around him. Big Charlie had proved himself to be a brave, stalwart friend and support with an uncannily accurate talent for throwing grenades.

Liam's courage was unquestionable. He was tenacious and determined in attack but the constant, good humoured banter in stressful situations that, in the past, had so often helped to reduce the tension, was now missing. He had, alarmingly, issued a challenge, once this show was over, to the athletic giants of the New Zealand Division for a game of rugby. On another occasion, after drinking in an estaminet in a small French town, he had told a fresh faced young officer who had enquired as to the whereabouts of the toilets, to join the group of men who were sitting on the stairs. When, finally, his turn came, the nervous young man was shocked to discover that he had been waiting in the five franc queue for the services of one of the establishment's ladies.

Although Edward knew that he could rely on Liam implicitly when they were in any action, he worried deeply about the dark, thunderous gloom that he withdrew into as soon as they were away from the front line. Liam now never wrote to his wife, whom he loved to the point of worship, but for whom he felt himself unworthy. Whenever the rest of the men received mail, Liam would disappear and Edward knew, from the smell on his breath, that he had been drinking.

More worryingly, Edward felt that he himself was now being drawn down into this darkness. He had tried many times to find a way to help Liam but the efforts only exposed Edward's own fragile methods of coping. Like most of the men, he now tried not to think about his family and his home except when receiving or sending letters. Then he wallowed for a while in the love that he felt and in the pain and misery of separation. But Liam's determination to confront what he perceived as the collapse in those ethical values that he felt his wife cherished in him, had left Edward with increasingly disturbing doubts about himself.

When they were involved in any action with the enemy, Liam's mood now changed to the point that, at times, he seemed almost crazed. The fear that had slowly developed in Edward's mind, that his friend was inviting injury, had grown into the numbing realisation that Liam was suicidal. An injury itself would not resolve his mental turmoil. It would have to be terminal.

317

The breakfast was fit for a king. They had French eggs, Irish bacon and Bury black puddings with some army baked fried bread. They were in Loupart Wood near Grevillers, to the north east of Miraumont, and the breakfast had been conjured up for them by the inventive catering corps as a late evening treat. It was a reward for the success of the previous night.

The operation had gone well and, in just less than half an hour, they had regained control of Beauregard Dovecote. Casualties had been high on both sides but the Lancashire soldiers fought with the spirited ferocity of a boxer who knows that he has gained the upper hand and burns to finish off his opponent. They had taken fifty German prisoners and captured eight machine guns and a Field Dressing Station.

In the end, the Germans had seemed almost grateful to have been captured and, with a man on each corner of a blanket, they cheerfully carried their wounded down to the British lines for treatment. They happily submitted to the irony of having their wounds treated by British medics using captured German equipment and they were awed by the food that they received for their meals. They explained that the German soldiers were almost starving because of the failure of their supply lines.

Early in the day, the Allied soldiers had mounted a successful attack on Miraumont. Edward's Battalion had moved through on the left flank of the pincer movement which had advanced following the bombardment of the town by the British artillery. Stories were now coming through of how many of the Germans had been almost anxious to give themselves up.

Spirits were high amongst the Allied soldiers but the drawn faces and the black, sunken eyes betrayed the lack of sleep.

Edward noticed the number of his comrades that were, like him, almost constantly coughing. They had been caught a few times by the gas when they had thought an area was clear. Small clouds of it would lie in ditches and copses, or it would drift in on a breeze during the night. Now they all had gas masks, although they didn't always manage to get them on in time. He remembered when they had first arrived in Northern France and they had all been fascinated by the green cloud that had been rolling slowly towards them.

'Its chlorine,' a sapper had shouted out. 'Pee on your hankies and fasten them over your faces. That will protect you.'

'I've only just been,' Edward had protested. 'Am I going to die because I can't pee?'

'Pass me your hankie and I'll do yours as well,' Big Charlie had offered with immediate generosity.

Edward had hesitated for a moment as he considered the implications of this offer. 'Errh, no. It's OK Charlie, thanks. I think that I might be able to squeeze another one out, after all.'

Assisted by the stimulating sight of the gradually approaching green cloud of chlorine gas, Edward had managed a modest flow. It had inhibited, but not totally stopped, the gas intake.

Edward glanced up and saw Liam sitting about thirty feet away, both hands clasped round his enamel cup, shoulders hunched forward and a cigarette dangling from his lips. His whole being seemed to be gripped by some deep gloom.

Frank Williams wandered up to the group. 'It's not been a bad day. We're in Miraumont, thanks to you lads. You did a good job taking the Dovecote. There is a downside though.'

'What's that?' enquired Big Charlie. 'Have we got to clear them out of Bapaume by tomorrow morning?'

'Not quite,' laughed Williams. 'There's hundreds of prisoners and they're eating us out of house and home. Poor sods haven't eaten properly for weeks'

'I'll have to write to the missus then,' Edward said. 'See if she can organise the women at Central Mission to come up with some cakes.'

'Well, they've done a pretty good job in the past,' replied the Lieutenant. 'But there's some more interesting news.'

He paused with a theatrical silence. 'Come on Frank, out with it,' urged Edward. 'You'll be giving us a few lines from Hamlet next.'

Williams smiled. 'It's about your favourite Major.'

Liam's head came up and Big Charlie put down his cleaning cloths. 'What's happened, then?' Liam snorted. 'He's not been given a Victoria Cross for outstanding gallantry in opening whisky bottles?'

'Well, no, not quite,' Williams replied. 'He's dead.'

Edward was on his feet. 'Dead?' he shouted. 'Fforbes-Fosdyke dead? How's he managed that, then?'

'Well he didn't really manage it. He got killed in Miraumont.'

'In Miraumont?' Edward was astonished. 'What was he doing in Miraumont? Are you saying that he was there when the fighting was going on?'

'No way,' Big Charlie scoffed. 'He wouldn't be seen dead involved in the fighting,' he said, smiling as he, at least, appreciated his attempt at ironic humour.

'Well, in the end, he was,' chortled Williams. 'He was there because he had been sent. The Battalion has lost so many officers that we are finding it a bit of a struggle. The CO told him that he had to go. He said that it was going to be an easy show. Just walk in to the town and take over. He said that it was going to be his last opportunity to get a citation to impress his old man with. That did it for him. He knew that he would have to take something back to prove that he'd been there. If the word had got out that he'd spent all the war backsliding then he'd have been finished.'

'Aye. Knew which side his bread was buttered on' Edward said quietly.

'Funny thing is, he was shot in the back.' The Lieutenant waited, indulging himself with a theatrical pause whilst the full impact of the words sank in. 'Well away from the action.'

Edward put their thoughts into words. 'What do you mean? He was running away from the Germans?' He would not have been at all surprised to hear that this was the case. The man who had showed such barbaric cruelty to his own men was known for his rank cowardice in the face of the enemy.

'Well, no. He never got near the Germans. He was doing what you would expect – directing operations from the rear and staying as far away as he could from any fighting. He had sent the lads in, giving them orders that they fortunately ignored because they could see that they would be wiped out. He stayed hidden behind a corner on the outskirts of the town, shouting and bawling at them to think of England and to take no prisoners. All of a sudden he shut up. They found him later with a bullet hole in his back.'

'Is there going to be an inquiry?' Big Charlie asked. 'You know, with his old man having a bit of influence, like.'

'No, I don't think so. He's been marked down as a killed-in-action. That's a better outcome for his Dad anyway. He wouldn't have been too happy with too many stones being turned over.'

'Who found him?' Edward enquired.

'The 7th. They were in support.'

Edward's jaw dropped open. 'The 7th. That's Chopper Hennessy's outfit. I don't suppose that he was too upset.'

The news had transformed Liam. He was on his feet now, smiling as he joined the rest of them. He clenched his fist and held it in the air. 'Great news, Chopper,' he said victoriously. 'That settles the score for your kid.'

29 Myrtle Street
Cross Lane
Salford 5
Great Britain

15th July 1918

Dear Dad,

Has Billy Murphy's Dad been killed because Mrs Murphy says that she never gets any letters from him but she hasn't had a letter from the Army so she doesn't know what's happened to him? Billy is worried that she might die because she has gone very thin and doesn't eat anything properly. When I went round there she asked me did we still get letters and when I said that we did she got upset again. Billy said that his Dad might have been shooting the Germans and they might have shot him back and nobody can find him or perhaps a bomb has blown his hand off like the man down the street. His Mam got even more upset and she said a Jesus, Mary and Joseph and said that what his Dad was doing was a hard job but it had to be done and he was doing it to protect her and the kids and if any of those Germans so much as harmed a hair on his Dad's head then she would go over there and rip the limbs off their evil bodies.

Me and Billy were a bit frightened of her so I told Billy that I would ask you because you might know. She used to be alright when she got letters but now she keeps doing Hail Marys and things like that and Billy says that she doesn't do the washing sometimes, but he's not bothered because he doesn't have to put clean things on every Saturday.

We're on summer holidays now and we have been told that we have got to catch as many white butterflies as we can because they eat all the cabbage on the allotments. That's cruel because they are only delicate and they can eat as much cabbage as they want for all I care. It's horrid. Uncle Jim has built a shed on his allotment and I take our Ben and our Sadie in there to play hospitals.

Our Edward still won't let me play cricket with them in Ordsall Park even though he makes me bowl to him all morning in the backyard but then he won't be out when he's supposed to be. He says that I can't play just because I am eleven because, anyway, I am a girl. Mam said she used to play football with the boys when she was my age but then he says that he couldn't take me because I'm his sister and I am supposed to be learning knitting and sewing. Mam made me stay in all day because I thumped him and told him that even a spotty butcher's boy pinched his girl friend. Me and Mam made some cakes to send to you but I would rather have played cricket.

The coalman up the street has been asking all the women to save scraps for his horse because he can't get enough hay. He said it is supposed to be rationed because so much goes over to France but he said the corporation horses don't look as though they're starving. Mam told him to take it up to Peel Park and put it on the grass and it will feed the grass at the same time with the manure. The coalman said that they are supposed to be having another meeting with the Mayor about it. Mam told him that you'd get more sense out of Soft Mick.

Will you be able to bring some horses back with you when you come home?

Love

Laura

Chapter 17

Ruyaulcourt September 1918

The area was one of gently undulating hills. The wooded tops, relieved sparsely by the copper hues of early autumn, wore a barbed, golden crown where the setting sun touched the tops of the trees. Much of the low lying land had been devastated by the years of destructive warfare. Stricken stumps of trees surrounded the gaping mouths of the shell holes, the shredded, splintered fingers of the branches pointing aimlessly from mutilated arms.

The whole landscape was surmounted by the strangling metal collar of the deep fortifications in front of the Hindenburg Line. Edward could see the massive barbed wire structure reaching to a depth of around a hundred yards which represented only the first line of this formidable defence. Hidden behind that, he knew, was row upon row of sturdily built, interconnected trenches, each with its own protective lines of barbed wire. Strategically placed around these massive defence systems were concrete machine gun emplacements and the whole of this was supported in the rear by the thousands of the German Army's heavy artillery guns.

The Hindenburg Line, stretching for over one hundred miles and, at this point, two miles deep, had been substantially fortified since Edward had been here at Havrincourt Wood in June of 1917. This was an area that the Allies had held for most of the last three years but, in the offensive that they had begun in March, the Germans had pushed the Allied lines back, in some places, a distance of thirty miles to the West. They had believed, then, that victory was theirs for the taking and the Kaiser and his subjects had been celebrating the approaching end of the war.

Their jubilation, however, was premature. By pushing sections of their front forward they had stretched their line beyond the ability of their forces to defend the exposed flanks and beyond the support that could be given by the supply line. In Germany, most of the population already had to survive on a diet of potatoes and occasional other vegetables and now the front line troops were going hungry. In their push forward, the German soldiers had come across stores that the Allied troops had left behind and were shocked to find that their enemy's rations, although basic, were more plentiful and much superior to their own.

The losses that they had incurred in gaining this ground had been massive and, by July, the German Army on the Western Front was starving and demoralised. They knew that the Americans were bringing in greater numbers of troops to support the Allied effort, but they feared most the British and Anzac soldiers. After four years, these battle hardened men had proved their mettle and had adapted their tactics and honed their skills to meet the demands of modern warfare.

In August, the early morning peace on the German line had collapsed into a deafening chaos of smoke, fire, poison gas and the thunderous roar of the artillery bombardment. The Allies had begun their response and the mighty German Army began to slowly disintegrate.

In the four weeks since they had retaken Beauregard Dovecote, the Third Army, including Edward's Battalion of the 1/8 Lancashire Fusiliers as part of the 42nd Division, had continued to push the retreating German Army back towards the Hindenburg Line. As they had progressed, their line had become more compressed into a shorter front, and there had been some greatly appreciated opportunities both for rest and retraining.

Both sides had suffered heavy casualties but the Allies had taken thousands of prisoners. The temper of the battle had changed and they felt that victory was there for the taking.

Now they were facing what would be, the following morning, their most formidable challenge. They were going to attempt to break the seemingly impregnable Hindenburg Line. They knew that the German Army believed, not only that it could be held, but also that it must be held. Their rather bookish Captain had told them that the Germans had taken the names for the trenches from the final opera in Wagner's 'Ring' which translated into English as 'The Twilight of the Gods.' The possible irony here had probably not been recognised by the fiercely defiant German high command, but it was savoured by the British soldiers.

Edward stood on the firestep and gazed out through the slit in the sandbags at the clumsy beauty of the tangled landscape that was gripped by a strained stillness. There was no wind, no sound and no life in this battered, grey domain but he knew that there were thousands of German soldiers embedded into the rolling French plains.

His battalion had been brought up to Ruyaulcourt at 7.30pm and from there they had made their way up to the front line. Now they must wait a lifetime for a battle that could be decisive but might prove impossible.

He went over in his mind, once again, the plan for the attack which had been detailed out for them that day. The strategy for the whole of the Third Army had been explained so that they could see where they fitted into the broader picture. There were five objectives for them to achieve, each of which had been given a colour reference. There was to be a series of massive onslaughts along the whole of the Western Front with the intention of smashing both the Hindenburg Line and the resolution of the German Army.

Edward lit a cigarette and looked out over the low land of the Ribecourt Valley, flanked by two great ridges, where they would mount their attack. Three spurs protruded into the valley from the Beaucamp Ridge on the right. If all went well then they would be camped on the furthest of these

– the formidable Highland Ridge – by the following night. It was a distance of around two miles and achieving this target would mean that they had broken through the main defences of the Hindenburg Line.

He knew that when the Allied bombardment opened, the Germans would respond by shelling the stretch of land where they believed they would find the approaching British soldiers. The ground was fairly soft and pock marked by shell holes so that would give the British soldiers a better chance. If the shells landed on hard ground the shrapnel could kill soldiers up to half a mile away but, if the ground was soft, it would cushion the fall and the circle of destruction would be limited.

Edward tried to envisage the route that they would take to keep up their position just behind the creeping barrage provided by the artillery. Things had changed so much in the last two years both with the design of the big guns and with the accuracy that was achieved by the men of the Royal Artillery. There was also a lot more of it. Many lessons had been learned by the infantry Battalions about the tactics to be used. Now they tended to go in fairly small groups and would keep quite close to the creeping wall of shell fire. They also attacked strategic targets on a compact front, often taking the enemy by surprise rather than announcing their attack by heavy artillery bombardments for hours, or even days, before they moved. That had only resulted in the enemy taking shelter in deep dugouts, to emerge when the Allied infantry approached

Lieutenant Frank Williams was to lead one of the platoons in the Company whilst Edward, subsidiary to Williams, would be leading another. The shortage of officers was becoming a profound problem for the Army because so many were being killed. The ones that were coming in were often straight from the officer training school and most of the Captains appeared to be only in their early twenties. Edward had admired and respected the majority of these young men. Despite their lack of experience, they invariably showed great courage in their leadership, often to the point of foolhardiness. Although some of them were haughty, arrogant and uncaring the majority of them worked hard and thoughtfully to earn the respect of the men that they led.

The only real exception to this that Edward could think of was the detestable Fforbes-Fosdyke, but he had received his just reward. He felt sure that Frank Williams knew a bit more about the Major's demise than he was letting on. There had been something about his face when Liam had mentioned about Chopper Hennessy being with the 1/7 Lancashires who were in support. Maybe an old score had been settled for the killing of his younger brother in the trench in Gallipoli but, there again, some things are better left unsaid.

Edward's thoughts turned, as they so often did, to the unfathomable torment that was torturing his friend, Liam. The previous week he had shown him the letter that he had received from his daughter, Laura, and Liam had read it over carefully without comment. His face had been a blank mask that had betrayed nothing of his feelings. Edward had watched him closely looking for a sign of contrition or remorse; any indication that he had been touched by the plaintiff message or become aware of the hurt that he was imposing. There had been nothing. The door had been slammed so tightly shut that nothing could pass through it. After reading it over four or five times he had handed it back to Edward with just a cursory 'Thanks' and had wandered off towards the New Zealand camp.

Edward was becoming desperate to find something that would help to free his friend's manacled mind. He was certain that Liam's unfailing good humour and ebullient personality had helped most of the longer serving members of their platoon to survive mentally. When a fellow soldier had bad news from home, Liam was available with an attentive ear and a cheery word, if they were depressed he would lift them with his quick wit, and when anybody seemed to be showing signs of shellshock or abject fear, his arm would be round their shoulders and he would weave a protective web of caring attention. Now, as he withdrew deeper into the dark recesses of his mind and needed, in turn, the help from his friends, they were unable to provide it. Liam's silences were so powerful and affecting that Edward felt his own mental state being gripped by a deep unease.

He had thought that young Laura's letter might jar Liam off this downward spiral but, once again, it seemed that he had failed. Liam's cavalier conduct in battle was likely to prove fatal and Edward had no ideas left that might avert it.

His cough was troubling him again. He took out another cigarette and enjoyed the soothing smoke. He watched Big Charlie collecting large, rounded stones together and throwing them at a distant tree. He guessed that it was around 80 yards away but Big Charlie's accuracy was amazing. Not too surprising, though. Big Charlie could kick penalties from anywhere within the opponents' half so he obviously had a good eye.

Edward hoped that, at least, he might have helped to resolve Big Charlie's marital problems. His wife, Laura, had bumped into Dorothy's cousin and she had given her the new address. Edward had passed it on to a grateful Big Charlie who had then spent several days laboriously writing a letter in his own words.

As he gazed out across the darkening valley his cheek was cooled by a sudden gentle breeze; his wife's soft hair brushing his face as he kissed her goodbye. Memories of his home and family that he tried to keep locked away but, so often, they floated like unbidden shadows into his consciousness.

They had been in their assembly positions since 2.00am on the 27 September 1918 and there had been three hours of tense waiting until just after 5.00am. The silence had been broken by the single shell being fired from one of the big guns in the artillery line behind them that signalled the start of the bombardment. Within seconds, the morning stillness was shattered by a raging cacophony of shrieking shells that flew over them and exploded into a wall of flame over the German lines.

So many guns were firing that the whooshing and screaming of the shells in flight blended with the echoing roar of the explosions as they thudded into the ground and created a melodrama of deafening sound. Huge spectacular plumes of orange, blue and yellow flames and dust rose into the air surrounded by dramatic showers of cracking sparks as ammunition dumps were hit.

Edward's Battalion was timed to go off at 7.52am to give the chance for the groups on the flanks to clear the higher ground. The wait seemed interminable. The noises coalesced into a wall of sound and their minds closed themselves against it. They had their tots of rum and Edward checked his letters and his pockets and had sudden misgivings about the nature of the letters that he had sent to Laura and each of the kids. His own anxieties had, maybe, flavoured the words with a sense of finality.

He watched Big Charlie going through his cleaning and checking routine again. Others were whispering their mantras, brushing their uniforms, reading favourite letters and saying Hail Marys. He felt a comfort from watching his fellow soldiers attaching themselves to these familiars.

His gaze fell on Liam sitting by himself on the fire step. His eyes were animated but distant. He was silently, but vehemently, mouthing his side of a conversation with an unseen participant. Liam's sometimes anguished face reflected the telling points that the other person was making. Maybe it was his beloved, though absent, Bridget who had invaded his troubled thoughts. The Captain called out 'Ten minutes to go' and patted Liam gently on the shoulder. Liam's head momentarily dropped as his muted conversation stopped and then he stood up, wiped his boots on the back of his trousers and crossed himself.

Edward watched the men make the final adjustments to their kit. They all carried trenching spades strapped to their back packs and some also held wire cutters. Three of them formed the Lewis Gun team and they had to bring the heavy packs of ammunition in addition to the gun. Most of the soldiers had grenade pouches fastened round them as well as the spare rounds of ammunition for their Lee Enfield rifles. They all had their carefully polished bayonets fixed. The soldiers were increasingly surprised by the apparent fear that was growing in the German ranks for the British bayonet. They seemed happy to exchange rifle fire but, as soon as the Tommies entered their trenches brandishing fixed bayonets, panic filled their eyes.

The Captain came over to Edward, shook his hand and wished him luck. Edward guessed that the officer was probably only in his early twenties. Mind you, he himself had been married two years by that age and he had a baby son. The young man's armoury consisted minimally of a pistol and a walking stick.

The Captain signalled that it was time to go but held up his hand. 'Have a good run lads. Look out for each other. This is going to be a tough one so keep your eyes peeled. Hang on until the big fella goes through then we'll follow.'

They heard a rumbling clatter and a Mark IV tank went by trailing a thick rope with a huge grappling hook attached to it. It thundered across the massive barbed wire barriers of the German defence system, snagging them and dragging them like an immense, contorting, whipping metal tail. It then turned to the side hauling its rapidly growing burden behind it. The soldiers looked on in with utter amazement. The tank had accomplished within a few minutes what hours of artillery bombardment had often failed to do.

The young Captain held his stick aloft. 'Let's go lads. Don't forget the 8th's motto. 'Go one better.' Good luck.' He was up the ladder and over the parapet. Hundreds of men went over the top following the track cleared by the tank. They kept their heads low and walked at a fast pace behind the curtain of shell fire that was progressing slowly forward in front of them. The artillery gunners had developed their skills in positioning to a high science, firing into the tightly defined coordinates that they had been given. The soldiers didn't get too close. The shells contained a deadly weaponry of shrapnel.

Rolling banks of smoke began to form into a blanket, held in the valley by the cold morning air. The Hindenburg Line became a wall of dusty orange and red flame. The Captain stood starkly outlined against this dramatic backcloth waving his pistol in one hand and his walking stick in the other. He was directing the platoons in the Company along the most effective routes. Like so many of his fellow officers did, he was leading and inspiring with a self sacrificing display of bravado. Most of the rank and file soldiers would have preferred less inspiration and more continued leadership.

Within minutes, they heard the fearsome staccato chatter of machine gun bullets and men began to fall. Edward's heart sank. They were caught out in the open like ducks sitting on a pond. He motioned his platoon into a shallow shell hole and tried to determine the direction of the hail of bullets. He looked round to check if the men were alright and he saw that the Lewis Gunner was lying dead about ten yards away. Liam, following Edward's gaze, jumped out of the hole and ran to retrieve the gun. When he got back

Edward asked him where the gunner had been shot. Liam told him that it was in his right temple. Edward looked at the other casualties. Most had received bullet wounds in the right side of their bodies although some had been hit in the front.

Edward told them that it was enfilading fire coming from the Beaucamp Ridge on the right. The groups that had left early to clear the higher flanks must have been stopped. Edward pointed in the rough direction that he adjudged, from the position of the wounds, the machine guns were positioned. The soldiers peered through the shroud of smoke and soon one of them spotted the concrete bunker in front of which were piled camouflaging dead trees. It was over a hundred yards away.

Big Charlie got to his feet saying that it was worth giving it a go and Edward urged him to be careful. Big Charlie nodded and grunted then, keeping his head low, he ran to the next shell hole. Seconds later he was standing on its rim with a grenade in his hand, his body absolutely still as he stared fixedly at the bunker.

'Jesus, Charlie. Get on with it,' Liam muttered with a shudder as seemingly interminable seconds ticked by. Then, with mechanical precision, Big Charlie withdrew the pin, reached his arm far behind him and, with a mighty throw, he released the grenade. It soared the huge distance to the bunker and exploded the moment that it landed. The machine gun fire faded in intensity. Taking out another grenade, he repeated the process whilst his friends watched the heart-stopping performance making urgent supplications to their often maligned God to bring the big man back quickly and safely.

The machine gun fire from that bunker had stopped but Big Charlie threw a third just to be sure. He returned to the shell hole grinning. 'That's sorted them buggers out, anyway,' he said, settling himself back down. They all congratulated him and climbed over the rim.

Machine gun fire was still coming from the right but from a higher position on the ridge and was inflicting less damage. It was clear now that there were also a number of emplacements around the bunker towards which they were heading. When he looked over to his left he could see that the companies on that side were also being cut down by enfilading machine gun fire from the ridge above them.

Edward could see the platoon led by Frank Williams in front and headed in that direction. He was disturbed to see the number of casualties lying about; some obviously dead, others screaming in pain whilst others were grimly trying to fix their field dressings in place over spurting wounds. They were only fifteen minutes into the operation and already they had lost up to half of the attacking troops.

They worked their way slowly forward and eventually re-established contact with the forward platoon. Lieutenant Williams had lost three of his men and was setting up the Lewis Gun, pointing out a copse of trees where he thought some machine gun emplacements were established. He directed Edward's platoon towards a low ridge which would give them a vantage point.

They set up their Lewis Gun and opened fire on the copse from a slightly different angle to that taken by Williams' group. All the infantrymen joined in with their rifles but it was almost half an hour before the machine gun fire had decreased sufficiently to move forward. The two platoons approached the copse of trees in a pincer movement, eventually getting within one hundred yards of the German position.

Edward soon realised that they faced a formidable task. There were at least two machine guns still in action and they were positioned underneath a natural escarpment. There was no possibility of getting to a high position behind them as the ground in front was open and they were in a hollow under the rock with a massive sandbag palisade around them.

Whilst the machine gunners obviously knew that the British soldiers were in the area, a less well defended emplacement having already been taken out, they didn't seem overly concerned and were concentrating their fire on the British troops down the hill. Edward could see that many of his colleagues were falling and there was an urgent need to resolve this.

'Special breed, these machine gunners,' observed Liam. 'They never come out with their hands up. They're never finished until they're in a bag.'

A grenade attack didn't seem feasible as they were so far away and, as soon as they broke cover from the trees, the Germans would turn their machine guns on them. Edward turned to Big Charlie. 'What do you reckon, mate? Is there any chance?'

'It might be possible from over on that ridge,' Big Charlie nodded. 'It's worth a try.'

'Not much by way of throwing-off points though.'

'I'll find somewhere,' Big Charlie grunted. He shrugged his bags into place and set off before Edward could say anything else. He skirted through the trees to the right and for a while they lost sight of him. Moments later he emerged from the trees and stood in the open ground with a grenade in his hand. He stood immobile for a few long seconds, fixing the image of the German machine gunners in his mind. For the time being he remained unnoticed by the enemy.

Finally he looked down at the grenade, pulled out the pin, drew his arm back and flung the deadly device, accompanied by an intimidating grunt. The grenade flew across the gap and landed in one side of the emplacement flinging rocks, body parts and ammunition into the air as it exploded. Big Charlie took out another grenade but one of the guns had not been taken out and now they knew where he was. As he pulled his hand back to make his throw, the machine gun started up again. Before he could release the grenade, the bullets found their mark and blood spurted from his stomach. He hesitated for a moment, then summoned up the last reserves of his strength and threw the grenade. It landed on its target but Big Charlie was on his knees, clutching at the wound in his stomach.

Edward, followed quickly by Liam, dashed over to help his friend. By the time that they got to Big Charlie he had rolled over on to his back, his face had turned a deathly white and blood poured out of his mouth. Liam lifted Big Charlie's head onto his knee whilst Edward cut the shirt away to reveal the wound. There was a huge, gaping hole from which the intestines were gradually emerging. He knew that the situation was hopeless but he had to try; he couldn't let the life of his mighty friend ebb away without trying. He told two men to go and find some stretcher bearers whilst he tore open his field dressings and stuffed them into the wound.

A large, red muddy pool was forming underneath Big Charlie and Edward struggled desperately to stem the flow. Big Charlie lifted his head and said weakly 'That's sorted them buggers out as well.'

'Aye. You did a fantastic job, Charlie,' Edward said, searching for words that wouldn't betray his increasing despair. 'Now what we want is to get you back on your feet so that you can sort a few more of them out.'

His ears thudded and sweat dripped off his face into Big Charlie's wound as he fought feverishly to stop the draining blood. 'There's nowt you can do, Eddie,' Big Charlie coughed as he slowly lifted is hand to grasp Edward's. 'Don't worry about me. Get the lads off the hill.'

'The lads are ok. Just keep going, mate. Keep going. I can't let you go out here.'

The blood gurgled in Big Charlie's throat as he struggled to speak. In a rapidly weakening voice he said 'Tell our Dot... I'd have been... right suited about... giving her...

those babies. Tell her... as how... she's the most... important thing... that's... ever...'

The big man's voice trailed away and his eyes closed.

Liam stared rigidly with disbelieving eyes at his dead friend's face, unable to accept the awful truth. He grasped Big Charlie's jaw and shook his head despairingly. As Edward turned away to find his own space to hide the welling grief, Liam bent his face down and kissed Big Charlie's forehead.

Edward sank to the ground and gripped his bursting head between his hands. Some part of his own life had been ripped from his body and he fought against an overpowering nausea. Big Charlie had been essential to their lives since they were small children. They had looked together, with the wonderment of young boys, at the grass growing under broken glass between the sets in their street. As older boys they had played football on the same cobbled streets and stony grounds. The three of them had started school together, played rugby for the same team, joined the Territorials at the same time and enlisted as regulars on the same day. Simple, honest lives. Not bloodied. And dead. At which second, as the blood had dripped into the dusty stones of this French hillside, had Big Charlie's life force left him? Edward felt guilt in his unwitting involvement in the death of his friend and incapable of resolving in his mind the void created by his absence.

His shame became a haunting cry that echoed in his mind then plundered his memories. He shuddered as he thought of this big man, gently shy and modest in life, lying shamelessly ruptured and exposed in death. Big Charlie would become carrion, claimed callously by the French earth whose freedom he had sought. Would he scoop out this alien soil and take home the Salford blood?

The wailing cry became that of the ravaging birds that would fall from the high stone slabs. It rose in harsh sounding words and yearning notes and lifted his consciousness. He heard a voice that he knew to be Liam's but which had taken on a haunting, nasal quality as he sang. The notes held in the air and floated around the valley, mournful, tragic and inextricably part of the bleak cliffs and the torn stumps of the trees. A bird that soared and probed as it searched amongst the black crevices for its dead mate.

Edward turned and watched Liam as he knelt at the side of the body of their lifelong friend, his head tilted back slightly and his wet eyes tightly closed.

Liam's voice rose in earnest supplication then fell in pitiful remorse. The strange words held no meaning but the sounds probed hidden depths of emotions, assaulted senses that had been boxed securely away from the numbing devastation of warfare. They scraped starkly across the stretched nerves of the constantly bereaved. Liam's voice was an instrument of anguish and despair that reached through the dark curtain of death. It rose in the air and shared its grief with the spirits that waited to guard the soul of the dead man on its long journey.

Edward felt disturbed and troubled yet stimulated, provoked and ravaged yet uplifted, as the song pillaged emotions from his locked up mind. He bent his head and prayed for the sacrificed life of Big Charlie.

They used their trenching spades to silently dig the grave then retched as they stuffed back the intestines and reluctantly threw soil on the still clothed but lifeless body of their friend. Two bleached and torn branches formed a rough cross on which they hung his identity tag before performing a simple ceremony. 'Thanks for everything, mate' Liam said quietly as he held his hand on the cross. 'We'll miss you more than you'll ever know.'

Edward reached for the identity tag and pressed it to his lips. 'Bye Charlie. We'll have to see if we can win this one without you. God Bless.'

A small stone dislodged itself from the pile on the grave and formed a curving track down the side of the mound.

'That song that you sang just before, it was a bit unusual,' Edward ventured hesitantly.

'It was an ullalulla that my old Irish Granny used to sing at a wake,' Liam responded. 'It goes better with a glass of whisky.'

Minutes later, they had rejoined the platoon and surveyed the devastation that Big Charlie had caused in the machine gun emplacement. The silenced guns and the scorched and dismembered bodies of the dead German soldiers lay scattered around the area.

'How many more does there have to be?' Liam whispered, addressing the question to an unseen listener. He turned to Edward and placed his arm across his shoulder. 'I'm sorry to do this to you, mate, but I'll be going with him,' he said quietly but firmly before joining the others.

They collected a few trophies from the corpses before burying them and shouldered the three machine guns and ammunition. Moving off again in the direction of the first objective, the Black Line, they could see the young Captain some distance ahead, standing on a small rise as he urged the men forward and directed the field of operations. He died instantly as the bullets tore into his body and he collapsed in a heap at the side of the dishevelled corpse of yet another once proud Salford soldier.

The ferocious artillery bombardment from behind them was lifted forward and was now peppering the trench system that was their first objective. Another of his platoon fell with a bullet through the heart followed by a second with a gaping wound in his shoulder. Edward detailed a man to get him into a safe hollow and apply a field dressing.

Soldiers from the support companies passed through their platoon and then progressed up towards the north east.

The Salford men moved forward, rifles in front of them, firing as they went.

The shelling was taking its toll on the enemy soldiers and the machine gun fire was lessening. They worked their way slowly towards the German lines, incurring five more casualties between the two platoons. Finally, three hours after they had commenced the attack, they were in the German trenches. There was some strong resistance initially but this soon collapsed in the face of the fierce bayonet assault by the British troops.

Grey faced, grey uniformed soldiers began to emerge from tunnels dug into the sides of the trenches with their hands held above their heads. Grateful for the chance to give themselves up. Their war was ended and they were still alive. There were so many of them that they presented a problem. Lieutenant Williams detailed a man who was already injured and needed medical attention to accompany them and they set off back towards the Allied jump off lines. On the way back, the German soldiers willingly collected their injured British counterparts and assisted them back to the Allied medical posts.

The Lieutenant showed them on the detailed map prepared by the air ordnance where they were in the trenches and outlined the plan for the next stage. It was now four hours since they had mounted the attack and they munched on some dried biscuits and sipped their water. Edward's group was to progress up the communications trench then cross over some open ground to meet up with the Lieutenant's platoon which was going to clear up the adjacent trench.

Because the achieving of the Black Line had been more difficult and more slowly gained than the planned time, the curtain of artillery fire had now moved some distance ahead. The communications trench, however, was fairly clear and minutes later they were up on the open ground. There was a small barn about two hundred yards ahead but little else. The ground was flat and offered little by way of cover. They would have to check out the barn; perhaps they would find some abandoned stores.

The men approached carefully using whatever limited cover was available and found themselves on a rough track that led up to the ramshackle building. Trees along either side of the track offered some protection and Edward split the group to utilise the cover on both sides. As they neared it they could see broken pieces of old machinery, a smashed water butt and a couple of ancient and long disused farm implements.

The sun was streaming through the broken roof of the old barn, lighting up the interior with bright, dusty shafts. Numerous missing planks from the side of the building revealed small drifts of old straw inside and a rickety wooden ladder leading up to a dangerously broken down mezzanine. There appeared to be no evidence of recent occupation but Edward urged caution as he waved the men forward. The distant rumble of the artillery bombardment marked an odd contrast to the rigid stillness that embraced this flat plain as they crept under the cover of the hedge.

They were within twenty yards of the building when a devastating torrent of machine gun bullets ripped into them from behind an upturned farm cart standing in overgrown innocence in the field on the right. Three men fell instantly and the rest dived to find whatever cover was possible.

'Bastards, stinking Boche bastards,' Edward heard Liam shouting vehemently behind him. The cart was around forty yards away and the men were firing at it more out of frustration than conviction. The ground in front of the cart sloped gradually upwards towards it and offered no cover at all.

Liam began to crawl up a very shallow ditch that curved off up to the right and Edward yelled after him. 'This one's for Big Charlie,' Liam shouted back.

After setting up the Lewis Gun team, Edward started to follow round the ditch after his pal. As he came within sight of him, Liam suddenly rose to his feet, pulled the pin on a grenade and flung it at the cart in one movement before dropping back down in the ditch. The cart rocked dramatically as the grenade exploded before falling slowly forward exposing the machine gun emplacement. Edward could see bodies of some of the German gunners on the ground but others were shouting and gesticulating wildly. Liam turned to Edward, who was yelling at his friend to come back. He grinned and stuck his thumb into the air. Then he was on his feet again and pulled the pin on another grenade.

The bullet hit Liam in the side of his forehead before he completed his throw and, as he fell, the grenade flew from his hand and landed some distance down the ditch. The explosion in the soft mud was muffled and Edward was on his feet and running towards Liam when he heard a great gasping sigh from where the grenade had landed. As he bent down to inspect his friend's wound, he saw the faint green gas escaping from the deep mud where it had been trapped since some previous action. Blood was pouring down Liam's deathly white face but he was still breathing. Edward knew that he must get him away from the gas before he could give any first aid.

He heaved on Liam's shoulders, praying for the strength to get him to safety, hoping that his men would deal with the German soldiers, wishing that the gentle breeze, rolling the bank of green gas towards him, would change its direction. It was bad enough losing Big Charlie but not Liam as well. His feet slipped in the cloying mud as he dragged the limp body, bullets flew around him and he searched the depths of his being for the strength to get him back. 'Come on, you awkward little sod,' he groaned as Liam's foot became entangled in roots growing through the side of the ditch.

Sucking in air to support his desperate struggle, he felt the familiar burning sensation in his throat. His eyes began to smart as he forced more steps from his aching legs. Within seconds, his eyes were flames and his throat rattled, his head began to reel and images from his past floated up in front of him like a picture show. Machine gun bullets splintered a branch of a tree close to his head, his lungs were on fire and his throat seemed to be filled with burning coals. With sweat pouring off him, he forced his legs to complete the vital steps to get Liam to safety. He could no longer see and his mind had become a swirling mist of dreams when he heard the soldiers' voices. The words were telling him to release Liam but they slowly drifted into the voice of his wife whispering 'Keep safe, Love.'

Chapter 18

11th November 1918 Salford

The front door burst open and young Laura's best friend, Amy, was standing there gasping, her cheeks glowing and her fists clenched with suppressed excitement. Edward found it difficult to comprehend how much the girls had changed since he had left four years before. Amy was taller now and more thoughtful, if somewhat constrained by a lack of funds, about her grooming and general appearance. The bloom of the young lady on her cheek only barely restrained the childish impishness which forever played around her eyes and mouth. She had the distracting fascination of a butterfly that wasn't totally convinced about leaving its rather dishevelled chrysalis.

'Eh up, Mr Craigie. Are yer still sitting there grumpy then?' she observed with her usual disarming candour. 'Is it the bad throat that's getting yer down?'

'Aye, well it doesn't help' Edward said smiling weakly. 'You're looking like the cat that's found the cream. What's up, then?'

'It's all the excitement going on outside. The fellas standing on the railings at the corner of Cross Lane reckon that the war is finished. They say that the Germans are signing some letter this morning then they're going 'ome.'

'Well, that sounds like good news, Amy. It's not before time.'

'Aye, it is. Perhaps me Dad 'll be back 'ome soon. Me Mam says she 'as a list of jobs to keep 'im occupied when he gets back,' Amy enthused.

Edward shuddered and turned away from Amy. He had seen Amy's Dad, a soldier in Lieutenant William's platoon, lying dead before they reached the Black Line. Amy's

Mother couldn't read and had obviously decided that there was always hope without confirmation of the worst.

'Is your Laura not in then?' Amy enquired. 'I was thinking as how we could 'ave gone a walk up to the Town 'all to see if the Mayor said owt about it.'

'They've all gone up to their Uncle Jim's with their Mam. Why don't you have a walk up there? You'll probably see them.'

'Why don't yer 'ave a walk up the Lane with me, then? Yer look as though yer could do with a bit of fresh air. Yer getting to look like Marley's ghost sitting in 'ere day in day out.'

Edward winced slightly. Amy always had a direct approach and an often dicomfiting honesty. He knew, in himself, that he was using his damaged lungs and throat as a not totally justified reason for hardly ever going out. Two weeks before, he had collected his navy blue demob trilby from the Drill Hall and come home. He knew that his breathing was permanently impaired and that he would have to adapt to it.

The family had been delirious to see him and he had been thrilled to be at home. But he wasn't home as a husband and father. He was only at home. It wasn't just the fact that he couldn't even begin to talk to his wife and family about his experiences during the last four years; it was as though his mind had set into some exclusive, distorted and incomm-unicative consciousness. He was going through the motions of playing the role of a Salford parent and spouse but it was on a different plane to the terrible and controlling reality of his mental state.

Their lack of dependence on him for almost any aspect of family life had developed in order to cope with his four year absence. Now, life for the rest of them just went on, with Edward occasionally caught in the orbit. His wife watched and waited with patience yet his existence, for so long ordered and organised and exposed to the most horrific manifestations of warfare, now seemed drifting and aimless. What he had had before the war couldn't be reclaimed and what he had been before had been destroyed.

'Do yer want me to spit on yer 'air so yer can comb it, cos 'appen yer've not got too much spit with that bad throat of yours?' Amy's offer shook Edward out of his reverie.

'No thanks, Amy. I'm ok. But I think that I'll stay here for now. I don't really feel up to going out' Edward said feebly.

'Well, yer nowt like someone who's ok to me. I don't know about Marley's ghost. Yer look as if yer sat here with a ghost on each shoulder. 'Appen a bit of a walk might do summat to bring a bit of colour to yer cheeks.' Amy's directness, decorously delivered with her strong Lancashire accent, was hard to resist but Edward was not to be persuaded. It was so much easier to leave things than to make decisions.

When he had woken up in the hospital in Arras with a white ribbon tied round his neck to indicate that he was only to be fed on milk, he had felt hopelessly lost. There was a deep void in the pit of his stomach and a sense of floating helplessly in the middle of a great ocean. There were other, equally redundant, patients and there were professional, caring nurses who fussed about the injured men and tended to their needs. But the sense of purpose that had dominated his life for four years, that had moulded his mind and cemented a mutuality with his pals, had been prematurely terminated.

His war was over and now he belonged nowhere.

'Well, yer should at least leave them cigs alone; they'll make yer throat a lot worse,' Amy counselled.

'They make it feel a bit easier, but thanks for caring,' Edward smiled. He didn't really know how to respond to her rough edged, frank charm.

'Right. I'll be off. Don't finish up like that miserable old divil next door to us.' She waved and disappeared up the street.

That afternoon, whilst the sirens on the ships in the Docks heralded the onset of peace and people danced in the street, Edward, working tirelessly with a cigarette dangling from his lips, painted the living room and the scullery stark, ascetic, purging white.

Chapter 19

April 1919 Salford

Edward stared at the dying embers in the grate. It would be out soon if he didn't move. This was a job that he had taken responsibility for, looking after the fire, but sometimes his mind drifted away. He got out of his chair, took some pieces of wood from the bag that his eldest brother, Jim, had sent and placed them carefully on the glowing cinders. There was an almost hypnotic fascination in watching the fire. It had comforting warmth. Coke gave a range of interesting blues and yellows as it burnt. Coal, when you could get it, and wood produced dancing, ever changing vistas of flames that drew you into their centre and painted flickering, shadowy shapes around the room.

The fire orchestrated groups of ethereal, wraith-like people that darted round the white walls; the carters and drovers in the early morning mists of the cattle markets; the dockers standing around the railings on Cross Lane corner in the late afternoons of winter; the weary soldiers, rifles at the ready, trudging across the barren, devastated fields of France bathed in the orange-red glow of the inferno of the bombardment; men being ripped apart by high explosive shrapnel shells or mown down by machine gun bullets; Big Charlie, his guts spilling out of his body and his life blood soaking away into the French soil, his face contorted by the pain as he struggled to make his belated avowal of his love for his wife; and Liam, the man at whose side he had walked for so many years and with whom he had shared those troubles and triumphs that are the quirky province of male pals, might also be lying under the cold, French soil.

He had been round to see Dorothy, just after he got back, to explain what a special and quietly heroic man Big Charlie had been, but he got no answer. The neighbours had

349

said that she had moved a month before. Perhaps it was as well. He couldn't share her grief – she had lost a husband, a lover and a breadwinner out of her sadly incomplete marriage and he had lost a friend with whom he had stood shoulder to shoulder and peered into the depths of hell.

He hadn't spoken about Liam other than to shrug his shoulders and grunt in reply when anybody enquired about him, and he never asked if there was any news. He knew that he should go and see Bridget but he couldn't formulate the words to explain how he had witnessed his friend's mind being torn apart by the polar forces of her purity and the corrosive evil of the war. He knew that his bumbling explanations would sound like a shameful admission of the guilt that he felt for his own complicity in Liam's degeneration.

The uncertain fate of Liam was a cancer that he could neither face nor resolve but whose eternal contemplation, sat in his chair in his Salford home with the lives of his family flitting around him, gave a discernible shape to the nightmare of industrial scale killing over the four years that had now become his life.

Young Laura came in and put her arm round his shoulders. She bent her head so that it rested against his. The shadows flickering on the wall became him and his childhood friends playing football in Turner Street. The girl from a few doors down, coming back from an errand for her Mam, had joined them but wouldn't take her turn at goalkeeper because she'd get into trouble if she tore her skirt. He turned and buried his face in the coal tar clean fragrance of his daughter's red hair. Young Laura was so much like her mother.

'Hello Pippin. Are you alright?'

'Yes thanks, I'm ok.' She answered him briefly but in a way that left an unspoken question hanging in the air.

'How come you're not playing out? I thought that you were playing school with Sadie and Mary.'

'They're fed up of that now. They've gone to play with next door's puppy and our Ben has gone to the coal yard to help the man clean out the stable. Uncle Jim gives him a penny for every bag of horse manure that he takes up.'

'Why don't you help your Mam then?' Edward asked.

'Mam's gone to do her cleaning job and she asked me to look after the girls,' Laura answered. 'Dad, you said that when you came home you would take me to see that big Hall on the other side of Ordsall Park.'

'Aye, well. We'll have to see when I feel up to it,' Edward answered evasively.

'Why don't we go today? It's a nice day and the sunshine will do you good,' Laura persisted. 'You hardly ever go out now and you're not going to get better sitting in front of the fire.' Like Mother, like daughter Edward thought wryly.

'I know that, Darling,' Edward said defensively. 'I just need to wait for my breathing to get a bit better.'

'Mrs Willoughby says that a breath of fresh air and a drop of cold water never did anybody any harm,' Laura countered. 'So do you want me to brew you a mug of tea, then?'

'Aye, that's not a bad idea love. Pour the kettle when it's just boiled, won't you.'

'Yes Dad. I am twelve in only five weeks, you know, so I do know how to brew tea,' she said, pursing her lips slightly.

'And anyway,' she added as she disappeared into the scullery, 'Amy said that I should tell you that the rest of your soldiers are due back in Salford tonight.'

'What's that? What did Amy say?' The casually delivered piece of news had hit Edward like a bullet shot and he felt shocked and stunned yet, at the same time, stimulated.

'She said something about the rest of your Battalion coming back tonight and she knows that her Dad isn't because he's dead,' his daughter answered with unsentimental detachment.

Edward had never known Amy's Dad very well and he already knew that he was dead but he, nevertheless, felt almost violated by the casual delivery of the news. 'Oh dear. That's an awful shock for her. Tell her that I'm very sorry to hear that. She must be really upset.'

'She's alright. She said that she'll get over it if her Mam is allowed to keep her job now that the men are coming back. She said that at least it will stop him coming in and thumping her Mam when he's been out for a drink.'

'Ah. I see. I didn't realise that he did that. It's still going to be difficult for her without a Dad.'

'She said that she would have adopted you as a Dad but you don't seem to have been too perky lately,' Laura said. 'Do you want one of these angel buns that me Mam made?'

'Yes please,' Edward accepted, reflecting once again on the penetrating honesty of young children.

After the evening meal was finished, throughout which he had sat silent and grim-faced, he went into the scullery and had a shave – he sometimes didn't see the point in having one each morning. The family watched as he quietly got himself ready, polishing his shoes and oiling his hair. He went upstairs and put on a clean shirt and tie before taking his suit out of the wardrobe.

Going back down, he adjusted his tie in the mirror and asked his wife to check him over. She affirmed that he looked very smart. 'Are you alright, love?' she asked, puzzled.

'Aye. I'm fine thanks. I'll just be having a bit of a walk.'

He took his cap off the peg, in preference to the trilby, brushed it down and placed it carefully on his head. 'I won't be too long.' He bent and kissed his wife briefly.

'Be careful, love,' she whispered to him. He gave an involuntary shudder. There was some resonance in her quiet supplication; it picked at disturbing memories. He walked slowly up Cross Lane, nodding at a few acquaintances, and then along the Crescent. He stopped for a long time staring into the flowing waters of the river bearing its half-hidden burden of debris. He gripped the rounded tops of the railings tightly as he saw the torrential storm waters of Gallipoli tumbling the bodies of dead soldiers down Gully Ravine.

He heard the faint strains of a military trumpet playing on W Beach, and the shouts of the transport men trying to drive their horses up to the front line. The increasing throb of the drum beat brought him slowly back to the Crescent and he realised that a band was approaching down Chapel Street. He joined the crowd gathered outside the Cathedral and tried to ignore the tightening pain in his chest.

The people lined up on either side of the road were mostly dressed like him in their suits and wearing flat caps. He recognised some of them as ex-army men although there were many older ones who were probably waiting to see returning sons. There were many wives and girlfriends amongst the agitated crowd and children ran excitedly along the road as the band approached.

As the soldiers drew closer the watching groups pressed forward to be nearer to their loved ones. The band passed followed by the officers and the flag bearers. People cheered and shouted greetings to the returning heroes who half turned their heads and allowed themselves a brief smile. Many of the men bore the scars of the hard battles they had fought but they wore them with pride as they marched rhythmically along the cobbled sets in front of this admiring and cheering audience.

Edward's spirit was sinking fast. He had watched hundreds of weary men in tired uniforms march past and scrutinised the face of each. His worst fears were becoming reality. His gloom was approaching black despair when he saw the familiar face set resolutely to the front. The scar on

353

the side of the head was still pronounced and the shoulders pulled back but the uniform bore the evidence of battle. The pocket on one side of his jerkin was rather clumsily stitched into place whilst the other was held in position by a German cap badge. Black patches on the back of the trousers just above the puttees bore witness to his habit of cleaning his still shiny toe caps there.

He called his name. Liam turned and grinned when he saw Edward. 'What happened to you?' Edward bellowed. 'I thought that you had copped one when nobody heard from you.'

Liam pointed a finger at his own head and mouthed the words 'Daft sod,' to Edward.

Edward smiled back and worked his way forward to get alongside Liam. He picked up the pace of the marching men and Liam, inclining his head slightly, asked 'Are you alright, Eddie?'

'I'm fine. What's more to the point is how you are.'

'I'm ok, thanks. Had a few weeks in hospital while they sorted out the bullet wound then I was great.'

'But…you know….' Edward said hesitantly, 'How are you in yourself, with these worries that you had and all that?'

Liam smiled. 'I'm fine now, thanks mate. It was the ullalulla that started me off, you know, singing it for Big Charlie. About the soldier boy going off to war and dying in some foreign field. It's the lament of the widow woman who cries in the night like a wailing wolf. She's got no home because her man has died and she's got no grave to weep over. Made me realise. All of us out there, you, me, Big Charlie, the German kids, we were all of us just the innocent victims. The bastards who start all these things, they're nowhere to be seen.'

'No. You're right,' Edward said, unconsciously matching his step to that of the marching men. 'But there's one thing that you can be sure of.'

'What's that?' Liam queried.

'Things will never be the same again. The working man has paid too high a price for that. We've all got to do our part to make sure of that.'

A warm feeling of relief was beginning to surge up inside Edward. Deep caverns were opening up and light was flooding in. He wanted to shout to the crowd, to jump around and punch the air. He had somebody that he could share the pained silences with.

'It's good to see you back, mate. I'll call round tomorrow,' he told Liam and turned off down the side street. He had a lot to do, a job to get, a family to bring up and provide for.

Edward bent forward and stifled the cough as he placed the rose at right angles to the shiny toecaps of his boots. He took out his handkerchief, blew his nose then folded his hands together across his front and bowed his head. Magpies bickered angrily with a seagull from the nearby docks until a yelping dog chased them off through the dandelion and daisy strewn field where the paupers were buried.

Liam, standing on the other side of the grave, crouched down with his head held upright to prevent the headaches and placed his rose alongside the other. 'What a waste,' he muttered, taking an oily rag out of his pocket and placing it under the stone flower pot. Pink blossom petals, blown by the warm May breeze, scuttered over the grave and nestled into the folds of the cloth as he replaced the heavy pot. 'Sorry, Dot. This is all we brought back of Big Charlie's.'

'Well, apart from he wanted you to know how much he loved you,' Edward added hastily. 'And to say, like, that he would have loved to have had a family with you.'

'Aye, you know, kids and that.'

355

A steam valve whistle ripped into the silence of the cemetery, startling a family of crows out of a tree. Cawing noisily, they flew over the head of the two friends before the gentle breeze regained its domain. Edward knelt down, sniffing as he awkwardly arranged the bunch of flowers in the stone vase that he and Liam had bought between them.

'Poor sod,' Liam said sadly. 'She had nobody left. At least she's been laid in here with her mother.'

A cloud of pink petals swirled round the gravestone and edged into the turnups of their trousers. Liam moved the drooping flowers to reveal the inscription on the side of the vase. *'Dorothy Jackson,'* he read. *'b.15ᵗʰ June 1885 d.24ᵗʰ December 1918. Wife of Charles k.i.a. Reunited.'*

'Perhaps we should have put a bit more on about Big Charlie. Like about him being brave and big hearted.'

'It's only a flower pot, Eddie, not an urn. He wouldn't have wanted that anyway.'

A rhythmic clopping of hooves heralded the parade of another family's misery. The horse drawn hearse was preceded by a tall, sombre, grey-faced man wearing a long black frock coat and a tall shiny top hat. The cortege emerged through the main gates of the cemetery and proceeded up the wide drive towards the chapel. The four horses, plumes of black feathers bobbing on their restless heads, were barely troubled by the glass enclosed carriage that they pulled behind them. The coffin, draped with a Union Jack, was piled high with elaborate wreaths and bouquets and a double line of smartly uniformed Lancashire Fusiliers marched at half pace behind. The sobbing family followed in a black curtained carriage and a long tail of dark mourners trailed gloomily in the rear.

'That'll be the young captain who was in the Reporter last week,' Edward said. 'Died of injuries that he came home with.'

'A lot more to see him off than would have been at Dot's,' Liam observed drily.

'I should have made more of an effort to see her when I came home,' Edward said. 'Poor Dot. She must have had nobody to turn to – nobody to even say goodbye to. She must have been pretty desperate.'

'She just needed to be back with Big Charlie.'

'That's as maybe, but I'm just surprised to realise that she was so dependent on him.'

'Eddie. There was a letter that she'd had from Big Charlie. I should have told you about it before.'

'Oh Christ. Where did that come from? What did he say?' Edward groaned. 'She must have misinterpreted something that he said.'

'When the neighbour smelled the gas coming from Dot's house she ran to get the priest. She was a bit scared. The priest let himself in by the back door. He turned the gas off but it was too late. He said that it was a bit odd; Dot had got together all Big Charlie's clothes and put them on. Everything. Work jacket, shirts, waistcoat, trousers. Even down to his vest and drawers. He said that you could hardly see her in there. You know, she was only like a tuppenny rabbit to start with. And she was still clinging to this letter.'

'Poor thing. She must have been reading it when she died.'

'Aye, that's right. The priest brought it round to Brig because he knew that she was a friend. Bit ironic, really, because she didn't even know that Dot was living only half a mile away on Cow Lane. She had enough problems of her own, though, worrying about me. The priest had sent for the police and he thought it best if the letter didn't get into their hands.'

'Phew. Sounds a bit incriminating. Not what you would expect from Big Charlie.'

'No. But it was loaded. He told her in the letter that he had killed the man who had blighted her life for so many years. It was Big Charlie who shot Major Gobshite, you know, that Fforbes-Fosdyke bastard.'

'Oh God. I knew that he had a grudge but I didn't imagine that it was that bad. There must have been some serious history there.'

'Aye, Big Charlie told me about it when we got back from Imbros. You know, when I told you about Brig's problems with the fat slug. Apparently Dot was fifteen at the time. There was only her and her Dad and he was seriously ill upstairs. They hadn't got the money for the rent when Gobshite came round and she asked if she could leave it for a week. He said that he had a better idea. He raped her in the living room. She was frightened of screaming for her Dad in case it killed him if he tried to come down.'

'He was an evil sod. He should have been put down at birth.'

'It would have saved us all a lot of grief if he had. The priest didn't know all that of course, but I suppose he might have put two and two together. He told Brig that Dot had started to come to church again in the summer. She hadn't been since her teens. She probably couldn't cope with the guilt. He said that she was in high spirits. Talking about having been cleansed and the cross that she had had to bear for so many years had been lifted.'

'She seemed to have had a real Hallelujah moment there,' Edward said.

'Aye. It must have been when she received the letter from Big Charlie. Trouble was that she then received another letter in November from the Army. It had taken them a bit to find her because she had moved a few times after that fracas with Big Charlie when he came home on leave.'

'That must have been the letter about him being killed?'

'Yes. I'm afraid so.'

'Oh sod it. I was back then. I should have gone to find her. Trouble was, I could hardly force myself out through the front door.'

'What could you have said, Eddie? She wanted the man who had finally freed her from her torment. Hearing about his heroics would have been about as much use as a sticking plaster for a severed arm.'

'What a waste. Big Charlie worshipped Dot but he never understood how she really felt about him.'

'Perhaps she has told him now,' Liam said quietly.

Edward stared at the corner of the oily cloth protruding from beneath the corner of the stone vase. Pink petals fluttered around it and collected in its folds. '*b.15th June 1885 d.24th December 1918.*' A clump of bluebells on the grave bowed their heads modestly. 'It was Christmas Eve when she went. Big Charlie said that she hated Christmases on her own.'

Liam picked up a rose and held it to his lips as he rocked on his heels. Bugles sounded the last post at a distant grave. As the final soaring note faded Liam began to sing, quietly at first then reaching up in pleading supplication, a beautiful but tortured sound that plucked at chords deep within Edward's body. A large black bird circled over them and cried its counterpoint whilst magpies on the ground chattered the chorus. There were no mountains in Weaste Cemetery to echo the ullalullah but in the rustling trees the souls of Salford wept for the spirit of another victim of that devastating war. A lament for Big Charlie's Dot; now given her absolution.

Made in Myrtle Street